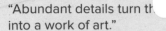

Follow Her Heart

MARTA PERRY

Previously published as *Heart of the Matter*
and *Her Texas Family*

Recycling programs for this product may not exist in your area.

ISBN-13: 978-1-335-40648-4

Follow Her Heart
First published as Heart of the Matter in 2010.
This edition published in 2021.
Copyright © 2010 by Martha Johnson

Her Texas Family
First published in 2016. This edition published in 2021.
Copyright © 2016 by Jill Buteyn

This edition published by arrangement with Harlequin Books S.A.

For questions and comments about the quality of this book, please contact us at CustomerService@Harlequin.com.

Harlequin Enterprises ULC
22 Adelaide St. West, 40th Floor
Toronto, Ontario M5H 4E3, Canada
www.Harlequin.com

Printed in U.S.A.

CONTENTS

A lifetime spent in rural Pennsylvania and her Pennsylvania Dutch heritage led **Marta Perry** to write about the Plain People, who add so much richness to her home state. Marta has seen over seventy of her books published, with over seven million books in print. She and her husband live in a beautiful central Pennsylvania valley noted for its farms and orchards. When she's not writing, she's reading, traveling, baking or enjoying her six beautiful grandchildren.

Books by Marta Perry

Love Inspired

Brides of Lost Creek

Second Chance Amish Bride
The Wedding Quilt Bride
The Promised Amish Bride
The Amish Widow's Heart
A Secret Amish Crush

An Amish Family Christmas
"Heart of Christmas"
Amish Christmas Blessings
"The Midwife's Christmas Surprise"

Visit the Author Profile page at Harlequin.com for more titles.

HEART OF
THE MATTER

Marta Perry

But seek ye first the kingdom of God,
and his righteousness; and all these things
shall be added unto you.

—*Matthew* 6:33

This story is dedicated to Pat and Ed Drotos,
my dear sister and brother-in-law.
And, as always, to Brian, with much love.

Chapter 1

Amanda Bodine raced around the corner into the newsroom, sure she was late for the staff meeting. She skidded to a halt at the sight of her usually neat, workmanlike desk that now bloomed with a small garden of flowers. Above it floated a balloon bouquet with a streamer that fairly shouted its message. *Happy Birthday.* Her heart plummeted to the pit of her stomach.

She glanced at her watch. Two minutes until the editorial meeting. If she could just get everything out of sight...

"Ms. Bodine." The baritone voice dripped with sarcasm, and she didn't have to turn around to identify the speaker—Ross Lockhart, managing editor of the *Charleston Bugle.* "It seems your personal life is intruding into the office. Again."

"I'm sorry." It wasn't her fault the her large family seemed to take it for granted that they were welcome in her workplace. One noisy visit from two of her cousins had occurred when Lockhart was addressing the staff. He was not amused.

She forced herself to turn and face the man. Drat

it, she never had trouble standing up for herself in any other circumstances. Why did her grit turn to jelly in the presence of Ross Lockhart?

Because if you get in his way, he'll mow you down like a blade of grass, her mind promptly responded.

"Get rid of it. Please." The addition of the word didn't do a thing to mitigate the fact that it was an order. "Editorial meeting, people." He raised his voice. "Conference room, now."

A rustle of something that might have been annoyance swept through the newsroom, but no one actually spoke up. No one would. They were all too aware that hotshot journalist Ross Lockhart had been brought in by the *Bugle*'s irascible owner and publisher, Cyrus Mayhew, to ginger things up, as he put it. Lockhart seemed to consider firing people the best way to accomplish that.

Lockhart stalked away in the direction of the conference room before Amanda needed to say another word to him, thank goodness. She should have made sure she'd regained her professional demeanor before coming back to the office from the birthday lunch with her twin sister. Lockhart already seemed to consider her a lightweight in the news business, despite her seven years' experience, and she didn't want to reinforce that impression.

She moved two baskets of roses and daisies to the floor behind her desk and grabbed a notebook to join the exodus from the newsroom.

"Happy birthday, sugar." Jim Redfern, the grizzled city desk editor, threw an arm around her shoulders in a comradely hug. "Too bad you have to spend it in another meeting." His voice lowered. "Sittin' around a table doesn't get a paper out. You'd think the man would realize that."

"He realizes Cyrus expects him to turn us into number one, that's what."

Jim snorted. "Not going to happen in my lifetime."

Nor in hers, probably. Everyone knew that the venerable *Post and Courier,* the oldest newspaper in the South, was Charleston's premier paper. The best the *Bugle* could hope for was to break a surprise story once in a blue moon.

And keep 'em honest, as Cyrus was prone to say. Everyone who worked at the paper had been treated to his lecture on the importance of competition in the news.

He'd probably like to believe his staff shared that passion.

Entering the high ceilinged, wood-paneled conference room, Amanda glanced around the table, assessing her colleagues. Cyrus's hope seemed unlikely to be fulfilled. His staffers were either just starting out, hoping this experience would lead to a more important job down the road, or they were old-timers like Jim, put out to pasture by other, more prestigious papers.

She was the only reporter who fit somewhere in the middle, with a year's experience at the Columbia paper, where she'd interned during college, and three years at the *Tampa Tribune* before the lure of the city she loved and the family she loved even more drew her home.

Except for Ross Lockhart, the exception to the rule— smart as a whip, newspaper savvy and ambitious. Above all, ambitious.

Lockhart took his place at the head of the long rectangular table, frowning as usual when he looked at them. He probably found them a pretty unprepossessing bunch compared to the company he'd kept at the Washington,

D.C., daily where he'd worked before a public scandal had nearly ruined his career.

She sat up a bit straighter. Maybe they weren't the brightest tools in the tool chest, as her daddy might say, but at least they hadn't fabricated a front-page story, as Lockhart had been accused of doing. And it must have been true, since the paper had made a public apology to the congressman concerned and promptly fired Ross Lockhart.

Lockhart's piercing gray gaze met hers almost as if he'd heard her thoughts, and her throat went dry. Juliet Morrow, the society editor, romantically claimed he had a lean and hungry look, like some crusader of old. The contrast between the steel-gray of his eyes and the true blue-black of his hair, the angular lines of his face, the slash of a mouth—well, maybe she could see what Juliet meant.

But the look he'd turned on her was more that of the wolf eyeing Little Red Riding Hood. She was already sitting near the end of the table. It was impossible to get any farther away from him. Only the obituary writer was lower on the totem pole than she was. She held her breath until his gaze moved on.

He began assigning the stories for the next news cycle. Knowing perfectly well he wouldn't have anything remotely important for her, she fixed her attention on a framed *Bugle* front page that announced VE Day and let her thoughts flicker again to that birthday lunch.

She and her twin were thirty today. Annabel was well and truly launched on the work that was her passion. The others at the meal, more or less the same age, were all either soaring ahead in careers or busy with husband and family. Or both. Only she was entering her thirties stuck in a job where her prospects grew dimmer every time her boss looked her way.

Which he did at that moment. She stiffened. Was there another dog show coming to town that needed her writing talents?

"Bodine." His tone had turned musing. "Seems to me I've heard that name lately. Something connected to the military, wasn't it?"

Her breath caught. Was this the way it would come out—the secret the family struggled to keep in order to protect her grandmother? Right here in the newsroom, in front of everyone, blurted out by a man who had no reason to care who it hurt?

The others at the table were looking at her, their quizzical gazes pressing her for a response. Finally Jim cleared his throat.

"Somethin' about the Coast Guard, maybe? Bodines tend to serve there." He said the words with the familiar air of someone who knew everything there was to know about old Charleston families...all the things their boss couldn't possibly know.

Lockhart's gaze slashed toward him with an air of clashing swords. Then he shrugged, glancing down at the clipboard in front of him. "Probably so. All right, people, let's get to work."

With a sense of disaster narrowly averted, Amanda followed the others toward the door. Two steps from freedom, Ross Lockhart put out a hand to stop her. "One moment, Ms. Bodine."

She stiffened, turning to face him. Maybe her relief had come too soon.

He leaned back in the chair, eyeing her. She held her breath. If he asked her outright about Ned Bodine, the great-uncle the community had branded a coward, what could she say? She didn't much care what he thought, but if word got out, her grandmother might be hurt.

Finally his focus shifted to the sheaf of papers in front of him. "Mr. Mayhew wants to run a series of articles on the Coast Guard—the functions of the base, its importance to the local economy, maybe some human interest profiles. It seems your family connections might be a help to us in that."

Excitement rippled through her. A real story, finally. "Yes, of course." She was so excited that she nearly tripped over the words. "My father, my brother and my cousins are still on active duty, several stationed right here in Charleston. I'd love to write about—"

He cut her off her enthusiasm with a single cut of his hand. "These will be in-depth pieces. I wasn't suggesting you write them."

Disappointment had a sharp enough edge to make her speak up. "Why not? I'm the most qualified person in the newsroom on the Coast Guard. I did a series when I was at the Tampa paper—"

"Knowing something about a subject doesn't mean you're the best person to write the articles." His tone suggested she should know that. "In fact, I'm taking these on myself. Your role will be to get me access and set up the interviews."

Something anyone with a phone could do, in other words. Naturally he wouldn't let her actually write anything. In Ross Lockhart's eyes, she was nothing but a sweet Southern belle filling in time until marriage by pretending to be a reporter.

Her jaw tightened until she felt it might crack. She could speak her mind, of course. And then she'd go right out the door onto the street behind the other eight people he'd fired.

Finally she swallowed. "I can take care of that."

"Good." He shuffled through his papers, leaving her to wonder if she should go or stay. Then, rising, he held out a half sheet of paper to her. "Get this in for tomorrow's news cycle."

He strode out the door, on to bigger and better things, no doubt. She glanced down at her latest assignment and sucked in an irritated breath.

At least it was a change from a dog show. This time it was a cat show.

Amanda Bodine wasn't quite the person he'd originally thought her. Ross paused at his office door, scanning the newsroom until his gaze lit on her.

Oh, she looked the part, with her chic, glossy brown hair and her trick of looking up at you with those big green eyes from underneath her thick eyelashes. A stereotypical Southern belle, he'd thought—pretty, sweet and brainless. But she wasn't quite that.

The charm was there, yes, and turned on generously for everyone but him. At the moment she was chatting with the kid from the mail room, seeming as interested in him as she'd be if Cyrus Mayhew himself walked up to her.

Everyone's friend—that was Amanda. Even a crusty old reporter like Jim would pause by her chair, resting his hand on her shoulder long enough to exchange a quip before heading for his desk. Every newsroom had its flirt, and she was theirs.

Amanda was a lightweight, he reminded himself. She didn't belong here. Even if she wasn't quite as shallow as he'd first thought, she didn't have the toughness it took to make a good reporter. Just ask him. He knew exactly how much that cost.

Sooner or later Amanda would take her sweet Southern charm and her big green eyes, marry someone suitable, retreat into her comfortable Charleston lifestyle and produce babies who looked just like her.

No, she didn't belong in a newsroom. He threaded his way purposefully through the desks toward her. But that didn't mean she couldn't be useful. Amanda could give him entrée into a world he'd have trouble penetrating on his own. And that wasn't exactly using her. She was an employee of the paper, after all.

The lie detector inside his mind let out a loud buzz. That was an asset when interviewing the many people who didn't want to tell the truth to a reporter. Not so helpful when it turned on him that way.

Well, okay. He *was* using her. He'd use anyone, try anything, that would get him back to the life where he belonged.

You don't have to trick her. You could tell her about the anonymous tip. Ask for her help.

The voice of his conscience sounded remarkably like that of his grandmother. She'd died when he was a teenager, but the Christian standards she'd set for him still cropped up at inconvenient moments. For an instant he wavered.

Then his resolve hardened. He'd tried being the Boy Scout before, living by his grandmother's ideals, and look where it had gotten him. Clinging to the remnants of his career with his fingernails.

If Cyrus Mayhew hadn't been willing to give him a

chance, the only newspaper job he'd have landed was delivering them. In Alaska.

So he'd do what he had to. He frowned. The called-in story tip had been annoyingly vague, as they so often were, but it had promised a scandal, fat and juicy, involving the Coast Guard base and kickbacks paid by local companies for contracts. A big story—the kind of story that, properly handled, could get him back on top again.

And Amanda Bodine, with her Coast Guard family, was just what he needed.

He stalked up to her desk, noting that just the sight of him was enough to send the mail room kid fleeing. Amanda had a bit more self-control, but she clearly didn't welcome his visit, either.

"Ms. Bodine." The balloons were gone from her desk. "Have you set up an initial meeting for me yet?"

"I…um, yes." A faint hint of pink stained her cheeks. "I spoke with my father. He'd be pleased to talk with you."

"Good." He'd done a little digging himself. Talking to Brett Bodine would be starting at the top. He was one of the head honchos at the local Coast Guard base. "When can we meet?"

Her flush deepened, and he watched, fascinated. When was the last time he'd met a woman who could blush?

"Actually, I'm on my way to a family get-together when I leave work. My daddy suggested you come along and have some supper with us. You can talk to him, and my cousins will be there…" Her voice petered out.

"I assume this is a birthday party for you." He lifted an eyebrow, remembering the birthday balloons and flowers. Clearly Amanda had some admirers.

"And my sister, Annabel. We're twins. Since our birthday is in the summer, we've always had a picnic at the beach." She clamped her mouth shut suddenly, maybe remembering who she was telling.

"It sounds charming."

Her eyes narrowed, as if she suspected sarcasm. "I explained to him that this was business, not social. If you'd rather meet at his office, I can tell him that."

The idea of taking him to a family gathering clearly made her uncomfortable, but it appealed to him. Get people in a casual setting where they felt safe, and they'd often let slip more than they would in a formal interview.

"No, this sounds good," he said briskly. "Give me directions, and I'll be there."

"It's at my grandmother's beach house over on Sullivan's Island." She kept dismay out of her voice, but her mouth had tensed and her hands tightened on the edge of her desk.

"Directions," he said again.

Soft lips pressed together for an instant. "I'll be coming back into the city afterward anyway, if you want to ride over with me instead of trying to find it on your own."

Her brand of Southern courtesy compelled the offer, he supposed, but he was quick to take advantage. A few moments alone in the car with her would give him a chance to get background on the people he'd be meeting.

"Fine," he said promptly. "Are you ready?"

Again the tension showed in her face, but she managed to smile. "Just let me close a few files." She flicked a glance at his shirt and tie. "But you'll want to wear something more casual at the beach."

"I keep a change of clothes in my office." He turned,

eager to get on with it. "I'll meet you in the parking lot in fifteen minutes."

He strode toward his office, nodding at the few staffers who ventured to say good-night to him. Most just hurried past, heads down, as if eager to escape his notice. It didn't work. He noticed, just as he'd noticed Amanda's reluctance.

She was both too polite and too worried about her job to argue with him. Even if she had, he'd have been perfectly capable of overrunning her objections.

Amanda didn't want him on her home ground, but that was too bad. Because the Bodines were going to help him get back to *his* native turf, and no other considerations would stand in his way.

Amanda had been treated to a sample of Ross's interview style on the trip over to the island, and she didn't much care for being on the receiving end. She pulled on shorts and T-shirt in the small room under the eaves that the girl cousins always shared at the beach house.

She glanced in the mirror, frowning at the transformation from city professional to island girl. Somehow she felt safer clad in her professional armor.

She pressed her fingertips against the dressing table that still wore the pink-and-white-checked skirt her grandmother had put on it years ago. Not that Miz Callie was a pink and frilly kind of person, but she'd wanted the girl cousins to feel that this room was theirs.

Dealing with Ross in the office was hard enough. Amanda still rankled over his quick dismissal of her ability to write the articles on the Coast Guard. Who was better equipped to write it—someone who'd lived with it her whole life or an outsider who didn't have a clue?

She wrinkled her nose at the image in the mirror. Ross had the answer to that, and he was the boss. He'd decided that her family was his way into the story, and if his aggressive, almost abrasive questioning in the car had been a sample of his style, they were in for some rough waters.

She headed for the stairs, the comparison lightening her mood. Daddy was used to rough waters. He could handle the likes of Ross with one hand tied behind his back.

And speaking of handling him, she'd left her boss alone with her grandmother. Goodness only knows what they were making of each other.

She usually skipped down the stairs at the beach house because of the sheer joy of being there. Now she hurried for fear of what Miz Callie might be saying. Catching Ross's gaze on her, she slowed to a more sedate pace as she reached the living room.

He was sitting in the shabby, over-stuffed chair near the wall of windows that faced the beach and the ocean. Her heart clutched. That had been Granddad's special seat after his first stroke had stolen away most of his mobility. He'd never tired of looking out at the sea.

"Is my grandmother takin' good care of you?" The tall glass of sweet tea at his elbow looked untouched.

"She is. She had to run back to the kitchen to deal with something." As if becoming aware of the glass, he lifted it and touched it to his lips.

She couldn't help but grin. "Obviously you aren't used to iced tea that's sweet enough to make your back teeth ache. Come on. We'll find the others. Someone will have brought a cooler of soda."

He put the sweet tea down quickly and stood, his gaze

sweeping over her. She usually felt he didn't see her at all. This gaze was far more personal. Too much so.

Her chin lifted. "Something wrong?" She edged the words with ice.

"No." He made an instinctive move back. "You just look different. From the office, that is."

"We're not in the office," she pointed out. If she could make him feel a tad uncomfortable, so much the better. She needed to keep a professional distance between them, no matter where they were.

"We're not," he agreed. His fingers brushed her bare arm, and the unexpected familiarity of the gesture set her nerve endings tingling.

He nodded toward the kitchen. "We were going in search of a soda," he reminded her.

"Right, yes." She took a breath. She would not let the man dismantle her confidence in herself. "This way."

But as she started for the kitchen, he stopped her with another touch. This time his hand lingered on her wrist, warming the skin. "In this setting, it's going to sound odd if you call me Mr. Lockhart. Let's switch to first names. Amanda," he added, smiling.

She nodded. What could she do but agree? But she'd been right. His smile really did make him look like the Big Bad Wolf.

She led the way into the kitchen, aware of him hard on her heels.

The kitchen was a scene of contained chaos, as it always was when the whole family gathered at the beach house. Her mamma and one of her aunts talked a mile a minute while they chopped veggies for a salad, her sister Annabel and cousin Georgia arranged nibbles on a huge tray, and Miz Callie, swathed in an apron that nearly swallowed her five-foot-nothing figure, peered anxiously at the contents of a huge kettle—pulled pork barbecue, judging by the aroma.

"Did y'all meet my boss, Ross Lockhart?"

"We introduced ourselves, sugar." Mamma stopped chopping long enough to plant a kiss on her cheek. "You comin' to help us?"

Miz Callie clattered the lid back onto the pot. "She'd best introduce her friend to the men first. I don't suppose he wants to be stuck in the kitchen."

"I'm afraid my cooking skills wouldn't be up to your standards, Mrs. Bodine," Ross said quickly. "It smells way too good in here."

Miz Callie dimpled up at him, always charmed by a compliment to her cooking. "The proof is in the eating, you know. You let Amanda get you settled with someone to talk to, and later on we'll get better acquainted."

"I'll look forward to it."

Amanda gave him a sharp glance, ready to do battle if he was being condescending to her grandmother. But his expression had actually softened, and his head was tilted deferentially toward Miz Callie.

Well. So something could pierce that abrasive shield he wore. That was a surprise.

Still, it would be just as well to keep him from any lengthy tête-à-têtes with her grandmother. Miz Callie was still obsessed with that old scandal about her husband's brother and they surely didn't need to let Ross Lockhart in on the skeleton in the Bodine family closet.

"This way." She put a hand on the glass door and slid it back. "Anybody who's not in the kitchen is probably down on the beach."

Ross followed her onto the deck that ran the length of

the house and paused, one hand on the railing. "Beautiful view."

"It is that." She lifted her face to the breeze that freshened the hot summer air. "On a clear day you feel as if you can see all the way across the Atlantic."

He turned his back on the ocean to have a look at the beach house sprawled comfortably on the dunes, its tan shingles blending into sand and sea oats. "Has your family had the place long?" The speculative note in his voice suggested he was estimating the cost.

"For generations." She clipped off the words. They couldn't afford to build a house on the beach at today's prices, but that was none of Ross Lockhart's business. "My great-grandfather bought this piece of property back when there was no bridge to the mainland and nothing much on the island but Fort Moultrie and a few fishing shacks."

"Very nice." He glanced toward the kitchen, and she realized he was looking at Miz Callie with that softened glance. "Did I understand your grandmother lives here year-round?"

"That's her plan. The family's been trying to talk her out of it, but once Miz Callie makes up her mind, you may as well save your breath to cool your porridge, as she'd say."

His lips curved. "I had a grandmother like that, too. A force to be reckoned with."

"Had?" She reacted automatically to the past tense.

"She died when I was a teenager." He turned to her, closer than she'd realized. Her breath hitched in her throat. "You're lucky to have your grandmother still. Very lucky."

The intensity in his low voice set up an answering

vibration in her. For a moment they seemed linked by that shared emotion.

Then she caught herself and took a careful step back. *This is your boss, remember? You don't even like him.*

But she couldn't deny that, just for a moment, he'd shown her a side of himself that she'd liked very much.

Chapter 2

The long living room of the beach house overflowed with Bodines. Ross balanced a plate of chocolate caramel cake on his lap, surveying them from a seat in the corner.

Clearly they were a prolific bunch. He'd finally straightened it out that the grandmother, Miz Callie, as they called her, had three sons. Each of them had produced several children to swell the brood.

Judging by all the laughter and hugging they were a close family, almost claustrophobically so. Who could imagine having a party with this many people—all of them related?

He certainly couldn't. His family had consisted of his parents, Gran and himself. That was it. His father had said more than once that having no siblings was a distinct advantage for a politician—they couldn't embarrass you.

That had been the creed by which he'd been raised. *Don't do anything to embarrass your father.*

And he hadn't, not even slightly, for all those years, until that final, spectacular event. His fingers tightened on the dessert plate, and he forced them to relax.

Forget his family. Forget his past mistakes. The thing to do now was to concentrate on the job at hand. If he could isolate Amanda's father for a quiet chat...

Miz Callie, a cup of coffee in her hand, headed in his direction. Tiny, probably not much over five feet, she was trim and lively, with a halo of white hair and blue eyes that hadn't faded with age. She sat down next to him.

"How's the cake? Can I get you anything else?"

"The cake is wonderful." He took a bite, realizing that the compliment was true. He'd been so busy thinking about the job that he hadn't even tasted it. "Thank you, Mrs. Bodine."

"Call me Miz Callie." She patted his arm. "Everyone does. We're just so glad to meet you at last. Amanda talks about you often."

He noticed she didn't specify what Amanda said. That wouldn't be polite. He could imagine that Amanda had broadcast her opinion of him to her clan.

"You have quite a family. I'm not sure I have them all straight yet. Several in the Coast Guard, I understand." Mrs. Bodine—Miz Callie, rather—might have some insights he could tap.

"That's a family tradition," she said absently. Her attention was on Amanda and her sister as they cut slices of cake. "Devil's food cake with caramel icing is Amanda and Annabel's favorite, so we always have it for their birthday. Funny that they like the same thing, because they're different as can be in other ways."

If this were an interview, he could get her back onto the subject of the Coast Guard with a direct question. In polite conversation, it wasn't so easy.

"They look nearly identical." Same honey-brown hair,

same deep green eyes, same slim, lithe figures. They were striking, seen together.

"Identical in looks, but not in temperament." Miz Callie's blue eyes crinkled. "Amanda is fifteen minutes older, and she's always been the big sister, the high achiever. And always trying to best her two older brothers, too."

He could tell the twins apart not by appearance so much as by body language and expression. Amanda was livelier, teasing and being teased, laughing easily.

"Annabel seems a little quieter."

"She goes her own way," Miz Callie said. "She always has. Never especially bothered by what everyone else is doing."

"Everyone else in this case being family?"

"I s'pose so." She twinkled at him. "There's quite a tribe of us, as you can see. And all the cousins are so close in age, too. Still, I guess family gatherings are all pretty much alike everywhere."

He nodded in agreement, although nothing could be further from the truth when it came to comparing this noisy crowd to his family. "They all seem very close."

That was not entirely a compliment, at least not in his mind. He wouldn't care to have this many people feeling they had a right to tell him what to do.

"Close." She repeated the word, but her tone gave it a different meaning. "I wish…"

Alerted, he studied her face. There was something there—some worry or concern evident in the clouding of those clear eyes, the tension in the fine lines around her lips.

"You wish…" he prompted.

She seemed to come back from a distance, or maybe

from thoughts she didn't welcome. She shook her head. "Goodness, I'm forgetting why you're here. You want to talk to the boys about the Coast Guard, and here I'm yammering on about everything else."

She was out of her chair before he could move. "Adam, come on over here and talk to Ross. He's wantin' to write something about the service."

Adam... Bodine, he supposed, they were all Bodines, came in obedience to his grandmother's hail.

"Sure thing, Miz Callie." He bent to plant a kiss on her cheek. "But I'll just bet he'd rather talk to you."

She gave him a playful swat and scurried off before Ross could do anything more than rise from his chair. Since Adam didn't take the empty seat, he remained standing, putting them eye to eye.

Tall, muscular, with an open, friendly smile—the man had been introduced to him, probably, but he couldn't for the life of him remember if this was Amanda's brother or cousin.

Adam grinned, almost as if he interpreted the thought. "Adam Bodine," he prompted. "Amanda's cousin. That's my sister, Georgia, pouring out the coffee. My daddy's the one standing next to Amanda's daddy. It's tough to sort us all out."

"I'm usually pretty good with names, but—"

"But we're all Bodines," Adam said, finishing for him. "Amanda tells us you're fixing to do some articles for the newspaper about the service."

"The Coast Guard seems important to the community, so it's a good subject for a series of articles." That bit ran smoothly off his tongue. "What made so many of you decide on that for a career?"

"Ask each of us, you'd get a different reason." Adam

nodded toward one of the laughing group clustered around the twins. "My cousin Win, now, he's a rescue swimmer. He always was a daredevil, so jumping out of a chopper feels normal to him. He'd say he's in it for the excitement. Me, I couldn't imagine a life that didn't involve being on the water. My daddy was the same." He paused, as if he looked deeper at the question. "Bottom line is serving our country, I guess."

"Patriotism." He tried not to let cynicism leak into his voice. Maybe he was jaundiced. He'd seen his father wave the flag too many times out of political expediency.

Adam's gaze met his. "That's somethin' we take kind of serious around here. Charleston's been a military town since the Revolution, and we have more military retirees here than most any place in the country our size."

"All the more reason to highlight what you do and the effect it has on the community," he said quickly, not wanting to get on the wrong side of the man. "Financially, for instance. I'm sure many companies in Charleston benefit from having the station here. It has to pump money into the local economy."

And into someone's pocket, if his informant was right.

"Sure, I guess so. My uncle Brett's the one you should talk to about that, though." He beckoned to Amanda's father, who veered in their direction. "Me, I just know about cutters and patrol boats."

Brett Bodine was probably in his early fifties, with a square, bluff face and a firm manner. He nodded, a little stiffly, and Ross wondered again what Amanda had been telling her family about her boss.

"Ross was just asking me about somethin' I figured you could answer better, Uncle Brett."

"What's that?" The man was measuring him with his gaze, and it looked as if he wasn't impressed with what he saw.

"He's wanting to know about the base doing business with local merchants, that kind of thing." Adam took a step back, as if leaving the field to his uncle.

Ross barely noticed. All his attention was on Brett Bodine. In the instant Adam had said those words, the man had reacted...a sudden tension in the erect figure, a flicker of wariness in the eyes, an involuntary twitch in the jaw.

Barely perceptible, unless you were looking. Unless your instincts were those of a trained interviewer, alert for the signs that you'd hit pay dirt.

Brett Bodine recovered quickly, Ross would say that for him. He'd managed a fairly pleasant smile in a matter of seconds.

"I'll put you in touch with our information officer," he said briskly. "She'll be glad to answer your questions."

She'd be glad to give Ross the canned speech, in other words. "In order to do a series of in-depth articles, I need to talk to the people who are actually involved in the work. Amanda thought you could help me with that."

The man's face tightened, as if he didn't like the reminder that Ross was his daughter's employer. "Our information office will—"

"Daddy." Amanda stood next to them, and they'd been so intent on their battle of wills that neither of them had noticed her. "I told you how important this is. You're not going to fob us off on someone else, are you?"

Us, she'd said. Apparently Amanda considered them a team. Well, if that's what it took to get him what he wanted, so be it.

Bodine's deeply tanned face reddened slightly in a flare of temper, but it eased when he looked at his daughter. He shrugged, seeming to give in to the inevitable.

"I guess not," he said. "We'll set it up for you to come in and talk in the next couple of days."

The words sounded right, but again, Ross read the body language, and it said exactly the opposite. Something was going on—something that Brett Bodine obviously knew about.

And something that, just as clearly, Amanda didn't.

For probably the first time in her life, Amanda was eager to leave the beach house. The party had been lovely, but she couldn't control the stress she felt at having her boss there.

That was all it was. Surely she'd been imagining the tension she'd thought existed between Daddy and Ross. They didn't even know each other. What did they have to be at odds about?

She popped her head in the kitchen door, looking for Miz Callie to say her goodbyes and thanks. Her grandmother probably shouldn't still be putting on birthday parties for the family, but no one had enough nerve to tell her so.

The kitchen was empty, the dishwasher humming, but before she could turn away, Miz Callie came in from the deck.

"There's the birthday girl. Come here, sugar, and let me give you a birthday kiss."

"And one to grow on," Amanda said, smiling, and kissed her grandmother's soft cheek. For a moment she stood, Miz Callie's comforting arms wrapped around her, and unexpected tears welled in her eyes.

She couldn't think of her vibrant, energetic grand-mother, the rock of the family, as growing old. It was too soon for that.

She blinked back the tears, knowing what had put that thought into her mind. For months Miz Callie had been obsessed with the idea of righting an old wrong. She kept saying that it must be done before she died; a constant reminder that their precious grandmother might not have too many years left hurt.

Miz Callie drew back and patted her cheek. "Amanda, honey, have you found out anything more about Ned?"

And there it was—the albatross that seemed to be hanging 'round all their necks these days. Ned Bodine, Granddad's older brother. They'd none of them even known him, except Miz Callie. He'd left long ago, run-ning off in 1942, never in touch with the family again. Every old-timer in the county believed he'd run out of cowardice, afraid to fight in the war.

Amanda's cousin Georgia, the first one Miz Callie had trusted with her quest, had found out that what ev-eryone believed wasn't true. Instead, after a sad love story and a rift with his father, Ned had left the island to enlist under a false name.

And there the story ended, as far as they'd been able to discover. How could you trace an anonymous man who could have gone anywhere, used any name?

Miz Callie's eyes grew suspiciously bright, and she patted Amanda's cheek again, her hand gentle. "It's all right, darlin'. You don't need to say it. I guess it's too much to hope for after all this time."

Pain twisted her heart. "We won't give up. There must be something else I can try."

She glanced toward the deck where her cousin Georgia stood with her fiancé's arm around her waist. Matt's little girl, Lindsay, leaned against Georgia trustingly. Lucky Georgia. She'd not only found the first clues to what had happened to Ned—she'd found love in the process.

Miz Callie shook her head slowly. "Maybe it's time to give up on learning anything more. The nature preserve is nearly ready to go. Maybe I'd best just make the announcement and be done with it."

"But Miz Callie, the scandal..." She bit her lip. The family might be satisfied that Ned hadn't been a coward, but they didn't have the proof that would convince anyone else. Plenty of folks would be unhappy at Miz Callie's plan to dedicate the nature preserve she planned for a small barrier island to a man they considered a disgrace to Charleston's proud patriotic tradition. She had a vision of scores of military veterans marching down Meeting Street in protest. Army, Navy, Air Force, Marines, Coast Guard—they'd all had a presence here at one time or another.

"I reckon we can live down a scandal if we have to." Miz Callie wiped away a tear with the back of her hand. "I just want to get this done."

"I know. But a little more time won't hurt, will it?" *Please.* They'd present a brave face to the world if it came to that. The family was agreed. But Miz Callie would be so hurt if folks she'd known all her life turned against her.

A fierce love burned in Amanda. She couldn't let that happen.

"I'll work on it. I promise." She was the reporter in the family, after all. Finding out things was her job. At least it was more important than covering pet shows. "You'll wait, right?" She looked pleadingly at her grandmother.

Miz Callie nodded. "I will. Don't worry so much, darlin'. God will show us the way."

She let out a relieved breath. She believed God would guide them, but she couldn't help wanting to chart this course herself. "Good. I'll…"

The sound of movement behind her stopped her words. She turned. Ross stood in the doorway. How long had he been there?

"I don't want to take you away from your party, but I do need to get back to the office."

"That's all right," she said quickly. "I'll just get my things."

Had he heard her conversation with Miz Callie or hadn't he? It worried at her as she gathered her things. She had to say goodbye to everyone, had to endure all the teasing about being a year older and exchange a special hug with Annabel, aware all the time that her boss stood waiting.

Finally, she got out the door, walking to the car with Ross on her heels.

The air between them sizzled with more than the summer heat as she started the car and turned the air-conditioning on high. And that was her answer. He'd heard something of what Miz Callie said. She wasn't sure how she knew, but she did. It was just there, in his concentrated expression.

They passed the island's park, the small collection of shops and restaurants, the old Gullah cemetery. Finally, as they approached the drawbridge that would take them off the island, she could stand it no longer.

"You heard what my grandmother said, didn't you?"

If that sounded like an accusation—well, she guessed it was. She spared a fleeting thought for her fired colleagues. Maybe she'd soon be joining them.

Silence for a moment. She saw the movement of his head at the edge of her vision as he turned to look at her.

"I wasn't eavesdropping, if that's what you're implying." His tone was surprisingly even. "I realized that your grandmother was upset, so I didn't come in. I'm not in the habit of listening in on the worries of elderly ladies."

She wasn't sure that she believed him. Still—

"You'd best not let her hear you call her elderly." She managed an apologetic smile. "I'm sorry. I hate it when she gets upset."

It was none of his business what Miz Callie had been upset about. Amanda had the sudden sense that the family skeleton had grown to an unmanageable size and was about to burst from its closet.

"You have a good heart." He sounded almost surprised.

"I love her," she said. "I'm sure you felt the same about your grandmother."

He nodded, staring out the window at the marsh grasses and pluff mud.

There didn't seem anywhere else to go with that conversation. She cleared her throat. "I hope meeting my people was helpful to you. For the articles, I mean."

"Very. You'll set up that appointment with your father as soon as possible."

"Right." When he didn't respond, she glanced at him. "Don't you want to talk to anyone else? My cousin Win is a rescue swimmer."

She held out the prospect enticingly. Win, an outgoing charmer, would be delighted to be interviewed, and surely that would be more interesting to readers than Daddy's desk job.

"What?" Her question seemed to have recalled Ross from some deep thought. "Yes, I suppose. I'll think about it and let you know."

Odd. Not her business, she guessed, how he approached the series of articles he said he was writing, but odd all the same.

She stole a sideways glance at him. His lean face seemed closed against the world, his eyes hooded and secretive.

Why? What made him so forbidding? The professional scandal they'd all heard of, or something more?

She gave herself a mental shake. This was the man who kept the entire news staff dangling over the abyss of unemployment. Maybe she felt a bit easier in his presence since this little expedition, but that didn't mean she knew him.

Or that she could trust him any farther than she could throw him.

He was going to have to tread carefully with Amanda, Ross decided. Something had made her suspicious of him after that family party the previous day.

He stood back to let the high school student intern precede him into the newsroom, assessing the young woman as he did. Cyrus Mayhew had chosen the recipient of his journalism internship on the basis of her writing, not her personality.

C. J. Dillon was bright, no doubt about that. She was also edgy and more than a little wary.

Suspicious, like Amanda.

The new intern had no reason for her suspicion, other than maybe the natural caution of a young black woman from a tough inner-city school toward the establishment, represented at the moment by him.

Amanda, on the other hand…well, maybe she did have just cause. He'd told the truth when he said he'd stopped outside the kitchen because he'd realized her grandmother was upset. He'd just neglected to mention that he'd heard the word *scandal* used in relation to her family. Or that all his instincts had gone on alert.

If he wanted to find out what scandal in the Bodine family would leave the grandmother in tears, he'd better find a way to mend fences with Amanda.

Assigning the student intern to her might disarm her. From what he'd seen of Amanda's relationship with everyone from the mail room kid to the cleaning crew, taking in strays was second nature to her.

"This way." He moved ahead of C.J. to lead her through the maze of desks in the newsroom. A few cautious glances slid their way. C.J. couldn't know that the looks were aimed at him, not her.

All right, so his staff didn't trust him. That was fine with him. He was here to turn this newspaper around, not make friends. He didn't need any more so-called friends who waited with a sharpened knife for him to make a slip.

Amanda's desk was at the far end of the row. Focused on her computer, a pair of glasses sliding down her nose, she didn't see them coming. She wore her usual version of business casual—well-cut tan slacks, a silky turquoise shirt, a slim gold chain around her neck.

That was a bit different from the way she'd looked at the beach house in an old pair of shorts and a Fort Moultrie T-shirt. He let his mind stray to the image. That had definitely been casual, to say nothing of showing off a pair of slim, tanned legs and a figure that would make any man look twice.

He yanked his unruly thoughts back to business. Amanda's only usefulness to him was the opening she provided to the Coast Guard base. And given that tantalizing mention of scandal, to the Bodine family in particular.

He stopped a few feet from her desk, feeling the need for a little distance between them.

"Ms. Bodine." *Amanda,* he thought, but didn't say.

Her gaze jerked away from the computer screen. The startled look she turned on him softened into a smile when she saw that he wasn't alone. No, the smile wouldn't be for him.

"This is C. J. Dillon. C.J., I'd like you to meet one of our reporters, Amanda Bodine."

"Hi, C.J. It's nice to meet you." Amanda held out her hand. After a moment, the young woman took it gingerly.

"C.J. is the winner of the journalism competition Mr. Mayhew set up in the local schools." The contest had been another of Cyrus's bright ideas for drawing attention to the *Bugle,* and all the staff should certainly be aware of it.

"That's great. Congratulations." She focused on C.J. "What did you win?"

Obviously the staff, or at least this member of it, hadn't kept up-to-date. His decision was even more appropriate, then.

"C.J. has received a six-week internship with the newspaper. A chance to find out if journalism is the right career for her, as Mr. Mayhew said in his editorial about the competition."

Which you should have read. The words were unspoken, but Amanda no doubt caught his meaning, since her lips tightened.

"You'll be happy to know I've decided to assign C.J. to work with you for the duration. You're going to be her mentor."

"I see." A momentary pause as Amanda turned to the young woman, and then came the smile that resembled the sun coming up over the ocean—the one she had yet to turn on him. "That's great, C.J. I look forward to working with you."

The ironic thing was that she probably did. For him, this brainstorm of Cyrus's was nothing but a nuisance. He had no particular desire to have a high school kid wandering around his newsroom.

Still, paired with Amanda, she couldn't do much harm. And if Amanda could persuade her that skin-tight jeans and a skimpy top weren't appropriate professional apparel, so much the better.

"Don't I have anything to say about who I work with?" The kid turned a belligerent frown on him. "I don't want to run around town covering stuff like boat parades and charity races. That's all she does."

He'd been so intent upon ridding himself of the problem that he was actually surprised when the kid spoke up. Irritation edged along his nerves. She was lucky to be here. Still, she'd obviously done her homework and paid attention to bylines.

"C.J., that's how everyone starts out," Amanda said quickly, as if to block out his response. Maybe she sensed his annoyance. "You're lucky you weren't assigned to the obit desk. This is much better than writing obituaries, believe me."

C.J. didn't noticeably soften. "Not much," she muttered.

"Hey, we do interesting stories. In fact, this afternoon we're heading down to Coast Guard Base Charleston for an interview. You'll have a chance to see the inside workings of the place."

"We?" He stressed the word. Taking Amanda along on interviews hadn't been part of his plan.

Amanda's eyebrows lifted. "My father is expecting us at three-thirty today. I hope that works for you."

He was tempted to make it clear that he didn't need or want her company. But if he did, that could put paid to any more help on her part. He might need her goodwill to gain future access.

"Fine." He tried to look as if he welcomed her company. "I'll see you then."

He turned away, startled to realize that on at least one level, he did.

Chapter 3

Amanda didn't know whether she was more relieved or surprised that Ross didn't fight her on the visit to Coast Guard Base Charleston, but he'd headed back to his office without further comment. Maybe he was beginning to see that she had something to offer. If this worked out well, maybe he'd...

She looked at C.J., and she came back to earth with a thump. Ross hadn't changed his mind about her. He just hadn't wanted to get into a hassle in front of the new intern.

No, that didn't sound like Ross. He didn't mind coming off dictatorial, no matter who was listening.

Thinking of him had brought a frown to her face. Amanda replaced it with a smile for C.J. Although, come to think of it, she wasn't exactly feeling warm toward the young woman. What had she meant by her outspoken distaste for working with Amanda?

She nodded toward a chair at the vacant desk next to hers—vacant since Ross had decided that its occupant was expendable. "Pull that seat over, so we can talk."

Wearing a sullen expression, C.J. rolled the chair to Amanda's desk and plopped into it, folding her arms.

Amanda had to hide a grin. C.J.'s body language was eloquent. Still, she'd have to learn that she couldn't call the shots at this point in her career. Any more than Amanda could.

"I suppose you've been working on your school newspaper," she ventured, wondering what the key would be to opening up this abrasive personality.

C.J.'s lips pressed together. After a moment, she shook her head. "Have to be a teacher's little pet for that, don't you? Anyway, I'm not gonna write stupid stories about poster contests and decorating the gym. I want to write about important things. That's why I entered the contest."

That hit a little too close to home. "Sounds like we have something in common then," she said briskly. "We both want to write more challenging subjects." She'd never really regretted retuning home, but the truth was that with the paper's already well-established staff, it was tough to move up. Especially when the new editor refused to believe she could write.

C.J. glowered at her for another moment, and then she shrugged.

Amanda resisted the desire to shake her. Working with this kid might be an exercise in suppressing emotions.

"Okay, then." Might as well go on the offensive, since nothing else seemed effective. "How did you know what kind of articles I write?"

Another shrug. "I know what everyone who works for the paper writes. It's my thing, isn't it?"

So she'd put time and effort into this chance at success. Did she even realize that her attitude was working against her? With a more accommodating spirit and some advice on what to wear, C.J. could come out of this on the road to success.

Dismayed, Amanda recognized her crusading spirit rising. It was the same irresistible urge that led her to one lame duck after another, always convinced that somehow she could help them.

And she had, more often than not. Her brothers insisted that her victims, as they called them, responded because that was the only way they could get rid of her, but she didn't buy that. That hapless Bangladeshi student at College of Charleston would have been sent home before he finished his degree if not for her organizing his fight to stay. And the article she'd written about endangered sea turtle nests had helped move along a new lighting ordinance.

Given C.J.'s attitude toward her, it was unlikely that the young woman would be one of her success stories. Still, she had to try.

"If you really mean to make journalism your career, an internship is a great place to start, especially getting one while you're still in high school. I didn't have one until the summer between my junior and senior years of college."

C.J.'s eyes betrayed a faint spark of interest. "Where did you go?"

"University of South Carolina. I interned at the Columbia paper that summer. Writing obits," she added, just in case C.J. had missed that part. "What schools are you looking at?"

C.J.'s dark eyes studied the floor. "Can't afford USC,

that's for sure. Maybe I can work and take classes at Trident," she said, naming the community college.

Amanda opened her mouth to encourage her and closed it again. She didn't know what kind of grades C.J. had, or what her home situation was. It would be wrong for her to hold out hope without more information.

She hadn't ever had to doubt that she'd be able to attend any college she could get into. Her parents had put a high priority on education for their four kids, no matter what they might have to sacrifice. C.J. might not be so lucky.

"How long you been here, anyway?" C.J. glanced around the newsroom, gaze lingering on Jim for a moment. As well-informed as she seemed, she undoubtedly knew that he wrote the kinds of stories Amanda could only dream about.

"Three years." She'd had her reasons for coming home, good ones, but maybe it hadn't turned out to be the smartest career path.

She was closing in on her ten-year college reunion, and still near the bottom of the journalism ladder, writing stories no one read but the people immediately involved.

C.J. eyed her. "If I had the edge you have, I'd sure be doing better by the time I got to be your age."

Was C.J. the voice of her conscience, sent to remind her that it was time she accomplished something worthwhile? Or just an obnoxious kid who would alienate everyone who might be willing to help her?

She slapped one hand down on her desk, making the silver-framed photo of her family tremble. "Now you look." She put some fire into her voice. "This internship can be the chance of a lifetime for you, but not if you go into it determined to annoy everyone you meet. You may be bright and talented, but so are a lot of other people. Talent won't get you anywhere without hard work and plenty of goodwill. Got that?"

She waited for the kid to flare up at her. C.J. pressed her lips together for a long moment. Finally she nodded. "Yes, ma'am," she muttered.

Well, that was progress of a sort. Maybe C.J. had what it took to get something from this experience. She prayed so.

As for C.J.'s opinion of her—there wasn't much she could do to change that, because like it or not, it was probably true.

Ross's finger hovered over the reply icon for a moment, then moved to delete. Finally he just closed the e-mail. He'd consider later what, if anything, he should say to his mother.

How long had it been since she'd been in touch with him? A month, at least. And that previous message had been much the same as this latest one—an impersonal recitation of his parents' busy lives. A perfunctory question as to how he was doing. A quick sign-off.

As for his father...well, he hadn't heard from his father since he left D.C. The last thing Congressman Willard Lockhart needed was a son who'd made the front page in the headline rather than the byline.

"Ross? Do you have a minute?"

He swung his chair around and rose, startled at the sight of the *Bugle's* owner, Cyrus Mayhew. "Of course. What is it?"

"Nothin' much." Cyrus wandered in, moving aimlessly around the office.

Ross felt his hands tighten and deliberately relaxed them. When Cyrus got aimless and folksy, it was a sure sign there was something on his mind. He might not know a lot about his employer yet, but he did know that.

Cyrus picked up a paperweight and balanced it on his palm, then put it back. He moved to the window, walked back to the desk. Peered at Ross, blue eyes sharp beneath bushy white brows. Someone had compared Cyrus to Mark Twain, and he seemed to deliberately cultivate the similarity.

The tension crawled along Ross's skin again, refusing to be dispelled. "Something special you wanted, sir?"

"Just wondering if you got that intern settled. Seemed like a nice youngster—maybe a little rough around the edges, though."

That was an understatement. "I assigned her to work with Amanda Bodine."

"Good, good. Amanda will take her under her wing. Might be a good role model for her."

She would, but somehow he didn't think that was all that was on Cyrus's mind today.

"Was there anything else?" he prompted.

"Well, now, I wondered what's going on with that tip we discussed. Anything in it?"

"It's too soon to tell."

Maybe he'd have been better off to keep that tip to himself. Was Cyrus really the elderly gadfly, intent on keeping the establishment honest? Or would he, like so many others, sell anyone out for a big story?

His stomach clenched. The face of his former mentor and boss flickered through his mind, and he forced it away. It didn't pay to think about the mentor who'd sacked him without listening to explanations, or the friend who'd stabbed him in the back without a second thought.

"But you're lookin' into it, aren't you, son?"

"I'm following up on everything we have, which isn't much. An anonymous call from someone who said businessmen were paying graft to get contracts at the Coast Guard base. A couple of anonymous letters saying the same thing, but giving no other details."

Cyrus nodded, musing, absently patting the round belly he was supposed to be dieting away. "We need to get on the inside, that's what we need."

"I'm working on that now, sir. I have an appointment with someone down at the base this afternoon."

Maybe it was best not to mention who. And even more important not to mention that tantalizing fragment he'd overheard from Amanda's grandmother.

"Good, good. Keep at it." Cyrus rubbed his palms together, as if he were already looking at a front-page spread. "We can't afford to let this slip through our fingers. This is the real deal—I can feel it."

"I hope so." For more reasons than one.

Like Cyrus, he wanted a big story for the *Bugle,* but even more, he wanted one for himself. He wanted to erase the pain and humiliation of the past year.

Irrational. No one could erase the past.

But one great job of investigative reporting could get his life back again. The need burned in him. To go back to the life he was born for, to dig into important stories, to feel he was making a difference in the world.

This was the best chance he'd had since he'd come to the *Bugle.* As Cyrus said, he couldn't let it slip between his fingers.

* * *

Amanda stood outside the redbrick building on Tradd Street that was headquarters of Coast Guard Base Charleston, waiting with C.J. while Ross parked the car. She was beginning to wish she'd had a chance to talk to the intern about proper professional clothing before taking her out on this initial assignment.

Ross came around the corner of the building, and before he could reach them C.J. nudged her. "So, you and the boss—are you together?"

"Together?" For a moment her mind was a blank. Then she realized the implication and felt a flush rising in her cheeks. "No, certainly not. What would make you think that?"

C.J. shrugged. "Dunno. Vibes, I guess. I'm pretty good at reading them."

"Not this time." Her fingers tightened on the strap of her bag. What on earth had led the kid to that conclusion? Were people talking, just because she'd taken him to the beach house?

Well, wouldn't they? The inner voice teased her. *You'd talk, if it were anyone else.*

That should have occurred to her. The newsroom was a hotbed of gossip, mostly false. She could only hope Ross hadn't gotten wind of it.

"Our relationship is strictly professional," she added. Obviously she'd have to make that clear to C.J. and to the newsroom in general. To say nothing of herself.

He joined them, and that increased awareness made her feel stiff and unnatural. She nodded toward the door. "Shall we go in?"

Fortunately she knew the petty officer on duty at the desk. That would make it simpler to ask a favor.

"Hey, Amanda." Kelly Ryan's smile included all of them. "You're expected. Go on up." She thrust visitor badges across to them.

"Is anyone free to take our intern on a tour while we're in with my father?" Sensing a rebellious comment forming on C.J.'s lips, she went on quickly. "I'd like her to gather background color for the articles we're doing. Okay?"

C.J. subsided.

"Sure thing. I'll handle it." Kelly waved them toward the stairs.

They headed up, leaving C.J. behind with Kelly, and she was still too aware of Ross, following on her heels. Drat the kid, anyway. Why did C.J. have to suggest something like that? It wasn't as if she didn't feel awkward enough around Ross already.

Ross touched her elbow as they reached the office. "One thing before we go in. This is my interview, remember."

"How could I forget?" She just managed not to snap the words. She'd like to blame C.J., but the annoyance she felt wasn't entirely due to the intern's mistaken impression.

She shot a sideways glance at Ross and recognized what she felt emanating from him. Tension. A kind of edgy eagerness that she didn't understand. What was going on with him?

They walked into the office. Her father, imposing in his blue dress uniform, rose from behind his desk to greet them.

Under the cover of the greetings and light conversation, she sought for calm.

I don't know what's going on, Father. I'm not sure

what Ross wants, but it must be something beyond what he's told me. Please, guide me now.

Her gaze, skittering around the room as the two men fenced with verbal politeness, landed on the framed photo on her father's desk. The family, taken at the beach on their Christmas Day walk last year. It was the same photo she had on her desk. Somehow the sight of those smiling faces seemed to settle her.

She focused her attention on Ross. He was asking a series of what seemed to be routine, even perfunctory, questions about her father's work and the function of the base.

"The Coast Guard is now under the Department of Homeland Security," her father said, clearly not sure Ross knew anything about the service. "Our jobs include maritime safety. Most people think of that first, the rescue work. But there's also security, preventing trafficking of drugs, contrabands, illegal immigrants. We protect the public, the environment and U.S. economic and security interests in any maritime region, including lakes and rivers."

This was her father at his most formal. He could be telling Ross some of the kinds of stories she'd heard over the dinner table since she was a kid—exciting rescues, chemical spills prevented, smugglers caught. Why was he being so stiff?

A notebook rested on Ross's knee, but he wasn't bothering to write down the answers Daddy gave. Maybe he was just absorbing background information. She often worked that way, too, not bothering to write down information she could easily verify later with a press kit.

But that didn't account for the level of tension she felt in the room—tension that didn't come solely from

Ross. Her father's already square jaw seemed squarer than ever, and his lips tightened at a routine question.

"I don't see why you need information on our local contractors." He bit the words off sharply.

"We'd like to show how much money the base brings into the local economy." Ross's explanation sounded smooth.

Too smooth. She'd already sampled his interview style, and this wasn't it. As for her father...

Ordinarily when Daddy looked the way he did at the moment, he was on the verge of an explosion. No one had ever accused Brett Bodine of being patient in the face of aggravation.

There was no doubt in her mind that he found Ross's questions annoying. But why? They seemed innocuous enough, and surely that was a good angle to bring out in the articles.

"So you'll let me have the records on your local contractors?" Ross's expression was more than ever that of a wolf closing in for a kill.

She braced herself for an explosion from her father. It didn't come.

Instead, he tried to smile. It was a poor facsimile of his usual hearty grin. "I'll have to get permission to release those figures."

He wasn't telling the truth. Her father, the soul of honor, was lying. She sensed it, right down to the marrow of her bones. Her heart clenched, as if something cold and hard tightened around it.

Her father, lying. Ross, hiding something. What was going on?

Please, Lord.

Her thoughts whirled, and then settled on one sure

goal. She had to find out what Ross wanted. She had to find out what her father was hiding. And that meant that any hope of keeping her distance from Ross was doomed from the start.

Chapter 4

Ross paced across his office, adrenaline pumping through his system. Lt. Commander Brett Bodine had been hiding something during their interview. He was sure of it. His instincts didn't let him down when it came to detecting evasion.

Too bad those instincts hadn't worked as well in alerting him that his so-called friend had been preparing to stab him in the back to protect the congressman.

He pushed that thought away. He'd been spending too much time brooding about what had happened in Washington. It was fine to use that as motivation—not so good to dwell on his mistakes.

This was a fresh case, and this time he would do all the investigative work himself. He wouldn't give anyone a chance to betray him.

He'd have to be careful with Amanda in that respect. All of her wariness with Ross had returned after that interview with her father. Was it because of Ross's attitude? Or because she, too, had sensed her father's evasiveness?

He didn't know her well enough to be sure what she was thinking, and he probably never would.

Pausing at the window, he looked out at the Cooper River, sunlight sparkling on its surface. A short drive across the new Ravenel Bridge would take him to Patriot's Point and its military displays; a short trip downriver to the harbor brought one to Fort Sumter. Everywhere you looked in the Charleston area you bumped into something related to the military, past or present.

The Bodine family was a big part of that, apparently. Brett Bodine's attitude could simply be the natural caution of a military man when it came to sharing information with the press. Ross didn't believe that, but it was possible.

He'd have to work cautiously, checking and double-checking every fact. Still, he couldn't deny the tingle of excitement that told him he was onto something.

Once he had the list of suppliers that Bodine had so reluctantly agreed to provide, he could start working from that end of the investigation. Finding the person who was paying the bribes would lead inevitably to the one accepting them.

Sliding into his chair, he pulled out the folder containing the anonymous notes and the transcript of the phone calls. He hadn't felt this energized in over a year. This was the real deal—he could feel it.

He'd just opened the folder when a shadow bisected the band of light from the door he always kept open to the newsroom. He looked up. It was Amanda, with an expression of determination on her face.

"I'd like to speak with you."

Closing the folder, he leveled an I-can't-be-disturbed stare at her. "This isn't a good time."

Instead of backing off, she closed the door behind her and advanced on the desk. "It's important."

"Not now." He ratcheted the stare up to a glare.

Her gaze flickered away from him. Good, intimidation still worked. Amanda believed that her job depended on his goodwill.

Whether it really did, he wasn't so sure. Cyrus seemed to have a soft spot for her, for some reason. But as long as she believed it, she'd do as she was told.

Except that right now, she wasn't. She clasped her hands together as if she needed support, but she didn't back away.

"What exactly is the slant of the story you're planning to do on the Coast Guard?"

He raised a dismissive brow. "I thought we were clear on this. Your only role is to arrange the interviews, not to contribute to the story, no matter how well you feel you know the subject matter."

"I'm not talking about my contribution. Or lack of it. I want to know what you're after."

"My plans for the story don't concern you."

"They do when you use me to get to my father." She shot the words back at him like arrows.

"Get to him?" Annoyance rose, probably because she was exactly on target. "That implies that he has to be protected from the press."

Those green eyes widened. In shock? Or because she agreed and didn't want him to know it? He expected backpedaling on her part. He didn't get it.

"My father doesn't need protection. But he also doesn't deserve some kind of hatchet job, if that's what you have in mind."

Apparently Amanda could overcome her fear of him when it came to her family.

"Why would you assume that? I'm sure my interview style isn't quite as laid-back as the one you generally employ in your painstaking search for the facts about the latest dog show or charity ball, but that doesn't mean I'm planning a hatchet job."

That was below the belt, and he knew it. After all, he was the one who assigned her those stories. And he'd been the recipient of enough sarcasm from his father to dislike using it on anyone else. Still, he had no choice but to keep Amanda away from the truth.

A faint wash of color came up in her cheeks. "You're after something more than a profile piece, aren't you?"

He stood, forcing her to look up at him. "*You're* an employee of this newspaper, Amanda. If you want to continue in that, I'd suggest you keep your imagination in check. Anything I print about your father or anyone else will be the exact truth."

"I trust it will be." She took a cautious step back. "If it isn't…" She stopped, apparently not able to think of a sufficient threat to end that sentence.

"You don't need to worry about that. I'll make sure of it."

Amanda couldn't know just how much he meant that. He wouldn't make the mistake again of rushing into print without being sure of his ability to back up his facts.

But he also wouldn't give up. He had no desire to hurt Amanda or her family. But if Brett Bodine was involved in a kickback scheme, the world was going to know about it, thanks to him.

She was actually shaking. Amanda detoured to the restroom instead of going straight back to her desk.

One of Cyrus's nicer eccentricities had been to have the women's room copied after the one in an elegant downtown department store, with plush love seats in a small sitting area and art deco black-and-white tile in the restroom. She went straight through, headed for the marble sink with its beveled mirror.

Ridiculous. This was idiotic, to let herself be so affected by what that man said or thought of her. She stared at herself in the mirror, disliking the flushed cheeks. Not only had she been affected, but she'd undoubtedly let him see it.

Grabbing a paper towel, she wet it and pressed it against her cheeks. She couldn't let him get to her like this. This wasn't who she was.

And he hadn't really answered her questions. He hadn't denied or explained anything. He'd stonewalled her, like a crooked politician fending off the press.

She tossed the towel in the trash and touched her hair, smoothing a strand back into place, regaining the polished facade she was careful to present to the world. Well, even if she hadn't gotten the answers she'd gone into Ross's office for, something had been gained. She'd actually confronted Ross Lockhart, and she was still in one piece.

She grimaced at her face in the mirror. More or less, anyway. And she still had her job, although he'd issued a not-so-subtle threat on that score.

Ross had implied that she was imagining the emotional currents that had swirled through the office during that interview. Little though she wanted to believe that, she forced herself to consider the possibility.

She couldn't deny that she tended to rush headlong into her latest crusade. If she did deny it, her loving family would stand in line to protest. There was that incident with the woman who claimed her lawyer had stolen her inheritance. It turned out she had neither lawyer nor inheritance.

Tension had existed between Ross and her father. She certainly hadn't dreamed that up. But it was possible that the two men simply disliked each other. Daddy could well have picked up on her feelings for her annoying new boss over the past few months. She hadn't made a secret of them, certainly.

But that didn't account for her conviction that her father had been hiding something. Brett Bodine never hid anything—everything he thought came right out his mouth. Anyone who knew him knew that. He should have exploded at Ross. He hadn't.

She pushed herself away from the sink. Standing here brooding about it wasn't doing the least bit of good. She had to think this through logically. If she talked to Daddy—

The reluctance she felt to broach the subject shocked her. She'd never hesitated to talk to her father, even though sometimes she'd known she'd have to be prepared to ride out a storm if she did. But then, never before had she suspected that Daddy was lying.

Enough of this. She strode out of the restroom and headed for her desk. She'd forget the whole thing, go and get some supper, maybe call Annabel, just for the assurance of hearing her twin's voice.

But when she rounded the corner of the newsroom, she realized she'd forgotten something. C.J. was there, apparently waiting for her. In Amanda's chair, in fact.

C.J. got up hastily when she spotted Amanda coming. "Hey." She seemed to take a second look at Amanda.

"Is somethin' wrong?" Her tone was laced with a kind of reluctant concern.

"No, nothing." She pasted what she hoped was a convincing smile on her face. "I didn't realize you were still here. We don't expect our interns to work late, you know."

C.J.'s face tightened, as if she interpreted that as a criticism. "I was writing up the descriptions of the Coast Guard base, like you asked me to. Or was that just busywork to keep me out of the way?"

Amanda pressed her lips together. The truth was that she'd forgotten all about giving C.J. that assignment, and the kid was astute enough to know that. She cleared her mind and prepared to deal with the problem in front of her.

"The assignment isn't busywork, but it's true that I need to get a sense of where your writing is now. And it wouldn't have been appropriate to take an intern to that sort of interview. You see that, don't you?"

C.J. nodded, perhaps a bit reluctantly.

"Okay, then. Let's have a look at what you've written."

The intern put a couple of sheets of paper in front of her on the desk. "I was just doing some rewriting on the printouts. If you want, I can input the changes and print it out again."

So C.J. wanted to present her with the best work possible. That was a good sign.

"Not necessary. Believe me, I've deciphered worse than this."

She breathed a silent prayer as she bent over the sheets, hoping she wouldn't have to correct too much. Cyrus had handpicked his intern, and Cyrus was erratic enough to make the decision based on whatever standard he thought important at the moment.

But C.J.'s writing proved to be surprisingly smooth and insightful. She read it once, quickly, and then went back over it again, checking a few places. Finally she looked up at the young woman, recognizing the tension that emanated from C.J.

"Relax, C.J. This is good, very good."

C.J.'s breath came out in a whoosh of relief. "Thanks." She seemed to make an effort to sound blasé, but a hint of eagerness showed through. "You marked some things, though."

"Let's take a look." At her gesture, C.J. pulled up her chair. She held the papers flat so that they could go over them together.

"This is a very effective word picture." She tapped one paragraph. "Notice how you've used exact details to get the image across. Now, down here, the observation isn't quite as visual. Do you see what I mean?"

"Got it." C.J. scribbled a few words on the sheet, seeming determined to get it exactly right. She flipped to the second page. "It's the same thing here, isn't it?" She stabbed another paragraph with her pen.

"You've got it."

C.J. slashed an arrow and then began making notes on the back of the sheet.

"You can go home," Amanda said gently. "You don't have to work on it right now."

C.J. moved her shoulders restlessly. "It's hard to get anything done there. The landlord turned off the air-conditioning. He says it's broke, but everyone thinks he's just trying to save money."

"In this heat? How long has it been off?"

"Ten days, maybe. My grandmother's been takin' a walk to the market every day, just so she can go in where it's cool."

That was unconscionable, as hot as the weather had been. Her mind flickered to the cool, welcoming dimness of her small carriage house apartment.

"Hasn't anyone complained to the landlord?"

"Doesn't do any good. He's always cutting corners like that—keeping it hot in summer and cold in winter. Besides, folks figure if they complain too much, he'll treat them even worse."

"But—"

C.J. shook her head. "No use talking about it. I'd rather work."

A relatively polite way of telling Amanda it was none of her business. She watched as the intern went over her work again, scribbling eagerly.

Had she had that sort of initiative at C.J.'s age? She doubted it. She'd been excited to get off to college, true, but she'd been looking forward to starting over with new people, creating a different identity for herself other than just being one of the Bodines. She'd been as excited about football games and parties as about what she might learn.

C.J. looked up from the page. "If I do this whole thing again, will you read it and tell me what you think?"

"Sure thing." She smiled, pleased at the sign C.J. was willing to accept criticism and learn from it. "You have a lot of drive, don't you?"

C.J. shrugged, but this time there wasn't any sullenness attached. "My grandmother always tells me that if I want something, it's my job to do what it takes to get it."

Her thoughts flickered to Miz Callie. "You know, my

grandmother would say exactly the same thing. I guess we have that in common."

Amanda half expected C.J. to back away from that suggestion. Instead, she got a tentative smile that revealed an eager, slightly scared young woman behind the tough exterior.

Another piece of Miz Callie's advice popped into her mind. *God sends people into our lives for a reason, Amanda. Always watch for that, because He might have a special job for you to do.*

Maybe C.J. was destined to be one of those people for her.

Ross locked his office door and started down the hallway, his steps echoing emptily on the tile. He'd stayed at the computer long after the editorial offices had grown quiet, familiarizing himself with every tidbit of information that might possibly affect the investigation.

Speaking of tidbits, his stomach had finally convinced him it was time to quit. Lunch was a distant memory, and he wouldn't achieve anything useful by checking out the snack machine.

He paused automatically at the newsroom door. His attention sharpened. Someone was still there. In a few quiet steps, he had a clear view.

Amanda sat at her desk, her attention riveted on the computer screen. A strand of that sleek brown hair swung forward, brushing her cheek, and the glasses she habitually wore for computer work had slid down her nose, giving her a slightly disheveled look. Charming, but not her usual polished veneer.

Staying late to work didn't fit with the image he had of her as the belle of the social ball. But then, he'd already figured out that there was more to Amanda Bodine than his snap judgment of her.

She'd found the courage to stand up to him today. While he didn't welcome opposition, especially from a subordinate, he had to admire the grit it had taken.

He'd come down too hard on her, that was the truth, and it had been nagging at him for a couple of hours now. That conscience his grandmother had instilled in him could be a troublesome thing at times.

He didn't want to feel that he'd been unfair to her. But he couldn't ignore the truth.

Besides, he still needed her. Threatening to fire her wouldn't encourage her father to come across with any information.

He realized he was gritting his teeth, and he forced his jaw to relax. Mending fences was clearly indicated. He'd never been especially good at that.

He walked toward Amanda's desk. At the sound of footsteps she looked up, startled. When she recognized him, she slicked her hair back behind her ear with one finger and slipped the glasses off her face. He couldn't mistake the aura of defensiveness that wrapped around her.

"Amanda." He lifted an eyebrow, trying not to look intimidating. "What keeps you at the office so late?"

Her eyes widened, as if his genial tone was cause for astonishment. "I… I came back after supper to do a little work."

He leaned against the corner of her desk, moving a silver-framed photo so that he wouldn't knock it over, looking at it as he did so. Amanda and her twin, her parents, the two older brothers, all in jackets and jeans and looking windblown as they walked on the beach. A nice family portrait. His gut tightened.

"Doing some research for a story?"

"Not exactly." Her lips pursed, as if trying to decide how much to tell him. The sight distracted him for a moment.

He managed a smile. "It doesn't matter to the boss if you're doing some early Christmas shopping online."

That surprised her into a smile, and some of the wariness evaporated from her face. "It's nothing like that. I'm looking into some family history for my grandmother, and I can get better access to records through the newspaper."

"Family history?" He perched on the edge of the desk. It was proving easier than he'd expected to get past the barriers he'd erected between them this afternoon. "I should have thought your grandmother was an expert on that."

"She is the family historian, but…" She paused, fiddling with the silver chain that hung around her neck. He had a sense that she was weighing what and how much to tell him.

"But what?"

"It's sort of a…a bit of a family mystery."

The stammer was a dead giveaway that poised, in-control Amanda didn't want to tell him about it, whatever it was. That just increased his curiosity.

"A mystery?" he said lightly. "Sounds intriguing. Tell me about it."

"Well, I…" She bit her lip. "It has to do with a distant relative who dropped from sight during World War II. My grandmother is determined to find out what happened to him, and I promised to help her."

It didn't escape his attention that she was carefully editing what she said to him. Well, fair enough.

If he could gain her trust by helping her with her little genealogical problem, it might ease things between them in other ways.

"This relative—was he in the service?"

She nodded. "He ran away from home to enlist, as far as we can tell."

"That's simple, then. The military records—"

She was shaking her head, and that recalcitrant strand of hair swung back against her cheek again. His hand itched to smooth it back for her, and he clamped down on the ridiculous urge.

"It's not that easy. He apparently signed up under a false name. That's what upsets my grandmother—the possibility of never knowing what happened to him."

He didn't know a lot about World War II, but the problem intrigued him. "You're assuming he died in service, are you?"

"I guess we are. I'd think he'd have gotten in touch with the family sometime if he'd come back safely."

He prodded the problem with his mind, intrigued in spite of himself. How would you go about tracing someone in those circumstances?

"That is tricky. Would he have enlisted locally?" He shook his head. "Probably not, if he didn't want to be recognized. Unless he wasn't very well-known."

"That's a thought." She absently slid the hair back behind her ear, frowning at the screen. "I was trying to look at enlistments from Charleston, but you're right. He'd have been recognized for sure if he'd gone there. But if he went someplace else, how do I begin finding him?"

He pulled over the office chair from the adjoining desk and sat down next to her. He didn't miss the involuntary darkening of her eyes at his closeness. Didn't miss it, but tried to ignore it, just as he tried to ignore his own longing to put his hand on her arm.

"Do you know anything about the circumstances? Exactly when he enlisted? Did he have a car? Any other means of traveling very far? Where were the enlistment centers in the area?"

"Some of that I know." A smile tugged at the corners of her mouth. "But you're pretty good at this investigative stuff, aren't you?"

"I should be. It comes with the job. Any journalist should have an overdeveloped sense of curiosity."

Her eyebrows lifted. "I have to admit I'm wondering why you're so eager to help me with this. This afternoon…"

"Maybe that's why." He forced the words out, not used to apologizing. "I guess I owe you an apology. I came on pretty strong."

Her eyebrows lifted. "Are you sure you want to admit that?"

"All the books on managing staff say that the good boss admits when he's wrong."

"I see." The dimple next to the corner of her lips showed briefly. "I'm delighted to know that you're trying to be a good boss. Is scaring everyone in the building half to death part of that?"

Was he really enjoying this semiflirtatious exchange? Maybe he ought to back away, but he discovered that he didn't want to.

"You're exaggerating. Nobody is that intimidated by me."

Her eyes widened in mock surprise. "Then why does Billy run in the other direction every time he sees you?"

"Billy?" He tried to think of a newsroom staffer by that name and failed. "Who's Billy?"

"Billy Bradley. The mail room boy who delivers mail to your office several times a day." Her expression said that he should have known that. "I'm sure those books of yours would tell you that a good boss knows something about all of his people."

"Maybe so." He could pull back from the intimacy of this conversation at any moment. Maybe he should. But he didn't want to. "If you're so smart, tell me three things about Billy Bradley."

"That's easy. Billy helps his mother support two younger brothers. He plays soccer in the little spare time he has. And he longs to be an investigative reporter."

"Wants to break big stories, does he?" He knew that feeling. "He won't do that from the mail room."

"He has those two little brothers and the widowed mother, remember?" Her tone chided him gently. "At this point, he's happy just to be working for a newspaper while he dreams of big stories. He's determined to be the best mail room boy ever."

"I see he has a big cheerleader in you." He could almost empathize with the kid. Still, he'd never had to work his way up through the mail room. A position had opened up automatically for the congressman's son.

"I like to encourage people." The dimple peeked out again.

Intrigued by the dimple, he leaned toward her, his gaze on her face. He saw her eyes widen and her pupils darken as he neared. A pulse beat visibly in her neck, and he fought the urge to touch it, even to put his lips over hers.

Whoa. Back off. He couldn't do that. He was her boss. They were in the newsroom. Was he asking to be charged with harassment?

He eased away from her, seeing the recognition in her eyes that must mirror his. They were attracted. Okay, they both got it. And they also both got that they couldn't act on that attraction.

He got up, the chair rolling soundlessly back. "Well. I'd better get on my way. Let me know if any of my suggestions pay off."

"Suggestions?" For an instant her eyes were glazed. Then she blinked and glanced toward the computer screen. "Yes, right. Thank you." She took an audible breath. "Good night, Ross."

"Good night." He turned and walked quickly away before he could give in to any of the impulses that rocketed through him.

Chapter 5

Amanda's steps hastened as she went up the stairs to the beach house. It had been a tense day in many ways, mostly because of Ross, and she was relieved to be on the island, safe from the pressures of the newsroom.

She wasn't sure what she'd expected after those moments she and Ross had alone in the newsroom last night. Maybe a little easing of his attitude toward her, at least, or a sense that he remembered.

Instead he'd been curt to the point of rudeness all day. She'd finally escaped the newsroom, taking C.J. with her. They'd wandered around the Market—Charleston's venerable open-air institution. She'd been gathering photos and interviews over the summer with some of the women who made sweetgrass baskets, hoping at some point she'd be able to do a story on them. Certainly it was more interesting than most of the pieces she did.

She hurried inside. "Miz Callie?"

"Right here, darlin'." Her grandmother emerged from the kitchen, beaming at the sight of her, and enveloped her in a hug. "Did you remember the rolls?"

"I sure did." She handed over the bag of still-warm

rolls from the Magnolia Bakery and brushed a kiss on Miz Callie's soft cheek.

Sometimes she thought that no one in her life ever expressed such obvious pleasure at the sight of her. It was a good feeling, to be so clearly loved, and every one of Miz Callie's grandchildren knew it.

"Supper's almost ready, and Georgia and Matt and little Lindsay are joining us. Come along in."

They found Georgia in the kitchen, forking fried chicken onto an ironstone platter. Through the glass doors, Amanda could see her cousin's fiancé, Matt Harper, and his eight-year-old daughter, Lindsay, knocking the sand off their shoes. They must have walked across the beach from Matt's house next door.

She went to open the sliding door for them and stood for a moment, inhaling the wind-borne salt scent of the sea. The tide was out, leaving long tidal pools and a swath of wet sand that glistened, beckoning her to plant some footprints there among the ghost crab trails.

"Hi, Amanda." Matt, tall and tanned, bent to press his cheek briefly against hers. "It's good to see you. Lindsay, come give Amanda a hug, honey."

Matt was beginning to sound like a good old boy after nearly a year on the South Carolina coast. As for Lindsay, she looked like all of them had when they were children, sun kissed and wind tousled.

"Hey, sugar, how are you?" Amanda gave the child a quick hug. "I declare, you've grown an inch this summer."

Lindsay grinned, displaying a space where a front tooth used to be. "Maybe I'll be the tallest one in my class when school starts."

"Could be." If she'd inherited Matt's height, she might well be.

Lindsay crossed the kitchen immediately to wrap her arms around Georgia's waist. Georgia said that she and Matt were taking their relationship slowly because of the child, but it looked to her as if Lindsay was ready to claim Georgia as her mother.

"Everyone grab a dish to take to the table," Miz Callie declared. "It's ready."

Amanda watched her cousin during the cheerful bustle of getting the food on. Georgia had never looked happier. The glow in her face when she looked at Matt and Lindsay shouted her love to the world.

Amanda suppressed a tiny pang that might have been jealousy. Georgia deserved every bit of the happiness she was experiencing. It was childish to use that as a reason to wonder when or if it might happen for her.

Once the blessing had been said and the platters of food started around the table, Georgia fixed her with an enquiring glance. "What's wrong, Manda? You look like someone's been picking on you. Is it that boss of yours again?"

"Not exactly." She forked a golden chicken breast onto her plate. "He's…" Her wayward imagination took her back to those moments when she'd felt lost in Ross's warm gaze. "Sometimes he can be human. He actually gave me a few pointers on the search for Ned."

Georgia dropped the spoon she held into the mashed potatoes. "You didn't tell that newspaper editor about Ned. For goodness' sake, Amanda…"

"Relax, honey. I didn't tell him anything except that I was trying to find out what happened to a relative of my grandmother's. He's an outsider. He's not going to know that old story."

"You said he helped you?" Miz Callie leaned forward, blue eyes bright with the question. "Did you find something?"

"Not exactly, but he gave me some ideas. For instance, Ned wouldn't have enlisted in Charleston, because he'd have been recognized there. And if he didn't have access to a car—"

"He didn't," Miz Callie said surely. "Goodness, it was so tough to drive then, with gas rationing and all, that folks just didn't drive anyplace they could get to by some other means."

"That's what I thought, so I've started checking up on buses and trains. Seems like he'd go someplace within fairly easy reach."

"I suppose he could have gotten someone to drive him," Miz Callie cautioned. "Though if so, he still couldn't have gone far, what with the rationing."

"Is there a record of where all the enlistment offices were in '42?" Matt asked.

"There must be. I'm working on that. And on what name he might have used."

"Eat, sugar," her grandmother said. "You don't need to let your supper get cold while you tell us."

Amanda put a forkful of fragrant fried chicken into her mouth, relishing the flavor. Maybe Miz Callie's fried chicken wasn't good for you, as her mother reminded the family each time she tried yet another vegetarian entrée, but it surely was delicious.

"What name would he have used?" Matt asked. "A middle name? A family name?"

"That's a thought. We ought to make up a list of possibilities to check out." Georgia traced her fork along the tablecloth, as if writing a list. "I'm getting excited all over again, just talking about it. I think Manda's really onto something."

She could search through military records, using some of the family names this time. For an instant she was back in front of her computer, with Ross so close she could smell the fresh scent of his aftershave.

She didn't want to keep remembering that, but she couldn't seem to stop herself.

She'd have to find a way. Ross's curtness today had to mean that he regretted what happened. Recognized it and regretted it.

That was the best course, surely. Nothing real could ever develop between them, and she'd be smart to accept that.

She forced her attention back to the table. Matt had begun telling an anecdote about one of his clients, an elderly man who wanted to sue his landlord for letting pigeons roost on the gables of the house he rented over in Mount Pleasant's old town.

She laughed with the rest of them, but the story reminded her of C.J.'s housing problems. Matt, as an attorney, might have some insight.

"What if you had a tenant with a real problem? For instance, he or she had a landlord who refused to fix the air-conditioning in a building where folks were really suffering from the heat."

"I'd have to know a bit more about it to give advice." Matt focused on her. "But certainly they have legal recourse if they have a signed lease that includes air-conditioning. It's a violation of the warrant of habitability. Is this someone you know?"

"In a way. My intern at work. She lives with her grandmother somewhere in Charleston, and they're having a lot of trouble with the landlord."

Matt frowned. "Too often, people are afraid to fight in situations like that. Or they can't afford to." His lips twitched as Georgia and Amanda both looked at him. "And, yes, I would take a case like that pro bono, if that's what you're planning to ask me. But as I said, I'd need a lot more information."

"I can talk to C.J., my intern, about it." Amanda recognized the enthusiasm that gripped her. It was what her brothers liked to call her Joan of Arc response to the little guy getting hurt.

Well, good. Maybe it would keep her distracted from the stupid attraction she kept feeling for Ross.

"Well, now, Amanda, it seems this might be just what you've been looking for."

Amanda stared blankly at her grandmother. Had Miz Callie been reading her mind?

"You've been talking about wanting to write an important story, haven't you?" Miz Callie said. "Seems to me you've just found one."

The idea took root with a sureness that made it seem as if God was sending a message to her through Miz Callie. She reached over to squeeze her grandmother's hand.

"You know, you might be right about that."

If this guy got any more evasive, Ross decided, he just might slide right out of the booth at the coffee shop and on out the door.

"Your contracts with the Coast Guard base must be pretty important to your business, Mr. Gerard," he prompted.

The list of suppliers had finally come through from Amanda's father, and he'd picked Gerard Plumbing as a good place to start. Now he was starting to wonder about that. Amos Gerard had balked at coming to the newspaper, but finally agreed to meet for a cup of coffee at the coffee shop across the street. So far the coffee was the only thing that had crossed his lips.

Gerard shrugged, wiping a ham-size palm on his jeans. "I guess so. They're good folks to work with." His gaze shifted from the coffee cup to the spoon to the sugar bowl without coming to rest on Ross.

"How did you come by that contract?"

He considered himself pretty good at reading the people he interviewed, but he couldn't decide whether the man had something to hide or was just nervous at talking to someone from the press.

"Saw the announcement and bid on it, like everyone else." Now Gerard's gaze did meet his, but with a suspicious glare. "If you're saying there was anything wrong with my work, you're way off base. The Coast Guard got exactly what they ordered from me, and at a fair price, too."

"I'm not questioning your work at all," he said quickly. If Gerard thought that, he'd clam up entirely. "I'd just like some insight into how the contracts are awarded. Who decides on the supplier, and how they make that decision."

Gerard's cheeks rounded, and he puffed out a breath. "I guess they decide who can do the job cheapest, same as everyone else does."

"It's a valuable contract for the supplier. Maybe there's a little extra consideration expected if your company is chosen."

He'd expect an honest man to take offense at the comment. Gerard just stared at him blankly. Then his gaze slid away again. "I guess..."

He let that trail off, his eyes riveted on the person who had just come into the coffee shop and was coming straight toward them. Amanda Bodine.

Something that might have been anger washed over Gerard's face and was gone so quickly Ross couldn't be sure of what he'd seen. Then he slid from the booth, tossing a handful of change on the table.

"We're done," he said, and walked quickly away with a curt nod to Amanda as he passed her.

Ross stared after him, speculation flooding his mind. Had Gerard been about to admit something? And if he had, was it the sight of one of the Bodines that had changed his mind? He didn't want to read too much into that, but Amanda's entrance had done something.

She paused at his table. "I'm glad I caught you. There's something I'd like to—"

He cut her off with a jerk of his head in the direction of the closing door. "Do you know the man who just left?"

She turned to look out the plate-glass window at the retreating figure. Gerard's Plumbing was clearly visible on the back of his shirt. Her brow furrowed.

"Gerard's Plumbing? I think they've done some work for my folks over the years. I don't think I know him personally. Is there some work you need done?"

That encounter could mean something or nothing, but all his instincts told him that Gerard had been a little too eager to get away from him once he'd spotted Amanda Bodine.

In any event, he couldn't afford to let Amanda start inquiring into what he was doing.

"Just a casual conversation." He rose, putting his payment on top of the bill. "I'm headed back to the office. I'll let you get your coffee."

Instead of heading for the counter, she fell into step beside him. "I really wanted to talk with you. About a story idea."

"Bring it up at the editorial meeting."

She stayed doggedly at his side, and her face was alive with enthusiasm. "C.J. told me about something that's going on in the apartment block where she and her grandmother live. It seems the landlord is refusing to take care of routine maintenance, not even getting the air-conditioning fixed in this heat."

They stepped out onto the sidewalk as she spoke, and the hot, humid air settled on him like a wet wool blanket. Trying to ignore it—ignore her—he strode across the street.

"That's not a story, Amanda. It's a personal annoyance. C.J. and her grandmother should complain."

"To whom?" She had to hurry to keep up with him. "The landlord ignores the tenants, and from what I can tell, they're too afraid of being kicked out to raise a fuss. He shouldn't be allowed to get away with that. If we ran a story—"

He stopped in front of the building, then immediately wished he'd taken the conversation on inside to the lobby. Where it was cool.

He scowled at her. That didn't seem to dampen the zeal that shone in her green eyes. "I repeat, it's not a story. The landlord could have a dozen perfectly good explanations, and you don't know any of them."

"But—"

"You're a reporter, Amanda, not a social worker or a crusader."

She flushed a little at that. "If I got more information about the landlord, talked to the tenants, then would you consider running it?"

That was the last thing he needed, to have Amanda running off half-cocked and getting herself into trouble. He was starting to feel responsible for her, and that annoyed him.

"Just let it go, Amanda. Get on with the article you already have on tap. If there's anything in this—"

"There is," she interrupted, anger sparking in her eyes.

"That decision is mine to make, not yours."

He held the door open, welcoming the blast of cool air. He could have someone look into the situation and get a handle on whether this was worth an investigation, but that someone wasn't going to be Amanda. If by any chance that landlord was pulling something underhanded and probably illegal on his tenants, he wouldn't be too happy to be confronted by a reporter.

For a moment Amanda stood on the hot sidewalk, glaring at him. Then, chin held high, she marched into the building.

He followed, letting the door swing shut behind him. Amanda was already almost to the elevator. Maybe he'd use the stairs.

She'd taken offense at his decision, not surprisingly. What else was new? It seemed impossible for the two of them to meet on neutral ground. He constantly fought the urge to throttle her.

Or kiss her.

Chapter 6

"Come on, can't you give me a smile?" Amanda coaxed, watching the child's face in the screen of her digital camera. "Please?"

The little girl sat at the top of the sliding board, dark hair in multiple braids tied with pink ribbons that matched the pink shorts and T-shirt she wore, her lips pressed together firmly.

Amanda glanced at C.J., who'd accompanied her on this assignment. "She'd be an adorable example of the summer playground program if we could get a smile."

C.J. took the hint and crawled onto the bottom of the slide. "Hey, is this the right way to use this thing?" She planted her palms on the slide and made as if to pull herself up toward the girl. "Is it?"

The child shook her head, solemn for another moment. "No." The corners of her lips curved up just a bit.

"It must be." C.J. pretended to scramble upward. "How'd you get up there? You slid up on your tummy, didn't you?"

"No, ma'am!" The child grinned, eyes lighting up.

She grabbed the sides of the slide. "You get yourself outta the way, y'hear? 'Cause I'm comin' down."

Amanda snapped quickly while C.J. scrambled out of the way. The child sailed off the end, bounced on her feet, and was headed toward the ladder again when a whistle blew.

"Crafts!" she yelled, and darted off toward the pavilion.

A smile lingering on her lips, Amanda shaded the camera with her hand to check the photos she'd taken, aware of C.J. watching over her shoulder. To Amanda's amusement, C.J. now wore a neat pair of tan slacks with a shirt in Amanda's favorite shade of turquoise.

The intern's attitude had steadily improved since that pugnacious exchange the first day, which was certainly an answer to prayer. Maybe the plain talking Amanda had done had gotten through to her.

Amanda knew perfectly well that she was putting off another serious discussion. She'd spent a couple of hours with C.J. today, and she hadn't mentioned the housing issue or the possibility of doing a story on it.

Maybe because that wasn't really a possibility, not as far as Ross was concerned. Amanda's jaw tightened at the thought. He was being unreasonable, dismissing the idea just because it came from her.

"Why didn't they send a photographer with us?" C.J.'s question was abrupt, as if she was ready to take offense at their lack of a photographer. "I thought they had pros to do the pictures."

"The paper does have a few photographers, but not enough to go around." And too often, the stories she was assigned weren't considered important enough to warrant a photographer. "If you have a chance to learn anything about digital photography, grab it. That ability improves your chances in a tough job market, believe me."

C.J. frowned a little, but she nodded. "Did we get enough material from Miz Dottie for the story, do you think?"

Amanda glanced across the playground to the pavilion. A couple of eager high school volunteers were teaching crafts under the benign gaze of the elderly black woman who'd spearheaded the fight to provide this program for the poorest of the city's children.

"I hope so. There's plenty more I'd like to say about Miz Dottie, but we're going to have limited column inches for this story."

That fact annoyed her. In her opinion, Miz Dottie was a true hero—a woman who'd dedicated her life to her community, sturdily walking over the forces that would have stopped her.

But the paper, in the person of Ross, wouldn't spare precious space for what he'd dismiss as a "feel-good" story. The old newspaper adage that "if it bleeds, it leads," seemed to be his motto.

She lifted damp hair off her neck. The stifling heat didn't seem to bother the kids, but she was wilting. "Let's head back to the office and pull this together."

They walked across the playground together, Amanda mentally composing the lead to the story.

"So if I learn to use a camera, I should put that on a résumé." C.J.'s mind was obviously on her future, not the current story, but Amanda didn't blame her for that. This internship ought to prepare her for a career.

"Definitely," Amanda said. She hesitated, knowing the intern was prickly on the subject of higher education for herself. "You know, there are still plenty of loans and scholarships—"

"Not for me," C.J. cut her off. "You don't get it. I have my grandmother to take care of. She took me in after my mamma died. Now it's my turn."

"I understand. Really." Wouldn't she do the same for Miz Callie, if she were in C.J.'s situation?

They got into the car, and she turned the air to high, the movement reminding her again of C.J.'s problem with her landlord. But this time Miz Callie's opinions on that subject came to the forefront of her mind.

Miz Callie thought she was meant to tackle this issue. If so, she'd have to risk disobeying Ross's orders. And now was the time.

Come on, Amanda. Are you a woman or a mouse?

She glanced in the rearview mirror and pulled out into traffic. "Is the situation with your hot apartment any better?"

C.J. concentrated on fastening her seat belt. "Not much. I bought a fan. Gran sits in front of it and works on her baskets."

"Baskets?"

"She makes sweetgrass baskets for the Market."

"I didn't know that. I wonder if I've talked to her there. I've been collecting interviews and photos to do a piece on the sweetgrass basket weavers."

C.J. glanced at her, lifting her brows. "D'you actually think he'll let you run it?"

There was no doubt in Amanda's mind as to who that "he" was. She probably shouldn't encourage C.J.'s attitude toward Ross, but she had to be honest in her answer.

"I don't know. But I want to try. Preserving that heritage seems important to me." The Gullah people of the islands had brought their basket-weaving skills with them from Africa generations ago. Without the dedication of the few who remained, the art would be lost, just another beautiful thing swept away by changing times. "Would your grandmother talk to me about the craft?"

"I guess. Long as you're not going to make her look like an ignorant old woman."

She gave C.J. a level look. "Do you think I'd do that?"

C.J. returned the look, seeming to measure her. "No," she said finally.

The level of trust contained in the word pleased her, but now she had to ask the more challenging question.

Please help me, Lord, to do the right thing for the right reason. That was the tricky part, wasn't it? Miz Callie would say that the Lord expected not only the right actions, but the right heart.

"I was thinking about what you told me about your landlord. Would your grandmother and some of the other tenants talk to me about it? Maybe—"

"You can't put them in the paper." C.J.'s voice rose. "He'd kick us out for sure."

"But maybe just the threat of publicity would be enough to make him mend his ways." Amanda hoped she was right about that. "I have a friend who's an attorney. He's willing to make sure your rights are protected."

"We can't afford a lawyer." C.J.'s face closed, turning her back into the sullen teenager she'd seemed in their first encounter.

"It wouldn't cost you anything. He's a friend of mine." She smiled. "And you're a friend."

C.J. averted her face, staring out the window at the busy sidewalks, crowded with locals headed for their favorite lunchtime restaurants and tourists bedecked with cameras. The intern was silent for so long that Amanda was sure she'd blown it.

C.J. traced a line down the crease of her slacks with one finger. "I guess maybe we could talk about it, anyway. See what my gran says."

Amanda let out a breath she hadn't known she was holding. "I can't ask for more than that. I'll stop by this evening, okay?"

C.J.'s gaze, dark with what seemed a lifetime of doubt, met hers. "Okay."

Surely, if the door was opening to this, God meant her to walk through.

"This isn't one of your brightest ideas, Manda." Hugh, Amanda's next older brother, peered disapprovingly at the apartment building where C.J. lived that evening. "Reminds me of the time you rushed into the neighbor's house, convinced it was on fire because you saw an orange glow in the bedroom window, which turned out to be mood lighting."

Would no one ever let her forget that? "This is different."

"Let me go in with you, okay?"

"No way. C.J.'s leery enough of talking to me. Confronted with you, she'd clam up entirely."

"Why?" He tried to make all six foot four of himself look innocuous. He didn't succeed. "I'm harmless."

"You know that and I know that, but oddly enough, most people find you intimidating. Useful in law enforcement, but not in this." She patted his tanned cheek. "Thanks for driving me. I sure wouldn't want to leave my car on the street in this block."

"Then you ought to understand why I don't want to

leave my sister in this block," he retorted, fixing her with the look that probably made wrongdoers confess on the spot.

"Just be a good brother and come back for me in about an hour and a half. If I'm going to be longer, I'll call you."

Hugh, probably knowing from a lifetime of experience that he couldn't dissuade her, nodded. "Daddy would scalp me if he knew I let you come here after dark. And you, too."

True, this wasn't an area she'd normally frequent, but she hadn't been able to come until C.J. got home from her job waiting tables. At this hour, the stoops and sidewalks were empty of children playing and women gossiping. A couple of men came out of the tavern across the street, talking loudly, and a group of teenage males drifted down the street, silent as smoke.

"I'll be fine." She slid out before she could change her mind. "See you later."

Despite her bravado, she was relieved that he waited at the curb, his size intimidating, until she'd been buzzed into the building. Once the door shut behind her, she waved through the glass. Hugh got back into his car and drove off.

There were definite advantages to having big brothers, annoying as they could be sometimes. She checked the row of mailboxes to be sure she had the number right and headed for the stairs.

She picked her way up, avoiding a few broken risers, her forehead damp with sweat before she reached the landing. The air was stifling, and the handrail had come away from the wall, dangling uselessly. That couldn't make it easy for C.J.'s grandmother to get up and down. Whether the landlord had done anything illegal she didn't know, but he certainly wasn't taking care of his building.

The apartment C.J. shared with her grandmother was on the third floor. She arrived slightly out of breath and knocked. C.J. opened the door almost before she'd taken her hand down.

"Hi, C.J." She hoped she sounded as if this visit was a normal thing for them. "I hope I'm not late."

C.J. shook her head, glancing back over her shoulder into the apartment. "My gran's not... Well, she's not real happy about this. She doesn't feel so good tonight."

"No wonder, hot as it is." She looked pointedly beyond the intern.

C.J. opened the door wider and motioned her in. "You're welcome to come in. I'm just letting you know how things stand."

Amanda stepped into a living room that was hot and airless, but scrupulously clean. Handmade lace doilies topped the backs of chairs and set under lamps. But it wasn't the doilies that captured Amanda's interest. It was the baskets.

Sweetgrass baskets, handmade by a master weaver, sat on every surface. A large one held newspapers and magazines, while a half dozen smaller ones were in use for everything from fruit to balls of yarn.

She picked up a shallow serving basket, its top edge intricately braided, the base striped in tan and brown that reminded her of the marshes in winter. "This is beautiful."

"You know what that basket is for?" A sharp voice cracked the question.

Amanda turned, basket balanced on her palms, to

see the erect elderly woman who stood in the doorway of what must be a bedroom. She was tiny, but she held herself erect with the dignity of a judge. Maybe she was a judge, at that, because she studied Amanda as if weighing her heart.

"Yes, ma'am. It's a pie basket, isn't it? My grandmother has one like it."

The woman inclined her head in a slight nod, as if awarding Amanda a point. "I heah from my granddaughter that you're a Bodine. Miz Callie your grandma?"

"She is."

Another point. She set down the basket. Judging by the perspiration that glistened on the elderly woman's skin, they ought to sit down and take advantage of the breeze from the fan C.J. must have put in the front window. But she could hardly suggest it. Apparently, the woman hadn't made up her mind whether Amanda was welcome or not.

"Gran, this is Amanda Bodine." C.J. rushed the introduction, sounding rattled. Well, she was standing between two of the authority figures in her life. "Amanda, I'd like to introduce my grandmother, Miz Etta Carrey."

"Miz Carrey, I'm glad to meet you. We think a lot of C.J. at the newspaper."

That must have been the wrong thing to say, because the woman's lips tightened. "My grandchild says you're talking about putting something in the paper about our troubles with the landlord. She shouldn't have mentioned our business. It's private."

Nothing like getting right to the heart of the matter. "If your landlord is breaking the terms of your lease, it's not right. Maybe the threat of publicity will do what complaints won't."

"Maybe it would, maybe it wouldn't. We're not going to know, 'cause you're not writing anything about us for that newspaper."

"Gran—"

"You, hush." The woman turned on C.J., dark eyes snapping. "You think he's not gonna know it came from us if something's in that paper, with you working there every day? Next thing we'll be out in the street, lucky if we get our belongings out with us."

"Amanda has a lawyer she says would help us."

"No!" The woman showed the first sign of strain, reaching out to grasp the door frame, her hand twisted by arthritis. "It can't be, Catherine Jane, and you should know that. You can't go against your family, just because of that job at the newspaper."

For an instant Amanda didn't know who she meant, but of course C.J. must stand for Catherine Jane. An elegant name, but one that must sound hopelessly old-fashioned to a teenager.

C.J. went quickly to put her arm around the elderly woman's waist. "I'm not, Gran. I'm not." She sent Amanda a look that seemed to say this was her fault. Which, she guessed, it was. "You'd better go."

Miz Callie would say that a lady always knew when to end a call. That apparently was now.

Amanda nodded and moved to the door. "I'm glad to have met you, Miz Carrey. I hope sometime you'll let me talk to you about your baskets."

C.J. pulled the door open, all but shoving Amanda through. "Just go," she muttered. She closed the door firmly in her face.

Amanda started back down the stairs, her stomach twisting. That had been short, but not sweet. She hadn't handled it well. She ought to have… Well, she didn't know what. She felt as if she'd stumbled in the dark and didn't know where she was.

She'd thought she was doing the right thing. Maybe the truth was that she was doing what she so often did rush into a situation on impulse instead of waiting for guidance. Just as Hugh had pointed out.

She'd reached the sidewalk, with the building door closed behind her, before she recognized an unpalatable fact. She was in trouble. Hugh wasn't coming for her for over an hour, and this wasn't a place to stand around with a handbag and a camera slung over her shoulder. At night. Alone.

A burst of noise and music spilled out of the bar across the street. She took a couple of hurried steps toward the curb. The bar wasn't the sort of place she'd normally enter, but at least there'd be people around while she waited for Hugh. She dragged her cell phone out to call him, its screen a welcome light in the dark.

She'd reached the curb when she saw them—figures, hardly recognizable in the dim light. The teenage boys she'd noticed going in? Maybe. They drifted closer, and her stomach turned over.

Hugh really would have something to say about this. She should have called him before she ever left the building. She glanced behind her. If she ran for the door, could she get inside before one of them reached her? With a shiver that must have been fear, she knew the answer was no.

Fragments of advice from the self-defense class she and Annabel had taken jostled in her mind. Fight? Run?

Before she could decide, a car sped down the street

and screeched to a stop next to her. The driver leaned across to open the door.

"Get in. Now." Ross sounded fully as angry as she'd been imagining her brother to be. Maybe more so.

Never mind. She was too glad to see him. She slid into the car and slammed the door.

Chapter 7

Ross wasn't sure which emotion was stronger—sheer anger that Amanda had put herself in danger by disobeying a direct order or the fierce protectiveness that had swept him when he'd seen her on that curb. Now that he knew she was safe, it was probably anger.

"What were you thinking?" he erupted, accelerating down the dark street. "Did I or did I not tell you to leave that story alone? Instead of listening, you walk right into a situation a ten-year-old child would know better than to get into."

Speaking of listening, she didn't appear to be paying the least attention to his tirade. Instead, she was twisted around in the seat, staring out the back at something behind them.

"What are you doing? Is someone following us?"

"No." She turned around again.

In the light of an overhanging streetlamp, he caught a quick, clear image of her face before shadows fell over it again. Her expression stifled any words that were on his lips.

Fear. Amanda—behind that cool, competent facade, Amanda was afraid.

"You're safe now." Reluctant sympathy softened his voice. He ought to be delighted she'd been scared. Maybe that was what she needed to keep her from committing such idiocy.

But he wasn't. Instead, he had an equally idiotic urge to stop the car and take her in his arms. He clamped the steering wheel nearly as tightly as he was clamping his jaw.

"Thank you." She was staring down at the cell phone in her hand. At least she'd had sense enough to call for help. She shot a sideways glance at him. "How did you happen to come along at just the right moment?"

"No happen about it. I called C.J.'s number earlier this evening and reached her grandmother. She told me you were coming."

Amanda's expression said she didn't quite know which question to ask first. "Why did you call her? You said there was no story."

He was afraid she'd zero in on that. "I said there was no story without more facts. That's what I was after."

"And that made you decide to come down here? Because you thought I might be in trouble or because you wanted to take over the interview?"

Just about any answer would only make the situation more uncomfortable. "I was late at the office. It was no trouble to swing by and make sure you were okay."

Which wasn't really an answer at all. Amanda probably knew he was late at the office every night. Probably thought he was a compulsive workaholic who had no life outside of work. She might just be right.

Amanda's brows knitted. "Were you going to come into the building?"

"Judging from C.J.'s grandmother's reaction to my call, I didn't think I'd be welcome. You have any luck?"

"Not much," she admitted. "But what were you doing? Waiting for me to come out?"

She was nothing if not persistent. It was a good quality in a reporter, but at the moment it annoyed the heck out of him.

"I was just pulling up when I saw you were alone on the curb." He ground out the words. "Speaking of which, where is your car?"

"I didn't want to leave it on the street, so—" She cut that off, consternation filling her face. "Good heavens, I forgot about my brother." She punched a button on the cell phone. Pressing it to her ear, she effectively ignored him.

He turned onto King Street and wondered where they were going. He had a vague sense she lived down in the historic district someplace, so he was probably headed in the right direction.

"Hugh? Listen, I got finished early, so I've already left. You don't need to—"

A male voice interrupted her, so loudly irate that Ross could hear it. He couldn't make out the words, but clearly Amanda was getting a much-needed earful from her brother.

"Yes, I know, but I wasn't in trouble—"

Annoyance prickled. She was sounding a lot more apologetic to the brother than she had to him.

"I'm telling you, I'm fine, so stop yelling. No, you don't need to get me. A…a friend is taking me home. Love you, okay?"

The resulting murmur sounded placated, if also a bit exasperated. Being Amanda's brother must be a full-time job, given her penchant for trouble.

She dropped the cell phone into her bag and brushed a wing of hair behind her ear. His hand tingled, as if he had touched the silky strand.

"You didn't fool him," he said, distracting himself.

"You mean about not being in trouble?" She blew out a breath. "It's tough to con Hugh, him being in law enforcement and all."

"To say nothing of knowing you since birth."

She grinned, the tension between them popping like a bubble. "That, too."

He'd probably be better off without being on the receiving end of too many of those impudent smiles. "One question? Where are we going?"

"Oh, sorry. I can call a taxi—"

"Just tell me." Maybe putting her in a cab was safer, given the level of attraction he felt in the close confines of the car, but...

She leaned forward, as if just noticing where they were. "It's not far, if you really don't mind driving me home. Just take the next left."

In a few minutes they were pulling to the curb of one of the narrow residential streets down near the Battery. "That's it?" He leaned across the front seat to peer through the window at the tiny house tucked between two graceful antebellum mansions.

"Small, but my very own." She opened the door, and the dome light showed him a faint embarrassment in her eyes. "Would you like to come in for a cup of coffee or an iced tea?"

He didn't want coffee, but he did want to see Amanda

in her own setting and to say something to her where they could be face-to-face.

"I'd like to come in for a moment." He got out quickly, before she could think of a way to uninvite him, and walked around the car to join her on the curb.

Amanda pushed open the black wrought-iron gate that led to the tiny front garden of the equally tiny cottage. She hurried up the brick walk, pulling a ring of keys from her bag.

"My place was originally the gatehouse for that property."

She nodded to the house on the left. It loomed over its small neighbor, and he realized that the trim and paint color of the two was the same, despite the difference in their sizes.

"You were lucky to get something in the historic district." He'd been here long enough to know that finding an affordable place to live was a major preoccupation in Charleston.

"It belongs to a friend of a family friend," she said, opening the door and switching on lights. "Come in."

He stepped inside, feeling as if he had walked into a child's playhouse. At first sight the living room seemed cluttered to him, with chintz upholstered pieces, lacy curtains drawn back from plantation shutters, and photos covering every horizontal space, but after a moment's study he decided that *cozy* was a better word. It was a far cry from the sterile furnished apartment he occupied when he wasn't at the paper.

"It's nice," he said, feeling some comment was called for.

"All castoffs from the rest of the family. You wouldn't believe what my folks and my aunts and uncles have in their attics, to say nothing of Miz Callie." She tossed her handbag on a cherry drop-leaf table. "Now, what about that coffee?"

He could say yes. They'd sit close together on that chintz love seat… No, that would be a mistake. He might end up doing something he'd regret, like kissing her.

"No coffee." He took a step that closed the distance between them, seeing her eyes widen. "I came in to say something to you."

"W-what?"

He was close enough to hear the hitch in her breath, and that set his pulses racing. "You put yourself in danger tonight for a story. You will never do that again, or I will fire you. Understand?"

She nodded. Her lips trembled, drawing his attention to them.

He could sense how they'd feel under his—the shape of her mouth, the softness of her lips, the sweetness of her breath. He leaned toward her—

Back off, he commanded himself. That would be a mistake. Even if he weren't pursuing a story that might lead directly to her father, he couldn't get involved with someone who worked for him.

Amanda, despite her veneer of sophistication, was really a small-town girl at heart, giving up a promising job in Tampa to come home because of her family, from what he'd seen. A woman from a close-knit family like hers would believe in love and fidelity and happily-ever-after. All the things he dismissed as fiction.

She looked up at him from beneath her lashes, the glance tentative, questioning, as if she wondered what he was thinking. And he couldn't resist. He covered her lips with his.

The kiss was sweet…an almost platonic touch in comparison to some of the women he'd dated. But the impact rushed through him and headed straight for his heart, pummeling it unmercifully. He touched her arms, drawing her closer, and she leaned into his embrace with a little sigh that seemed to say she'd come home.

It was the sigh that brought him back to himself. He couldn't do this. It was a mistake—a gigantic one.

It took more willpower than he'd known he possessed to pull away. Amanda's green eyes held a dazed expression that probably matched his own.

He had to search for the right words to say. "I'm sorry. I shouldn't have done that." He took a step back, feeling as if he'd left a part of himself behind.

Amanda shook her head, seeming to shake off the dream that held her dazed. "Don't apologize. You weren't the only one involved."

"No." He hadn't been, and that made things infinitely more complicated. "I'd better go." Before he made the situation even worse, if that was possible. "Good night, Amanda."

He turned and walked quickly away, because if he didn't, he wasn't sure how much more foolish he might have been.

The fact that Amanda was expected for supper at Mamma and Daddy's the night after her adventure at C.J.'s apartment was trouble on so many levels she wasn't sure how to count them. There was the fact of her having been stuck there, to begin with, and then there was that kiss, which she'd been trying all day to forget.

But the thing that made her chest tight and her palms damp as she went up the walk to the front door was what she had seen when she'd climbed into Ross's car. She'd looked back, just a quick glance to be sure no one was coming after them.

The door to the bar had opened, and a man stepped out onto the sidewalk. Not just any man. The last man she'd expect to see in a place like that—her father.

She paused on the walk, ostensibly to admire her mamma's dahlias, blooming their hearts out along the veranda. But she wasn't really seeing them. She was seeing something furtive about that familiar figure in that place. Out of uniform.

Ask him. The voice of her conscience was blunt. *Just come right out and ask him.*

She could, of course. Make it light, as if it meant nothing at all. Which it didn't, she assured herself quickly.

That meant revealing her presence in that part of town, and Daddy wasn't going to be happy about that. But that wasn't really what held her back, and she knew it.

That odd interaction between her father and Ross lay at the bottom of her uneasiness. She'd tried again and again to tell herself that she'd imagined it. Unfortunately, she hadn't been able to make herself believe it.

Ross was still working on the Coast Guard story, even if he hadn't asked her for any more introductions. Maybe she'd already served his purpose when she'd introduced him to the family. She just didn't know what that purpose was.

She touched the brilliant face of an orange dahlia and straightened, heading for the door. She didn't know what she was going to do, but she'd best get inside before Mamma sent someone out to fetch her.

The brass knob was familiar to her hand, and the

frosted glass sent back a dim reflection of her face. She turned the knob and walked inside, dropping her bag on the table under the mirror in the center hallway. Her heels clicked on the parquet floor.

"I'm here," she called. "Anybody home?"

"We're in here, sugar." Hugh's voice. If he'd told Mamma and Daddy what she'd got up to last night...

She walked into the parlor. Hugh's long legs were stretched out comfortably in front of him as he leaned back, looking practically boneless, on the couch. Annabel, in her usual jeans and T-shirt, perched on the arm next to him, her thick braid swinging across her shoulder.

Mamma was probably in the kitchen, but Daddy sat bolt upright in his chair, hands planted firmly on his knees, looking as if he wanted to give someone a piece of his mind.

She exchanged a wordless glance with her twin. *Danger, danger...* Annabel didn't need to speak to convey the warning.

"What's this I hear about you gettin' into trouble last night, Amanda?"

She swung on Hugh. "You told."

He spread big hands wide. "I was makin' a joke of it, honest. I didn't know Daddy'd get so het up."

"Yeah, right. Tattletale."

"Right." Annabel weighed in instantly on her side. She swatted Hugh lightly on the head. "Troublemaker."

He grinned. "Daddy, the twins are picking on me."

"You ought to know better." Mamma appeared in the doorway, a wooden spoon in her hand, but it wasn't immediately clear whether she was talking to Amanda or Hugh. Or both.

"Do you need some help, Mamma?" She'd be just as glad to get into Mamma's less volatile company until Daddy forgot about this.

"No, no." Mamma waved the spoon. "It's just about ready, so don't settle down too much."

She vanished again.

Amanda turned to her sister, ready to change the subject with a question about Annabel's horses, but Daddy got in first.

"Amanda, where exactly were you last night?"

She pressed her lips together for an instant. This would be all right. She'd say where she'd been, and Daddy would comment on being in the same place, say he'd have come to her rescue if only he'd known, and her doubts would be wiped away.

"Down on Joslyn Street. The three hundred block. It's where my intern lives."

Where you were last night, Daddy. In a bar I'd never have expected you to touch with a ten-foot pole.

"It's not as bad as it sounds, I promise." Hugh sat up straight, bumping his legs on the coffee table. "I dropped her off, and I was coming back to get her."

Daddy frowned. "At least you two had that much sense. If I hadn't been stuck on base last night, I'd have taken her myself, if it was that important."

It struck her like a blow to the stomach. Daddy. Lying. She could hardly put the words together. That just didn't happen.

"Hugh took care of it," Annabel said, with the air of someone who didn't see what all the fuss was about.

"Actually, I didn't." Hugh's gaze met hers and then slid away. "Manda got done a little early, so a friend drove her home."

"Friend?" Daddy's voice cut like a knife. "What friend?"

She swallowed. "Not a friend, exactly. My boss. Ross Lockhart."

She saw the impact on her father. Saw it, saw him try to hide it. And knew that whatever had taken him to that bar last night, she couldn't ask him about it. She couldn't put him in a position where he'd lie to her again.

Amanda still worried about the situation the next evening when she walked the short two blocks to the home of Cyrus Mayhew. The *Bugle*'s publisher was having a party, and apparently the whole staff was invited.

That meant she'd be seeing Ross in a social setting. A business setting was bad enough. He'd been cool and distant at the office, as if to deny that their kiss had ever happened.

At least Ross had allowed her to do some minor investigating into the landlord situation. She'd discovered the owner was an absentee landlord, living on one of the gated barrier island communities off Beaufort, not here in Charleston at all.

She crossed the street toward Cyrus's place, cautious of the cobblestones of the historic district, never easy to navigate when wearing heels, and felt the breeze off the water. The Mayhew house proudly faced the Battery and Charleston harbor. Cyrus was fond of talking about the window glass that had broken during the siege of Fort Sumter, which was visible from his second-floor balcony during the day.

The wrought-iron gates stood hospitably open. She stepped into the walled garden where tiny white lights glistened in the trees, reflected from the surface of the

oval pond and echoed the light summer colors of the
women's dresses.

She hadn't gotten two feet when a waiter swept down
on her with a tray of drinks, followed by a second with
an array of canapés. She took an icy glass of lemonade
and a mushroom tart, turned away and narrowly escaped
the waving champagne glass of the *Bugle*'s society editor, Juliet Morrow.

"Evening, Amanda." Juliet beamed in her direction.
Juliet did enjoy a party. "Be sure you get some of those
crab turnovers, y'heah? They are superb."

"I'll do that." She bit into the flaky pastry of the
mushroom tart, feeling the flavors explode in her mouth.
Cyrus had been a widower for years and showed no
signs of wanting to change his marital status, to the despair of Charleston's female population, which thought
he needed a hostess, at least. Instead, he employed the
best caterer in town for his parties.

"Nice, isn't it?" Juliet's glass gestured to take in the
garden, the caterer's people, even the graceful lines of
the antebellum house. "Cyrus is lucky it didn't rain tonight. He wouldn't want this horde tramping on his
Oriental carpets and puttin' their glasses down on his
piecrust table."

"The air's heavy enough for a storm." Amanda
quelled an inward shudder at the thought, never having managed to quite conquer a childish fear of thun-
derstorms. "I'm sure he'd be welcoming if we had to
go inside." She glanced around, nodding to people she
knew. "Where is he?"

Juliet lifted a perfectly plucked brow. "Our esteemed
publisher? Or our hunky new managing editor?"

"Hunky?" She kept her voice level with an effort.

She certainly didn't want to raise suspicions in Juliet's fertile imagination. "Really, Juliet, if you use that kind of language in your column, folks will think your beat is gossip, not society."

"This is just between you and me, darlin'." The society editor's smile held only a trace of malice. "You should know how attractive the man is, as much time as you've been spending with him. Tell me, what's really behind that gruff exterior?"

The memory of Ross's kiss flooded through her, and her cheeks heated. She could only hope the light was dim enough to hide it.

"Ah, I see I've hit a nerve." Juliet sounded as satisfied as a cat in the cream pitcher.

She should have known the woman could see in the dark, again like a cat. "Don't be ridiculous." Her voice was pitched higher than she wanted. "There's absolutely nothing between me and Ross Lockhart."

She turned, hoping to make a graceful exit from the conversation, and found Ross standing behind her. Juliet's soft laughter faded as the society editor walked away.

If there was a graceful way out of this situation, Amanda couldn't see it. "I'm sorry."

The words didn't seem to penetrate the stony mask that was Ross's face. Not much like the way he'd looked when he'd kissed her, was it?

"People are talking." He said the words as if they tasted bad.

"Just Juliet," she said quickly. "She's always imagining relationships that aren't there."

Except that something *was* there between them. One kiss didn't make a relationship, but it meant something, if only that he was attracted. As for her feelings—well, she wasn't going to explore that right now.

"It has to stop." That icy glare would make anyone quake.

A tiny flame of anger spurted up. She wasn't the one who'd initiated that kiss, after all. "Stopping gossip isn't in my job description."

One thing—she wouldn't have to worry about avoiding him. He'd never come near her after this. A quick retreat seemed in order, but before she could implement that, Cyrus swept down on them.

"Just the people I wanted to see." He put his arm around Amanda's shoulders, effectively cutting off her flight. "Now, I don't want to spend the evening talking business, but I do want to hear what the latest is on that troublesome landlord."

Amanda blinked. She hadn't realized Cyrus knew anything about that, given the reluctance with which Ross was pursuing the story.

"We've finished a lot of the background research." Ross shifted into editor mode in an instant. "Jason Hardy owns several buildings in the area of C.J.'s apartment building, most of them in a questionable state. It looks as if he puts in barely enough repairs to keep on the right side of the housing inspectors, but he's skirting the line. I think we could make a case that he ought to be looked at more thoroughly."

"Maybe it's time we interviewed the man. Let him know the press is interested," Cyrus said.

The concerns C.J.'s grandmother had voiced echoed in Amanda's mind. "If you do that, he's going to think that C.J. is involved."

"Hardy lives down near Beaufort," Ross said, ignoring her as if she hadn't spoken. "I can go down and talk to him."

"Take Amanda with you." Cyrus squeezed her shoulders. "I want her involved."

Oh, no. That was what her heart was protesting. It was what Ross's expression said, as well.

"I don't think—" he began.

Cyrus cut that off with a wave of his hand. "It was her idea, after all."

"But if we interview him…" Neither man listened to her.

"Very well." Ross's voice was icy. "We'll go tomorrow."

Great. Ross didn't want this. She didn't want this. But they were both going to have to deal with it.

Chapter 8

Amanda felt as if she'd been arguing with Ross all the way from Charleston to Beaufort. That wasn't quite true, of course. Most of the way she'd actually been arguing with herself.

How did I get into such a mess, Father? I thought this was going to help C.J., and instead it could cause her all kinds of heartache. I meant well.

That was a feeble excuse. How much of the world's trouble had been caused by people who were well-meaning? Too much, probably, and now she'd contributed her little bit.

Please, help me see what's best to do. Help me show Ross that we can't pursue the story if it's going to hurt more than it helps.

Was that the right thing to pray for? She slid a sideways glance toward Ross, his face impassive behind his sunglasses as he concentrated on driving across the bridge from Beaufort to Lady's Island. Her chances of diverting him from a course he'd decided upon seemed slight, at the least.

She tried to still her doubts, staring out at the expanse of water, sky and islands. Beautiful, as always, but the dark clouds that hung on the horizon seemed to echo her mood.

I'll do my best to listen, Lord. Please show me the right thing to do for C.J. and her grandmother. And for Daddy.

Her heart clenched into a tight, cold ball at the thought. Daddy. What was going on with him? What was Ross's interest in him? Neither of them was likely to tell her, but she couldn't just do nothing.

Guide me, Father. She came back, in the end, to the simplest words. *Guide me.*

Ross turned his head to look at her. She caught the movement in the periphery of her vision and tried to unclench the hands she'd had clasped in her lap.

"Is something wrong?" He sounded reluctant to ask the question, as if he wouldn't like the answer. Which he wouldn't.

"Just the same thing we've been talking about for the past hour or so. I don't want C.J. and her grandmother to get hurt for the sake of a story."

Ross blew out an exasperated breath. "Maybe you should have been a social worker instead of a reporter. Our job is to get the story, that's all."

"No matter who gets hurt?"

His jaw clenched so hard that a tiny muscle twitched under the skin. "I'm not hurting anyone. The cheating landlord is the bad guy, remember?"

"I know. I agree." Why couldn't he understand this? "But if C.J. and her grandmother get kicked out of their building because of what we did, I'm not sure they're going to agree."

"May I remind you that you're the one who brought me the story?"

"That was before I'd talked to C.J.'s grandmother and realized what was at stake." She shouldn't have gone to him without more information.

"I don't want to see them get hurt," he said. "They ought to have an attorney represent them in this, but I don't suppose that's occurred to them."

"I've already taken care of that."

He lowered his sunglasses so that he could look over them at her face. "*You* took care of it?" He didn't sound as if he approved of that, either. "If it comes out that an employee of the *Bugle* is paying an attorney for the tenants, it will look as if we're manipulating the story."

"That's ridiculous. Anyway, I'm not paying anyone. My cousin's fiancé is an attorney, and he sometimes takes pro bono cases. Surely no one can make an argument out of that, just because I'm sort of related to him. I'm sort of related to half the county, if you go back far enough."

He glanced at her again, seeming to weigh what he saw there. "You really do go the extra mile, don't you?"

It almost sounded as if he cared. "I didn't think of it that way," she said slowly. "It just seems to me that people are more important than any story."

"That's a fatal mistake for a reporter." He snapped the words. Clearly he was back to being annoyed with her after what had seemed a moment's respite. "Besides, if this story pans out, it will benefit more people in the long run."

"Is that really why you're doing it?" The question was out before she thought that it might be offensive. She bit her lip. "I'm sorry. I didn't mean—"

"I know exactly what you meant." His voice turned icy. "I'm doing my job. If you can't do yours, maybe you're in the wrong line of work."

There didn't seem to be anything to say to that. In fact, there didn't seem to be anything to say at all. As far as their values were concerned, she and Ross were miles apart.

Following the signs, they drove along the narrow road, salt marshes pressing close on either side, until they reached the gated community that occupied its own small island. To her surprise, Ross stopped before he reached the gatehouse, turning to zero in on her face.

"I'll focus my questions on the other buildings Hardy owns," he said abruptly. "This is about more than just the apartment house where C.J. and her grandmother live. That should keep him busy defending himself. There's no reason he'd assume C.J. was involved. If he does, between your lawyer friend and the newspaper's clout, we'll protect them."

Funny. He sounded as annoyed at himself for the concession as he was at her. His offer wasn't a great solution, but it looked as if it was the best she was going to get.

Ross kept what he hoped was a pleasant smile on his face as he surveyed Jason Hardy. The man had met them on the putting green that was apparently part of the landscaping of his luxurious property. The sprawling low country-style home was screened from other, equally expensive properties by the artful use of palmettos and crepe myrtles. Yes, Jason Hardy had it made, and he was clearly eager to show off.

"Had to have a putting green right here."

Hardy gestured expansively with a gloved hand. He

couldn't be much over forty, tanned and groomed to perfection, from the carefully tousled hairstyle to the tips of his costly leather golf shoes.

"With the hours I work, it can be impossible to get in eighteen holes on a regular basis." He cast a look at the dark clouds massing on the horizon. "Wouldn't you know? I've cleared my schedule for the afternoon, and now there's a storm moving in."

"You don't find it inconvenient for your work to live clear out here?" Ross would gladly keep the man bragging about his success for a few minutes before letting him know that this interview wasn't going to be a puff piece about the rising young businessman.

"Cybercommuting," Hardy said quickly. "With the right use of technology, a busy man can be anywhere in the world in seconds."

"Is that right?" he murmured, as if he'd never heard of such a thing.

Amanda moved quietly around them, taking one photo after another. Without a word being spoken, she'd picked up on his idea. Show the man playing with his expensive toys while his tenants sweltered in the heat, his buildings falling down around them.

Amanda had good instincts. Unfortunately, she also had a soft heart that was going to get in her way when it came to being a decent reporter.

He was abruptly tired of buttering up this sleazeball. "So, your investments in slum housing in Charleston—are they doing well for you?"

Some of the bonhomie slid from Hardy's face. "I'm not sure what you mean. I am invested in some rental properties in the city, I believe."

"You're underestimating yourself, aren't you?"

He held out his hand. Amanda put the file folder into it without missing beat. He flipped the folder open and pretended to study it. Never mind that he'd committed its contents to memory. Hardy didn't need to know that.

"Let's see," he said. "That's twenty-six rental buildings all together, owned by you either directly or through a subsidiary company."

Hardy's eyes narrowed. "I guess that might be about right. It's a small part of my portfolio."

"And out of those twenty-six, there have been two hundred and forty-seven complaints to the housing department. A hundred and ten investigations ensued. Fifty-four citations issued, ranging from broken heat pumps not fixed to questionable evictions to contaminated water."

Hardy held the golf club between them as if he felt the need for weapon. "What is all this? I thought you wanted to do a profile piece on me."

"A profile has to include both sides," he said gently. "Surely you realize that. Now, about the situation with the broken air-conditioning at...let me see...hmm, twenty of twenty-six buildings. That's a fairly large number, don't you think? A person might almost think the air conditioners in your buildings were deliberately put out of commission so you didn't have to pay those high electric bills this summer."

He let a smile play around his lips. There was nothing like it when an investigation came together—that wave of exhilaration knowing that the creep wasn't going to wiggle off the hook this time.

"You don't dare print that. It's speculation, that's all." Snatching his putters, Hardy stalked off the green. "Get off my property. You're not going to get away with ambushing me like this."

"Don't you want to give us a statement, Mr. Hardy? I'm sure our readers would like to hear directly from you."

This story was small potatoes, he knew that. CNN wouldn't pick it up; there'd be no national interest. But for the first time in months, he felt like a reporter again.

Amanda moved around, the camera up to her face, snapping picture after picture. Hardy swung toward her, anger darkening his face.

"Stop taking pictures. Give me that." He grabbed for her.

Fury swept through Ross, but before he could move, Amanda slipped easily away from the man.

"You don't want to do that." Her voice was cool. "Think how bad it would look on the news if you assaulted a photographer."

Baffled, Hardy swung back to Ross. "Any of those pictures get in your second-rate rag, and I'll sue. I'm calling your publisher. We'll see about this."

Ross couldn't help but grin at the thought of Cyrus being intimidated. It would make Cyrus's week if Hardy actually called and threatened him.

"You do that, Mr. Hardy. I'm sure he'd like to hear from you." He gestured to Amanda and started walking toward the car. "Thanks for the interview."

Ross spent the first ten minutes of the drive back recording his impressions with the aid of a microcassette recorder. He was pleased with the way the interview had gone. Amanda could hear that in his voice.

And see it in his eyes, for that matter. As the sky continued to darken, he'd pulled off his sunglasses, allowing her to see the intent focus of his gaze.

He took pride in what he was doing. She might not like the "ambush" aspect of the interview, but she had to admit that probably nothing else would have worked with a man like Jason Hardy. She'd have been out of her depth if she'd been alone.

The thought was sobering. Maybe Ross was right. Maybe she wasn't meant to be a reporter, if that was what it took.

A few fat raindrops splattered on the windshield, and Ross clicked on the wipers. "It looks like Hardy isn't going to get in his golf game this afternoon."

"He's probably too busy anyway, what with needing to exert his influence to kill the story." A rumble of thunder sounded, and her hands clenched on her pant legs.

"Is something wrong?" He darted a look at her. The man had eyes that noticed every little thing.

"Nothing," she said, knowing it wasn't true. "I wanted to say...you handled him exactly right, even though I don't suppose much that he said will actually make it into the article."

"No, but it would be a shame to run the piece without having interviewed him."

"Do you really think he'll call Cyrus?"

Ross grinned. "I hope he does. Cyrus will have him for lunch, and probably get a quote out of it besides. But he won't. Hardy has undoubtedly called his attorney, who'll tell him he was an idiot for even talking to us."

"Hardy thought we were there to do a profile piece on him." That still bothered her.

"He's not smart enough to play with the big boys, then."

Obviously it didn't bother Ross.

"I'll tell you what's going to happen next," Ross said. "By the time we get back to the office, we'll have received a carefully worded statement from the lawyer, which we'll be obliged to print." He smiled thinly. "This is one place where your photographs will speak more loudly than his words, I think."

A clap of thunder punctuated his words, and then the storm was on them. Rain came down as if someone had emptied an immense bucket over their heads. In a moment, it was so dark it might have been dusk except when lightning forked toward the ground, illuminating everything in flickering bursts like a crazy series of still pictures. She couldn't keep a gasp from escaping.

"You really don't like storms, do you?" Ross said.

"Not much." She had to loosen tight lips to answer. "I'm such a wimp about it. When I was a kid, I used to hide in the closet. Or under the bed." She tried to smile. "No closets here, unfortunately. Just ignore me." She was thirty now, for pity's sake. It was time she acted like a grown-up.

"We can do better than that." He flicked the turn signal on. "Looks like a restaurant of some kind ahead, though I never really trust a restaurant whose sign just says 'eats.'"

"You don't need to…" she began, but he was already pulling into the crushed-shell parking lot.

"I'm getting hungry anyway. We'll get something to eat and wait out the storm." He pulled up next to the porch so that she could get from the car to the shelter of its roof in a quick step. "Ready?"

She nodded, took a shaky breath and opened the door. Wind and rain struck her, but almost before she felt it, Ross had grabbed her arm and propelled her into the restaurant.

"Hey, folks." The grizzled elderly man behind the counter was the only occupant. "Y'all brought the rain with you."

"Not our idea," Ross said. "How about some coffee?"

"Comin' right up. You, missy?"

"Sweet tea, please." She headed for a booth on the inside wall, safely away from the windows, and slid in. She looked up at Ross in belated apology. "Sorry. Is this okay?"

He smiled, face relaxing. "Fine. Would you like me to ask him if he has a closet?"

The arrival of their drinks saved her from answering that. "What you folks want to eat?" The man, who was apparently server as well as cook, and maybe the owner, too, didn't seem inclined to offer a menu, but his apron was spotless and the aromas from the grill were all good. "The shrimp-burgers are nice today. And I got me some sweet potato fries."

"That sounds good to me." She'd learned, hitting some questionable roadside cafés coming and going from school in Columbia, that it was usually safest to order the day's special.

"A burger." Ross obviously didn't hold to that philosophy.

She lifted her brows after the man returned to his kitchen. "Don't care for the local cuisine?"

"Some things. What exactly is a shrimp-burger?"

"That depends on the cook. It might be a cold shrimp salad on a roll. Or it might be something like a crab cake, only made with shrimp. You take your chances."

"Thanks, but I'll just play it safe."

"You don't strike me as someone who plays safe." She took a sip of the tea. Sure enough, it was sweet enough to make teeth ache.

Ross frowned down at his coffee, as if he suspected an insult she hadn't intended. "You asked me something earlier," he said abruptly. "You asked if publishing the truth was my only reason for pursuing this story."

She didn't know what to say. Luckily she didn't have to, because he went on.

"I chase the story because that's who I am." He gave a wry smile. "An investigative reporter. This pretense of being an editor is wearing pretty thin. Cyrus knows that. That's why he pushed me to do this story."

"But if this job isn't what you wanted, why did you take it?"

If he hadn't, they'd never have met. She wasn't sure where that thought had come from, but she didn't like it.

"I didn't exactly have a lot of choices." His lips pressed together for an instant. "You must know what happened to me in D.C. Big story…made the wire services and the television talk shows. It's too bad I didn't write it."

"I know what people said about what happened," she said carefully. "I don't know if that's the truth."

"The truth can be an elusive thing."

Ross stared at the checked oilcloth that covered the tabletop, looking as if he didn't see it. Rain clattered against the tin roof, making so much noise that it would be impossible for anyone else to hear them, even if anyone had been there.

Would he go on or was that all he was willing to say, at least to her?

"I was after the story of my career." He seemed to

force the words out. "I'd been following leads on congressional misdeeds for a couple of weeks. That was a shade on the ironic side for me."

"Because your father was a congressman." That fact had received a lot of play in the reporting, she remembered.

"Right." Tension cut deep lines in his face. "I wasn't getting very far. I heard plenty of rumors that a particular popular congressman was letting special interests line his pockets, but no way to prove it. Then I ran into a old buddy of mine from law school. When he heard what I was working on, he said maybe he could help."

He began playing with his spoon, turning it over and over in his fingers.

"Vince was a lobbyist. People talked to him who would never talk to a reporter. Anyway, he came back to me in a couple of days. Said he'd found someone who could deliver the goods—photos, statements, everything. For a price, of course." The spoon flipped from his fingers to land on the table, and he picked it up again. "The paper was willing to spring for it. The editor was salivating at the idea. Pushed me to go ahead. Move fast, before someone else got onto it."

She could see where this was headed, and she hurt for him. "Your friend set you up."

"They did a great job. It was like something out of Woodward and Bernstein, right down to the meet-in-a-parking-garage. I turned over the money, the guy turned over the pictures, the paper rushed into print the next day. And then found out we'd been suckered when the whole story was easily disproved by the congressmen's staff." He shrugged. "Long story short, someone had to take the fall for it. I was the one whose byline was on the story."

Without thinking, just needing to comfort, she put her hand over his. "I'm so sorry. If he hadn't been your friend…"

"If he hadn't been my friend, I wouldn't have fallen for it so easily. Even so, I should have taken a few more days to check it out. I didn't. My fault." His hand turned, and he clasped her fingers.

"It's not a bad thing to trust a friend. Or to want to succeed." She discovered that her breath was playing tricks on her…catching in her throat just because he was touching her that way.

He folded his other hand over hers, so that hers was enclosed in his warm grip. His fingertips stroked the inside of her wrist almost absently, as if he didn't realize he was doing it, but took some comfort from the touch.

"I had everything going for me then. The right connections, the right job, a fast track to the top. And then it was gone in an instant, and I was a pariah. No one in Washington wanted to speak to me."

"They judged you without bothering to find out the truth." Guilt pierced her heart. Hadn't she done the same when she'd first heard the story?

Forgive me, Lord. I was so quick to judge. I'm ashamed of myself. I didn't think I was like that.

"If not for Cyrus's eccentric charity, I'd be looking for a new profession."

"You want your career back." She said what she sensed under his words.

"Of course I want it back." His grip tightened almost painfully. "All I need is one story big enough to hit nationally. If I get that, someone will take a chance on me. I can get back to a national market."

All he wanted was to leave here. The thought made a hollow spot in her heart.

She tried to rally. Naturally he'd want to get back to Washington. With his family background, he'd probably dreamed all his life of working there.

"Your family…" She let that trail off, not sure what she wanted to say.

He let go of her hands, and she was cold without his touch. His face hardened into a mask to shield his feelings.

"You know what the motto of my family was? Never embarrass your father. And I never did, until I really did it up right, with stories in every major daily."

The bitterness in his voice shook her. "But he must have understood that it wasn't your fault."

"He must?" His ironic expression mocked her words. "I don't know, because he was never willing to talk to me about it. He sent a message via one of his aides. A check, actually, accompanied by the suggestion that a new life somewhere far away might be a good idea."

The pain she felt for him was a knife in her heart. If she lived to be a hundred, she could never understand a parent acting like that. "I'm sorry." It came out as a whisper, earning her one of his sardonic smiles.

"Don't look so tragic, Amanda. It wasn't exactly a surprise. I knew what to expect from him."

That made it all the sadder, but she didn't suppose she'd better say that to him.

She'd add that to the other thing she'd never say to him. That she'd realized, while he was holding her hands and telling her his private grief, how much she cared for him. Cared deeply.

Because she cared, she wanted him to have what he wanted, even if that meant she'd lose him.

You can't lose what you've never had, she reminded herself. Somehow that didn't comfort her. When—not if, when—Ross left, he'd take a piece of her heart with him.

Chapter 9

Amanda consistently turned to two people when she needed to talk—one was Miz Callie, the other was her twin. Mamma sometimes complained about that, but in a good-natured way. She said she'd get her own back when Amanda and Annabel had daughters, and they turned to her.

"If I'd known you were going to put me to work, I'd have gone to see Miz Callie today," Amanda said in mock complaint.

She scooped a bucket of feed from the bin her sister indicated.

"Miz Callie would give you cookies and sympathy," Annabel retorted. "Since you came here, you must need something else. Or you know what Miz Callie would say, and you want a different opinion."

"Who made you so smart? You're the kid sister, remember?"

"Only by twenty minutes."

The familiar banter with her twin was comforting. She had tight relationships with her brothers, but that was nothing like the bond with Annabel. Her twin was almost her other half.

She followed Annabel down the row of stalls. Her sister's menagerie seemed to have grown a little each time Amanda came to the farm Annabel owned out in the country north of Mount Pleasant. Her latest addition was a small gray donkey.

Amanda stopped at his pen and poured the feed into the bucket. "What's this guy's name?" She reached out to pet the donkey, but he yanked his head away, showing the whites of his eyes.

"Toby." Annabel leaned against the stall bar, frowning a little when she looked at the donkey. "He's still pretty skittish, I'm afraid. More so than I imagined he'd be. But you'll be okay, won't you, Toby? You just need a little time to learn you can trust us."

The donkey, apparently reassured by the love he heard in Annabel's soft drawl, edged his way back to the feed bucket and began to eat, his eyes still rolling at the slightest move.

"He was treated badly." Now that he was close, Amanda could see the scars.

Annabel just nodded. She didn't like to talk about the things that had happened to the animals she sheltered, but every vet and animal control agent in the county knew he or she could count on Annabel to take in their worst cases.

"The vet says he's healing okay, but the scars go deeper than the physical."

Amanda found those words echoing in her mind as she followed Annabel through the chores. Some scars did go deep. The story Ross had told her—how much was he still hurting from the betrayal of his friend? His parents, too, had let him down, as had the employer who hadn't trusted him enough to look for the truth.

Ross had let her see more deeply into his heart than she'd dreamed he would. She wanted to help him, but for the first time in her life, she doubted her ability.

Annabel let her alone, maybe knowing she needed time. Finally, when they leaned on the pasture fence admiring the horses that stood in the shade of the live oak, Annabel turned, eyebrows lifting.

Amanda knew that expression. After all, she had one exactly like it. Looking at Annabel was like looking in a mirror, aside from minor differences in hairstyle and clothes. Her sister was waiting to know why she was here today.

"It's complicated," she said, as if Annabel had asked the question aloud. She propped a sneaker on the fence slat and frowned down at the stain on the toe. Her own fault— she knew better than to wear new sneakers to the farm.

Her sister nodded. "It usually is. Is this about your boss?"

She didn't bother asking how Annabel knew. Twins just did. "Ross is different from anyone else I've ever... well, cared about."

She couldn't say they were in a relationship, because they weren't. But there was that kiss. And the way he'd confided in her. That meant something, didn't it?

"He's not your usual lost soul, that's for sure." Annabel leaned against the fence, absently adjusting her ball cap to keep the sun out of her eyes.

"Come on. I don't *always* go for needy guys, do I?" That was the family's running commentary on the guys she dated. Annabel collected stray animals; Amanda collected stray people.

"Pretty much."

"Well, maybe so. Anyway, Ross is different." He needed healing, just like the creatures who found their way to Annabel's care, but he wouldn't admit that easily. "I'm not even sure how it happened, but I care."

Love? She wasn't going to say love, not yet.

"What about him?"

"I don't know. He's attracted, but it's complicated. I mean, he's my boss, for one thing. And besides that..."

She couldn't tell even Annabel what Ross had told her. That shook her. She'd always been able to tell Annabel everything.

"Besides, I don't think he's going to be around that long. His goal is to get back to a big metropolitan market. Charleston is just a stepping stone for him."

"Honey, don't go falling in love with a man who'll take you away from us. I don't want to go chasing all over the country every time I need some twin talk." Annabel's tone was light, but her eyes were serious.

"It's not just that." She blew out a breath. "Ross wants his career back, and I'm not sure what he'd do to get it."

That was the crux of the matter, she realized. As usual, talking to Annabel had made things clear to her.

Ross had shown her pieces of himself, and she had come to understand what drove him. But she still didn't know who he was, soul deep. She didn't know what he'd sacrifice to get back the life he felt had been stolen from him.

"Manda..." Annabel touched her hand lightly. "Be careful, okay?" Her tone was troubled. "I don't want to see you get hurt by caring for someone who isn't going to put you first."

The words weighed on her. Annabel knew what that was like, and Amanda had gone through that hurt with her. She didn't want to open herself up to that.

"I'll try." Her throat tightened. "But I'm afraid it might already be too late."

This trip to the Coast Guard Base was probably a waste of time, but Ross felt stuck with it. Impatience prickled along his nerves as he followed Amanda through the check-in procedure and back outside again.

He should be following up on another interview with a local supplier to the base, not walking around like a sightseer. And the slumlord story waited on just a few more follow-up questions. He'd assigned that to Jim Redfern, knowing the veteran reporter would cover all the angles.

But he knew himself well enough to recognize the reluctance with which he'd let go of that story. He'd told Amanda that he was kidding himself, playing at being an editor instead of an investigative reporter, and he hadn't even known that until the words came out of his mouth.

He let his gaze linger on Amanda. She walked slightly in front of him with that quick, graceful stride, her silky hair ruffling in the breeze off the water. An enormous pair of sunglasses hid her eyes, but couldn't mask the eagerness in her expression at the thought of showing him something more about the service that was so important to her family.

He seemed to see her again across the table from him in that roadside restaurant, leaning toward him, her face filled with concern. Was that concern what had prompted those confidences? He certainly hadn't planned on telling her any of that, but it had spilled out. He'd been like the mail room kid, leaning on her desk to share his dreams.

That shouldn't happen again. She was too caring, and he found it too easy to respond to that.

Besides, the more involved he became in her life, the more it would hurt her if her father ended up the subject of a front-page exposé.

"Adam's due to meet us in a couple of minutes." Amanda stopped in the shade of one of the white buildings that dotted the area. "We may as well wait here for him."

He nodded, trying to block distractions from his mind. He'd be better off to focus on the moment—convince himself that he really was here to develop a story on the base. From what he'd seen of Adam Bodine, there was a sharp mind behind that genial exterior. It wouldn't do to make him suspicious of Ross's motives.

Leaning against the wall, he watched the play of light and shadow on Amanda's delicate features. Actually, maybe that wasn't a very good idea, either.

"Have you come here often?" He asked the question at random, trying to distract himself.

She turned toward him, her face lighting with eagerness. "This has always been one of my favorite places, since I was a kid. Even when my daddy was assigned elsewhere, there always seemed to be a Bodine who was posted here."

"I'm surprised you didn't go into the Coast Guard, too, then." If she had, he'd probably never have met her. That thought troubled him more than it should.

She tilted her head, considering. "I guess it is odd,

but I never even thought of it. I always knew I'd be a writer of some sort."

"Why journalism, instead of fiction?"

"I guess I've always been more interested in real people than imaginary ones."

"That's probably the secret to your popularity at the paper. Everyone wants to talk to you." Did that sound as if he was envious? Nonsense. It didn't matter to him how many admirers Amanda had.

He could see her eyes crinkle at that, even with the dark glasses she wore. "Sometimes what they want is to complain."

"About what?" Then he caught on. "About their hard-hearted new boss, I suppose."

"Oh, they have some better adjectives than that," she assured him.

"I can imagine." He found he was leaning a little closer, drawn into Amanda's orbit despite his best intentions. "Would you care to share some?"

Her lips pursed. "My mamma taught me not to use language like that."

He quelled a ridiculous urge to kiss those lips right here in public. Maybe it was just as well that her cousin Adam was striding toward them along the walk, looking ready for anything in his blue shirt and pants, a blue ball cap with the Coast Guard emblem square on his head.

"Hey, Manda. Ross. Sorry to keep you waiting." Adam shook hands with him and gave Amanda a quick hug. "I had to clear something up, but now I'm all yours. What would you like to see first?"

"Let's go down to the docks," Amanda suggested.

Ross nodded. It didn't matter what they saw today,

since that wasn't the story he was after, but he'd play along.

They started along the walk, and Adam fell into step with him. "What specifically is the aim of your article? If I knew that, I could tailor the tour to it."

The aim of my article is to expose somebody, maybe somebody named Bodine, as crooked. No, he couldn't say that.

"A general look at the different facets of your work," he said instead. "I'm not sure exactly what we'll be using in the finished series of articles, but it's all new to me."

"There's Win," Amanda said. She nodded toward a group of men and women jogging past.

One broke away and jogged toward them. Ross recognized the Bodine Amanda had pointed out as a rescue swimmer at the party. Probably a year or two younger than Amanda, Win Bodine had the long, lithe lines and the upper-body strength of a swimmer combined with the spark of a daredevil in his eyes. He stopped beside them, still jogging.

"Hey, how're you doing? Adam said you'd be comin' by today. I'll tell you all about being a rescue swimmer, if you want."

"What's to tell? You just have to jump out of a helicopter into the ocean now and then. Easy enough for someone who's half fish and half seagull." Adam's tone made it clear that this was familiar territory for the cousins.

"You're just jealous because women are more impressed by my job than yours." Win continued to jog with the easy manner of someone who probably wasn't even aware that he was doing it.

"Is that why you struck out and had to spend Saturday night playing air hockey at my place?"

The teasing was the kind that went on between men who knew each other to the bone. In this case, probably literally from birth. Amanda looked on with an indulgent smile.

He tried to ignore a stab of pure envy. The Bodines didn't know how lucky they were. Probably didn't even realize some people didn't have that kind of family bond.

Would that bond be enough to hold them together if Brett Bodine ended up convicted of extorting bribes? That was an ugly thought, and he didn't have a clue as to the answer.

"Your crew is getting away from you," Amanda pointed out, nodding to the group Win had been jogging with. "You two can save your macho teasing for another time."

Win laughed. "And I've got just the time. Miz Callie called, and she's fixing to cook up a ton of steamed shrimp and some pecan pie tomorrow night. She said to pass it along to you if I saw you. You, too, Ross. She'll give you a call herself, but don't you disappoint her, now."

He waved, breaking into a run toward his group, who jogged in place waiting for him, yelling out a few gratuitous insults as they did.

"Sounds like some good eating," Adam said. "You're coming, aren't you, Ross?"

He should make some excuse. He shouldn't socialize with people who were going to be slammed if the story broke the way he thought it was going to. But Amanda was looking at him with obvious pleasure at the prospect, and he discovered he loved seeing that look in her eyes.

He shouldn't, but he was going to, and he'd just have to deal with the consequences.

"Sounds good," he said. "I'll be there if I can."

Adam gave a quick nod. "Okay. So, what do you want to see first?"

"You know perfectly well where you want to start," Amanda said. "Go ahead, show us the cutters and patrol boats."

"Well, since you insist."

Ross followed the two of them, letting the easy banter between the cousins flow over him.

When they reached the docks, Adam stopped at a businesslike white-and-orange boat with an enclosed cabin. "Here she is. My patrol boat—home away from home."

"Your first love," Amanda teased.

"Maybe that, too."

Amanda turned at a hail from farther along the dock, obviously seeing someone she knew, and scurried off to talk to two young men in Coast Guard blue.

"Is there anyplace in Charleston where Amanda doesn't have friends?"

"Nope. That's our Amanda." Adam's open face filled with affection as he watched his cousin. "She's always been everyone's friend and confidante. There are times when I wish she wasn't quite so trusting."

Ross stiffened. Was that aimed at him? "That's a good quality, isn't it?"

Now the look Adam turned on him was distinctly serious. "I wouldn't change her if I could. But she does lead with her heart. I wouldn't want her to get hurt."

"Is that a warning?" His jaw tightened. Adam couldn't know there was anything more than a professional relationship between them.

"Well, now, I wouldn't say that. I guess the days are long past when the Bodine boys would threaten to land hard on anyone who messed with one of them. Just consider it a bit of friendly advice. Bodines stick together, no matter what."

Amanda rejoined them, giving him no opportunity to say more, but his mind spun with the implications of Adam's words. Was that just cousinly protectiveness? Or did Adam know something about the investigation?

How could he? But Ross couldn't shake the suspicion that something more was going on than met the eye.

Amanda marched toward Ross's office that afternoon, seething. She'd come back to the newsroom from a late lunch satisfied that Ross had been shown the best of Coast Guard. That surely he must feel the same patriotic pride that she did after spending time with the people of Coast Guard Base Charleston.

Jim Redfern had been waiting for her, his normally dour face wearing even deeper grooves than usual. C.J. wasn't there, because she'd learned that Ross planned to use her and her grandmother as examples in the slumlord story. She'd walked out.

Crusading spirit carrying her along, Amanda rapped sharply on the door frame of Ross's office and walked in without waiting for an invitation.

Ross, telephone to his ear, lifted level brows at her impetuous entrance and held up one hand, palm out, to stop her. The gesture just added fuel to the flame.

She stalked across the office, frowning at the large-

scale map of Charleston that filled most of one wall.
Ross faced it while sitting at his desk, while behind him
stretched a whiteboard, a corkboard and a flow chart
showing what everyone on the staff was working on.
That was it. There wasn't a single personal item on the
walls.

Or on the desk. Ross was, as far as his office was
concerned, a man without personal connections at all.

The reminder of what he'd shown her of himself
cooled her anger slightly. Just in time, as he hung up
the phone, dropped the pen with which he'd been making notes, and turned his frown on her.

"What?"

"I understand from Jim that you plan to use C.J. and
her grandmother as examples in the story about Hardy."
She tried for cool and collected. They were two profes-
sionals discussing a problem—that was all.

The small muscles around his mouth compressed.
"That's right."

"You can't do that," she said flatly, her air of detachment fizzling away as quickly as it had come. "I told
you how they felt about it."

He shoved his chair back, putting a little more distance between them. "This is about reporting a story,
Amanda. Not about catering to somebody's feelings."

"It's not a question of catering to someone's feelings,
as you so nicely put it." She'd find it so much easier to
argue with him if she weren't so aware of his every
movement—of the way his long fingers tightened around
the chair arm, of the narrowing of his eyes at her defi-
ance. She grasped after the detachment she'd lost. "All
I'm saying is that surely we can run the story without
hurting the individual."

He made an impatient, chopping motion with his right hand: "A dry recital of facts won't interest the reader or sell papers. We need the human element."

"Even if it hurts the very people you're trying to help?"

"Newspapers are in the business of reporting the news, not helping people, as I've told you repeatedly. The story serves the greater good."

He blew out an exasperated breath, as if he tired of having the same argument with her, reminding her of that moment when he'd said that if she wanted to help people, she should go into social work.

He couldn't really be that hardened, could he? Her heart twisted. This would be so much easier if she didn't know what was behind the cynical attitude. If she didn't care so much that he get what he longed for.

A memory flashed into her mind. Miz Callie, comforting her in the midst of some teenage crisis of the heart.

I love him, she'd wailed. Miz Callie's reply had contained a world of wisdom. *Then you'll want him to have his heart's desire, child. That's what loving is, even when it hurts.*

His taut posture eased a little, as if her silence meant the battle was won.

"What about C.J.?" If she couldn't fight him for herself, she could for someone else.

"What about her?"

"She found out. She's left."

Something flickered in his eyes at that. He hadn't known, and it mattered to him. She leaned toward him, hands on the edge of his desk, pressing the point home.

"This isn't just some faceless person you're throwing

under the bus for the sake of a story. This is C.J. This internship was supposed to help her, not make her life more difficult. Surely there's a way to write a story with an impact that doesn't hurt her."

For a moment the silence stretched between them, his gaze fixed on her face. Then…

"You write it," he said abruptly.

"What?" She stepped back, not sure what he meant.

"You work with Jim. You do the human interest aspect of the story. Get it from C.J. or get it from someone else, but get it."

It was a challenge. Did he think she couldn't rise to it? If so, he'd be disappointed.

She tried not to let satisfaction tinge her smile or her voice.

"Thank you, Ross. I won't disappoint you."

To her surprise, his lips twitched slightly. "You madden, annoy, bemuse and surprise me, Amanda. But you never disappoint."

Before she could respond, he'd turned back to his computer, giving her a chance to get out of his office, hoping he hadn't noticed the stunned look on her face at his words.

Chapter 10

Tradition had it that Charleston's Market had been on the same spot for a couple of centuries. Amanda didn't find that hard to believe as she stepped into the welcome shade under the roof that stretched along the aptly named Market Street almost to the old Customs House. Under its shelter, folks sold just about everything imaginable, with the emphasis on goods that would attract the tourists that flooded the historic district.

Amanda made her way along the crowded aisle, nodding to a few of the sweetgrass basket weavers she'd interviewed over the past couple of months for the story that might never see the light of day. And speaking of stories that might fail, she was here to find a way of convincing C.J. and her grandmother to cooperate.

If they didn't get on board with the story, she'd have to find someone else who would, and the clock was ticking. She couldn't kid herself that Ross would hold the article for her.

So she'd do this because she had to, and she'd show Ross in the process that it wasn't necessary to sacrifice someone for the sake of a story.

He should know that. He'd been the one sacrificed himself. Somehow that had only made him more determined to get back on top. Her heart twisted a little at the thought.

Please, Lord... She stopped, not even sure how to pray in this situation. *I want what's best for Ross. And for C.J. and her grandmother. Please show me what that is. Amen.*

She stepped into a band of sunlight where the roofs didn't quite meet, and then back into the shadows again. There, right in front of her, was another sweetgrass basket stand. C.J.'s grandmother sat weaving, her gaze moving over the people who passed by. When she came to Amanda, she made no sign of recognition at all.

C.J., manning the counter, hadn't mastered that impassive stare. Her brows lowered, her mouth tightened. If she'd had something in her hands, she just might have thrown it.

"C.J.—"

"Forget it. I got nothin' to say to you."

Amanda hesitated, her throat tight. "I think you have a lot that you'd like to say to me. You're angry."

"You just bet I'm angry." C.J.'s hands gripped the rough edge of the wooden counter on which the baskets were displayed. "You acted like you were my friend. But you just wanted to use me for a stupid article in the paper." Her lips twisted. "Your big chance to write somethin' besides dog shows, wasn't it?"

That hit too close to home. Hadn't that been in her mind the evening she'd gone to C.J.'s apartment?

"I wanted to write something more important. You know that. But not at the cost of hurting you." She pressed her fingers against the counter, willing C.J. to listen. To understand. "I only mentioned the situation to Mr. Lockhart because I thought the paper might help you."

"Fat lotta help that's going to be, when he prints our names and the landlord comes down on us for telling you. How's it help us when we're out on the street? Like my grandma says, none of the neighbors are fool enough to stick their necks out and talk to you."

"It's not just a question of you and your neighbors," Amanda said. The grandmother was listening, even if she made no sign of it. This argument was for her, as well as C.J. "We looked into Mr. Hardy's business dealings. He owns a number of buildings in your area, and he handles them all in the same way. There are a lot of people besides you and your grandmother hurting because of that man, and he gets away with it because everyone's afraid to complain."

C.J. looked taken aback at that, but then she shook her head. "Well, go get some of them to be in your story, and leave us alone."

"I could." *Maybe, if I had the time.* "But you're the one my attorney friend offered to help. And I want to do the story about you, because I believed you're a fighter. Maybe I was wrong."

"Don't you say that." C.J.'s grandmother rose, dropping the half-made basket onto her worktable. She held her head as proudly as if it bore a crown. "This grandchild of mine sure enough is a fighter."

"Leave it be, Gran." C.J. took her arm, urging her back to her seat. "We're better off not having anything to do with her. You were right."

Mrs. Carrey shook her off. "Why?" she demanded.

"Why you giving in so easy on this? You were all het up about it before I talked you out of it."

"For you." C.J. put her arm gently around the older woman. "You took care of me all these years. Now's my turn to take care of you."

The woman reached up slowly, laying a worn, wrinkled hand on C.J.'s smooth cheek. She shook her head, tears gleaming suddenly in her eyes. Without looking at Amanda, she spoke.

"Miz Bodine, your grandmamma is a strong woman, I know."

Amanda thought of Miz Callie, determined to brave the disapproval of her entire community in order to right a decades-old wrong. Tears filled her eyes. "Yes, ma'am, she is a strong woman."

The woman nodded slowly. She patted C.J.'s cheek. "That's what I want this grandchild of mine to think about me."

"Gran, I do," C.J. protested. "You're the bravest woman I ever knew. I just think you shouldn't have to fight anymore."

Mrs. Carrey looked over C.J.'s shoulder to meet Amanda's gaze. "This child's something special, you know that? She's the only one of the family who has the brains and the gumption to make something of herself, and here I was, telling her to be afraid. Not to fight. I'm ashamed of myself."

"But Gran…"

"No buts." She gave C.J. a smile so full of love that it took Amanda's breath away. "We aren't quitters. We're fighters. We'll show that *t'ief* something." She shot a glance at Amanda. "You know what *t'ief* means?"

"Yes, ma'am, I do." She couldn't help the grin that

spread over her face. The Gullah expression she'd applied to Mr. Hardy was only too appropriate. A thief.

"Well, that's what he is, and I guess your story is gonna show that to the world." She shoved the counter to make room for Amanda to squeeze through. "You come back here and let's get started."

Amanda rinsed dinner plates that evening while Miz Callie cut generous slices of pecan pie for dessert. Miz Callie's shrimp feast had been a small party by Bodine family standards. She'd invited only Hugh, Win, Adam and Georgia, along with Georgia's fiancé, Matt, and his little girl. And Ross.

Amanda stacked the plates and turned to her grandmother. "So, Miz Callie, you want to tell me why you invited Ross to this particular little group?"

"Well, now, I just thought it'd be a bit easier to get acquainted without the whole kit and caboodle of Bodines here tonight. So I invited the ones I thought he'd enjoy getting together with."

Amanda leaned against the counter, surveying her grandmother. Something about that innocent blue-eyed gaze made her suspicious. "Are you sure that's all?"

Miz Callie's lips twitched. "Well, I did notice a little bit of tension between him and your daddy, so I thought we'd do without your folks tonight. I always thought Brett would take on at the idea of his baby girls getting serious about anybody."

Her cheeks warmed. "We're not… I mean I don't think…"

Might as well give up on that sentence. She didn't think her romantic attachment, or lack of one, had anything to do with Daddy's attitude, but maybe it was bet-ter not to trouble Miz Callie with that.

Her grandmother gave her a probing stare. "Is that what has you so distracted tonight, child?"

Distracted? Who, her? She'd fully expected Ross to make some excuse to get out of this dinner tonight, given how exasperating he seemed to find her lately. But there he was, sitting next to her through dinner, his arm brushing hers each time he moved, sending her senses shivering.

"I'm not distracted. Well, I guess I'm a little worried."

"About what?" Miz Callie paused in the act of putting pie on a tray, apparently ready to keep everyone waiting for their dessert to hear what troubled her.

"I'm just…" She tried to frame her worries in a coher-ent way. Her concerns about C.J. and her grandmother, her worries about the unaccountable animosity between Daddy and Ross…maybe they all amounted to the same kind of fear.

"I'm worried about whether I'm doing the right thing in a couple of situations," she said finally. That pretty much covered it.

"Have you prayed about this?" That would always be Miz Callie's first response to trouble.

"Yes. But probably not enough."

Miz Callie smiled. "You know perfectly well, Manda, that you rush right into doing things because they're good, and that's a beautiful quality. But maybe you need to take time to find out if they're the good things God has in mind for you."

That was a complicated and sobering thought. Car-ing about Ross was good, but was it good for her? She didn't know.

"Sometimes it's hard to know what God's plan is, even when I'm trying to pay attention."

"I know what you mean." Miz Callie patted her cheek, and she flashed back to C.J.'s grandmother doing the same thing to her. "I find the more I'm trying to steep myself in prayer and God's word, the easier it is to see what's right. Just wait and trust."

"I'll try." She blinked back tears. "Thank you, Miz Callie. You're a wise woman." If she and C.J. turned out half as well as their grandmothers, they'd be doing fine.

"Go on with you." Miz Callie waved away the compliment. "You take that coffee in before they think we've forgotten them."

But when she got into the dining room with the coffee service, no one seemed to be missing her. Instead, they were grouped around Ross, looking at some papers on the table in front of him.

Georgia waved a sheet of paper at her, her cheeks pink with excitement. "Manda, just look what Ross found for us. Miz Callie, look."

Miz Callie set down the tray of pie and pulled glasses from her pocket to perch them on her nose. "What is it?"

"Ross got us enlistment records for the month of August of '42 from every recruitment center in a hundred-mile radius of Charleston." Adam sent Amanda a questioning look. "I didn't realize he was in on our little hunt."

"I explained that we're trying to find out what happened to a relative of Miz Callie's," she said quickly, a note of warning in her voice. "He had some helpful suggestions, but I didn't know about this."

Why on earth had Ross pursued the matter on his

own? She'd have expected him to forget it the instant they'd finished talking about it.

Faint embarrassment showed in Ross's expression when he shrugged. "It's no big deal. Amanda and I talked about how you'd track someone who'd enlisted under a false name under those circumstances, and I just got curious. I contacted a researcher I used to use in D.C., and he was able to locate the records for the centers that seemed the most likely."

Miz Callie sat down, seeming to realize all of a sudden what this might mean. "Goodness gracious." She pulled the papers toward her. "If Ned is in here—well, I guess we just have to hope he used a name that meant something. If he did, maybe I'll know it when I see it." She looked at Ross. "I purely don't know how to thank you. Words just aren't enough."

"Thanks aren't necessary," Ross said quickly. He was clearly embarrassed at being the center of so much appreciation. "Really, it was nothing."

"It was a kind deed," Miz Callie said, her voice firm as she reached out to clasp his hand. "Don't you ever go discounting the power of a kind deed."

Ross clasped Miz Callie's fine-boned hand in his, and Amanda wondered if he was thinking of his own grandmother and what he'd said about her that first time he'd given her a glimpse of the man behind the mask.

"It was my pleasure to help you," he said.

And her heart turned over, seeming to unfold like a flower.

I love him, she thought, surprised. *I love him.*

Ross leaned on the deck railing, looking out at the ocean that moved softly in the dark, lit only where the moon traced a shimmering pathway on the water. He heard the door open and close behind him and knew without looking that it was Amanda.

"They're still at it," she said, coming to lean on the railing next to him. Her arm brushed his, sending a flare of awareness through him.

Where had it come from, this instinctive reaction to Amanda? He hadn't expected it or even necessarily welcomed it, but there it was. If she was anywhere within range, he knew where. If she touched him, no matter how impersonally, he felt it to the marrow of his bones.

"This hunt of yours seems important to them."

"It'll make Miz Callie happy. She's frustrated at the idea of never knowing what happened to Ned."

She was editing what she told him, and he seemed to know that, also by instinct. "I heard someone say he was a Bodine. I thought he was a relative of your grandmother's."

"He was Granddad's older brother," she said. "There was a family quarrel, and he just disappeared. She feels as if she has to know."

He suspected that still wasn't the whole story, but that didn't seem to matter. At the moment nothing seemed to except being here with Amanda.

He knew all the reasons why this was a bad idea. He'd listed them to himself plenty of times. But for once his intellect and his feelings were not working in tandem.

"Take a walk on the beach?" he asked abruptly.

"Sure thing." She lifted her head, as if sniffing the breeze. "The wind's off the ocean, so the bugs shouldn't be biting too badly."

"That makes sense, I guess, but every time you drop

a little bit of nature lore, it confuses me." He followed her down the stairs.

"Why?" She stopped at the bottom to wait for him, her face a pale oval in the dim light.

"Out here, you're nature girl in your shorts and T-shirts, knowing all about the tides and the flora and fauna. Back in the office, you're Ms. Sophistication. Or at least you look that way. I'm not sure which is really you."

"You noticed that, did you?" She started toward the water, and he followed along the narrow path through the dunes. She sounded relaxed, all the tension that had been between them earlier wiped away. "That's an easy one to explain."

"So go ahead, explain." They reached the hard-packed sand where the walking was easier, and he fell into step with her.

"When I'm here, I revert to the kid I used to be here, growing up. All the cousins do. Just watch sometime when we're doing a crab boil on the beach." She made it sound as if it was a given, that he'd be here to share that. "The boys act like they're about ten, and the girls… well, maybe a year or two older."

"That fits in with something Adam said about the Bodine boys landing on anyone who caused trouble for any one of you."

She glanced up at him. Out here in the moonlight he could see her face better, or maybe his eyes were just growing accustomed to the dark. Right now, her expression was questioning.

"The Bodine boys were terrors, there's no doubt about that. But how did Adam come to say that to you?"

"It was when we were at the docks." How would she

react? "He implied that you were protected. I figured he was warning me off."

If he could see colors in the dim light, he'd probably find that she was blushing.

"That nitwit. He shouldn't have said anything of the kind. He certainly ought to have outgrown that kind of nonsense."

She didn't seem to be reading anything into the comment except the surface meaning, and maybe that's all there was.

"So did they really beat up guys who bothered you girls?"

"I don't think it ever went that far." She paused, seeming to examine the tracks of some tiny creature in the glistening wet sand. "There was one kid who came close. He stood me up for my senior prom."

"Sounds like he deserved some grief for that." He was surprised to discover his fists clenching in response to that years-old insult.

"It wasn't as bad as it sounds." She looked up at him, as if to reinforce the point. "Really. I mean, he was just a guy friend. He never even thought of me romantically. I was just a buddy." She gave an exaggerated sigh, as if laughing at herself. "That was the story of my high school career. I was every guy's best buddy, the one they asked for advice on their girlfriends."

"That doesn't excuse him for dumping you after he'd asked you."

She looked a little disconcerted at his persistence. "It wasn't a big deal, except of course I'd gotten the dress and all. You see, his girl had broken up with him. He told me all about it, and then he asked me to go. But they made up at the last minute, so naturally he wanted to take her."

Naturally. The guy really had deserved pounding. From his limited experience with girls and proms, he'd guess it had been a very big deal indeed.

"So you missed your senior prom." He pictured her crying her eyes out in her crushed gown.

"Goodness, no. Oh, I spent about a half hour moping and crying. Wailing that I loved him. Miz Callie said that if I loved him, I'd want him to have his heart's desire, even if that wasn't me." A smiled touched her lips. "Which pretty much convinced me I hadn't loved him. And Daddy lined up all the Bodine boys who were old enough and told me to take my pick for a prom date."

That was a diverting thought. "Who did you pick?"

"Adam. He was the big football hero. Not that my big brothers weren't impressive, but going with a brother would really have been humiliating. I figured a cousin would be bad enough, but all the girls actually envied me. He was considered quite a catch, believe it or not." She shook her head. "He'll never let me forget that he took me to my senior prom. But it taught me one thing."

"What's that?" Hopefully not to date jerks anymore.

"That August I was off to Columbia for college, and I decided to make myself over. No more being the spunky kid sister and listening to the boys' troubles. I turned myself into the datable girl, not the best buddy girl, and I had fun doing it, too."

The odd thing was that she really thought she'd changed. Oh, she might have altered the exterior, but she was still the good friend everyone relied on, whether she realized it or not.

"I'm still thinking about that idiot who gave up a

prom date with you. Didn't he know what he was missing?"

"Missing?" She sounded disconcerted. They'd come to a stop and stood very close on the shining sand. The breeze off the water ruffled Amanda's hair, blowing strands of silk across her face.

He reached out to slip his fingers into the strands, smoothing them back from her face, letting his palm linger against her cheek. Her eyes widened, and her face tilted toward his in what seemed an involuntary movement.

"He missed this." His voice had roughened, but he couldn't help that. Every cell in his body seemed independently aware of her. "He could have stood on the beach like this with you, touching you. He could have drawn you close." He suited the action to the words, bringing her into the circle of his arms.

She tilted her face back, her hair swinging in a shimmering arc. "I'm glad he didn't," she murmured.

"I'm glad, too." He ran his fingers back through her hair, holding her, caressing the nape of her neck, running his thumb along the smooth line of her chin. "I wouldn't want to be jealous that he'd kissed you."

One tiny part of his mind shouted that this was a mistake, and he shut it up ruthlessly. Mistake or not, they were going to have this moment. He lowered his head, and his lips claimed hers.

Chapter 11

Ross's hand clasped Amanda's warmly as they walked back toward the beach house. She might have stayed there locked in his arms forever, but the family would wonder why they were gone so long. Or guess why, more likely.

It didn't matter. Nothing mattered but being here, with him, feeling his hand swallowing up hers while warm waves washed over their bare feet and then receded, shifting the sand restlessly under them.

She should be cautious. Just because she'd tumbled headlong into love didn't mean that he felt the same. But she couldn't stop her feelings, any more than she could stop the ebbing tide.

She glanced up at his face, lit by the moonlight, and smiled.

"What's so funny?" His voice was a low rumble that echoed the sound of the surf.

"You, walking in the water with your pant legs rolled up and your shoes in your hand. A bit different from your usual persona."

His face eased into a returning smile. "It's nice." He sounded surprised.

"Didn't you go to the beach for vacations when you were a child?"

"I suppose, but that was a long time ago. I haven't taken a vacation in—" He stopped, obviously searching his memory. "Not since college, unless you count being unemployed for a time."

"You're overdue for a little relaxation time, then." She'd known he was a workaholic, but that was ridiculous. Everyone needed downtime in order to stay sane.

"I guess I am. You were lucky to grow up in a place like this. With a family like yours."

Only the fact that she was hypersensitive to his speech made her aware of some tension in those last words. Not surprising. The little he'd told her about his parents had made them sound as warm and caring a pair of boa constrictors. She sought for something that would encourage him to open up.

"Miz Callie has always held us all together, even when we were kids running wild on this beach. Tell me more about your grandmother."

He was silent for a moment. The wavelets washed over their feet, then sucked away toward the ocean again, drawn by its irresistible force.

"She was like your Miz Callie, I suppose. The kind of person who radiates caring. Knowing she loved me gave a center to my life when I was a kid. Whatever conscience and values I have came from her."

"She was a person of faith, then."

He nodded. "She hauled me along to Sunday school and church every Sunday, no excuses. Even after she was gone, I still felt guilty if I tried to sleep in on Sunday mornings."

"And now?" She held her breath, wondering if she was going too far.

He shrugged. "Now I guess I don't know. Somehow God doesn't seem to have much to do with my life."

Her heart clenched. "Miz Callie would say that God has everything to do with it, even if you don't believe."

They'd reached the bottom of the stairs leading up to the deck. Ross stopped, turning her to face him, his hands on her shoulders. "Is that what you'd say, too?"

She nodded. "Yes. I tried the 'sleeping in on Sunday mornings' when I went off to college. It never worked for long. I started feeling like a boat without a rudder when I ignored my faith."

His hands massaged her shoulders gently, and his touch seemed to go right to her heart. "You're pretty special, you know that?"

"Not me." She tried to deny the way her heart fluttered at his words. "Charleston is filled with women like me."

"Then why am I not compelled to kiss any of them?" His lips found hers, and he murmured her name against her mouth.

She wanted to stop thinking entirely, to give herself up to the sensation of being held and cherished in his arms. Of feeling a part of him. But she couldn't quite do that. What he'd revealed about his lack of faith troubled her, and she had to be careful.

He drew back finally, still holding her in the circle of his arms, but looking at her with a faintly troubled expression.

"What's wrong?" she murmured.

"You tell me. It seemed to me you're pulling away."

She wasn't sure what to say. "I guess maybe I don't want to move too fast."

"Maybe you're right." He touched her cheek. "I am still your boss. I wish…"

The sliding glass door above them opened, and footsteps sounded on the deck. "I don't see them," Georgia said. "They must have walked pretty far."

She must be looking down the empty beach, wondering where they'd disappeared to.

"We're here," she called, resigning herself to never knowing what Ross might have said if they hadn't been interrupted. "We'll be right up."

Georgia leaned over the railing to look down at them. "Sorry. I just couldn't wait." Her voice lifted on the words. "We found something."

She vanished again, and Amanda heard her say something to the others. It looked as though the romantic moments were over for now, but that was probably for the best.

Ross touched her shoulder. "We'd better go up before your cousin comes after me."

She started up the stairs, her thoughts returning to that odd exchange he'd mentioned with Adam. What had prompted that?

They walked back into the dining room to find Miz Callie looking slightly dazed. "We might have found him, Amanda. At least, we've found two enlistees who fit. Surely, once we look into them more closely, we'll know. One of them must be Ned."

"Miz Callie, that's wonderful." She bent to hug her grandmother, glancing from face to face.

Georgia was elated, hugging a smiling Matt. Win and Hugh looked pleased. Adam...

Adam didn't seem to be paying any attention to their find. Instead, he was staring at Ross with a look that sent a chill right down her spine.

Cyrus drifted into Ross's office the day after the dinner at Miz Callie's with such a casual look that it was immediately obvious to Ross that something was on his mind. For once, he didn't beat around the bush.

"Where do we stand with the kickback story? Anything happening?" He leaned against the corner of Ross's desk, running one hand over his bushy white hair in a futile attempt to tame it.

Ross lifted his hands, palms up. "Nothing. That's how much I've come up with. Rumors, yes. Hints, odd looks. Facts, no."

"You're not giving up." Cyrus straightened, offended at the thought.

"Of course not." Frustration put an edge to his voice. "As long as there's a thread, I'll keep trying to unravel it. Sometimes that's all it takes—one loose end. I have a lead on somebody who works for a guy who's gotten a suspiciously high number of contracts from the base."

Cyrus grunted approval. "If there's cheating going on, it's our job to expose it. And if we're first to break the story..." He let that trail off, but there was no doubt of the passion he felt. Much as Cyrus claimed to like his gadfly role, he'd give a lot to break this story.

"We'll do our best."

That was all he could promise, and his stomach tightened at the thought that it might not be enough. Maybe he didn't have what it took. Maybe, in this alien place, he'd never be able to come up with the contacts that had fallen so easily into his hands in Washington.

"You'll do it," Cyrus said. "I take it there's nothing to tie Bodine into the scam?"

"Nothing but his position." And Ross's gut instinct telling him that the man didn't like him. But there could be plenty of reasons for that—the main one sitting out in the newsroom right now.

"It'll happen. Look at the story you've nailed starting from a simple complaint from an intern about her air-conditioning."

"That did come together." He couldn't help the satisfaction in his voice. "Jim's writing a sidebar on low-income housing in the city to round it out, and we break it in tomorrow's paper."

Cyrus's eyes glinted, and he rubbed his palms together. "That'll show 'em. I read Amanda's piece, by the way. She did a great job with that interview. Heart-tugging without being maudlin, presented the people with dignity. There's more to that young woman than I thought, and I'll be the first to admit it. I was judging her on her appearance, and there's substance there."

"It wasn't bad." The lukewarm words hid a rush of pleasure at hearing Amanda praised. She had really risen to the challenge he'd thrown at her.

"Guess it's time to give her somethin' substantial to work on." Cyrus's bushy brows drew down. "Unless we have to expose her daddy for a thief. I reckon we'll see her back mighty fast if that happens."

When Cyrus started sounding folksy, that meant that he was worried.

Well, Cyrus had company in that. Ross had let himself get involved with Amanda, despite all the good reasons not to. If this situation turned sour, a lot of people were going to get hurt.

He seemed to see Amanda's face, turned up to his in the moonlight, and his heart clenched. If that happened, how was he going to live with himself?

Amanda dragged her mind back to the words on her computer screen. It was something of a comedown to go from the excitement of breaking the slumlord story to writing an article about the barbecue cook-off for charity the *Bugle* was sponsoring on the weekend. Too bad every story couldn't involve controversy.

Still, it made her understand a bit about Ross's attitude toward his profession. And why he felt his real life was back in D.C., where he could go from one important story to another.

He'll go back to that, a small voice whispered in the back of her mind. *He'll go back, eventually. And then where will you be?* And even if he didn't, were they really suited to each other? Each time they got close, it seemed she saw something in his values to push her away.

"Amanda."

She looked up, startled, to find her cousin Adam standing in front of her desk. By the patient look on his face, he must have been standing there for a bit.

"Adam, sorry. The receptionist didn't let me know you're here."

"She knows me by now. That must be some important story you're working on to take you that far away."

"Just daydreaming," she said quickly. She waved toward a chair. "Have a seat. What's up?"

He sat down, reaching over to drop a manila envelope on the desk. "Truth is that I need your opinion on something." He tapped the envelope with one finger. "I've been doing some research, trying to find something that will tell us which one of our possible candidates is Uncle Ned."

"If either," Amanda said. "I know Miz Callie is convinced we're almost there, but…"

"I know, I know. That's why I want you to look at this. Be sure it's not just wishful thinking on my part before I take it to Miz Callie."

"What?" She reached for the envelope, but before she could take it, Adam emptied its contents onto her desk. A black-and-white photo slid out, as well as a magnifying glass.

"Take a look." He put the photo in front of her. "You'll need the magnifier to make out the faces. Tell me if you see anyone familiar."

Amanda pressed the edges of the photo flat. It was a copy, she'd guess, of an old picture. Adam, with his latest photo software, would probably have sharpened it as much as possible.

The black-and-white photo showed a PT boat docked someplace where there was sandy beach and palm trees in the background. The boat's crew posed for the camera, grinning self-consciously.

Her heart clenched at those young faces, staring out at her from more than a half century ago. They were filled with so much bravado.

"That was taken when she'd just arrived in the war zone," Adam said. "She had a full complement then, not tested in battle yet." He spoke of the PT boat with as much familiarity as he'd talk of his own patrol boat. "See if you recognize anyone."

Obediently she took the magnifier. Were they going to find out what had happened to Ned Bodine at last? Her pulse beat rapidly, and she paused a moment to steady herself before bending over the image.

Take it slow, study each face methodically. Adam trusted her to do this right and not send Miz Callie off on a wild-goose chase.

She worked from the right to the left, focusing on each face, searching for any trace of familiarity. Nothing. Then she moved the glass to the group on the left.

The face jumped out at her, so clear that she couldn't help a gasp. She planted her finger on the figure. "There. That's Ned. It has to be."

"You sure, sugar? The features are pretty washed-out on an old photo like this."

"It's not just the features." She struggled to explain the sense of familiarity that gripped her. "It's not just the features, although they're right, what you can see of them. It's the way he holds himself, the way his hand rests on the boat's hull, like he's caressing it." She grinned, sure of herself. "I've seen you do the same, more times than I can count."

Adam's face relaxed. "I see something of our Win in him, myself. That tilt of the head, maybe."

Funny how gestures and movements could pass through generations as surely as coloring. "Which one of the two names Miz Callie picked out is he?"

"Theodore Hawkins." He didn't need to explain that Hawkins was the name of Granddad's mother's family. "I guess he wanted to take something of family with him."

"I guess he did." She touched the photograph lightly. "Do you know what happened to him?"

"Not yet, but it shouldn't take long now that we have a name. One thing I do know." His face sobered. "The PT boat went down in the South China Sea in '44."

Her eyes filled with tears, and she brushed them away impatiently. "Well, we thought from the beginning that he probably didn't survive the war, since the family never heard from him. Miz Callie will be relieved to know the truth."

He nodded, standing and scooping the photo and magnifier back into the envelope. "I'm gonna run over there a bit later to show her what we have. It'll take a couple days, probably, to get the complete military records. You want to come with me?"

"I can't, not tonight." She glanced at her watch. "I'm meeting someone for dinner. You go, and take all the credit. You deserve it."

That didn't bring the smile she expected. "This date—it wouldn't be with Ross Lockhart, would it?"

"Yes, why?" She sat up straighter, prepared to do battle. Adam's attitude toward Ross was just ridiculous, and she didn't mind telling him so.

"Look, sugar, don't fly off the handle with me." He obviously had no trouble interpreting her mood. "I just… I don't want you to get hurt. I don't trust him."

She blew out an exasperated breath. "For pity's sake, Adam. I'm a big girl now. I don't need the Bodine boys to protect me from my dates."

"That's not what I mean." Adam frowned, planting one fist against her desktop. "Maybe he's a nice enough guy in some ways, but I'd say there's not much he'd stick at when it comes to getting a big story."

True, but… "That's what makes him a good reporter."

"Even if he's after a story that involves your family?"

The question burst out of him, and then he clamped his mouth shut as if instantly regretting it.

She shot out of her chair, facing him over the width of her desk. "What are you talking about? What could he possibly want to write that would affect us? If you're talking about that business with Ned—well, we've practically got the proof in hand that he wasn't a coward."

Adam dismissed that with a wave of his hand. "His digging is more up-to-date than that. If he—" He stopped, shook his head. "Look, I can't say more."

"Adam." Her voice warned. "You tell me what's going on right this minute."

"I can't." To do him credit, he looked miserable at having brought it up. "Maybe I'm imagining things, but has it occurred to you that this series he's supposed to be doing about the Coast Guard base might be a cover for something else?"

"No." She tried for an indignant tone, but it didn't quite ring true. Daddy's unexplained animosity toward Ross, Ross's insistence on information that didn't seem to have much to do with the supposed purpose of the articles…

"I'm sorry, sugar." His voice went soft. "I don't want to cause trouble. Just—be careful."

Before she could say anything, he turned and walked quickly away.

Chapter 12

Amanda was still troubled by Adam's words when she stepped through the front door of the Shem Creek Café that evening. She shook the rain from her umbrella and shoved it into the old-fashioned milk can that held a number of similarly wet umbrellas. The storm that was making its way up the coast promised them a couple of inches of much-needed rain before all was said and done.

The rain hadn't kept folks away from the popular restaurant, and the tables and booths were already crowded. As the hostess moved toward her, she scanned the dining area and spotted Ross, half rising to catch her eye from a table next to the window.

"That's okay, I see my…" What? Date? Boyfriend? She wasn't sure either of those words applied to her tenuous relationship with Ross.

Fortunately, the waitress didn't bother to wait for her to finish the sentence, waving her into the dining room with a smile.

Amanda wove her way between the tables, trying to suppress the flutter that arose somewhere in her midsection when she saw Ross waiting for her, his eyes warming as he watched her.

Ridiculously aware of his gaze on her, she nearly stumbled into a tray rack that had been left between the tables to trip up the distracted. *Get hold of yourself,* she lectured. *This isn't just about being with Ross tonight. You have to find out if what Adam hinted at is true.*

If she didn't, the suspicion would poison whatever relationship she and Ross had. She couldn't pretend the feeling wasn't there. She had to deal with it.

Adam's words had crystallized the amorphous concern that had been drifting like fog in the back of her thoughts. She'd realized after he left that she'd already been wondering why she'd never seen any indication that Ross had written a word about the interviews she'd set up.

Certainly he'd been researching something. Jim had commented on that, saying he'd surprised Ross searching through some records late in the evening, when he'd thought the offices deserted. And Ross never had asked to see any of the photos she'd taken, or checked with her on anything to do with the Coast Guard.

"Amanda." He said her name with a caressing note that he'd never use in the office. "I'm glad you're here."

"I hope I didn't keep you waiting long." She slid into the chair he pulled out for her, too aware of the treacherous effect his nearness had on her as he bent to push the chair in. She could only hope the anxiety she felt wasn't written on her face.

Anxiety—that was probably the right word. The truth was that she'd rather not face this. She'd rather pretend everything was fine and enjoy the moment.

"I've just been here a few minutes," he said. "Cyrus

advised me to come early so I could get a table at the window to enjoy the view."

"Cyrus knows we're out tonight together?" She wasn't sure she liked that thought.

"Cyrus knows everything. Sometimes I wonder if he doesn't have a closed-circuit television watching our every move."

"Not here, I hope." She glanced around with a mock shudder.

"Just at work." His face relaxed in a smile.

Her heart clutched. She hadn't ever seen quite that much ease in his expression. Even when he'd been enjoying himself as he had, she felt sure, with Miz Callie, there'd been a hint of restraint, of things suppressed and guarded.

This was the way he could be, if he weren't so eaten up with the wrongs that had been dealt him.

Please, Father. The prayer formed almost without volition. *Please help him set himself free from all that holds him back from being an open, giving person.*

"Have you had a look at the menu?" She'd been silent too long, caught up in her reactions to him. "I highly recommend the she-crab soup. And the shrimp and grits."

"Do they guarantee that only she-crabs went into the soup?" The teasing note in his voice turned her determination to jelly.

"I'm sure they do. Anyway, it's the best I've ever eaten."

"Okay, then. She-crab soup and a grilled sirloin."

She raised her eyebrows at that. "You did notice that saltwater tank when we came in, didn't you? Why would you order steak in a place that has seafood only a step from the boats?"

She nodded to the window beside them. A lone fishing boat made its way up the creek, its captain swathed in a yellow slicker against the rain.

"You're not going to let me get away with this, are you?" He flipped the menu open again. "I'm not ready to try shrimp and grits yet. Will you be satisfied if I get the grouper?"

"I guess. But sometime you have to give in and try grits."

They could go on all evening like this, as far as she was concerned. Keep the tone light and easy, enjoy the moment. Not think about the questions she had to ask.

"Maybe I can have a bite of yours," he said softly, reaching across the table to touch her fingertips with his in a gesture that set her pulse fluttering.

The server came then, and after a consultation as to what the catch of the day was, she brought drinks and headed back to the kitchen with their order.

"This is in the nature of a celebration," Ross said, tipping his glass of iced tea toward hers.

"It is?"

He nodded. "We've put the story to bed. In the morning it will be all over the city. Cyrus was very complimentary about your writing, by the way."

Cyrus was? "I'll have to thank him," she said.

"All right." His fingers enveloped hers. "Your piece was better than good. You're not quite the lightweight I thought you were at first."

"At first? You've had me pegged as the stereotypical Southern belle right along, and I'm not sure you're over it yet."

"Maybe so," he admitted. "You have to admit, you do look and sound the part."

"Scarlett O'Hara has a lot to answer for," she said darkly. "And let me tell you, Scarlett was a lot tougher than she looked."

"Got it," he said, lifting one hand in a gesture of surrender. "I promise not to make that mistake again. I couldn't, not now that I know you." His voice deepened on the words, and his eyes seemed to darken.

Her breath caught in her throat. She couldn't have given him a flippant answer if her life depended on it. Adam's worry sounded in her mind, adding its weight to the doubts she couldn't get rid of.

Their food arrived then, and she was grateful for the distraction. They ate, they sampled each other's entrées, and then Ross pinned her with a direct gaze.

"I saw you and Adam in the newsroom today. It looked like a pretty serious discussion."

She smoothed her napkin out in her lap. It seemed she was being forced to have this talk no matter how she tried to avoid it.

"He brought a photo over to show me." She was still avoiding, and she knew it. "He's been trying to identify which of our possibilities is the right one, and he found an old picture of the crew of a PT boat that Theodore Hawkins served on. It was Uncle Ned. I'm sure of it." Her eyes filled with tears at the memory of that young face. "The family will be so relieved to know the truth about him at last."

"After all these years," he said, shaking his head a little. "There's a human interest story there, if you're not too close to write it."

"I hadn't thought of that."

Her nerve endings prickled. She hadn't, but that could be the resolution to all their worries about Miz Callie

and the memorial to Ned Bodine. If the world, meaning Charleston in this case, learned first that Ned hadn't
been a coward, but had served honorably, then no one
could argue about Miz Callie establishing a memorial
to him.

"Is that everything?"

She looked up, meeting his gaze, to find a question
in his eyes.

"I... I don't know what you mean." She certainly was
feeble as a liar.

"Yes, you do. Something's been weighing on you."
His dark brows furrowed, setting three vertical lines
between them. "Was Adam warning you against me
again?"

"Not the way you mean." She couldn't leave it at that.
Despair settled on her. What she said next was going to
send Ross back behind his armor. She'd prayed that he'd
be set free, but accusing him wouldn't do that, would it?

"What then?" His tone turned impatient.

She took a breath. There was no way out but to say
it. "Are you really writing a series of human interest articles about the Coast Guard base? Or is it a cover for
something else going on?"

She watched it happen. His face tightened into a
mask. His eyes grew cold and suspicious.

"What makes you think that?"

They were both answering questions with questions.
That didn't get them anywhere.

"I don't just think it. I feel it. There was something
going on when you talked with my father. You went in
there with an agenda, and it didn't have anything to do
with writing a profile piece."

She waited for the ax to fall, knowing she'd said nothing more than the truth.

"People who haven't done anything wrong don't have to worry about publicity," he said finally. "That's all I have to say about it, so you might pass that on to your cousin. And the form these articles take is my business and Cyrus's."

Not yours. The words were unspoken, but there.

All the barricades had gone up between them again. And any chance she had of finding out who Ross truly was at heart had just moved further away.

Amanda tried to put aside her worries and enjoy the air of celebration that permeated the newsroom the next day. The slumlord exposé had been everything Cyrus might have wished for—a splashy story of wide interest, a clear villain and, best of all, the *Bugle* had beaten out the competition.

The television in the corner of the newsroom was turned on, with local stations belatedly jumping on the bandwagon, promising exciting new revelations about Hardy on the noon news.

A grumble greeted this, but Cyrus, watching with the others, turned away with a shrug. "That's their advantage, going on the air right away. People are still going to come to us if they want something more than a couple minutes' worth of sound bites."

"Right." Even Jim, whom no one could remember seeing smile since a certain prominent local politician had been caught trying to pick up an undercover policewoman, had a broad grin on his face. "We do our job, they do theirs. Good work, everyone."

Most of the staff had had little or nothing to do with

the story, but its success affected them, too. Amanda suspected that the old warhorses, like Jim, were reminded of what it had been like in their glory days, while the eager kids saw their dreams of journalism coming true.

The buzz died off suddenly. If it was Ross...her stomach lurched. They'd parted with an uncomfortable truce last night, and she couldn't imagine that there would be any more romantic dinners on their horizon for a while, at least.

But it was C.J. who'd come in. She paused, looking around rather truculently, as if prepared for a fight.

Jim walked over and threw an arm over her shoulder in a hug that would have staggered Amanda, but didn't seem to faze C.J. "Good work on that story, kid. You led us to a really fine piece. We couldn't have done it without you."

Following Jim's lead, the others in the newsroom added their congratulations. By the time C.J. made it to Amanda's desk, she wore a broad grin.

She dropped into the chair beside the desk, a little doubt creeping into her eyes. "D'you think they really mean it? I didn't do much. If it wasn't for my gran, I'd never have talked to you about it."

"They mean it," Amanda assured her. "Even if you had second thoughts, your instincts were right on target."

"That's right." Ross's deep voice startled her, even as it reverberated right down to her bones. How did he manage to get within a few feet without her knowing he was coming? "Instincts are a solid part of being a good reporter. You can learn how to construct a story, but you can't learn instinct."

C.J. ducked her head, embarrassed at being singled out by the managing editor.

"Trust your instincts," he said, this time looking right at Amanda.

She lifted her chin. "Sometimes your instincts can tear you in two directions at the same time." Between the man you cared about and your family, for instance.

"If you're in doubt, go with the truth." He'd given up any pretense that he was talking to C.J., his gray eyes focused laserlike on Amanda's face. "That's the only thing reporters have going for them in the long run."

"And if you're not sure what the truth is?"

"Then you'd better find out, if you're any kind of a reporter." He spun and stalked off.

"You want to tell me what that was all about?" C.J. was probably too astonished to be tactful, if she ever was anyway.

"Nothing." She took a breath and shook her head. "Well, nothing I can talk about. How are things between your grandmother and the other people in your building?"

C.J. shrugged, seeming to accept the new subject. "The other folks are all over the place. Some of them are complaining about the news crews out front, and some are offering them guided tours and acting like they broke the story themselves. Some of them are blaming us for bringing all this fuss on them. And I guess some are just plain scared."

"How's your grandmother taking it?" That was exactly the thing they had feared would happen to Miz Callie if she went through with her plans—that people she cared about would turn against her.

"She just holds her head high and ignores them." C.J. gave a little shrug that probably expressed bafflement. "I want to punch someone. Not sure I'll ever get to where she is."

"Give yourself some time." That was probably good advice for her, too, when she wondered if she'd ever be the woman her grandmother was. "And don't forget about calling the attorney if there's anything you don't understand. He's there to help you."

"I won't forget. And no chance I'll forget what you did."

"What I did? It was you and your grandmother who did it. And Mr. Lockhart, of course, who started the investigation."

"I didn't mean that." C.J. lowered her gaze in embarrassment. "I mean what you said that day at the Market. About having courage. It seems like that really affected my gran. She's got her nerve back in a big way, ready to conquer the world. Says I'm going to college if she has to bully me all the way. She'll do it, too."

"I don't doubt it." She smiled, thinking how alike C.J.'s grandmother and Miz Callie were under the skin. Miz Callie would do that, too, if she thought one of her grandkids needed it.

"She sent this for you." C.J. put a paper bag in Amanda's hands. "She said don't you give me no arguments about takin' it, either."

Even without unwrapping it, Amanda knew by the touch what it was. A sweetgrass basket. She opened the bag and pulled it out, her breath catching.

Not just a sweetgrass basket, a work of art. It was an egg basket, the delicate oval shape complemented by striations, layering dark against light in an endless spiral.

"It's beautiful." She knew better than to try to return

it. That would be an insult to the woman and to C.J. "I don't know how to thank her. I'll cherish this."

"I guess that's all the thanks she'd want." C.J.'s eyes were suspiciously bright. "She said to tell you something else. She said to remind you that strong women have the courage to do what's right."

Amanda turned the words over in her mind as she turned the basket over in her hands. C.J.'s grandmother had echoed her own words back at her, with a twist. Was she that kind of strong woman? She wasn't sure, but it was time she started acting as if she was.

Chapter 13

The rain had stopped by the time Amanda arrived on Isle of Palms that afternoon to cover the festival the newspaper was cosponsoring to benefit the elementary school that served the two barrier islands. Cyrus's philanthropy could be erratic. It was hard to tell what worthy cause would catch his fancy, but he regularly used the newspaper to sponsor events that needed a bit of help.

She moved among the crowds along Front Street, past the Windjammer Café and rows of shops. The street was lined with booths of all sorts, many of them featuring local delicacies or handcrafted items. Beyond the buildings, the dunes ran down to the sea, gray and angry-looking today. Somewhere out there the slow-moving tropical storm had stalled, a situation that made coastal dwellers edgy.

She had more than the weather or the festival in mind at the moment, though. Daddy was off duty today, she'd learned by a phone call to her mother. He'd announced his plan to stop by the festival, even though Mamma couldn't come because it was her day to volunteer at the hospital; everybody knew that, and she couldn't possibly disappoint folks who were counting on her.

Assuring her mother that she understood, Amanda had gotten off the phone. Mamma didn't know why it was so important to Amanda to catch up to Daddy today, and Amanda surely didn't plan to tell her.

She had to confront Daddy and find out what was going on between him and Ross. She hadn't had much success with Ross, but she certainly could manage her own father better than that.

And there he was. Not giving her nerves a chance to fail, Amanda hurried her steps, catching up with him in front of a fishing game booth, where small children were dipping with their nets in pursuit of colorful plastic fish.

"You plannin' on going fishing, Daddy?" She slid her arm in his.

He jerked around, nearly throwing her off balance. "Manda. What on earth are you doing here?"

Keeping her smile fixed with an effort, she gestured to the camera slung around her neck. "I'm covering the event for the newspaper. Didn't you know we were a cosponsor?"

What was going on with Daddy? He'd jerked around like a…like a criminal, feeling the hand of the law on his shoulder. She shoved the thought away.

"No, no, can't say I did." He sounded distracted. "I just figured one of us ought to come and support the school, and your mamma was tied up at the hospital today." He loosened her grip on his arm. "Well, I'll let you get on with your work. I'm fixin' to pick up a shrimp burger for my lunch and see if I can find some little somethin' to take to your mamma."

She caught his arm again. "Not so fast, Daddy. I need to talk to you."

"If you're working—" he began, but she cut him off.

"Daddy, I have to know. What's going on between you and Ross Lockhart?"

There was the faintest hesitation, and then he was shaking his head. "I don't know what you're talking about, child."

"You know exactly what I'm talking about." She wanted to shake him. "For goodness' sake, I even had Adam coming by the office to tell me to stay away from the man because of it, whatever it is."

Daddy scowled, his square face flushing. "Adam ought to know enough to hold his tongue."

"Adam is worried about me. I think he's afraid I'm going to get squashed like a bug between the two of you. And I'm worried about you." There, it was a relief to say the words. "Everyone's stumbling around in the dark. Just tell me."

Her father's color deepened. "You ought to know that there's some things I can't talk to you about, Amanda. Can't even talk to your mamma, for that matter, and I tell her everything."

She felt it slipping away from her, and she tried to hang on with both hands. "Ross Lockhart is my boss. That means I'm involved, whether I want to be or not. Why does Adam think I need protecting? Why did you and Ross act like you were old enemies the first time you met? What were you hiding from him?"

"Hush up." Daddy darted a quick look around, but no one was close enough to hear their low voices. "I can't talk about it, Amanda. If you want to know something about your boss, you'd better ask him."

"I have." She met his gaze steadily. *Oh, Daddy. I trust you. Just don't shut me out.*

Daddy's face tightened. "What did he say?"

"He said the innocent don't need to worry about publicity."

She expected him to explode at that. Expected, but didn't get it. Instead, her father seemed to be looking at someone or something over her shoulder. His muscles had gone tight, and his expression actually scared her.

"I can't talk anymore right now." He gave her a little shove. "Take yourself and your cameras off, and forget I'm here."

"Daddy—"

"I mean it, Amanda." It was his tone of command, the one she'd never disobeyed in her life. "I'll talk to you later. Right now, just go."

There was no arguing with that. She turned, tears blurring her eyes. What on earth was her father mixed up in?

Ross ducked behind an ice cream stand when Amanda turned to look in his direction. If she saw him, she'd think he didn't trust her to cover the event.

The truth was far from that, but he didn't intend to enlighten her. He'd had another tip, and this time he'd realized that the informant had to work for Cliff Winchell, the contractor who'd been so evasive each time Ross had called.

He couldn't make too much of that fact. Plenty of innocent people didn't want to talk to the press. But Winchell was also the man whose company seemed to get more than its share of contracts from the Coast Guard base.

According to the informant, Winchell was meeting today at the festival with his contact from the base. And sure enough, there the man was, working his way from booth to booth as if he had nothing better to do with himself today but buy a candy apple.

Ross stationed himself by the ice cream stand, to the annoyance of the vendor, and casually watched the man. Still, he couldn't keep himself from glancing at Amanda from time to time.

She moved, and he was able to see who she was talking to. His stomach jolted. Amanda turned, walking away from her father, the distress on her face plain even from this distance.

Her pain caught at his heart, turning it cold. He should never have let things go as far as they had between them. She was going to be hurt—was already hurting, and he'd probably make it worse before he was done.

But how could he have resisted her? He'd come from a situation where everyone he knew and trusted had turned against him. Even the rescue Cyrus offered had been conditional.

But Amanda—there was nothing conditional about Amanda. Interest in everyone whose life she touched poured from her like a welcome stream in the desert. She had a good heart. His grandmother would have said those simple words in the highest of praise.

Winchell started moving oh so casually, along the row of buildings that lined the street. Ross followed, cutting through the crowd at an angle that would keep him well away from Amanda.

He could avoid encountering her, but he couldn't dismiss her from his mind that easily. That talk they'd had about faith—he hadn't been able to stop the flow of memories that had loosened.

He'd drifted far from the faith to which his grandmother had led him, maybe too far to go back. After her death, he'd gone along with the people who were his friends at school—high achievers who focused on success and achievement. Faith seemed to have little to do with that.

Winchell was walking along the sidewalk, stopping to stare at a restaurant menu posted in a window. Looking at that, or using the plate glass to see if he was being followed? Ross kept back, well out of range of the glass.

Amanda had admitted drifting, too, when she went away to school. Probably a lot of people did. But she'd come back to the faith of her childhood. Back to the center of her life, she'd implied.

He didn't have that. Maybe she didn't, either, his cynical mind retorted. Maybe she just thought she did, under the influence of the family she loved. How could she know?

Winchell, apparently satisfied no one was watching him, slipped between the buildings and disappeared. Ross elbowed his way through a group of teenagers blocking the sidewalk and narrowly escaped being hit by the swinging camera of a sunburned tourist.

He reached the place where the man vanished. A narrow passageway ran between the buildings. At the end of it, he could glimpse dunes and sea oats. Nothing else, but Winchell had gone this way, so he would, too.

When he neared the end of the passageway, he slowed, moving cautiously, and peered around the corner. There was his quarry, perhaps twenty yards away in the dunes, gesticulating wildly, facing another man. Amanda's father.

Oddly, there was no satisfaction at seeing a difficult case come together. Just sorrow and anger at what the man was inflicting on his family. On Amanda. Brett Bodine would hurt so many innocent people with his duplicity.

Pain had a grip on his throat, but he pulled the small camera from his pocket. This time he wouldn't be caught by faked photos. He'd provide the proof himself, and no one would be able to question it.

If she concentrated hard enough on her job, Amanda decided, she just might be able to ignore that unsatisfying conversation with her father. Or pretend to.

She'd interviewed one of the organizers of the event and picked up a quote from a teacher at the school. A few grinning students had been happy to have their picture taken. They'd been enjoying the festival as much for the fun it provided on an uncharacteristically gray July day as for the money it would raise for their school.

Still, that was okay. It was their engaging grins she'd been after.

What else might Cyrus think was important to her report? Since he was a sponsor, he'd cast a particularly critical eye on whatever she brought in. It was a wonder he wasn't here in person, supervising.

She rounded the corner of a white-elephant stand, run by the ladies of one of the island's churches, and spotted the one person she definitely hadn't expected to see here. Ross.

He hadn't noticed her yet. She could slip back around the stand and avoid another awkward conversation.

Then she noticed the camera he carried, and annoyance swept away any other consideration. She walked up to him with quick strides. As if he sensed her approach, he swung around to face her.

"Amanda." He looked almost startled to see her, as if he didn't remember sending her.

"Amanda," she agreed. "The person you sent to cover this event." Disappointment that he so obviously still didn't have confidence in her lent an edge to her voice. "What's wrong? Didn't you trust me to do this? You even brought your own camera."

He seemed to give himself a mental shake, and he slid the camera into his pocket. "Don't be ridiculous." His tone was just as sharp as hers had been. "If I didn't think you could handle the assignment, I assure you, you wouldn't be here."

That she almost believed. When it came to work, Ross didn't know the meaning of the word *tact.*

"I see. Then do you mind my asking why you're here, too?"

He shrugged, glancing away from her as if fascinated by the daily specials chalked on a board in front of the nearest restaurant. "Cyrus thought a representative from the paper should be here all day. He's tied up in a meeting at the moment, so I'm his deputy."

It was perfectly plausible, knowing Cyrus. She'd buy the story if she didn't know him so well. He wasn't meeting her eyes.

"Have you met with the organizers yet?" she asked, sure she knew the answer.

"Not yet. I'll do it." He gave her a baffled, irritated look. "If you have what you came for, you can head on back to the office."

"It sounds as if you want to be rid of me. What's going on?"

"Nothing except that I don't want you to waste any more of the *Bugle*'s time."

She almost wished she couldn't read him so easily. This connection between them was going to be difficult enough to end without that.

She'd come to know him so well in such a short time—had gone from disliking him to grudging admiration to caring to love. And now it was over.

The angry glance he directed at her didn't bother her, because she could see something else lurking in the depths of his brown eyes. Something that might almost be pity.

Her heart lurched. Why would Ross be looking at her as if he felt sorry for her?

"Amanda."

The curt voice had her spinning to face her father. He looked—frozen. Bleak. And suddenly she couldn't breathe.

"Daddy, what is it?" Who is it? That was the question. Who is hurt, or worse, to make you look that way?

"I need you to go out to the beach house to stay with your grandmother."

She nodded, trying to find the words to ask.

"A fishing boat swamped." He jerked his head toward the gray ocean, seeming to force the words out. "Win went after a survivor. He's missing." He held up his hand to still her questions. "I don't know anything else. I'm headed for the post. I'll call you at the beach house as soon as I have anything."

Anything. Like whether her laughing, loving, daredevil of a cousin was alive or dead.

Daddy drew her close for a quick, hard hug. She resisted the urge to cling to him. He didn't need that now.

"I'll take care of Miz Callie. It's okay. I'll call the others. Just go." Her voice choked, in spite of her effort to keep it level. "I love you, Daddy."

Chapter 14

Amanda wasn't fit to drive after a shock like that. At least, that's what Ross told himself as he took the wheel of her car. He pulled onto Palm Boulevard and turned toward Sullivan's Island. He wasn't all that familiar with the barrier islands, but finding his way around them wasn't hard, since each had only one main street running its length.

He sent a sideways glance toward Amanda. For the first few minutes of the drive she'd huddled in the passenger seat, gaze turned inward, hands clasped in her lap. He realized she was praying.

Then she straightened, pulling the cell phone from her bag, and began calling. The first few calls ended in left messages, it seemed. *Call me, right away.*

Finally she reached someone. Her brother Hugh, it sounded like. After a few emotional exchanges she disconnected and turned to him.

"Hugh knows a little more than what Daddy told me. Not much." She was making an effort to keep her voice steady, he could tell, and his heart twisted.

"What did he say?"

"A fishing boat capsized about thirty miles out. Not a commercial one—a twenty-two-foot private boat, from what he'd been able to find out." She pressed her lips together for an instant. "They shouldn't have been out that far, not in six-to-eight-foot seas. Most likely a wave swamped them, and they were in the water before they even knew what happened."

"How many people were onboard?" He couldn't keep his mind from working like a reporter's, even in these circumstances.

"He didn't know. Two or three, from what he'd heard." Her hands clasped together in her lap, straining until her knuckles were white.

"Win was in the chopper that went out." That much was obvious, so he'd save her from saying it again.

She nodded. "They radioed back that they'd spotted the overturned boat with two survivors clinging to it. One of them didn't have a life jacket. Win insisted on jumping. Hugh said the account got sketchy after that. He didn't know what happened with the chopper, or how Win went missing, or…" Her voice broke.

He covered her hand with his. "Hold on. They should know more soon." He had no idea if that was true, but his heart ached for her and it was the only comforting thing he could think of to say.

"Hugh's on his way to the base. He'll call back as soon as he gets on duty."

"I thought Hugh was a cop." Wasn't that what she'd said when she talked about her brother?

"Coast Guard. Maritime law enforcement," she said briefly.

Of course. He would be. And what would Hugh think if his uncle was exposed as a crook?

They crossed the bridge between the islands at Breech Inlet, and he glanced out at the gray, angry-looking ocean under an equally gray sky. How long could someone survive in that? Win was in good shape, but even so...

"I'm surprised they let Win jump when it's this bad out."

She looked surprised. "That's what he does. 'I'm a Coast Guard rescue swimmer. I'm here to help you.' That's what they say when they go after someone. The other boys tease him about that." Her voice trembled a bit on the words. She took an audible breath. "But that says it all, really. I know Win can come across as flippant and brash, but underneath, he's solid. *Semper Paratus.* Always Ready."

"I don't doubt that." It was steadying her to talk, it seemed. A good thing, given what she'd have to deal with this day.

She nodded, picking up the phone again. "I'd better try to make a few more calls. Daddy will call Win's folks, but everyone else has to be told." She paused. "Thanks. For driving me. For listening."

"Anytime."

Anytime, he thought as she started calling again. There wouldn't be any other times, probably, to talk or listen or anything else.

The camera weighted his pocket. It was like carrying a loaded grenade. Once those photos hit the paper, the lives of all the Bodines would change immeasurably. And Amanda would never speak to him again.

He couldn't change who he was. He couldn't change the truth.

She was talking to her twin. He recognized the note

in her voice that only seemed to be there when she spoke with Annabel.

"Love you," she said, clicking off just as he pulled up at the beach house.

She was out of the car in an instant, and then she stopped, clinging to the car door. He hurried around to her and took her arm.

"Okay?"

Her eyes were dark with hurt. "No one else has gotten here yet. They wouldn't tell Miz Callie on the phone. I'll have to tell her."

"You can do it." His fingers tightened on her arm. "She's a strong woman. She can deal with it."

"You're right." Her eyes focused on his face. "I appreciate—" She stopped, as if suddenly realizing something. "I forgot that you drove my car. You can take it back, if you want. Or I'll call a cab for you—"

"Forget it. I'll stick around, as long as I can be useful."

Her expression went guarded. "Not to write about."

"No. Just to help."

He'd do this, and it was the last thing she'd ever let him do for her.

He followed her up the steps to the beach house, trying to find a little extra armor for what was to come. He couldn't pretend he was very good at dealing with other people's emotions.

Maybe that was why he'd never be able to write the sort of story that Amanda had done about C.J. and her grandmother. He just didn't have that sort of caring in him, apparently.

Amanda opened the unlocked front door, calling out as she did so. "Miz Callie?"

A quick, light step sounded, and Amanda's grandmother emerged from the kitchen, shedding a straw hat and sunglasses as she did so.

"Amanda. Ross. What a nice surprise. I just came in from—" She broke off, looking from one face to the other, and her smile vanished. There was silence for the space of a heartbeat.

"Who?" she asked.

"It's Win, Miz Callie."

Amanda went to put her arm around her grandmother. He moved to her other side, ready to grab her if she started to sag. But Miz Callie, it seemed, was made of sterner stuff than that. She leaned against Amanda for just a second, and then she straightened.

"How bad?"

"He's missing. We don't know much more." Amanda guided her grandmother to the sofa and sat beside her, holding her hands. "He went in after a victim…"

The phone rang. Amanda signaled to him to answer it. She continued talking to Miz Callie, her voice steady.

Amanda was a strong woman in a family filled with them. Too bad he'd let himself be blind to that for so long.

He took the cordless phone into the kitchen to answer it. "Bodine residence."

"Hugh Bodine here. Who is this?" A male voice barked.

"Ross Lockhart. I drove Amanda over."

"Good. She shouldn't be alone." Hugh, at least, didn't seem to share the family suspicion of him.

"She's talking to your grandmother now. Do you want me to get her?"

"Don't bother. I'll tell you what I've found out, and you can relay it to them." If anything, Hugh sounded relieved to have someone who wasn't emotionally involved take over that chore.

"Amanda's told me what she already knows, so just go from there." *And don't expect me to break the worst news, because I won't.*

"The weather was bad, but I guess you can see that for yourself. Two survivors. The pilot radioed the coordinates, said he was having trouble keeping the helo steady in the wind. Win jumped, we know that."

"What happened to the chopper?"

"Nearly went down, but the pilot managed to pull it out. They limped back to base." Frustration edged Hugh's voice. "Choppers are grounded. You'll have to tell them that, of course, but be sure they know every available craft is out looking."

"I will." Even from a layman's viewpoint, he knew that had to be bad news.

"Give me your cell number," Hugh said abruptly. "That way, I can be sure to get you if…"

He let that trail off, but Ross could fill in the blanks. If he had to relay something bad, Hugh wanted it told in person, not over the phone. Ross reeled off the number, hung up and walked back into the living room, carrying the phone.

Amanda and her grandmother stared at him, their expressions nearly identical. Hope. Fear. Need.

"That was Hugh." Sitting down across from them, he repeated the substance of Hugh's message. "He said to tell you that every available craft is out there. He'll call back the instant he has anything more."

They were silent for a moment. Then Miz Callie held out her hand to him. "Let's pray."

He couldn't refuse, any more than he could have refused his own grandmother, and he hoped his reluctance didn't show on his face. If God was there, Ross couldn't imagine He'd want to hear from him.

Amanda took his other hand, her grip firm, and his pulse accelerated.

"Dear Father," Miz Callie began, sounding as if she talked to a close friend. Her voice was calm and confident as she prayed, asking for God's protection for all those in peril, especially Win and the two people he was trying to save.

The sense that he was a fraud slipped away from Ross as she prayed. He might not have been able to pray himself, but as he listened, he found his heart gradually creaking open to the possibility that not only was God there, but He cared what happened to Win, to the victims, to those who waited and those who struggled to find them.

"Amen," she said softly, and the word felt like a benediction.

Ross opened his eyes, shaking his head a little as if it needed clearing. What had just happened? He didn't want to start wondering, start questioning. He wasn't looking for God.

Feet pounded on the outside stairway, and the door flew open. Annabel rushed in, followed by Georgia and a couple of other people he didn't know but vaguely recognized from the birthday party. The Bodines were arriving in force. He backed away, giving them access to Miz Callie, divorcing himself from the family group.

He should leave. Amanda had her people here now, and she didn't need him.

But he'd given Hugh his cell number, so he couldn't very well go off without letting him know. More steps sounded on the stairs. A retreat was in order, if he didn't want to be inundated by Bodines.

He'd head into the kitchen and start some coffee. That was what people did while they waited for news, wasn't it? He'd make coffee and hope Hugh called soon.

He'd found the coffee and filters and started a pot when his cell phone rang. He jerked it out of his pocket. "Lockhart."

"Hugh Bodine here." It was a growl. "There's not much new, but I told my father I'd check in. How's Miz Callie doing?"

"Praying," he said. "She's handling it. Some other family came in."

Hugh grunted. "I can hear them in the background. That'll help, I guess. Just try to keep them focused on the positive. Adam's out there. He's not gonna come home without his cousin."

"I'll try." He hesitated, knowing he was involving himself still further, but feeling unable to stop. "Just between us, what are the chances?"

"Wish I knew. Win took a second life vest with him when he jumped. If he didn't lose it on the way down and managed to get it onto the victim, they can hang on for a time, warm as the water is."

"What if he lost it?"

"If he lost it, Win will give his vest to the victim." Hugh's flat tone suppressed a world of emotion.

"I see." He did. If Win was out there without a vest, trying to help two victims, with night falling…

"I've got to go," Hugh said quickly. "Hang in there. I'll get back to you when I can."

The call ended, and he hadn't told Hugh he was leaving.

Amanda came in, lifting her eyebrows when she saw the phone in his hand. "Was that Hugh?"

"Nothing new," he said quickly. "He just wanted to touch base."

If she thought he was hiding something, she didn't betray that. "Coffee. Good, thank you. I'll take some to Miz Callie." She stopped, hand on the cabinet door, and looked at him with such sweetness that it jolted him right in the heart. "Thank you for staying. It means a lot."

"No problem," he said, realizing the question had been decided for him. He was staying.

The beach house was beginning to crowd with people, reminding Amanda of a pot coming to a boil. Every Bodine was here except for Uncle Harrison and Aunt Miranda, Win's parents, who'd gone to the base along with anyone who had the credentials to get on base.

She was beginning to feel useless. To say nothing of the stress that bubbled along her nerves, threatening to explode.

Her gaze met Ross's. As if they'd communicated without words, he started making his way toward her.

Her heart gave an odd little twist. In spite of the unanswered questions that lay between them, he'd been a rock in this crisis, and she wasn't ashamed of clinging to him.

He stopped beside her, his dark brows lifting in a question.

"I can't stay here any longer. I've got to go down to the base."

"Can you get in?"

"Press credentials will do it. They might send me packing if I went alone, but they're not going to turn away the managing editor of the *Charleston Bugle*."

He gave a short nod. "Let's go."

It took minutes to explain to Miz Callie, and then she and Ross slipped away. Without seeming to think about it, he got into driver's seat.

Ordinarily that might raise her hackles, but not now. Today she needed to keep her thoughts, and her prayers, focused on Win.

Father, be with them. I know so many people are praying for them now. Please hear our prayers.

She glanced at Ross. She hadn't missed how uncomfortable he'd seemed at praying with them, and it had touched her heart when he'd taken her grandmother's hand with such tenderness.

"Thank you. I don't know how—"

He cut her off with a shake of his head. "Forget it."

The words were rough to the point of rudeness, but she sensed that they covered pain instead.

As if to fill the silence, Ross snapped the radio on, just in time for a local news bulletin about the rescue. She listened to it, fingers digging into her knees. Nothing that they didn't already know.

"They'll be trying to identify the missing rescue swimmer," Ross said.

"Yes." She swallowed, hating the thought of newspeople descending on her family while they waited. "Sometimes I don't like our profession much."

"Right."

They didn't speak again, and in a few minutes they'd reached the base. The procedure moved smoothly until they entered the building that housed the command center, where the press was being gently but firmly shepherded into a briefing room by Petty Officer Kelly Ryan.

Breathing a silent prayer of thanksgiving, Amanda

caught her friend's eye and jerked her head toward the stairwell. Kelly gave the most minuscule of shrugs and nodded her head.

Grasping Ross's wrist, Amanda let the rest of the mob flow past them and led him quickly up the stairs. They reached the upper levels without incident.

"You'd make a good spy," Ross said.

"It helps to know the territory, but it's going to get harder now. If my father sees us…" She didn't need to finish that. Ross knew as well as she did what his reaction would be.

They'd just started down the hallway when an office door opened right in front of them. With no time to do anything else, Amanda met Thomas Morgan's startled gaze.

"Ms. Bodine." The young ensign who was her father's assistant glanced from her to Ross. "What are you doing here? The press is supposed be—"

She silenced him with an urgent hand on his arm. "That's my cousin out there. I can't just sit home waiting for news. You can help us, can't you, Tommy?"

His reluctance was palpable, reminding her that Daddy had said how intent his assistant was on promotion. Tommy wouldn't want to get into trouble.

"If we're caught, we won't say a word about you. Just get us someplace where we can know what's going on. Please."

He hesitated a moment longer, but then he shrugged. "Go up the next flight of steps and in the second door on the right. That's the best you'll be able to do without your father spotting you."

"Thanks." She squeezed his arm. "And we never saw you, right?"

"Right." Looking relieved, he backtracked into the office he'd come out of.

Following his directions, they reached the indicated door in moments. Amanda paused for a moment, refreshing her memory of the layout. If anyone she knew was on duty in the communications room, they'd probably be all right. Whispering a silent prayer, she opened the door and slipped inside.

The woman at the nearest station turned at their entrance. Thanking heaven for a familiar face, even if she couldn't come up with a name at the moment, Amanda gave her a pleading look.

With a hint of a smile, the woman turned back to her instruments as if she didn't see them.

"We're okay," she murmured to Ross.

He nodded, taking in the room with a thoughtful glance. "I was right. You can't go anywhere in Charleston without finding someone you know."

"It's really a small town, despite appearances." She watched the intent faces, longing for a sign. They were as tense as she was, focused on their jobs with lives in the balance. All the more so, because one of those lives was one of their own.

She fought to untangle the radio chatter she picked up, knowing that it must sound like so much gibberish to Ross.

"Reports are coming in from ships engaged in the search," she murmured quietly. "Negative, so far."

He clasped her hand warmly in his. "They'll find him."

She nodded, but dread began to pool in the pit of her stomach. The need for action had driven her this far, but what could she really accomplish here? Win was out there, somewhere. There was a lot of ocean to cover, and in a few hours it would be dark.

A hand went up, halfway down the row of technicians, beckoning to them. Amanda moved almost without awareness, grasping the back of his chair to steady herself. There was a chatter of static, and then a voice came through, identifying sender and location.

"That's Adam's patrol boat." She reached for Ross's hand, found it and gripped it hard.

The anonymous voice suddenly came through clearly. The room around them fell silent as others strained to hear.

"...have the wreckage in sight."

Please, Lord, please...

"Sighting two victims. Preparing to attempt the transfer."

Two. Where was the third? Win... Her heart seemed to stop. She felt Ross's arm go around her, supporting her.

Static. An endless wait. Static again. Then...

"Two victims, one rescue swimmer on board. All alive."

The room erupted in cheers. Amanda couldn't cheer. She could only sag against Ross, grateful for the strength of his arms around her.

Thank You, Lord. Thank You.

Chapter 15

"This surely was one good news day." Cyrus looked down at the *Bugle,* spread across his massive oak desk and rubbed his palms together. The front page of the *Bugle* covered the rescue, lauding Win Bodine as a hero.

Which he was, Ross agreed. "We don't have a heroic story with a happy ending that often."

As Hugh had said he would, Win had given his life jacket to one of the victims and then managed to keep both of them safe and together until help arrived. You didn't get much more heroic than that.

"Those Bodines have more lives than a cat," Cyrus said. "Good thing, considering the jobs they go into."

"It's hard on the people who are waiting to hear if they're dead or alive." Ross would never forget the time he'd spent with Amanda and her grandmother yesterday. Never.

Amanda had leaned on him in a time of crisis. That was a sign of trust he hadn't expected, given how things had been between them recently.

That trust would be gone soon. He faced that bleakly. In a few days the story would break. Then she'd need all that strength she'd shown yesterday to get through the scandal.

She'd go through it with her head high. He had no doubt about that. But it would cut her to the bone, and she'd never be quite the same.

He'd like to say he'd give anything to protect her from that, but he couldn't. It wasn't true. He wouldn't give up his career.

He tried to assure himself that it wouldn't make a difference if he did. Cyrus would run the story anyway. Somehow that didn't make him feel any better.

"Too bad." Cyrus closed the paper and put it aside with an air of finality. "They're going to go from rejoicing today to grief tomorrow."

"Tomorrow?" That shook him. "You're surely not thinking to break the story that soon."

"There's no point in waiting that I can see." Cyrus's tone expressed sorrow laced with determination. "Besides, we've had the public's attention for the past few days. We can't afford to lose it at this point, you know that as well as I do."

Ross had rushed into print once before, eager to get the story out, and lived to regret that. At least this time he wasn't depending on anyone else's information, but even so, he wanted it ironclad before it went out with his byline. "Let's take it slower. We can't afford to make accusations without proof."

"We have the records of Winchell's contracts, one after another awarded to him by Bodine's office. We have the photos of the two of them meeting yesterday." Cyrus ticked off the facts.

He was being swept along too fast. "It's not enough.

There's no law against the two of them meeting at the festival, despite appearances."

Cyrus's shaggy eyebrows lifted. "What about the packet?"

Ross felt as if he'd missed a step in the dark. "Packet?"

"Didn't you look at the pictures you took?" Apparently taking the answer for granted, Cyrus grabbed a folder from his desk, shaking the contents out onto the surface. "Look. If that's not incriminating, I don't know what is."

Ross took the photo Cyrus held out and saw the thing he'd completely missed in his efforts to get as many shots as he could. Winchell, holding out a bulky envelope to Brett Bodine.

Wordlessly, Cyrus passed him another. In this shot, Bodine was stuffing the envelope into his jacket pocket. Maybe that explained why the man had been wearing a jacket on such a hot day.

"I never saw them." He shook his head. "Just snapped as many as I could get without being seen. With everything that happened afterward, I…"

He'd been too busy worrying about Amanda. Trying to help her in any way he could. And all the time, the proof about her father was in the camera he carried.

Here was the big story he'd been looking for since he came to the *Bugle.* A step back toward the life he wanted.

So why wasn't he happier?

Amanda entered the newsroom later than her usual time, but with a light step. The family had been up until all hours, rejoicing over Win's safe return.

Of course Win had wanted to downplay it, so they'd

tried to go along, but tears had never been far from the surface.

"Amanda!" C.J. was the first to spot her, and she came at a half run to envelop her in a hug. "Nobody thought you'd come in today."

"I didn't think that." Jim elbowed C.J. over to get in on the hug, pressing his cheek against Amanda's. "I knew all along that this gal was a pro. Glad everything turned out okay, sugar."

Those treacherous tears threatened to spill over again. "We are, too. Thanks, Jim."

The rest of the newsroom staff had gathered around her by then, wanting to share in the happiness, and her heart swelled. It really did feel as if all of Charleston had been praying with them and now shared their happiness. That had been the message on the flowers Miz Callie received that morning from Cyrus, coming so early that he must have had to wake up the florist.

Flowers for joy, not for condolence. A shudder went through her at the thought of how easily it could have gone the other way.

She pulled back, squeezing C.J.'s hand. "Thanks, everyone, so much. I just can't tell you how much it helped to know folks were praying with us." She wiped away a tear that had escaped. "I've got to thank Cyrus, too, and then I'd best get back to work."

She escaped down the hall that led to Cyrus's office, blotting her eyes with a tissue. Maybe in a day or two she'd have gotten over this tendency to cry at the least little thing. Though even time probably wouldn't erase the memory of those hours when they hadn't known whether Win was alive or dead.

She couldn't think of that without thinking of Ross.

He'd stayed with her through it all. At the time she hadn't even questioned turning to him in the crisis. It had seemed the most natural thing in the world. For all his sharp edges and occasional cynicism, he'd been a rock when she needed him.

Oh, she'd have gotten through it without him. She had her family and her faith to see her through. Her heart chilled. Ross didn't seem to have either of those. Small wonder that he'd turned cynic.

Maybe she could make a difference. Things had been rocky between them, but maybe, given time and patience, there could be a future for them. After yesterday's seemingly miraculous rescue, she could believe in another happy ending, couldn't she?

Cyrus's door stood ajar, and she paused, hearing voices. He had someone with him. She'd have to come back later.

Then she realized that the second voice belonged to Ross, and her heart gave a silly little leap. Smiling, she reached toward the door.

"...the Bodine story." Ross's voice was a low rumble. They must be talking about the coverage of Win's rescue.

"The photo of Brett Bodine has to go above the fold on page one." Cyrus's voice rang out clearly. "Showing him accepting the bribe tells the whole story in a single picture."

Her breath caught in her throat, feeling as if it would strangle her. Brett...bribe...what on earth were they talking about? Those two words didn't belong in the same sentence.

"...seems pretty clear," Ross was saying.

Ross...plotting against Daddy. Her heart seemed

caught in a vise that tightened cruelly as she tried to comprehend what she was hearing.

Her fingers closed on the edge of the door. She'd confront them, tell them—

Wait. Stop and think. She took a steadying breath, then another. Pulled her hand away from the door.

That was always her default reaction, wasn't it? Rush in without thinking.

Not this time. Not if Daddy was in trouble and Ross was his betrayer. The vise on her heart gave another, stronger twist.

She had to find out what they were planning so she'd know what she was fighting. There had to be a logical explanation for this. Would Jim know?

She rejected that. Jim was many things, but not much of an actor. He couldn't have greeted her the way he had if he'd been in on a story that would discredit her father.

No, this had Ross's fingerprints all over it. Ross had been lying the whole time he'd been supporting her. Comforting her. Kissing her.

Her cheeks flamed. She had to find out the truth. She backed silently away from the door and headed for Ross's office.

There'd be no euphoria at the breaking of this story, Ross knew. Just a dogged determination to do his job, coupled with a bone-deep despair over what that was going to do to Amanda.

God, if You're there, if You still listen to me, help her.

Once this broke, she wouldn't appreciate the thought that he prayed for her. The dagger in his heart dug a little deeper.

Could he warn her? Totally unprofessional, but how could he let her be blindsided?

He swung his office door open and froze in his tracks. Amanda wouldn't be blindsided. She stood at his desk, reading the file of notes on the investigation.

She looked at him, face white, eyes blazing, and shook a sheet of paper at him. "How can you possibly believe this? You've met my father. He wouldn't do anything like this."

He closed the door behind him. No one else needed to know what they'd say to each other.

"I wouldn't have thought you'd go through my desk, either. Looks like we're both wrong." But the indignation he tried to drum up rang hollow.

Twin flags of scarlet burned in her cheeks. "I was coming to Cyrus's office to talk to him. To thank him for the flowers he sent to my grandmother. And guess what I heard? You and Cyrus planning a front-page story framing my father."

"We're not framing anyone." He took a step closer, trying to keep his voice low. Trying to keep some control over the situation. "We're not printing anything but the truth. If you wanted the truth, you should have asked us, not come searching in my desk."

"I had to know what I was fighting." She slapped the paper down on the stack.

"There's no fighting about it. The decision has already been made. The story runs tomorrow." He reached toward her, knowing she didn't want him anywhere near her, but unable to stop the gesture. "At least you're forewarned now."

"Forewarned?" Her voice rose. She was teetering on the edge. Hardly surprising after everything that had happened the previous day. "You're going to print lies about my father. Don't you know that will destroy his career? And the family…" She stopped, her voice breaking.

"I'm sorry for all the people who are going to be hurt." She probably didn't believe that. "But you have to realize that your father's the one who brought this down on you. Not the newspaper."

"He's innocent. He would never—"

"Look." He pulled the condemning photograph from the folder he held. "Just look at it and accept the truth. That's your father taking money from a contractor who's gotten way more than his fair share of business from the base, thanks to your father's influence."

The picture shook her. He could see that in the way her eyes darkened and her lips pressed together as she tried to assimilate the pain.

Her reaction shook him, too. The need to comfort her nearly overwhelmed him. Yesterday she'd leaned on him, and he'd been there for her. Today—

Today he could do nothing.

She shook her head, thrusting the picture away from her. "There's an explanation. There has to be. Just talk to him."

"I can't."

"Why not? You at least interviewed that slumlord before you ran the story."

"This is Cyrus's decision, not mine. I'm an employee of this paper, just as you are."

"Not anymore." She straightened, bracing herself with her fingertips on his desk for a moment, and then walking around it toward the door, avoiding him as she might a skunk in the road.

"Amanda—" But what could he say? Naturally she wouldn't keep working here after this.

"It's funny." She paused, hand on the doorknob. "I spent all this time trying to show you that you were wrong about me." She turned to face him. "But maybe you were right all along. I really am that sweet Southern girl you thought I was. And my family is more important to me than anything else."

She yanked the door open and walked out of his office and out of his life.

Chapter 16

She'd been looking for her father for hours without success. Amanda's stomach churned as she picked up her cell phone to try once more. Why wasn't he picking up? If she didn't get to him in time to stop that story from going to press…

The call went immediately to messages. Gritting her teeth, she ended the call. Little point in adding yet another "where are you?" to the ones she'd already recorded.

She crossed her tiny living room in five steps and stared out the front window, catching a group of tourists with cameras pointed in her direction.

Letting the curtain fall between them, she took a deep breath. A few tourists was nothing compared to the crowd that would descend on Mamma and Daddy's house if that story ran. She couldn't let that happen.

She picked up the phone again. Time to bring in the big guns. She hadn't wanted to call Mamma, fearing her mother would read the anxiety in her tone, but she couldn't waste any more time, not when her mental clock ticked away the hours until the paper went to press.

"Mamma? Hi, it's Manda."

"Sugar, what's goin' on with you? How about comin' over for supper tomorrow? I'm making Brunswick stew."

"That sounds great, Mamma. Maybe I will." Or maybe they'd all be too busy dealing with fallout to eat. "Right now I need to get hold of Daddy. He's not picking up his cell phone. Do you know where he is?"

"Goodness, I… I don't know. He had to go out this evening, but I don't believe he said…"

"Mamma, this is important." She couldn't keep up the facade that was just a casual call, not when the need for action pounded in her brain and tightened every muscle. "Where is he?"

"Sugar, you make it sound like life and death." A thread of uneasiness laced her mother's voice.

She took a breath and sent up a wordless prayer that she wasn't making things worse. "It's important. You and Daddy don't keep secrets from each other, no matter what he says. Whatever he's involved in, the newspaper is about to blow it wide-open. I've got to get to him."

Silence for a long moment. "He's at Battery Park, meeting with…someone."

She suppressed the urge to press for more answers. Time enough for that once she'd found Daddy. "Thanks, Mamma." She hung up and darted for the door.

A few minutes later she was pulling into a parking space bordering the park. She could have walked, but if she missed Daddy here, she'd waste time running back for her car. She stepped up the high curb and stood on the sidewalk, surveying the park.

Battery Park, covering the end of the peninsula that was Charleston, was a popular tourist destination, but by now most of them had probably headed for dinner or back to their hotels to put their feet up. Stilling her nervous impulse to rush through the park, she stood where she was, scanning the area methodically.

No sign of him, and her heart sank. Time was running out. If she—

There he was, leaning against the wall, looking out over the water toward Fort Sumter. Another man stood next to him. Not, she realized with relief, the contractor who'd been in the photo Ross showed her.

She hurried across the grass toward them, her heartbeat quickening as she approached. How did she say this? How could she tell her father that the world was about to hear he was a liar and a thief?

The other man saw her first, and she saw the quick flare of recognition in his eyes before he turned away to point out in the general direction of Sullivan's Island.

How did he know who she was? She'd never seen him before. Casually dressed, middle-aged. Military, she thought automatically. When you were around it all the time, you knew.

"Daddy."

He turned around. "Amanda. What are you doing here?"

"Looking for you. We have to talk."

The other man spoke up. "Thanks for the sightseeing tips. I'll be sure to check out the places you mentioned."

"What? Oh, yes." Daddy was rattled. "Glad I could be of help."

Too late, she thought. She'd seen that betraying look of recognition. Whatever was going on, this was no casual meeting. This man was in on it.

"It's no good," she said. "I know."

"Honey, now's not a good time. How about I stop by your place in a little bit, okay?"

She shook her head. There was nothing to do but come out with it.

"The *Bugle* is after you," she said flatly. "They're running a story in tomorrow's paper. They've got a picture of you at the festival taking money from some contractor." She got it all out on a rush of words and came to a stop, feeling as if she'd been running.

Her breath caught in her throat. Daddy looked dismayed. Not guilty, thank the good Lord. Just unhappy with the news she'd brought.

She grasped his hand, feeling the strength of it close around hers as it had when she was a little girl. She blinked back tears.

"I know you didn't do anything wrong. You couldn't have. But unless you do something to stop it, all Charleston is going to read about that in tomorrow's paper."

Still holding her hand, her father looked at the other man. "What do you think?"

For a moment the man's face tightened in denial. Then he shrugged. "I guess we'd better go down to the newspaper and resolve this."

"That's it, then." Ross stared across the width of the office at Cyrus, the weight of the decision pressing on him. "I'll…"

The rap on the door gave him a welcome respite. "Come in," he called, despite Cyrus's frown.

Brett Bodine stalked in, followed by another man— lean, graying, with a closed face that gave nothing away. Bodine, with his flushed face and clenched jaw, was easier to read. He'd like to take Ross's head off.

Ross thrust his chair backward as he rose. If Bodine thought he could intimidate the press—

The thought broke off when he saw who else was there. Amanda. A quick glance was all he could allow himself, but even that was like a blow in the gut.

Cyrus took a step forward, the light of battle in his eyes. "If you're here to talk us out of the story, you've come to the wrong place."

Bodine's hands curled into fists, but before he could speak, the other man interrupted, pulling an ID from his pocket. "This isn't precisely what you think, gentlemen."

He held it out to Cyrus. Whatever it was, it stopped him cold. He looked, grunted, and passed it to Ross with an air of handing the situation over to him.

"Agent Baker." He let the realization sink in. "What's the federal government want from the *Bugle?*"

Baker permitted himself the briefest of smiles. "Ordinarily, nothing. But Ms. Bodine told us about the story you plan to break."

He couldn't prevent his gaze from slipping to Amanda. She hadn't known about the federal agent, he could see that.

He forced his focus back to the agent, preparing to negotiate. This was familiar territory, after all. He'd often played the game of getting as much information as possible from tight-lipped officials.

"And what exactly is your interest in our story?"

"We'd prefer that you refrain from printing it."

Ross sensed Cyrus's feathers ruffling at that, but the older man kept silent. With a little luck, he'd let Ross handle this.

"I'm afraid we can't accommodate you." Ross's mind worked furiously, trying to sort out the possibilities.

Bodine might be cooperating with the feds, ready to give up his fellow conspirators. In that case, they could be playing for time.

"I'm not trying to pressure you, Mr. Lockhart. Only to prevent the *Bugle* and you from making an embarrassing mistake."

Ross stiffened at the expression, but kept a slight smile pinned to his face. It was all part of the elaborate dance, with Baker determined to give away as little as possible while Ross was equally set on getting the whole story.

"It's good of you to be concerned for the *Bugle,* but you'll have to convince us with facts."

"Tell him and be done with it," Bodine snarled. "He's not going to cooperate for less."

"Daddy…" Amanda began, and then stopped, hands moving in a small gesture of helplessness.

The gesture seemed to clutch his heart. For a moment he could barely breathe for the desperate need to protect her.

Agent Baker shrugged, "You realize that this is off-the-record." He looked from Cyrus to Ross. Seeming satisfied with their nods, he went on. "Several months ago, we received a report of possible irregularities in the awarding of contracts at the Coast Guard base here. The report came from Brett Bodine."

A small gasp escaped Amanda.

"We investigated." Baker went on as if he hadn't heard. "With his assistance, we were able to identify the officer involved."

The facts Ross thought he knew flew into the air, rearranged themselves and came down in a new pattern. "But the meeting with Winchell. The packet of money."

"Not money," Baker said. "We've managed to persuade Mr. Winchell to cooperate with us. He handed over a list of the deals made by the officer."

Bodine's expression tightened, if that was possible, and Ross understood. The man was in pain at the idea that someone under his command had abused his position.

"We need you to kill the story until we've completed our investigation," Baker said. "I can assure you, it's in your country's best interest."

"Who is the guilty party?" Ross planted both hands on the desk. Baker had to give them more than that.

"I can't tell you that."

"You can give us an exclusive," Ross countered. "If we don't jump the gun on you, that's the least you can do."

Baker's noncommittal mask was probably hiding some furious calculating. How far could he go?

"Forty-eight hours," he said at last. "You don't mention anything in the press for forty-eight hours, and we'll give you a couple hours' head start on the story. That's the best I can do."

"It's a deal," Cyrus said, clearly unable to contain himself any longer.

"Good." Baker shook hands briskly, first with Cyrus, then with him. "We'll be in touch."

Bodine took the hand Cyrus extended. For Ross, he had nothing but a furious glare. And Amanda...tears had spilled over, trickling down her cheeks.

Bodine and Baker turned to the door, Cyrus behind them, probably trying to get another fragment or two about the story.

He didn't bother to listen. All he could see, all he

could think of, was Amanda. He reached out, not quite daring to touch her.

"Amanda, please. Stay. Just for a moment."

Her father spun at the words. "My daughter has nothing to say to you."

Amanda wiped away tears with the palm of her hand. "It's all right, Daddy. I'll be along in a few minutes."

She closed the door behind them and turned to face him.

She didn't want to stay. Amanda pressed her palms against the solid wood of the door behind her. Talking to Ross was only going to make the pain in her heart worse. But she wouldn't be a coward about it.

Ross's face was a taut mask, revealing nothing of the feelings behind it. If any. Did he feel anything but ambition? Want anything but success?

A cold shudder went through her. "There's no point to this." She turned away, groping for the doorknob.

"Wait. Please. You need to see something."

She didn't move.

"Please." His voice softened to a husky rumble. "Just look at this, and I won't ask you for anything more."

She turned back slowly to face him, and he swung his computer screen toward her.

"Look. This is the front page of tomorrow's edition, made up before we heard the agent's story."

She had to brace herself before she could look at it. Had to prepare herself to see the photo of Daddy. Above the fold, Cyrus had said.

She stared. Blinked. And took a step toward him, shaking her head to clear it.

"What? Where is it?" The lead story was a follow-up to the rescue. She leaned closer, scanning the page. Nothing. There was no mention of anything else to do with the Coast Guard Base.

She touched the screen, reading it through to be sure she wasn't making any mistake. Then she looked up at Ross's face.

"I don't understand. You were going to run the story in tomorrow's edition. Why did you give it up before you'd even heard the explanation? Did Cyrus change his mind?"

"Not Cyrus. I changed my mind. Cyrus…well, he went along with me in the end."

Meaning Cyrus hadn't wanted to. She tried to still the spinning of her mind. Tried to hold out against the hope that began to blossom inside her.

"You convinced him not to run the story. Why?"

He turned away slightly, as if he didn't want her to see his face. His fingers pressed against the desktop until they were white.

"You." He stopped, cleared his throat. "When I saw how much you were hurt, it forced me to take a good look at myself." He darted a glance toward her. "I didn't like what I saw. The man my grandmother had hoped I'd be—he's pretty well buried by now, isn't he?"

He didn't seem to expect an answer to that, which was fortunate, because she didn't have one.

"I've been blaming everyone else for what happened to me back in D.C., but the truth is that a major part of the blame falls squarely on me."

That she could respond to. "Your friend betrayed you. That wasn't your fault."

"I'm the one who fell for it. I'm the one who rushed into print. I was too proud, too sure of myself." The muscles in his neck moved convulsively. "I never stopped to ask myself whether I might be wrong."

The chill that had gripped her heart began to fall away. Ross was taking down his protective barriers, piece by piece. He was letting her see who he really was.

"My grandmother expected me to become an honorable man who relied on God for guidance. Instead, I became a cynic who relied on nothing but his own ambition. That's not who I want to be."

He was facing her now, close enough that she could see the pain that darkened his eyes and twisted his lips.

"No," she said softly. "It isn't who you are, not really." She tapped the computer screen. "You put your job on the line with Cyrus to delay the story, even before you knew the truth."

"Cyrus thought I was crazy." He shook his head. "Crazy was what I was before, when I let myself be eaten up by anger and ambition. Maybe being humbled by losing everything I thought was important was the only road back to finding out who I really am."

Tears spilled over again, but they were good tears. "I'm sorry you went through that. But if you hadn't, I'd never have met you."

"Maybe you'd be better off if you hadn't."

"Don't say that." She hesitated, wanting to put into words the effect he'd had on her. "Being challenged by you made me realize what's really important to me."

He reached out slowly, letting his fingers brush her cheek. Warmth flooded through her, erasing the last bit of tension.

"I already know. Your family. Your faith. Any chance there's room for me on that list?"

She couldn't breathe for the happiness that filled her,

bubbling up until she felt she might lift off the floor. "There's plenty of room for you."

"I love you, Amanda Bodine."

She caught his hand, pressed it against her lips and said the words. "I love you, Ross."

"Enough to marry me?" There was the faintest trace of uncertainty in the words.

"Definitely," she said.

He drew her against him, his lips claiming hers in a kiss that promised a love that would last a lifetime. Her arms went around him, holding him close, knowing this was meant to be. God had planned them for each other from the beginning. They'd just both been too stubborn to see it.

Ross pressed his cheek against hers. "My grandmother would be delighted."

Joy bubbled up in her again. "Miz Callie will be, too."

He held her back a little so that she could see the love burning steadily in his eyes. "I'm afraid your father is not going to be exactly pleased."

"He'll come around when he sees how happy you make me," she said. "He'll see that God meant us for each other. Forever."

Epilogue

Miz Callie had insisted on a family dinner to celebrate Amanda's unexpected engagement. Amanda wasn't so sure that was a good idea. Maybe it would have been better to wait until everyone had gotten used to it—in this case, everyone being her father.

Still, so far they all seemed to be behaving themselves. Against Miz Callie's will, everyone had brought something, with the result that there was enough food spread out on the long table at the beach house to feed half the island.

Since they'd long since outgrown the number of available tables, folks had spread out all over the place, and the volume of Bodine chatter was faintly overwhelming, even to someone who was as used to it as she was.

She glanced at Ross, sitting next to her on the living-room floor. He smiled, seeming unaffected by the clamor, and leaned over to kiss her cheek lightly.

"Everything okay?" he asked.

"Very much okay." She moved a little closer. "You're officially accepted, I do believe."

"More or less," he said, but it didn't seem to bother him that Daddy wasn't quite reconciled.

"Of course you're accepted." Miz Callie, sitting behind them in her favorite rocker, touched Ross lightly on the head. "Brett is even being pleasant."

"Maybe he's just relieved that this investigation is wrapped up and moved off the front page," Ross suggested.

"Well, now, I wouldn't be surprised." Miz Callie's face clouded a little. "He took it hard, knowing that an officer under his command betrayed the service that way."

They'd all been shocked to learn that her father's aide, Thomas Morgan, had been using his position to take money under the table from contractors in exchange for doctoring the bids.

"Nobody wants to hear that a fellow officer is crooked." Adam, arms wrapped around his knees, leaned forward to join the conversation. "That's someone you might have to trust your life to one day, besides the fact that it gives all the honest men and women in the service a black eye."

"I think most folks know enough not to blame anyone else for what one person did." Miz Callie rested her hand on Amanda's shoulder. "As for us, I'd say we have a lot to celebrate."

She'd raised her voice a little on the words, and the room seemed to fall silent as she spoke. Miz Callie's descendants turned their faces toward her.

"We celebrate our Win's safety after a dangerous mission."

Win smiled, looking a little embarrassed as sounds of thanksgiving echoed through the room.

"We celebrate the fact that truth has come out in a difficult situation." She looked at Amanda's father, her eyes bright with unshed tears. "Your daddy would be proud of you, Brett. You did your duty."

More than one person blinked back tears, Amanda knew. They realized, none better, just how hard that had been for her father.

"And we celebrate the truth coming out about another family member who did his duty." Now a tear did trickle down Miz Callie's cheek, but her hand on Amanda's shoulder was strong. "We know now that Ned Bodine served his country in the navy during the war, and he's going to be honored as he should be for that service. Adam has learned that Ned didn't die in the war."

A murmur of surprise went through the room at that. Most of them had just assumed that Ned hadn't come back.

"We'll find out what became of him afterward, Miz Callie." Ross took her hand. "I promise."

Miz Callie touched Amanda and Ross, her touch seeming to link them to all the generations that had gone before. "And we share the happiness of Amanda and Ross. May their love grow and flourish all their days."

Amanda let her gaze move from one face to another around the room—her kin, the people she knew best in the world, linked by faith and by love. She had them, and now she had Ross. Her heart was filled to overflowing with thankfulness.

* * * * *

Jill Lynn pens stories filled with humor, faith and happily-ever-afters. She's an ACFW Carol Award–winning author and has a bachelor's degree in communications from Bethel University. An avid fan of thrift stores, summer and coffee, she lives in Colorado with her husband and two children, who make her laugh on a daily basis. Connect with her at jill-lynn.com.

Books by Jill Lynn

Love Inspired

Colorado Grooms

The Rancher's Surprise Daughter
The Rancher's Unexpected Baby
The Bull Rider's Secret
Her Hidden Hope
Raising Honor
Choosing His Family

Falling for Texas
Her Texas Family
Her Texas Cowboy

Visit the Author Profile page at Harlequin.com for more titles.

HER TEXAS
FAMILY

Jill Lynn

I praise You because I am fearfully and wonderfully made; Your works are wonderful, I know that full well.

—*Psalms* 139:14

To my husband: God blessed me big when
He gave me you. Thank you for being better than
I could have ever imagined, for making me laugh
and for always cleaning my mess of a car.
I love you!

Chapter 1

Climbing a tree in heels? Not one of her better decisions.

Lucy Grayson held her cell phone toward the Texas sky and prayed for reception. The prayer didn't work, nor did her ascent, which she'd hoped would somehow get her closer to a cell tower. Just beyond the tree, Lucy's pitiful car sat on the side of the road with a flat tire, stranded like a woman with a broken high heel.

Her whole life was packed into that car...all of her shoes, most of her clothes and everything else she could cram in. Which made the thought of clearing out her trunk in order to reach her spare tire daunting. And so not necessary. Not if she could get hold of her sister and brother-in-law and borrow their truck, loading everything into it instead of dumping her things on the side of the road.

She was mere miles from their home, so she *could* walk. But surely her phone was just being ornery. It had to have some reception. Another impatient glance at the screen told her nothing had changed in the past twenty seconds of her life.

Drat.

Lucy wiggled her left foot, attempting to free it from her red ankle bootee without reaching down to untie it. She certainly couldn't climb down in these shoes. She'd slipped a few times on the way up and didn't want to risk the same during her descent.

A look down had her stomach tripping all over itself. Lucy had climbed higher than she realized, hoping just a little more height would give her the results she wanted.

Averting her gaze to the limb directly in front of her, she shimmied out of her left ankle boot. It dropped to the ditch below with a muted thud. The sole of her bare foot met rough bark, and she started the same process with her other shoe. One final kick of her heel against the tree limb sent it flying from her foot. Perfect. Now to get down.

A yelp sounded.

At the bottom of the tree, a man stood staring up at her, his hand pressed against his forehead. Oh, no. She hadn't...

"Is there another shoe coming that I need to be aware of?"

Lucy pressed her lips together to hold back the ill-timed amusement that begged for release. Keeping her right arm wrapped around the tree trunk, she pointed to her other shoe, which had landed a few feet away from him. "No. Sorry about that."

"It's okay. I think." He stopped rubbing his forehead, leaving the red mark from her boot weapon visible. "What are you doing up there?"

Now, *that* was a tough question to answer. Picnicking? Going for a climb? Moving to Texas? Nothing seemed quite right. And her actual answer, now that she had an audience, did sound a bit…unusual. Or for her, usual. Her family would definitely call this a typical Lucy moment.

"I was making a phone call." Or trying to.

The man's brow crinkled, and he continued to peer up at her with confusion. Lucy scrambled down the tree, each bough swaying under her now bare feet. Despite feeling somewhat like a monkey, the sensation of being free did give her a thrill.

She landed in front of him with a very ungraceful, un-dancer-like crash.

During her descent, he'd crossed his arms over a white-checked oxford he wore with crisp jeans and brown leather shoes that even her fashion sense approved of. He was a head taller than her, with chocolate hair and midnight-green eyes.

A wave of recognition rushed through her, causing her skin to prickle with awareness.

Lucy remembered this man from her sister's wedding. She didn't know his name. She just recalled seeing him that night.

At Olivia and Cash's reception, he'd been dancing with a little girl. The small child had worn glasses and a frilly dress, and her shoes had been propped up on his toes as they'd twirled around the dance floor. Lucy had melted at the sight. After all, she was a dancer.

Right. That was what had attracted her attention. Not the fact that the guy was totally droolworthy and hadn't noticed her for a second. Usually when guys tried to gain her attention, she couldn't care less. This one hadn't known she existed…although now that she'd clocked him in the head with a shoe, she'd be unforgettable. For all the wrong reasons.

Did it really matter that he was looking at her without an ounce of recognition?

It wasn't as if Lucy wanted to follow her sister's path and sign up for a wedding ring while in Texas. She didn't do serious relationships. She did fun. Lucy had made the decision way back in high school, and she'd stuck to it ever since. It had taken only one experience—one moment of going gooey over a guy—to teach her she much preferred to keep things light. And it was a lesson that had served her well over the years.

"I saw your flat tire and thought you might need help." The look of bewilderment still etched across his face had her fighting a smile. Not everyone knew what to make of her personality. But did he have to look *so* shocked? So he'd found her up a tree trying to make a phone call. She wasn't acting *that* crazy. "Where are you headed?"

"I'm actually moving here. Right now I'm trying to get to my sister's house, which is just—" North? East? Lucy searched for the Rocky Mountains that had declared which way was west for the whole of her life, but was only met with the low green hills that permeated Texas Hill Country. Finally, she just pointed. "That direction."

He reached forward and removed something from her hair, tossing it to the side. Looked like a baby branch by the size of the thing. How had she not noticed that monstrosity hitchhiking a ride on the way down?

"Your sister?"

"Yeah. Olivia Maddox." Even after seven months of her sister being married, that new last name still felt so weird to say.

"Graham Redmond." He offered his hand, and Lucy shook it, introducing herself. "Cash is a friend of mine."

Lucy just nodded. *I know. Men.* This conversation only served to support her philosophy of keeping them in the fun/friend category instead of getting overly involved with one.

"So, are you moving to Texas for work?"

"For fun." For the most part. Lucy could also mention that she couldn't get along with her previous employer and that the move had been perfect timing for getting away from a certain guy, but she didn't feel like delving into those things now. Or maybe ever. "And partly for work. I have a part-time job lined up teaching dance." Although teaching one measly dance class wasn't enough to pay her bills. Lucy's first priority in town was to find a job that did. Scratch that. Her first priority was to get to her sister's house. The second would be to make sure she could pay for rent and groceries.

But at least she knew she was doing the right thing in moving. After the trouble with her old boss, she'd prayed for an out. Olivia had called about the dance-instructor opening a few days later. Moving to Texas had been an answer to prayer and just the kind of adventure Lucy craved.

She reached out and gently touched the mark on his head. "I'm sorry about hitting you with my shoe. Does it hurt?"

He flinched as if her hand inflicted more pain than her boot had. "It's fine."

"But it looks so red." A perfect match for the color of her shoe. And it was forming a rather large bump. "How do you know? Maybe you should get it checked out."

"I'm a doctor." He tenderly touched the spot. "I'm not worried about it."

"Okay." She shrugged. Why did she care so much? Sure, her shoe had caused the welt, but he obviously didn't want her interference. Fine by her.

She could say the same back to him. Since he'd so nobly stopped to help her, she would reassure him she didn't need his assistance. He could keep heading wherever he'd been heading, and she'd figure out how to get to her sister's or change the tire on her own.

Graham Redmond didn't need to fill the role of dashing hero in her life. Because, as the residents of Fredericksburg would soon find out, Lucy wasn't a damsel in distress who needed to be rescued.

She could rescue herself.

Usually people worried about pulling over to help with a stranded vehicle because a dangerous person could be planning some kind of highway robbery...not because they feared shoes falling from the sky and almost knocking them out cold.

The place where Graham's forehead had been introduced to a high heel still smarted, but he ignored the throbbing in order to figure out the woman in front of him. She seemed...young. Flighty. And not just because she'd been up a tree when he'd pulled over at the sight of her stranded Volkswagen Beetle. She twisted long, blond curls over one shoulder as she bent to pick up her shoes, sliding them back on her feet and then tying the small black laces. Skinny jeans met with a blue-and-white-checked shirt extending from under a navy sweater. How old could she be? Early twenties? She acted a bit like a teenager, though her looks didn't support that theory.

And neither did the math. If Graham remembered correctly, Olivia's sister was just a few years younger than she was.

He pointed up the tree she'd just climbed down like some kind of gymnast. "Did you say you were making a phone call?"

"Yeah."

"If you were calling for help, I can change the tire for you."

She huffed, crossing her arms. Had he said something offensive?

"I know how to change a tire. At least, I'm sure I could figure it out," she said, voice quieter. "There's probably instructions. How hard can it be?" She motioned to her car. "I was calling my brother-in-law because my car's packed full. Every inch of it. I'd have to unpack the back to get to my spare, and since I'm almost to my sister's house, it made more sense to see if they could bring the truck. That way I could load everything into it, and I wouldn't have to move all of my stuff onto the side of the road."

Her convoluted logic made sense. Graham must be losing his mind.

"So, you need a ride to Cash and Olivia's? That I can do."

Her eyes narrowed to slits. "Were you...headed in that direction?"

"No, but it's not far."

The toe of her boot tapped as she contemplated. A quick shake of her head was coupled with tight-pressed lips. "No, thank you."

No? What did she plan to do? Walk? Hope for cell

reception? She was crazy to think he'd leave without helping her.

"I don't want to interrupt your plans."

What plans? Graham hadn't done anything social in the past…five years or so. Not since Mattie was born and then losing Brooke. He didn't exactly have a busy social life. Work? He had plenty of that. And colored pictures on his fridge. He had lots of those. Plus, he played a mean game of Go Fish on Saturday nights.

"My daughter and I were just headed home. It will only take us a few minutes to drop you off." If he had to be direct or demanding in order for her to accept his help, so be it. Anything to make this encounter go a bit faster. Lucy made him feel…uncomfortable. As if he wanted to loosen his tie, even though he wasn't wearing one today.

After a minute of contemplation, she let out an earth-shaking sigh. "Fine." The word came through gritted teeth. "I appreciate your help."

He got the impression she didn't like his offer of help one bit, especially when her forced tone was accompanied by crossed arms and eyes that flashed with displeasure. Their bright blue color punched him in the chest. Unique. Brilliant. He wasn't sure exactly how to describe them. Not that he needed to write a report. What he needed to do was drop this woman off at her sister's and then head home to get his week organized before the craziness of Monday hit. No doubt his medical office would be slammed tomorrow morning as it was almost every Monday. But at least there he felt useful. At least there he was too busy for the images of his past failures to haunt him.

"Let me grab my purse."

While Lucy did that, Graham opened the trunk to his car and checked the bolt pattern on his spare. It didn't match the one on Lucy's wheels. Just as well. Graham wasn't sure he'd live through the experience of changing a flat tire with this woman. He'd seen what Lucy could do with a shoe. What harm could she accomplish with a lug wrench?

He started his BMW and pulled up parallel to her car. She came over with full hands, so he leaned across the seat and popped the passenger door open. Lucy slid in, dropping a purse and jacket on the floor of his car. When she shut the door, the scent of lime and coconut came with her.

It was the end of January, and she smelled like summer. Graham hadn't known the season had its own scent before.

He motioned to the backseat. "This is my daughter, Matilda Grace. Everyone calls her Mattie."

Lucy buckled and twisted to face the backseat while he put the car in Drive. "Hi, Mattie Grace. It's nice to meet you."

In the rearview mirror, Graham could see the name earned a smile from Mattie. A shy one.

"I'm Lucy."

"*Ms.* Lucy," he said.

Those eyes of hers jutted to him, giving off a spark of something close to annoyance before she softened and turned back to Mattie. "What grade are you in?"

"Kindergarten."

Graham could feel the mix of interest and shyness oozing from Mattie in the backseat. His daughter tended to be on the serious side with an older-than-her-years nature. She was compliant, sweet and entirely more than he deserved. He thanked God for her every day.

The short distance to Cash and Olivia's took only a few minutes. When they arrived, the three of them got out, making their way up the wide porch steps.

Lucy knocked, then opened the door, calling out her arrival. She stepped inside, and Olivia squealed, tugging her into a very enthusiastic hug.

Cash Maddox appeared at the door, surprise evident. "Hey, Red. Mattie. Come on in."

At thirty-one years old, Graham was a few years older than Cash, but the two of them had grown up together and they'd always had an easy friendship. Cash was one of the few people who understood losing someone—not that he'd lost a wife, like Graham had, but grief was one emotion they shared knowledge of.

Even though Graham was close to six feet tall, Cash towered over him. His friend passed him in inches... and brawn. The fact that Cash ran a ranch from dawn till dusk and Graham saw patients inside all day might have a little something to do with that second thing.

"I can't believe you're finally here!" Olivia took a step back from her sister, her brown hair contrasting with Lucy's sunshine blond. "Where have you been? I thought from the last time I talked to you that you were going to get here an hour ago."

"Flat tire." Lucy grimaced.

"Where's your car? Did you change it? What happened?"

Lucy laughed, a lyrical sound that tightened Graham's throat. Was he coming down with something? There'd been a lot of rash/fever combinations in the office last week. It was either that or this woman had some strange effect on him.

Definitely had to be germs.

"Still on the road. No, I didn't change it because I didn't want to unpack everything. And Graham stopped and ended up giving me a ride."

Olivia's gaze jumped to him. Seemed she hadn't noticed his arrival. But then, he would guess Lucy's entrance anywhere would pretty much overshadow anyone else's.

"Thanks for taking care of my little sister, Graham." He nodded.

"Yeah." Lucy flashed bright white teeth in his direction. "Thanks for the ride."

He opened his mouth but no sound came out.

Olivia bent to eye level with Mattie while Graham still choked on his words. Or lack of them. Honestly. What was wrong with him?

"Hey, Mattie. It's good to see you." Her hand trailed along one of Mattie's brown pigtails, coaxing a grin from his daughter.

"Mattie is practically a superhero. She swooped in and saved me from having to make the choice between a long walk or unloading my car." Lucy shared a fist bump with Mattie, her head tilting in his direction. "Along with her trusty sidekick."

Graham's mouth gave in to a slight curve at the acknowledgment. He'd take the demoted status just for the look on his daughter's face.

Lucy turned to Cash. "About my car. I thought maybe I could borrow your truck. I'll change the tire. I can do everything if you'll just let me—"

"What?" Cash snorted. "You really think I'm going

to send you back out to take care of a flat tire on your own? What kind of brother do you think I am? I'll take care of it."

By the way Lucy's chin jutted out, she wasn't satisfied with that answer. "I don't want you to have to deal with all of my stuff. The car's jammed full."

"I have a thing for taking care of little sisters, and since Rachel up and left for college, you're stuck with my overprotective nature. I might even have a spare out in the garage we could use. And if I don't, not that much can fit into that tin-can car of yours anyway."

"Listen, McCowboy." Her finger poked into Cash's gray T-shirt. "I'm absolutely helping with the tire. Don't even think about going without me."

McCowboy?

Cash shook his head, glancing at Olivia with amusement. "You did mention what a complex your sister has about accepting help."

So it wasn't just Graham she fought. Good to know.

Lucy squeaked. "That's not true! I just accepted a ride to your house." The woman beamed as if she should win a prize.

"Lucy's car is near the big oak tree that got hit by lightning when we were in high school." Graham's lips twitched, and Lucy's eyes started dancing with mischief. She certainly wasn't embarrassed about her tree climb. He got the impression not much caused her to experience that particular emotion.

"So, Graham." Olivia turned to him. "It's actually perfect that you picked up my sister. I wanted the two of you to meet."

A cold sweat snaked under his collar. Was Olivia trying to set him up with her flighty sister? *Not* going to happen. Graham had already had the love of his life. Now he had Mattie and absolutely no desire to remarry. Olivia would just have to take her matchmaking ideas elsewhere.

"Lulu, Graham's office manager is out on maternity leave and he needs someone to fill in."

What?

He hadn't expected that. And this conversation sounded like trouble. Yes, the woman who ran Graham's front office had gone on maternity leave unexpectedly early last week, leaving him completely strapped, but that didn't mean Lucy Grayson was the right person for the position.

"I think it would be a perfect start for you, Lulu." Olivia gave Graham a look he couldn't quite decipher. Did she expect him to offer Lucy a job right here and now? Bend down on one knee and start begging?

Lucy studied him long enough to make him squirm, determination sparking in her eyes. "I do have a business degree. I don't have experience in a medical office, but I could learn."

How was he going to get out of this? Graham wanted someone for the position who could walk right in and know what they were doing. Someone with experience. Exactly the type of person he'd been looking for since well before Hollie went into early labor. Unfortunately, after three different temps had filled in last week, Graham was beginning to think that person didn't exist.

Olivia was still talking about the possibility of Lucy working for him, how it would be a great fit, how it would be beneficial for both of them.

Graham could only stare. He felt as though he was

sliding down a treacherous slope with little chance of rescue.

"Sorry, Red." Cash looked far too amused and not nearly concerned enough. "I don't think there's any saving you from this one."

"Seriously? You're just going to leave me hanging? I am never prescribing anything for you ever again."

Cash laughed. "I can't imagine anyone going up against Liv and coming away with a win. Trust me, I know from experience." His gaze slid to his wife, filled with enough admiration that a twinge of jealousy came over Graham.

Graham remembered that look, that feeling, well. He'd give anything to look at his wife like that again. But those days were gone, and he was healing. He was moving on. Just not into another relationship.

Unfortunately, at the moment, his friend was right. By the look on Olivia's face, she was going to win this battle. Graham wanted to run for the door. Either that or rewind the evening and not stop at the sight of a stranded yellow Beetle.

"What do you think? Should we give it a try?" Lucy looked so hopeful that something in him tugged. She couldn't be worse than the temps, could she? Maybe he was overreacting about the fact that he'd found her up a tree on the side of the road. Perhaps they could help each other out.

She'd have to be trained, but he'd figure out that part. Besides, it wasn't as if he had any other choices lined up.

Graham would usually pray about a decision like this. Take his time. Wait on God's guidance. But he was desperate. Desperate enough to hire a woman who looked like a model, smelled like sunshine and didn't have a lick of experience.

Her words came back to him. A try, she'd said.

The tension in his body untangled. That was what he would do. He'd hire her on a trial basis. That way, when she couldn't do the job, he'd have no issue letting her go.

Chapter 2

On Tuesday morning, Lucy sat behind a wide receptionist desk in Graham's medical office and stared at the blinking black beast in front of her. Some might call it a phone. Lucy deemed it an instrument of torture. It boasted a number on the small gray screen—one that kept growing as the number of people waiting for her to answer increased. When Graham's nurse, Danielle, had trained Lucy on it early this morning, she'd called it the queue. Lucy didn't have such a nice name for it.

It scared her more than spiders or spam.

On Sunday night, she and Graham had hammered out a few details. An agreement of sorts. They'd agreed to give working together a try. He'd put a lot of emphasis on that last word, and Lucy felt an underlying sense of tension that normally didn't invade her life. Graham probably thought she was completely unqualified for the position. And he'd be right. Which meant she needed to prove herself today.

She knew her opportunity to work for Graham had everything to do with God and Olivia making it happen and very little to do with her office skills—which were nonexistent.

On Monday, when Lucy had moved into her above-garage apartment in town—the one her sister had lived in last year—she'd scanned the paper for any other job openings she might be qualified for, just in case working for Graham didn't pan out.

There weren't any.

Since her move to Texas had come up quickly, Lucy hadn't had time to save. She didn't have any reserves for covering an extended period of time without work. And since she absolutely refused to ask her parents or Olivia and Cash for money, she needed this job.

How hard could it be? she'd thought. Answer a phone. File some charts. But after a few of the calls she'd already fielded this morning, Lucy was afraid to touch the flashing beast in front of her. Since timidity wasn't in her nature, she took a steadying breath and yanked the receiver up, pressing it to her ear.

"Dr. Redmond's office. May I help you?"

"This is Walt Birl. Who's this?"

Another favorite question of the morning. Who was she? What was she doing in town? And from two grandmothers—was she interested in meeting their grandsons?

"Lucy Grayson. I'm new to town. I'm running from some unsolved crimes in Colorado. What can I do for you, Mr. Birl?"

Stunned silence.

Lucy winced and looked at the phone as though she could see his reaction through the small black holes. Oops. Perhaps not her best move. Wasn't she planning to be professional today? Prove to Graham he hadn't made a mistake in hiring her?

When she put the phone back to her ear, loud cackling greeted her. "I like you. Listen, I have a rash I need to discuss with someone."

Don't pick me. Don't pick me.

"It's kind of round, though there's a few spots—"

"Mr. Birl, you really need to speak with the nurse or schedule an appointment with Dr. Redmond. I'll be no help at all."

"Okay. Transfer me to Danielle, then."

Lucy sighed with relief, then pressed a few buttons on the phone, hoping the call actually went to Danielle's phone and voice mail in the back.

She dived into the waiting queue. It took her almost two hours to wade through the calls, partially since everyone had to get the lowdown on her before talking medical business. Finally, the screen didn't show anyone on hold. Lucy did a happy dance, chair sliding back and forth with her movements.

"What are you doing?"

She screeched. Graham had come down the hall during her happy dance...with a patient. Thankfully the frazzled mom with a toddler on her hip simply waved and walked out the front doors.

Lucy motioned to the phone. "Just celebrating getting through the phone calls."

"Oh." Graham sported the same look of confusion he'd been wearing when he'd stopped to help with her flat tire. "Okay." He shrugged and disappeared down the hall again. Even slightly snarly, the man still managed to look good. He also had impeccable taste in clothes. A crisp white button-down shirt and black dress pants. A tie that teased some of the lighter flecks of green from his eyes. He reminded Lucy of an actor on a television show she used to watch. Definitely Hollywood for this small town.

Digging into her purse, Lucy plucked out her phone and texted her sister.

What are you doing?

When it beeped a response, Lucy gave a silent cheer. Liv almost never responded to texts during the day because she was normally in the middle of teaching one of her French classes at the high school.

Between classes. How's the first day?

How to answer that?

Exciting.

Lol. Yeah, rt. R u still at work? Have u caused any trouble?

Lucy's lips curved. Her sister knew her too well.

Yes and no.

Though Lucy had simply meant to answer Liv's questions in order, the humor in it made her perk up. Let her sister wonder a bit at that.

Lucy?!!!??

She laughed and slid the phone back into her purse. It took her a few minutes to figure out how to print the updated appointment schedule so she could pull the patient charts for the rest of the day. Once she did, Lucy did a pirouette on her way to pick up the sheet from the printer located in the far left corner of the reception space. Now that the phone calls had slowed, she was doing okay. Maybe she'd get the hang of this job faster than she'd expected.

Graham walked into the reception space and dropped some charts on top of the pile on her desk that needed to be reshelved, then turned and scanned the files.

"Just grabbing my next appointment. I'm sure you haven't had time to pull anything with handling the phones this morning."

"Thanks." That was nice. Maybe the man didn't just speak in grunts all the time. Actually, she knew he didn't. She'd heard him being great with the patients. And she'd seen him interact with Mattie the other night. Graham looked at his daughter as if she made the sun rise and set each day. From what Lucy had gathered in the short time they'd been together on Sunday, she agreed with that assessment. Mattie was supercute with her red glasses, glossy hair and bright, inquisitive green eyes that seemed to quietly observe everything around her.

Seeing Graham act so sweet with Mattie had melted Lucy a bit.

But he certainly hadn't sprinkled any of that sugar in her direction. With Lucy, he kept a polite distance and only spoke caveman.

She considered the way Graham obviously adored

Mattie to be his best quality. Second best? His choice in cologne.

Inhaling, she inched closer to his back as he faced the charts. Woodsy. Spicy. Definitely worth a second sniff. She leaned in just a bit more.

Graham grabbed a chart and turned, almost bumping into her. Lucy jumped back, not realizing how close she'd migrated in her efforts to breathe him in.

He stared at her, those dark, stormy eyes wide.

"Sorry." She took a step back. "I—" *Want to smell you?* Nope. Not first-day-on-the-job words.

Graham's brow furrowed. "You okay?"

"I'm great." *You just smell distractingly good. What kind of cologne is that? Would it be weird if I requested you wear it every day? Would it be even worse if I grabbed your perfectly knotted grass-green tie, tugged you forward and buried my nose along the collar of your shirt?*

Graham made his way past her, pausing by the edge of the desk. "We'll turn off the phones for lunch. I need to grab Mattie from school. She has a half day today. But Danielle can answer any questions you have after you're done eating."

"Sounds good." Lucy pasted on a bright smile and waited until Graham disappeared down the hall before letting it fall from her face. Phew. That had been a close one.

She searched the shelves filled with rows and rows of manila folders reaching up to the ceiling behind her desk and along the wall. Looked as though the chart she needed was on the top row. She glanced around. Not a stool or chair to be found besides the rolling one behind her desk. At five and a half feet, Lucy wasn't necessarily short—unless she compared herself with her sister or father—but she was pretty sure she needed some assistance to reach the top row.

She rolled the office chair over, aligned it in front of the shelves, then dropped to the ground and locked the wheels into place. Lucy stood and put one foot on the chair, then changed her mind and unzipped her brown, high-heeled boots. She removed them from her feet, rather proud of herself for taking the time to ensure her safety. She'd learned her lesson about climbing in heels.

Her outfit for the day—an army-green dress that swished above the knee, cinched with a multicolored belt and accessorized with an assortment of mismatched beaded bracelets—wasn't exactly ideal for climbing on a chair. But Lucy would make it quick. She'd grab the chart and be back down before anyone knew what she'd been up to.

After giving the chair a test shove to make sure the wheels didn't roll, Lucy stepped up, toes digging into the leather. She heard the front door to the office open but kept her concentration on the charts. Scanning the names until she found the one she needed, she slid it from the shelf. The chair moved under her feet. She gasped and reached for the shelf, dropping the file in order to hang on with both hands. The grip stopped her movement. A shaky, relieved breath whooshed out, causing dust to fly off a few files in front of her. Another close one.

She jumped from the chair before it could cause further damage, bare feet landing on the floor with a thud.

Lucy found herself face-to-face with a young man who'd appeared behind the receptionist desk during her chart hunt. He screamed cowboy. Broad shoulders in a blue plaid shirt. Boots peeking out from jeans.

The skin around his brown eyes crinkled. "I apologize for being in your space, ma'am. When I walked in, I saw you wobbling on the chair and thought you might need a hand. Looked like you were about to take quite the tumble. And yet, here you stand."

He had a Southern drawl and he'd called her *ma'am.* Yee-haw. "I appreciate the backup."

"I'm the one who called to see if Doc Redmond could squeeze me in for this." His right shirtsleeve was rolled up, a nasty-looking gash visible. He situated the cloth he was holding to fully cover the wound. "I'm Hunter McDermott. My family's ranch edges your brother-in-law's."

She introduced herself, and dimples sprouted in his cheeks.

"The famous Lucy Grayson. Do you really think anyone in this town doesn't know who you are?"

At least one person hadn't.

"Sooo…" He stretched the word out. "I suppose you saw a bit of Rachel back in Colorado." Hunter's gaze flitted away before meeting hers again. "How's she doing?"

Oh. Now Lucy knew the lay of the land. Wonder if Rachel Maddox knew she'd left behind one interested cowboy in Texas when she'd headed to Colorado for college.

"Rachel's great. Busy with classes and off-season volleyball training. And not dating anyone that I know of."

Interest flashed on his face before he cleared his throat. "That's good, then. I mean, not that she's not dating anyone. Just that she's doing well. I—"

Hunter shrugged and shook his head, and Lucy's amusement and pity for the guy doubled. He grabbed the chart she'd dropped—amazingly the contents had stayed anchored inside—and handed it to her. "Here you go."

"Thanks." Lucy stepped toward the desk to set the file down and stumbled over her forgotten boots on the floor. Though she didn't *exactly* need it, Hunter reached out, grabbing her arms to steady her. They shared an amused grin.

"I'll let Dr. Redmond know you're here."

"No need." Graham spoke from behind Lucy, his curt tone zinging along her spine. "Come on back, Hunter."

Hunter nodded at Lucy, then stepped around to the front of the reception desk.

"I'll meet you in exam room two."

At that, the cowboy disappeared down the hallway, leaving Lucy with a disgruntled Graham.

Uh-oh. Why did he look so upset? Was it something she'd done? She could just imagine the long list of complaints Graham could have against her. After all, she'd literally been thrown into the job this morning with very little training. Lucy hadn't been taught much more than how to deal with the phone and a quick lesson on the appointment scheduling system. Had she mis-scheduled an appointment? Lost a chart? Offended a patient?

She didn't know the answer. She only knew by the tension tugging on Graham's mouth and the crease cutting through his forehead that whatever he had to say couldn't be good.

And Lucy really, really preferred good.

Graham didn't usually have to count to ten when dealing with Mattie, but Lucy Grayson might be harder for him to handle than his five-year-old daughter.

He couldn't shake the sight of Hunter and Lucy standing so close when he'd walked into the front office. What had they been doing? There had to be a good explanation for why they'd been tangled up together. For why Hunter had been behind the receptionist desk in the first place.

Had to be.

"What were you just doing?" Though he attempted to keep calm, his voice dripped with irritation. And then, instead of giving her time to answer, the rest of his thoughts spilled out without permission. "I walked down the hall to find you practically in a patient's arms, and a young man at that. How do you think that looks? What kind of reputation do you think that gives the office?"

Her mouth opened but no words came out.

Didn't she have anything to say to defend herself? And why did *she* look upset with *him*?

A glance over his shoulder told him Hunter was in the exam room, door closed. Waiting. Graham couldn't deal with Lucy right now. His patient needed sutures and that came first.

He faced her again. "I need to help Hunter." Plus, he needed to finish this appointment in time to grab Mattie from school so she didn't have to ride the bus. He knew she didn't like it, though she rarely complained. His daughter seemed to think it was her job to take care of him instead of his job to protect her.

"But I—" Lucy had finally found her voice. "I wasn't—"

"We'll talk about this later."

Without letting her finish, Graham turned and walked down the hall. Exasperation snaked under his collar, mixed with a faint touch of guilt for being so short with Lucy. He paused outside the door to exam room two, loosening the knot of his tie. Somehow, he needed to get his mind out of the fog that had descended on him this morning.

For being a Tuesday, today definitely felt like a Monday.

Nothing was going according to plan. First, he'd wanted a qualified person to fill in for Hollie. Instead, he'd got Lucy. He'd known after their conversation Sunday night that Lucy didn't have any experience working in a medical office. Her résumé sounded like an audition for a Broadway show. Yet he'd been desperate. And he knew she was, too. That, coupled with the pressure from Olivia, had prompted him to give working with Lucy a shot.

No pun intended.

The morning had been crazy busy, and Graham hadn't really had time to observe Lucy. Except for the time he'd found her dancing in her chair, their close encounter by the charts…and then finding her and Hunter behind the desk together.

The unprofessional nature of what he'd seen grated. Graham had the niggling sense that he was missing some piece of the puzzle with Lucy. When he'd questioned her about previous employment on Sunday night, Lucy had been vague. She'd mentioned working at a dance school back in Colorado. Until…what? She hadn't really said why she'd left. Only something about a "difference of opinion" with the owners of the studio. Now he wondered if there was more to the story. Had she been unprofessional there? What had gone on between them?

It was obviously something he needed to figure out. Along with whether he'd made a bad choice in hiring her. Did he need to let her go already?

The thought came with an underlying sense of relief. Why?

Graham didn't want to go anywhere near the answer to that question, because if he did, he'd have to analyze the fact that Lucy Grayson flustered him. She was… young. Flighty. And entirely too beautiful for her own good.

If Brooke were still alive, she'd never be okay with someone like Lucy working in his front office. Graham wouldn't be, either. But Brooke was gone. And Graham should be able to have a receptionist without thinking of her as anything but that.

Only, seeing Lucy in Hunter's arms…something had sparked in Graham that he hadn't expected. A sense of jealousy. Where had it come from? He didn't know. Nor did he want to explore it.

Lucy might be a good fill-in for Hollie on maternity leave, or she might not. The jury on that was still out. But as for any attraction Graham felt for the young woman?

That, he knew his answer to. He'd already had the love of his life. Dating, marriage, love…those things weren't for him. Which meant attraction to his off-limits receptionist wasn't an option.

Chapter 3

Lucy pushed out the doors of the medical office and screamed up at the mocking bright blue sky. *Oh, my.* Her heartbeats settled from outraged racing to annoyed drumming. That scream had felt good. She'd like to indulge in one more—this time in Graham's presence. But he was still dealing with Hunter.

After Graham had headed down the hall, Lucy stayed until it was time to turn the phones over to the answering service. Then she'd waved goodbye to Danielle—who probably thought she was just ducking out to grab something for lunch—and headed outside.

She didn't want to leave the only real job option she had in this town, but Lucy knew better than to let someone treat her the way Graham just had. His accusations had stolen the air from her lungs and the words from her mouth.

She and Hunter had been totally innocent in that situation, yet Graham assumed the worst.

Lucy didn't like thinking a person was one thing and then finding out they were something completely different. At least with Graham she'd found out right away.

Unlike before.

Words spoken about her years earlier tumbled back. She could still hear Nate talking to his best friend, still picture his arrogant behavior.

After that, she's all yours.

Indignation flared at the memory. Lucy had vowed never to let someone treat her with such disrespect again. Her independent, take-care-of-herself streak had started growing the day she'd overheard Nate, and it hadn't slowed since.

Which meant she couldn't stay working for Graham. Not if that was what he thought of her. Not if that was how he planned to treat her.

She *should* feel relieved leaving. Instead, pinpricks of disappointment riddled her skin.

She needed this job. Too bad Graham had reacted the way he had. Lucy could see now he'd never really given her a chance. He'd thrown her into the position with hardly any training and then he'd jumped to conclusions.

It wasn't as though working as a receptionist in a medical office would end up on her Pinterest board for dream work. If Lucy let herself travel down that road, she'd wish her way into owning a dance school she could run under her own philosophy. But that option wasn't on the horizon.

Lucy paused near her car as a school bus pulled up to the parking lot. The door opened and Mattie got off, clutching some things to her chest.

Hadn't Graham said he was going to pick her up?

The bus pulled away, and Mattie dropped the items she'd been holding on to the grass between the sidewalk and the parking lot.

Lucy approached. "Hi, Mattie Grace."

The little girl glanced up, shoving her glasses to the bridge of her nose. "Hi, Lucy." One shoe was untied, but the rest of her looked perfectly put together. A bright, white shirt without a mark on it—something Lucy could rarely boast of accomplishing—a jean skirt, light-up tennis shoes and a pink fleece sweatshirt. The sight made Lucy realize she'd forgotten her jacket inside.

Double drat. Maybe she could live without it. After all, the weather in Texas was warmer than Colorado.

"What's going on with your lunch?" Mattie's pink-and-purple lunch box was open, leftover contents and containers spread on the ground. Lucy knelt, helping her put the items back inside.

"One of the boys kicked my lunch box on the bus and everything fell out."

At Mattie's quiet explanation, Lucy's outrage spiked a few degrees. "Sounds like I should pay a visit to your school bus tomorrow."

The girl's smile was like the sun coming out from behind clouds. "It's okay. He doesn't bug me very often. My dad said he was going to pick me up so I didn't have to ride the bus today, but he must have forgot."

Oh, be still her heart. No matter how much Lucy didn't like Graham right now, she knew he'd never forget Mattie. "I don't think he forgot, sweetie. I think he just had a busy morning."

Lucy barely resisted scooping the girl up in a big hug. They closed the lunch box and stood, slipping it into Mattie's backpack.

After Graham and Mattie had left the other night, Olivia had told Lucy that Graham's wife had passed away from cystic fibrosis at a young age—only in her twenties. Since then, it sounded like Graham pretty much worked and took care of Mattie.

As if her thoughts had summoned him, Graham came out of the office and jogged to his car, the *beep-beep* from his key fob interrupting the quiet. Since he was parked on the other side of the building, he didn't notice them.

Lucy and Mattie shared a grin. "Told you he didn't forget. Think we should stop him or let him go?"

"Let him go."

Lucy laughed. "I'm not sure whether to be impressed or shocked."

That earned her a giggle.

The thought was tempting. A trip to school and subsequent freak-out would serve Graham right. Smothering her impulse to let him suffer a bit, Lucy called out to him across the lot. He looked in their direction, shoulders sagging when he saw Mattie.

Since his adorable daughter was standing next to her, Lucy would figure out how to talk to Graham in a civilized manner. She would put on her maturity cape—at least, until no little cars were listening—and if she could manage it, beyond that.

He came over, dropped in front of his daughter and pulled her into a hug. Lucy ignored the tug on her heart. *I will not like Graham. I will not soften toward him.* When Graham buried his face in Mattie's hair and inhaled as if he wouldn't live another second without smelling her, Lucy lost the battle. The chant wasn't working.

"Did you take the bus?"

Mattie nodded.

"Why didn't you wait? I told you I'd come get you."

"It's okay, Dad. I didn't mind."

Graham ran a hand through his hair, causing the dark locks to stick out in every direction and reminding Lucy of a young boy. She skipped over the thought, concentrating instead on the irritation she'd felt inside the office minutes ago.

"Next time, just wait for me, okay?"

The small shrug told Lucy Mattie's answer was far more of a "we'll see" than a "yes." Lucy liked the girl more and more by the moment. If only Mattie didn't have that look marring her features. Lucy couldn't figure out if she was sad or serious or both.

"Why don't you go inside and find Danielle?" Graham spoke to Mattie. "I'll be in in a sec."

"Okay. 'Bye, Ms. Lucy."

So they'd gone formal. Lucy offered Mattie a fist bump, which she answered with a small nudge.

Graham watched Mattie go inside before facing Lucy. She fought the temptation to squirm, knowing she hadn't done anything wrong. It might have looked strange to find Hunter behind her desk, but Graham could have given her the benefit of the doubt. He could have let her explain.

Instead, he thought she was so unprofessional that she'd throw herself at one of his patients.

Lucy sent up an SOS prayer that she'd be able to talk to Graham in a mature manner and that God would show her how to handle this conversation. After Graham had walked away from her inside, Lucy hadn't even considered asking God for guidance. She'd just followed her instincts. She was horrible at remembering to pray for help, usually barreling forward without stopping to think. Certainly without stopping to pray.

But in this situation, Lucy needed all of the direction

she could get. Because not only was she at a loss for what to do if this job didn't work out, she'd never been very good at keeping her thoughts to herself.

When Graham had realized Lucy was no longer inside the office, he'd wondered if she'd just left to grab some lunch...or if she'd taken off, never planning to return. After the way he'd acted, Graham wouldn't blame her if she had bolted.

Hunter had told Graham what had happened and why he'd been behind Lucy's desk. A very simple explanation. If only the sight hadn't sent Graham into thinking the worst.

He'd jumped to conclusions and been a jerk. Now he was going to have to grovel. The thought almost tugged a smile from his lips. He hadn't groveled in ages— not since Brooke. Though, even then, it had been more in teasing. They'd had a good relationship, not the constant back-and-forth bickering that some couples were prone to. Which was exactly why Graham didn't expect to have anything like it again.

But he did have a bit of experience in apologizing. What husband didn't?

"About earlier."

She crossed her arms, gaze defiant.

"I'm sorry for my reaction. I was short with you and I jumped to conclusions."

When she opened her mouth, he braced for her to be angry with him. Instead, like a slowly deflating balloon, her shoulders lowered. "Okay."

Not exactly accepting his apology, but he'd take it for now.

On to the second order of business. Before he asked

her to stay, Graham needed to know what had transpired at her old job. But he had the feeling she wasn't going to like his prying. "Lucy, what happened at the dance school you worked at in Colorado?"

"I don't want to talk about it." She mumbled a word that sounded a lot like *mature*. After fidgeting with the collar of her green dress, she let loose a frustrated exhalation. "Why do you want to know?"

"If you're going to be working here, and I'm going to trust you, I need to know."

"But I'm not—" Her sigh scattered across the parking lot. "Fine. It's not like I did anything bad there. I worked at the same school for years and loved it, but when they sold to new owners, we couldn't get along."

"Why not?"

A man could spend years deciphering the emotions that flickered through her gorgeous blue eyes. Graham focused on her mouth instead, but that didn't help. Her lips pressed together, broadcasting frustration with his questions.

"They were so into the correct dance positions, they were cruel. I mean, I get that they wanted to win competitions. What school doesn't? But they pushed too far. They were way too strict on all of the age groups, but especially the beginner's classes. Those little girls are there to learn to love dance, not to do a perfect plié at age four."

"That's it?"

"Um, kind of."

"Lucy."

"I confronted them about it, asking them to change the way they were treating the students. It didn't go over well. They said I didn't have the right attitude to be one of their teachers. That's when I knew I couldn't continue working there, so I packed up and moved."

Huh. Graham had thought there might be a skeleton in her closet. Instead, she'd been a defender for the young girls in her classes. Wouldn't he want someone to do the same for Mattie if she were in a class like that? He'd definitely had Lucy pegged as something she wasn't.

This woman surprised him. And Graham wanted her to stay working for him. In one morning, she'd accomplished more than any of the temps. His patients even liked her, and they reacted to change as though he was trying to personally offend them.

"Lucy, will you consider coming back to work?"

She rubbed her arms. "I'm not a huge fan of yours right now."

"I'm not a huge fan of myself right now."

Those lips curved ever so slightly. "You know, I wasn't doing anything inappropriate with Hunter. I'd been standing on the chair—"

"I know. He told me. I overreacted." *And seeing his hands on you*…hadn't bothered Graham in the least. Lucy was too young for him to be thinking about her in that way. Plus, besides his other list of reasons, she was his employee. *Possibly* his employee.

"I'll get a stool."

Her head tilted, loose curls cascading over her right shoulder as she studied him. "Why do you want me to stay, anyway?"

"You dealt with this morning's chaos better than the temps I've had in, and they had experience. All I've heard today is how delighted everyone is with you."

Lucy's eyes narrowed. "But I didn't get anything done this morning but handling the phone."

"But you did handle it."

She didn't look convinced, but at least she wasn't running for her car. "I'm not exactly qualified for this position." Her hand flew through her hair with agitation, sending the locks bouncing. One finger pointed at him. "You can't just throw me into a medical office and expect me to have a clue what I'm doing. You have to give me some time to adjust and figure things out."

"I—"

"And you have to at least try to like me. I'm not asking you to fall in love with me—" Good to know since *that* definitely wasn't on Graham's to-do list. "But you could at least make an attempt to get along. People don't usually have such a hard time with me."

That was exactly what he was afraid of. Lucy had this energy, this essence that just attracted people to her. Graham felt the tug, too, though he didn't plan to pursue anything more than a work relationship. A friendly work relationship. That he could handle.

"I accept your terms."

"Really? You're not just saying that?"

He raised his right hand. "I pledge to not be a jerk." He winced. "I'll do my best. And I really mean what I'm saying."

Lucy's eyes began to twinkle. "Do you think we can get one purse a month thrown into my salary?"

"No."

"How about one for the whole of Hollie's maternity leave?"

"No." His lips twitched.

"We could call it a briefcase, make it a business expense."

"Lucy." He groaned. What was he going to do with

this woman? He wasn't sure whether to laugh or run in the other direction.

Her shoulders inched up. "I would try to keep bargaining for more, but we both know I'm not that valuable of a commodity. I don't want to ruin my chances."

He had a feeling she would be more valuable—to his office—than she realized. Now that he was over his misconceptions, Graham felt relieved he'd found a fill-in for Hollie that his patients liked.

"I think we should shake on it. Graham Redmond, you promise to be patient with me as I figure out this job—*and* give me a real chance this time—and I'll do my best to be professional."

Lucy offered her hand.

"I already pledged an oath."

She raised one eyebrow, waiting.

Fine. Graham would shake on it. He cupped her hand in his. It was warm and soft and definitely didn't make him think about a business deal.

He pulled his hand back. Scrubbed it against his pants.

She was right. He hadn't really given her a chance. He'd been expecting her to fail. But Graham should know by now he was the one who excelled in the failure department.

He'd definitely made mistakes with Brooke. He'd loved her. That much he'd got right. But he hadn't been able to save her. He'd known when he married Brooke there were risks. She'd had cystic fibrosis, but she'd been on medication and always done well. Until her lungs had got worse and worse. Even then, Graham had assumed he could help her, that she'd get better.

They'd married young—just out of college. She'd

worked, putting him through medical school. And then they'd found out Brooke was unexpectedly pregnant. At first, Graham had been shocked. He'd been a wreck. Would Brooke's body handle the pregnancy okay? How would they make it? How would he provide? He'd planned to quit medical school until Brooke had given him a verbal slap, knocking him back to reality. She'd told him it would be fine.

And she'd been right.

At least for a while. They'd welcomed Mattie into the world, and Graham had fallen for her just as he had her mother. The years of residency had begun. Brooke had been a rock. Working, taking care of Mattie and shining like never before. Motherhood had fit her. Both of their parents had helped out as much as they could while living over an hour away. Things had settled in again. He'd been months from finishing his residency when Brooke got sick.

Graham should have been able to save her. He should have had the knowledge. He'd pushed her doctors for every detail, searched for answers himself—any treatment options they might be missing. But in the end, it hadn't been enough. He hadn't been enough. She'd faded quickly, no matter what he'd done. No matter what he'd prayed.

He still didn't know how he'd made it through those last months of residency without her. Prayers and family had carried him. Graham had come out stumbling. He'd followed through on his and Brooke's plan to move back to Fredericksburg and open a clinic near both of their parents, missing her as though part of his heart had been surgically removed.

He'd done it for Mattie. Graham would do anything

for Mattie. Which was why he'd continued to practice medicine while doubts about his abilities as a doctor assailed him.

If he thought too much about Brooke, about how he'd failed her and been unable to save her, then he wanted to crawl into bed and never come out.

Instead, Graham focused on Mattie. Her needs before his. He kept putting one foot in front of the other, hoping the whole town wouldn't notice he'd fallen flat on his face two years before.

"You still with me, Hollywood?" Lucy's question interrupted his sprint down memory lane. She'd moved closer, about a foot away, bringing the scent of lime and coconut with her.

"Hollywood?"

Her lips lifted. "So, you *can* hear me. I wasn't sure for a minute."

A light breeze tousled her hair, and Lucy pulled her curls to one side while the hem of her skirt flitted above her knees.

For a second, Graham questioned his sanity, asking Lucy to keep working for him. He only knew his decision had nothing to do with her looks and everything to do with his medical office. Lucy was good at the position—okay, maybe *good* was too strong a word at this point. She had the potential to do well, and that was what mattered.

Besides, it wasn't as if he was in love with the woman. He could simply admit she was beautiful and leave it at that. Anyone meeting Lucy would think the same.

Relief slid down his spine. A bit of attraction? That he could handle. He wasn't signing up for anything more than a businesslike friendship with Lucy Grayson.

Graham and Lucy started walking toward the office, Lucy a few steps in front of him. Without permission, his eyes slid down her belted dress, noticing the way it hugged her curves and showcased her legs. He quickly bounced his gaze to the sky and bit back a groan. The outfit was professional, he would give her that. But it was also distracting. To him. He was positive Hunter hadn't minded rescuing Lucy, though the man hadn't seemed as frazzled by the incident as Graham had been.

"You know, you could wear scrubs if you want. A lot of people working in medical offices do. It simplifies things."

Plus, maybe scrubs would help keep his thoughts focused on work instead of on the woman in front of him.

"Scrubs?" Lucy turned back, nose wrinkled. "I'm not really a scrubs kind of girl. I think I'll pass."

That was exactly what he'd feared.

Chapter 4

Before Lucy could even consider teaching her first Saturday-morning beginner's ballet class, she needed two things—a Diet Coke and her sunglasses.

Assuming she'd left her sunglasses at work yesterday, since they weren't on the floor of her car, Lucy had left early enough to swing by Graham's office this morning and then hit the drive-through. Some things were worth the sacrifice of a few minutes of lost sleep.

Graham had given her a key to the office on Wednesday, which she considered his peace offering after their confrontation Tuesday. The rest of the week they'd been cordial to each other. Lucy had been scrambling to learn about the job, and Graham had been Mr. Polite. He'd been patient with her and completely professional. He treated her the way she saw him treat everyone else— very respectfully. It bored her just a titch, and Lucy had *almost* found herself wishing for the snarly Graham back, if only for the entertainment value.

She pulled into the lot of the small redbrick building, surprised to see Graham's car there. Did he work Saturdays, too?

Lucy parked and walked inside, calling out her arrival. When no one answered, she checked the reception desk. Score. Her favorite Ray-Ban sunglasses—red on the front, multicolored on the inside—were peeking out from under some papers. She grabbed them.

"Hi, Lucy."

She placed a hand over her thudding heart and turned. "Hey, Mattie. What are you up to?"

"I was drawing in Daddy's office. He's working."

Huh. That did not sound like a fun Saturday to Lucy.

"What are you wearing?" Mattie's eyes traveled the length of Lucy's dance sweatshirt, striped fitted shirt that landed just past her hips, leggings and bright green Converse high-tops.

"Clothes for teaching dance. Except for the shoes. Those I have to change when I get there because you can't wear ballet shoes on the street."

"You teach dance?" Mattie's eyes grew large. She bounced on the toes of her pink tennis shoes. "And do you wear the pink slippers?"

"Yes and yes." Delight had erased the seriousness Lucy had come to expect on Mattie's face.

"And you do the twirls?"

A pirouette. "Yes." Lucy stooped to Mattie's height. "Do you...do you want to take ballet, Mattie?"

She nodded quickly, then looked down at the floor.

"Have you asked your dad?"

She shook her head.

Why hadn't she asked Graham? In the past few days, Lucy had learned the little girl was a miniature adult—possibly more mature than Lucy—and that she always seemed slightly sad.

That last one killed Lucy. She couldn't curb the deep

dcsire to make it better, to give the girl some fun. A little joy.

When Lucy had been ten, her uncle had died unexpectedly. Her dad had been devastated over losing his brother, and Lucy had taken it upon herself to cheer him up.

She'd done everything she could to bring happiness back into his life. She'd put on plays. Performed hilarious songs. Made him funny cards and left him notes. Sneaked silly faces at the dinner table. Eventually, it had worked. Dad had called her his sunshine, and cheering people up had become her thing. She already read people's emotions quickly, so delving into helping them came naturally.

And Lucy just couldn't resist bringing some cheer into sweet, serious Mattie's life.

"I think we should ask him."

Mattie bit her lip. "Okay."

Lucy glanced at her watch. She wouldn't have time for her Diet Coke run if she talked to Graham about Mattie doing dance. But when a little hand slipped into hers, Lucy knew it didn't matter.

Her decision had already been made.

Graham heard a noise down the hall and stood from behind his desk. Hopefully it wasn't a patient popping in. He wasn't exactly looking professional in jeans, an untucked blue cotton button-down and brown leather tennis shoes.

More likely the noise was just Mattie. She'd been drawing quietly in his office, but she must have wandered off. He'd promised her they'd do something fun this afternoon to make up for working on the weekend. Being Mattie, she'd agreed without an argument.

He really did not deserve her.

He poked his head out of his office door and found Mattie and Lucy coming down the hall hand in hand. His daughter had been pestering him with questions about Lucy all week. Turned out Graham didn't know that much about her, so he wasn't much of a help to Mattie.

He did know that the past three days with Lucy had gone much better than Tuesday morning. They'd settled into a working relationship in which Graham didn't have a ton of interaction with her outside of work questions—and he was thankful for that.

In the past few days, she'd managed to lose only one chart (Graham had later found it filed under the first name instead of the last), and she'd shredded a stack of notes he'd left that needed to be added to charts. He was working on rewriting those this morning. But, beyond that, she'd charmed his daughter, made friends with Danielle and managed to deal with his sometimes crazy patients and make it look easy.

Lucy and Mattie stopped in front of him, some kind of trouble hiding behind their shared glance.

In leggings and bright green tennis shoes with her hair piled on top of her head in a messy bun, Lucy looked the part of dance instructor. Maybe she'd forgotten which job she was going to this morning.

"Graham." She paused to wink at Mattie. "We have a question to ask you."

Unease trickled through him. "Okay."

"Mattie expressed an interest in going to dance class. The one I teach on Saturday mornings is beginner's ballet. It would be perfect for her."

Perfect? Lucy had no idea what she was talking about. The only activity perfect for Mattie was yoga. Although she could probably pull a muscle in that. Something with padding around her whole body and no physical contact would do. But since that sport didn't exist, he'd vote no.

His daughter had a major propensity for getting hurt. The last sport Mattie had played was soccer. She'd ended up with a concussion. Who got a concussion in peewee soccer? When she'd begged to take gymnastics, she'd sprained her wrist within the first week.

If there was a competition for reading fast, Mattie would rock it. Or a spelling bee. She could totally do that. He should check if her school had—

"What do you think? Can she come to class with me?"

"I think you're good, aren't you, Mattie?"

Mattie stared at him, seconds feeling like hours. "Okay, Daddy." Her hand slipped from Lucy's and she walked down the hall, her little shoulders slouching.

Graham rubbed a fist over his aching heart. He wanted to make her happy, but more than anything, he wanted to keep her safe. Sometimes parents had to make the hard decisions, and this was one of them.

"Are you joking?" Lucy's hands landed on her hips, and she looked as though he'd just told her she couldn't buy another pair of shoes all year. Guess it had been naive of him to think she'd walk away and let him handle his daughter's care without injecting her opinion. "You can tell she wants to go. It's obvious. Why won't you let her?"

"You're overstepping your bounds, Lucy. You don't understand."

"What I understand is that little girl will do anything for you—including give up a dance class she really wants to go to. You should have seen her light up when we were talking about it. She *wants* to go."

"Mattie struggles with athletics. I don't want her getting injured or feeling left out if she's not as good as the other girls." Rarely did he get heated, but right now? Not feeling so calm. "Plus, who are you to have an opinion about Mattie or question my parenting? You're acting like a sixteen-year-old."

"I'm offended for sixteen-year-olds everywhere. And you're acting like an ancient grump."

"At thirty-one, I am ancient compared to you. And since I'm Mattie's *old*, *grumpy* father, I get to make the decisions."

"I'm twenty-four. You're not *that* much older than me."

"I am in wisdom." *What?* That sentence didn't even make sense. "Age doesn't matter. I'm her father. It's my choice." Graham did the math in his head. "Wait—didn't you just graduate from college last year?" A fifth-year senior. The way Lucy acted, he could see her not finishing in four.

"Yes. Before I started college, I traveled with a dance team."

"And then you went to college after that?"

She nodded.

He was being a jerk. Again. Why did he expect the worst from Lucy? Most people wouldn't take time off and still go back to school. She should be commended. But while she might surprise him in certain areas, she was definitely driving him nuts right now.

They stared each other down. Graham wasn't planning to budge. He'd made his decision.

Eventually Lucy's stance softened. "Listen, Hollywood, I understand you're worried about her, but the class is really safe. I'll be there the whole time to watch out for her and help her so she doesn't feel lost or uncomfortable."

Hollywood. Why did she keep calling him that?

Lucy glanced at her watch. "I know you're my boss and all, but since it's the weekend, I don't think that counts. Do you?"

Strange logic. "Ah, I guess not?"

"Great. Then you won't fire me when I take her to dance anyway." Lucy headed down the hall, and it took a second for her words to register. When they did, Graham went after her. She and Mattie were standing by the reception desk, and Lucy was helping Mattie into her coat.

"You can't just take her. That's kidnapping."

Lucy faced his daughter. "Mattie, do you want to go to dance with me?"

Mattie looked at him with mournful eyes, then at Lucy before her gaze dipped to the floor. Finally, she gave the most imperceptible nod.

He felt like the worst dad ever. Especially since she rarely went against what he said. Must have been hard for her to admit. But even with seeing her blatant desire to attend ballet, letting her go was so hard. She'd had a lot of hurt in her life. Was he so wrong not to want her to go through more?

They were leaving. Mattie and Lucy were walking out the front doors while he stood there thinking. Graham followed them into the parking lot.

"It's illegal for her to ride without a booster seat."

Lucy marched over to his car. She wouldn't get anywhere with it. He always locked the doors. She pulled on the back door handle, and it popped right open.

Impossible. He *always* locked his car. That verse about everything being possible with God seemed to also apply to Lucy. Whatever she touched turned to gold. Did God just shine down on her life with rainbows and unicorns?

She grabbed Mattie's car seat and walked back over to her Volkswagen. After putting it in her backseat, she helped Mattie buckle in.

When she climbed into the driver's seat, Graham approached.

"I'm calling the cops. You can't just take my daughter."

Lucy shrugged. "Call the cops, then. The girl needs some fun in her life. You know I'm right or you would have already stopped me." At that, she slammed the door and drove off.

Turned out, Matilda Grace Redmond had some natural dance ability. And even if she didn't, the whole morning fiasco with Graham would have been worth it just to see the look of joy on the girl's face.

She'd missed a few steps—okay, a lot—but it was her first class. She'd improve. And, really, it wasn't about getting the steps perfect. It was about a little girl's delight when she learned the five positions and got distracted watching herself in the mirrors. The way she tried to stand on her toes the first time she wore ballet slippers, even though she shouldn't, just because she wanted to be like the older girls in pointe shoes. It was about falling in love with dance the way Lucy had so many years before.

When they'd arrived at the studio with barely any minutes to spare, Lucy had scrounged through the share bin—a place where dancers left items that no longer fit them—and found a skirt and shoes for Mattie. Total score. The dance school had a small area where they sold a few necessary items, and Lucy had snagged a leotard and tights there. A small price to pay for the way Mattie kept twirling in the outfit even though class had already finished.

Yes, the morning had been worth it. But now that Lucy was removed from the encounter with Graham, she really wished she would have handled things better. Niggling doubt about the way she'd acted snatched her joy at seeing Mattie so happy. Why couldn't she just be calm and reasonable? She'd always been passionate. Sometimes her emotions ran a bit…dramatic. She rarely thought too long before making a decision, usually jumping right in. But this time, she might have been a little too *Lucy*.

At least her intentions had been good.

She'd just wanted to help Mattie, not ruin her own newly improved relationship with Graham. Or hurt Mattie's chance to do dance in the future. She hadn't even thought about that. What if Graham never let Mattie come back and it was all Lucy's fault? That would be awful. Mattie really did seem to love it.

She sent up another of her trademark help-fix-what-I've-already-done prayers, hoping God could help her and Mattie out. They could certainly use some divine intervention.

Lucy corralled Mattie and Belle—the other little girl from class who hadn't been picked up by her parents yet—into the waiting area so that the next class could start. Just as they walked into the space lined with chairs and couches, the door to the studio opened and a female police officer walked in.

Panic climbed Lucy's throat. Graham wouldn't really... He hadn't...

The cop scanned the room, and Lucy broke out in a sweat worthy of a marathon runner. Had Graham seriously called the cops? She needed a place to hide. But would that be considered resisting arrest?

Mattie and Belle were chatting and comparing ballet shoes, completely oblivious to Lucy's turmoil.

She dived behind the closest chair, body barely fitting in the space. She was probably overreacting—as usual. Maybe the officer had already moved on. Lucy leaned ever so slightly from behind the chair and peeked out.

Drat! The woman's black boots were headed right for her! She ducked back behind the seat, hoping the officer hadn't seen her.

"Excuse me, but are you Lucy? Lucy Grayson?"

Oh, no. Oh, no. Oh, no.

Lucy winced, slowly standing from her position. She was going to use her one phone call to call Graham and yell at him. As if she had actually kidnapped Mattie. He could have stopped her if he wanted to. She wouldn't have left if the man had put up a fight. He'd been wavering the whole time. Lucy had simply taken advantage of his indecision.

And now she was going to suffer the consequences. Lucy squared her shoulders. Time to take it like a woman. "Yes. That's me. I can ex—"

"I'm Peggy." The officer extended her hand. "Belle's mom. It's nice to meet you."

Lucy's mouth flopped open. Belle's mom. Graham

hadn't really called the police. Yet… Lucy had just been hiding behind a chair.

"You are the new instructor for beginning ballet, right?"

"Yes." Lucy shook the woman's hand. "I am. I was just—" She glanced at the chair that had recently been her safe haven. "We were just…playing hide-and-seek."

It was the truth. Only Lucy had been hiding from a police officer, not Belle and Mattie. She could have told Peggy more of the truth, but *I hide from law enforcement* hadn't seemed like the better option.

Thankfully Peggy was gracious and didn't ask Lucy about her strange behavior. She did ask about Belle's time in class, and by the time they left, Lucy hoped she'd redeemed herself and her escapades would be forgotten.

Hoped, but didn't necessarily believe.

After Belle left with her mom, Lucy stuffed Mattie's ballet shoes into her own dance bag and helped her put on her pink tennis shoes.

They walked outside, and again, Mattie's hand slipped into Lucy's. The child still sported that dreamy look. One Lucy understood well. Dance had always been that place for her. Olivia had played volleyball, creating a bond with Dad, and Lucy had danced her way through life.

Even if Graham didn't forgive her, the morning had been worth it.

They got into the car, and Lucy pulled out her phone and texted Graham.

Are you still mad? She had THE BEST time. She's got natural talent. No injuries.

His reply came back in record time.

Maybe a little.

The man must have been glued to the phone. Remnants of guilt slithered across her skin. She definitely could have handled this morning better.

Lucy would have to work on that whole think-before-you-do thing.

I'm sorry I stole your daughter.

I'm still considering pressing charges. ☺

He'd included a smiley face? He was putty in her hands.

If it makes you feel any better, when one of the dance parents arrived in a police uniform to pick up her daughter, I thought you HAD called the cops on me.

Ha! That does make me feel better. Did she really have fun? She fit in okay? She didn't get hurt?

Overprotective man. His barrage of questions made Lucy grin.

"When are we going?"

"One sec, Mattie." Lucy had forgotten about the little girl in the backseat.

She looked so happy. Like she was living a fairy tale.

That might be overdoing it a little, but Lucy needed to plead her case a bit. She continued texting.

It's dance. There's not that many ways to get injured.

Not completely truthful. But at Mattie's age, the steps and classes were simple. The older girls had more chances of injury.

Any chance I can keep her for another hour? I think the first dance class deserves an ice cream celebration.

Crickets. No answer. Lucy glanced in the rearview mirror. Mattie was staring out the window. Patient, serious little thing.

Fine.

Graham's begrudging response made Lucy laugh. He didn't exactly sound excited, but she'd take it and run.

"What's so funny?" Mattie piped up from the back-seat.

"I was just texting your dad that I thought we should grab some ice cream before I drop you off. What do you think?"

Mattie's eyes grew to the size of quarters, and she nodded quickly.

Lucy's phone beeped again, and her mouth curved, picturing another text from Graham. Directions on what Mattie could and couldn't do, most likely.

When are you coming home? I miss you.

Disappointment sucked the air from her lungs. It was from Bodie. Not Graham.

Bodie Kelps. Lucy had gone on a total of three dates with him back in Colorado. After which, Bodie had started talking about the future and Lucy meeting his parents. He'd even brought up the relationship-defining talk, which was Lucy's cue to exit the scene.

The move to Texas couldn't have come at a better time in terms of Bodie. Lucy liked him. They'd been friends during college and after, and she didn't want to lose that friendship because things hadn't worked out between them. She'd told Bodie in clear terms that they were not in a relationship and that she didn't want to keep dating after she moved.

But the man didn't listen.

He must think she was using moving as an excuse and he could prove his affection by continuing to pursue her. She wasn't. Even if Lucy had stayed in Colorado, she wouldn't have continued dating Bodie.

He'd texted her every day since she'd moved and called twice. Once she'd answered and talked to him—after all, she didn't want to be rude—but she'd tried not to encourage him in a romantic way. Her hints definitely weren't working.

Maybe she could etch it into stone or something. Although that would be pricey to mail.

Lucy put the phone to the side, started the car and drove out of the parking lot. Bodie could wait for an answer on that text since she didn't know what to do about him. He obviously hadn't believed her when she'd told him she was moving and that they were over. Lucy just didn't do serious relationships.

She didn't have some heart-wrenching story like the

one her sister had endured. Lucy had just learned her lessons young. One time she'd attempted that whole *falling for someone* thing. The results hadn't been good. One time had been enough for her to realize she much preferred to love and embrace everyone in life without ever getting too serious.

Lucy had been young—her junior year in high school—the first time she'd been tempted to let her feelings for a guy progress beyond friendship. A senior had asked her to prom, and she'd accepted. He was gorgeous, and she'd let her imagination get the best of her. She'd started daydreaming about him, thinking maybe he was really interested in her, acting like one of the silly girls she usually detested. Then, one day after school, she'd needed someone to give her a ride home. She'd headed to Nate's locker to see if he could, but realized as she approached that he was talking about her to his friend.

At first she'd been giddy, thinking he must really like her. But then she'd realized they were discussing a plan regarding her.

They were talking about how long Nate would date her before passing her on to his friend who wanted a turn with her. Discussing her as if she were a piece of playground equipment.

She's already fallen for me. I have no doubt that by prom, I'll get what I want. After that, she's all yours.

If Lucy hadn't overheard, she'd never have known that all of Nate's flattery and attention had only been done with one goal in mind.

Thankfully it had been early enough in the relationship that Lucy had come out of the experience with her heart still intact. In fact, she considered that day, that conversation, one of her biggest blessings because of how it had changed her life.

From that point on—after telling Nate exactly what she'd thought of his plans—she'd made a few decisions.

First, she'd started rescuing herself. She hadn't called her parents or sister for a ride home from school. She hadn't found one of her girlfriends and bummed a ride. Lucy had walked. Granted, it had been only a few miles to get home, but that had been the beginning for her.

No more looking for a prince when she could rescue herself.

And second, she'd tossed out serious (not that she'd ever had an extra supply in that department) and stuck to fun. She hung with groups of friends and even went to prom that year with a bunch of people. Guys. Girls. Everyone knew her. Most loved her. She loved back. Simple. Easy. No mess to clean up when she went through life with the objective of having fun.

"Ms. Lucy?"

"Yeah?"

"This really is the best day ever."

The contented sigh that came from the backseat wrapped around Lucy. Good thing she didn't resist getting involved with people in general, just dating relationships. Because she feared she'd already lost her heart to the adorable five-year-old in the rearview mirror.

Chapter 5

He missed his daughter.

Graham was a big sap, and even one more hour without Mattie felt like a year. *Pathetic* would be a good word to describe him right now. Even though Mattie was likely having a ton more fun with Lucy at dance and now going to get ice cream, he wanted her here. He wanted to look across his desk and see her at the credenza in the corner where she kept her art supplies and liked to color. He was selfish, that was what he was.

And he was getting nothing done.

With time to himself, his workload should be dwindling. But since Lucy and Mattie had left, he'd only dealt with a few charts and organized his pens. Who didn't want to claim an accomplishment like that for their Saturday?

He wanted to ask Mattie about class. Sure, he'd got some answers from Lucy, but he wanted to hear from his daughter.

Graham checked his watch. Lucy had texted only a few minutes ago that they were going for ice cream. He could go meet them. But that would be overprotective of him. Which he wasn't. He was more…curious. Another good word.

He grabbed his keys.

If he happened to be at the same place as them, nobody could fault him for that. And Graham knew just where his daughter would want to go.

Lucy judged the ice cream places in town by the level of excitement coming from the backseat. Clear River, a red storefront that boasted bakery, ice cream and deli signs, garnered the most response, so Lucy found a parking spot, and she and Mattie walked the short distance. If the smell of sugar and cinnamon that greeted them when Lucy opened the door was any indication, Mattie had impeccable taste.

Red booths with white tables lined the space, and a curved glass display case held mouthwatering treats with the menu hanging behind. When it was their turn to order, Mattie still hadn't decided which flavor to choose, so Lucy ordered first.

"I'll have a double-scoop cone. Chocolate peanut butter cup, strawberry cheesecake and… Let's make that a triple. One scoop of caramel turtle fudge, too."

She felt a tug on her arm. "Can I have that many scoops?"

Lucy imagined her answer should be no, but she didn't know why. "Go for it."

Mattie told Lucy the flavors she wanted and Lucy conveyed the order to the person behind the counter. She paid and they scanned the place for a seat. Once they grabbed a booth and slid in, Lucy tasted her ice cream.

"Mattie, why didn't you tell me this ice cream was amazing?"

The girl's small shoulders lifted. "I kind of did." She gave a shy smile and took a lick of chocolate.

True. She had squealed.

Lucy had thought no one could top Josh & John's— her favorite Colorado Springs ice cream—but she might be wrong. She'd probably need to return to Clear River and taste all of their homemade ice cream before she could make a truly informed decision.

Mattie pointed toward the front windows. "Daddy!"

Lucy turned to see Graham stepping inside the restaurant. He spotted them and headed in their direction.

"How's my girl?" He slid into the booth next to Mattie, and she threw herself into his arms. For a second, Lucy had thought he'd said *girls*, as in plural. And for a moment, her heart had leaped.

Strange.

"You have some kind of tracking device on me?" Lucy patted down her arms.

"Ha. No. I knew where Mattie would want to go for ice cream and I just—" He shrugged, then kissed the top of Mattie's head, accepting a bite of her ice cream.

Oh. He hadn't been checking up on her. He'd missed his daughter. A forgivable trait.

"You just wanted some ice cream?"

"Something like that." Graham's answering grin absolutely *did not* make Lucy's knees the consistency of Jell-O. She must just be out of shape or something. It had been a few weeks since she'd taught dance. "But it's almost lunchtime. Shouldn't we be eating lunch?" He glanced at Mattie's cone, then back at Lucy. "Instead of a triple-scoop cone?" His voice had lowered to a growl. And that was why she should have said no. "She's five." He raised an eyebrow at Lucy.

"They didn't have a quintuple scoop."

He groaned. "You can't have ice cream for lunch."

"Um, whyever not?" Lucy finished the caramel turtle fudge and moved on to the strawberry cheesecake. Oh. My. If she could marry this ice cream, she would. "Haven't you ever had dessert for a meal?"

Graham's head tilted. "No. Can't say that I have."

"We're going to have to change that." Lucy winked at Mattie.

"I'm going to get us something to eat." Graham pushed out from the booth. "Mattie, you're going to get a stomachache if you only eat that."

Mattie just smiled and took another lick of her cone.

Graham ordered at the counter, returning a few minutes later. When their food arrived, Lucy accepted the sandwich he'd ordered for her, digging in. Her first bite was absolutely to die for. She swallowed, wiping her mouth with her napkin. "What in the world is this sandwich? It's amazing."

"Smoked beef brisket on a jalapeño bun. They make their own sauce for it."

"What if I was a vegetarian?" She took another bite.

"I've seen you eat at work."

"True. You're forgiven for making us eat lunch. This is really good."

"Thank you." Graham's dry response made her tamp down a smile. He handed Mattie an extra dish. "Here, honey. You can put the rest of your cone in this while you eat some lunch."

Mattie acquiesced, moving on to her sandwich while Lucy dug into her purse and found some cash. "Here." She held the money out. "Will this cover it?"

"Cover what?"

"Lunch." She waved the bills at him.

"I bought lunch, Lucy. I don't want your money."

"But you don't need to pay for mine." Again, she attempted to get him to take the money.

"Anyone ever tell you that being unable to accept help or gifts from others is not a good quality?"

Ouch. Lucy lowered her hand. If anyone had ever said that to her, she hadn't listened. "Fine." She shoved the bills back into her purse. "Be noble."

His lips twitched. "Besides, I see that Mattie's in dance clothes, which had to come from somewhere. I assume you paid for those. Now I owe you money."

"We found some pieces in the giveaway box."

"And the other ones Lucy bought for me."

"Ms. Lucy," he corrected his daughter, shooting Lucy an accusing look. "And that's interesting information, Mattie."

"Does she really have to call me Ms. Lucy? It's so old lady."

"Old lady would be Ms. Grayson."

"Oy. Fine. Mattie, you're welcome to call me Lucy when your father's not around."

Mattie giggled, and Graham shook his head while swallowing a bite of his sandwich. "You really don't have a mature button, do you?"

"I hope not."

"Look, Daddy." Mattie leaned across Graham and pointed. "It's Grandma and Grandpa!"

A couple approached the booth, both looking as though they should be going to a business meeting instead of out for lunch. Mattie's grandmother was dressed in black dress pants and a yellow shirt, her perfectly styled brown hair shining, and her grandfather wore charcoal-gray pants and a white polo.

Mattie scrambled over Graham's lap to get out of the booth. She wrapped her arms around her grandmother's legs. The woman's hair stayed in place as she hugged Mattie back. "Honey, it's so good to see you."

She looked at their booth, gaze resting on Lucy, then Graham. "This looks cozy."

Cozy. Interesting word choice. But it wasn't so much what she'd said as the way she'd said it. Lucy rubbed her bare arms. She hadn't realized the temperature in Texas could drop so fast.

"Hi, Grandpa." Mattie hugged him, also, and he visibly softened. "Do you know Ms. Lucy?" Mattie's bubbling excitement regarding Lucy didn't transfer to her grandparents. Two wary pairs of eyes swung in her direction. And stayed. They didn't miss a thing, traveling from her messy bun to her bright green high-tops. She must look about twelve. Maybe fifteen on a good day. Perhaps Mattie's grandparents would think she was the babysitter.

Graham made introductions, and Lucy received some polite nods from the couple, Belinda and Phillip Welling. Could their last name sound more regal? It definitely fit them. The name also meant they were Graham's late wife's parents, not his parents. That realization and the fact that they were looking at her as if she'd stolen their granddaughter made Lucy want to slide off her seat and hide under the table. Maybe Graham had called them this morning instead of the police. At least that would explain their tense faces.

Enough of this. Lucy could handle almost anything, these two included. "I'm Mattie's dance teacher."

"Mattie takes dance?" The woman's eyes widened before landing on Graham with accusation.

"She just started this morning," Graham answered. "Lucy's working at the clinic, covering for Hollie while she's on maternity leave."

This seemed to placate them somewhat. Perhaps the temporary nature of the position pleased them. Lucy wouldn't call them rude. They weren't even antisocial. There was just something about the way they looked at her. They almost seemed…hurt.

Lucy could totally go for a hole in the ground right about now. But a better option would be to simply leave them to their family affair. It didn't matter that she hadn't finished her lunch. Her stomach had suddenly turned. Maybe from eating dessert first.

Or something like that.

"It was great meeting you." Lucy pasted on her brightest smile and stood. "I'm going to take off."

"Are you sure? You're welcome to stay." Though he said the right thing, Graham's uncomfortable body language didn't support his words. He looked as though he wanted to hide in the same hole as Lucy. Only that would make them far too close for his comfort, she was sure.

He certainly wasn't confronting his in-laws about the way they were acting toward her. Not that she expected him to. After all, she was just the help.

Lucy would love to stay and keep feeling like a piece of gum stuck under someone's shoe, but she really did have to go.

She offered Mattie a fist bump. "You did great this morning." Mattie beamed, then switched to a pout with impressive speed.

"You're leaving? But Daddy's here and we're not done with lunch. Don't you want to stay?"

Her innocent question caused the tension in their small circle to triple.

"Actually, I've got to run. Graham, I'll leave Mattie's car seat by your car." No one would steal it in this town, would they? And with that, she bolted for the door. Once outside, she struggled for calm, but even the quaint Main Street didn't lighten her mood.

Lucy really needed to shake off that encounter. She knew better than to let other people's opinions affect her.

Back in high school when she'd overheard that horrible conversation that had reduced her to a pawn in a game, she'd instantly felt like a body—a shell—and nothing more.

She hated that she'd given Nate the power to impact how she felt. That was why ever since then she'd stuck to being carefree, to loving everyone without loving someone in particular. Because when things got serious, when she let herself get too involved, it gave far too much control to someone else. The encounter with the Wellings just now had brought back all of that turmoil. They'd treated her like an item that had outlived its shelf life and no longer belonged anywhere.

Lucy hadn't felt that unwanted in a long, long time.

And she'd do just about anything to avoid that feeling.

Graham felt as though he'd walked into a freezer. The way his in-laws were looking at him made him feel about two feet tall. What was going on? He'd always had a good relationship with the Wellings, so this scenario didn't make sense. They had to be upset about something.

He handed Mattie his phone, and she began playing a game while he stood and faced the couple. "Belinda. Phillip. What's wrong?"

"Are you…?" Belinda studied her perfectly manicured nails, then looked up, tears pooling. "Are you dating that woman?"

"Lucy?" Graham glanced from one wounded face to another. That was what was bothering them? "No. I'm not. Why would you think that?"

Belinda looked out the front windows to where Lucy had recently disappeared. "When we saw the three of you together, it just looked…" She trailed off and shrugged.

Somehow catching up with Lucy and Mattie after dance class amounted to him being in a relationship. Perfect.

"You already heard Lucy works for me. She took Mattie to dance class this morning and then I met up with them afterward. It was nothing more than that."

"How well do you know her?" Phillip's brow furrowed. "If she's spending time with Mattie, I assume you've checked her out?"

"Did I run a police report? No." Graham stifled his irritation at their unwarranted intrusion. "She's fine. Her sister is married to Cash Maddox." Though the Wellings were sometimes overprotective—even more than Graham—this conversation didn't need to continue. His in-laws should trust him.

Belinda touched his arm. "Be careful, Graham."
Of what?

"You wouldn't want to confuse Mattie or fill her mind with ideas."

In the past five days, he'd been closer to losing his

temper than he had in years. "Trust me, I'm not planning to date. Anyone."

His in-laws nodded, and while their tension lessened, Graham's grew. "Would you…?" He forced out the words. "Would you like to join us for lunch?" It was the right thing to say, but it came out wooden.

"Thank you for the invitation," Phillip responded, "but we don't have time. We're grabbing something to go since we're meeting with the foundation lawyers today."

The foundation. A charity started in Brooke's honor that raised money for cystic fibrosis research. One that always reminded Graham that he'd failed his wife. He knew it was for the best of causes, yet he'd never been able to help his in-laws with it when they asked. He attended only one charity function per year, and even that was a push.

The Wellings didn't understand why he wouldn't be a part of something that honored Brooke, why he wouldn't accept a position on the board. It had been the one point of contention between them. Until today. Now he could add Lucy to the list. Though that thought was absolutely absurd.

They said goodbyes, and Graham fought the annoyance churning in his gut.

Why did he feel so frustrated? The Wellings had only questioned him about dating—something he didn't have any interest in. So why did their interference bother him so much?

Graham slid back into the booth and Mattie put the phone down on the table.

"What was that about, Daddy?"

"How much did you hear?"

"Just Grandpa and Grandma asking if you were dating Ms. Lucy." Mattie munched on a chip, studying him with those inquisitive little eyes. "Are you ever going to marry someone, Dad?"

Graham had just taken a bite, and it lodged in his throat. He coughed, then took a drink of water. "I loved your mom so much, I really can't imagine that, honey. She was my best friend."

"Like me and Carissa?"

The image of Mattie and her best friend, Carissa, playing together made him smile. "Something like that."

"Only you kissed Mommy."

Good thing he hadn't taken another bite. He reached for his water again. "Right. When you're married, you get to kiss your spouse."

That seemed to satisfy her. Mattie went back to eating and playing her game, and Graham sorted through the day's events. Compared to their normal, peaceful existence, today had been rather crazy. And it wasn't even noon.

It seemed Lucy had that effect on their life.

The way she'd looked at the office this morning when she'd been ornery with him came flooding back. She did this thing when she was upset, though he doubted she realized it. She pressed her lips together, almost as if she was stemming whatever she really wanted to say from coming out. From what he'd learned about her, his assumption probably wasn't far off.

"Are you thinking about Mommy?"

Graham stole a chip off of Mattie's plate. "Why?"

"'Cause you're smiling."

"I was?"

Mattie nodded. Graham swallowed. "If I was smiling, then I was definitely thinking about Mommy."

At least, he should have been.

Chapter 6

It had been a week since the encounter between Graham, his in-laws and Lucy, and that freezer he'd walked into still hadn't fully thawed. It had warmed to refrigerator temps, but that was about it.

At work this week, he and Lucy had functioned *around* each other. Please and thank-yous had abounded. Graham had never thought politeness could kill him, but he was close to changing his opinion.

He'd dropped Mattie off at dance this morning—to Lucy and Mattie's delight—and Lucy was planning to drive her home after. He'd tried to refuse Lucy's offer, not wanting to add any more taking care of his daughter into her free weekend time. But the look she shot him had wilted his resistance.

Graham had let her win that battle. But when she got here, he planned to fix this thing between them. They had to keep working together, and he didn't want Lucy stuck in this place she'd been in all week. He kind of... missed the Lucy he'd first met. The one who did whatever she wanted—like taking Mattie to dance—and bulldozed her way through life.

Though that Lucy drove him a little crazy, seeing how she'd been acting this week threw him. He—or his in-laws—had obviously offended her. She hadn't said anything out loud, but her actions made it abundantly clear. Graham had noticed a lot less dancing in the front office than when Lucy had first started. She'd also been walking around sporting a *see how happy I am* smile that definitely seemed forced.

Even if Lucy didn't want to admit she was human and had feelings, Graham knew the encounter last week had wounded her.

It had messed with him, too. He hadn't realized his in-laws would be so upset by the idea of him dating. His own parents, who lived across town and whom he saw all of the time, had never given him that impression. In fact, his mother had started casually bringing up women who were single about a year after Brooke's death. Graham had ignored her at first. Then, when she'd continued to hint, he'd told her he didn't plan to remarry.

After that, his mom had stopped saying anything out loud. But he assumed she hadn't completely given up on the idea of making him "happy" again and procuring a few more grandkids. She had enough, between Mattie and Graham's nieces and nephews, but the woman was greedy.

Graham couldn't imagine wanting to date, but if he did change his mind, he now knew he'd have opposition from his in-laws. Brooke had been one of a kind—and their only daughter. He could have guessed his moving on would be hard on them, but he hadn't envisioned they'd react the way they had.

Good thing he hadn't really been on a date with

Lucy. He didn't want to hurt his in-laws. They'd suffered enough already.

He heard a car pull up, and suddenly the dishwasher he'd been unloading felt like the most important thing in the world. Graham would rather unload a hundred dishwashers than face Lucy right now. All week, he hadn't brought up last Saturday's encounter with his in-laws because he'd hoped it would blow over. But it obviously wasn't going to. Which meant he needed to fix it.

He just didn't know exactly how to accomplish that.

Lucy pulled up to Graham's house and put the car in Park. The desire to let Mattie run inside without going in herself was strong.

Superman strong.

During the past week, Lucy and Graham had flitted between professional and uncomfortable. Meeting Graham's in-laws had put a damper on her mood. While she didn't know what exactly they'd said after she'd left the restaurant, Lucy could guess.

She wasn't good enough for Belinda and Phillip Welling. The thought that they might not want her around their granddaughter hurt. Lucy might be carefree, but she only wanted the best for Mattie. She wasn't trying to compare or compete with Mattie's mother. She just wanted to bring some joy into the girl's life.

Right now, Lucy didn't feel so joyful herself—a feeling she'd really like to shake. Hopefully the day she had planned hanging with her sister would chase away the strange sense of melancholy that had sprouted in her over the past week. She wasn't used to this feeling and she didn't know what to do with it.

She'd even gone so far as to pull out her devotional

three times this week—practically a record for her. Olivia was great at doing her quiet time, but Lucy had never been able to stay on task when she attempted the same.

A knock sounded on the passenger window. Mattie stood outside the car, waving. When had she got out?

Lucy rolled the window down. "Yes? How can I help you?"

At her horrible British butler impression, Mattie giggled. "Why are you still sitting in the car?"

"I don't know."

"Okay, then, come on!" She ran toward the house.

As if life were so simple. Lucy turned off the car and forced herself to follow. Mattie had left the front door open, and Lucy walked inside.

Directly in front of her, a wooden staircase led to the second floor—where Lucy assumed Graham's and Mattie's rooms were.

Not that she'd be requesting a tour.

The living room was to her left. Wood floors, leather couches, a flat-screen TV on the wall and a small table in the corner covered with pink and purple Legos gave the space a homey feel. A large island was the only thing separating the kitchen from the living room. The older home had been remodeled...the charm of a midcentury house but with new amenities.

Graham came from the kitchen and met her in the living room, looking casual in jeans and a long-sleeved gray shirt. Lucy had got used to seeing him in business attire at work—dress pants and a shirt and tie. Unfortunately, she knew Graham's clothing habits way too well. By ten in the morning he loosened his tie, and by two in the afternoon he rolled his shirtsleeves up.

If Lucy was in an admitting sort of mood, she'd admit

that she liked today's casual look on Graham. Truthfully, she liked all looks on him. Her employer happened to be a very good-looking man. Thus, the Hollywood nickname that had quickly come to fit him.

Only, today he looked a bit more rumpled than he normally did. His short, dark hair disheveled. Eyes sporting some red. Was he stressed? What about? Work or personal life?

"Thanks for dropping her off. I could have picked her up."

"It's not a problem. I was going by anyway, headed out to the ranch."

"You're going to the ranch?" Mattie chimed in.

"Yep."

"Can I come? I want to ride a horse."

Graham's hand rested on Mattie's shoulder. "Matilda Grace. You can't just invite yourself places. Lucy has her own life. She's got plans today."

Mattie looked crushed. Lucy knew her sister would be fine with Mattie tagging along. They didn't have any big plans—just hanging out.

"If your dad says it's okay, you can come."

"Please?" Mattie started tugging on Graham's arm. "I'll do anything. I'll clean my room."

"Your room's already clean."

"Please, please, please?"

Graham's exhalation ricocheted through the first floor of the house. Finally, after a few more jumps from Mattie, he nodded.

"I'll go change!" She ran up the stairs, leaving Lucy and Graham alone.

"I don't want her—"

"Getting hurt. I know. I'll ask Cash to give her a ride. You trust him, right?"

Graham nodded slowly.

"Okay, then. Why don't you tell Mattie I'm in the car? I can wait for her there and you can get back to…" Whatever it was he'd been doing. What exactly did Graham do in his spare time?

Again, not her business. She turned to go.

"Lucy, wait."

Drat. Escaping sounded so much better. With a super-sized sigh, she faced him.

"I know things have been weird since last Saturday with my in-laws. I'm sorry they acted that way. I think they were just—" He shrugged. "They weren't very nice and I'm sorry. They're not usually that way."

Only for her. Comforting thought.

"They thought we were…" Graham looked at the television that wasn't on. He looked at the floor. Anywhere but at her. "They thought we were *together.*"

"Like dating?"

He finally met her gaze. Nodded.

So they hadn't been upset about her being around Mattie—though that sentiment probably wasn't far behind this one. They'd been upset about her being with Graham.

They must have thought she was encroaching on their daughter's turf. Lucy fought the desire to hunt them down and tell them she didn't have any plans to get involved with their son-in-law. The Wellings could keep Graham. Lucy would stay away from him as long as she got to continue having a relationship with Mattie.

"Well, I'm sure you set them straight."

He nodded again.

"There you have it. You don't need to apologize for them. I get it." Lucy wasn't Welling quality. She'd figured that out right away.

"It's not about you, Lucy."

Right.

"I told them I'm not planning to date anyone, because I'm not. I don't ever plan to remarry."

He didn't have to make up this whole story for her. So they weren't a match in the love department. The idea that Graham would never remarry was crazy.

"You don't have to explain anything to me. It's not like we *were* on a date."

"I know. But I'm telling you, I wouldn't be anyway. I'm really never getting remarried."

What? Graham definitely seemed the type to marry and grow old with someone. Lucy could picture him having more kids, a stepmom for Mattie. The girl would love it. Maybe having a mom again would take away some of Mattie's serious nature and let her be a kid.

What would keep Graham from considering marriage again? He was only thirty-one.

"Was—" Lucy tried to stem the words, but curiosity won, "Was your marriage…that bad?" Graham's frown told her what she already knew—she shouldn't have asked.

"No. It was that good."

Ouch. Why did those words sting? She hardly knew this man. She'd been in town two weeks, and yet his response made her feel as if she'd been shoved from a moving car.

This had nothing to do with her. Then why did it feel as though it did?

Mattie came bounding down the stairs and Lucy wanted to cheer.

"I'm ready. Is this okay?" Mattie pointed to her bright green, long-sleeved T-shirt that was covered in yellow and pink flowers. Coupled with older-looking jeans and scuffed tennis shoes, it was a perfect outfit for getting dirty on the ranch and riding horses.

"You look perfect, Mattie Grace."

She beamed and Lucy's heart did that gooey-melty thing she'd deemed "the Mattie effect."

It was good to see Mattie so happy. Lucy felt as though she'd been making progress with her. At dance this morning, Mattie had even volunteered to do the five basic ballet positions in front of the whole class, her face glowing with pride. While Lucy had befriended the girl in order to bring joy into her life, the opposite was also happening. Lucy was happier knowing Mattie. She already couldn't picture life without Mattie in it.

The thought made Lucy's stomach drop to the spotless mahogany wood floors. Graham's in-laws wouldn't try to stop her from having a relationship with Mattie, would they?

No. According to Graham, that wasn't what they'd been upset about. But Lucy imagined that could quickly change…especially if the Wellings saw her with Graham and Mattie again.

Lucy needed to be careful.

She'd have to keep her distance from Graham—as much as she could, considering she worked with him every weekday, Mattie now attended her dance class on Saturdays and they went to the same church on Sundays. Lucy didn't want to give the Wellings any more reasons to dislike her.

"We'd better go. I'll text you later about dropping Mattie off. Or you can always swing by and get her if you miss her." Lucy's mouth twitched.

Graham shook his head, though his lips did succumb to a slight curve. "I'm sure I'll be fine. I'll find…" He glanced around the living room. "Something to do."

"How about laundry?" Mattie offered. "We always have plenty of that."

"Thank you, Ms. Smarty-Pants."

Mattie grinned, gave Graham a hug and managed to fit in two pirouettes on her way out the front door.

Before Lucy could follow, Graham touched her arm, holding her there. She gently tugged away before he could feel the goose bumps that spread across her skin.

"I mean it, Lucy. I really am sorry for how they acted. You just moved here, but you already do so much for Mattie. She's so much happier with you in her life. I need to know you're not offended."

Graham couldn't have given her a higher compliment. The very thing she'd set out to do, she'd accomplished — or, at least, started to accomplish. Because Lucy definitely wasn't done yet.

"You do this thing when you're mad. Or thinking. You kind of—" Graham moved a hand to his face, then scrubbed it across his chin. "Never mind." He stepped closer. "Lucy." The way he said her name caused her stomach to do a backflip. "I need you to answer me."

Oh, he smelled *good*. "Why do you need this from me? Why do you care so much?"

"We were going to get along, remember? That was our original agreement." A slow grin claimed his mouth. "I was supposed to try to like you. And in that vein, I'd like you to be happy. Not offended by my in-laws."

Give me another whiff of your cologne and you can have anything you want. Lucy's eyelids drifted shut.

"Lucy?"

"Hmm."

"What are you doing?"

Her eyes popped open. Once again, *smelling you* didn't seem like a good answer. "Uh, forgiving you or your in-laws? I'm not sure which."

Graham brightened. "Good. I'll take it." He took a step back. Disappointing man. "I hope you mean it. Otherwise I'll have to make you take a vow."

Lucy knew what he meant. She *knew* he was talking about their previous oath, but the statement brought to mind wedding veils and white lace. He was never going to marry again.

Never.

That word held so much finality. It wasn't as though Lucy had thought they were going to date. And really, her views on serious dating weren't any different than Graham's.

So, technically, this conversation was a good thing. It just…didn't feel that way.

Lucy managed a strangled goodbye, then turned and walked out of the house. She made sure to walk slowly, as though to prove what she'd just learned in her conversation with Graham didn't matter. Because, of course, it didn't.

If anything, that feeling settling like cement in her lungs was relief.

Chapter 7

Lucy and Olivia stood near the corral railing at the Circle M and watched Cash and Mattie take a few slow circles around on horseback. Mattie sat perched just in front of Cash in the saddle, helmet on, smile stretching from ear to ear.

"She's adorable." Olivia waved, and though Mattie looked as if she wanted to wave back, she didn't let go of the saddle horn.

"She is," Lucy agreed.

Cash rode over to them. "Mattie wants to go out on the ranch."

Lucy shoved her sunglasses on top of her head. "You sure, Mattie?"

The girl nodded, lips pressed into a straight line. Serious but determined.

"Be careful with her." When Cash leveled her a look, Lucy raised her hands. "Hey, I trust you. I just know Graham, and you're carrying precious cargo there. Plus, I don't want to get blamed for anything. I already saw a small scratch on her arm. I can't imagine how much trouble I'll be in for that."

Mattie had been practicing lassoing with a small rope and propped-up saddle earlier. She'd also thrown rocks, dug in the dirt and jumped into a pile of hay. Her nails had enough dirt under them to fill a sandbox. She was filthy and happy and Graham was going to kill Lucy.

Olivia pushed away from the fence. "Give us a minute and we'll ride with you."

"Absolutely not." Cash's comment cut through the peaceful day.

It sounded nothing like her brother-in-law. Lucy glanced between Cash and Olivia as they had an old-fashioned Western stare down. Cash sported a *don't mess with me* look that, although serious, made Lucy want to laugh. She had that tendency in uncomfortable situations.

"You guys want me to get the guns so you can have a duel?"

"Nope." Cash gentled his tone, but the steel underneath stayed intact. "Mattie and I will be back in a bit. Why don't you two head inside? Liv, you can rest." With a tug on the reins, Cash and Mattie rode out of the corral.

Rest? What was going on between the two of them? "What was that about?" Lucy studied her sister's profile. Olivia let out a strangled sound and strode toward the house. Lucy caught up to her. "Is there trouble in marriage-land?"

"No."

"That's good to hear. I've never seen him be so bossy with you. It was kind of marvelous."

Olivia's lips succumbed to a slight curve. "Not funny. He's just being his typical self."

"Meaning?"

They reached the front door, and Olivia stomped inside. She went into the kitchen, got out two glasses and filled them with water from the fridge. "Meaning he's being overprotective." She gave one to Lucy, then went to sit on the couch.

Lucy followed. "Since when won't he let you ride a horse? Isn't that a little outrageous?"

"Yep." Olivia rested a hand on her stomach in a maternal gesture. "It is, sort of. Except he has his reasons."

Lucy's eyes widened and she leaned forward. "You're not…are you…?"

Olivia nodded, glowing and fighting tears at the same time. "I'm pregnant."

Lucy let out a whoop and grabbed her sister in a fierce hug. When she pulled back, Olivia was full-on crying, rivers of moisture running down her cheeks.

"Uh-oh. Have you turned into a crazy emotional mess?"

Another nod.

"It's kind of great to see my big sister, who's usually so put together, falling apart."

"Brat."

Lucy laughed. "Tell me everything. Is it really not okay to ride a horse when you're pregnant? I didn't know that."

Love and annoyance warred on Liv's features. "It's not a rule or anything, but a lot of people say not to. Of course, I didn't meet Cash until after my miscarriage, but he knows how hard it was on me. He's turned overprotective—even more than usual. I feel like I'm under some kind of Cash-prescribed bed rest. Not that he's gone that far. He's just being careful, which I do appreciate even if he drives me nuts sometimes. And I guess—" Liv sighed. "He *might* be right, since I don't want to do anything to harm the baby." Smile lines framed her eyes. "But don't you dare tell him."

"I'm totally Team Olivia. We have the same blood running through our veins. That's, like, impossible to trump."

Liv's smile grew. "I'm only a few weeks. We just figured it out. I probably won't tell anyone but you and Janie for now. And Mom and Dad."

"Boy or girl?"

"We won't know that for a while."

"Please tell me you're going to find out."

"I want to. I think we will."

Lucy sat back against the couch cushions and propped her feet up on the coffee table. "Now the whole—" she deepened her voice "—'go in and rest' comment makes more sense."

"That was a horrible impression of Cash. His voice is much more attractive than that."

"While I *might* agree that was a bad impression, I'm going to call a gag-me offense on the other part. Yuck! I don't need to hear any of those sentiments."

"You're really still a twelve-year-old girl at heart, aren't you?"

"Pretty much." Lucy would be offended if it weren't so true. "I cannot believe I'm going to be an aunt! We are going to get into all sorts of trouble together."

At Olivia's look, Lucy wiped the humor from her face. "And by that I mean I will be a perfect role model."

"You just might be. Watching you with Mattie is seeing you in a whole new light."

"It is? Why?"

"You're great with her. Almost…maternal."

What? At twenty-four, Lucy hadn't expected to hear

that word used to describe her for a long, long time. She had no idea what to say in response to that. "Mattie's pretty great."

"True." Olivia's mouth lifted as though she knew Lucy was sidestepping the conversation. "I thought we could invite Graham over for dinner tonight since the Smiths are coming."

That would be the social thing to do. "We should?"

Lucy was excited to hang with Jack and Janie Smith—great friends of Cash and Olivia's. She couldn't wait to get her hands on their newborn daughter, Abigail, and see their adorable three-year-old son, Tucker. But did they have to invite Graham?

Her sister quirked an eyebrow. "Of course. What's with you, anyway? It's not like you not to include the whole county. You never leave anyone out."

True. And since she and Graham were *friends*, she should want him there. Lucy was fine being friends with Graham. She just wasn't okay with losing a relationship with Mattie. And if Lucy and Graham got too close or spent too much time together and the Wellings found out, they would not be pleased. Lucy didn't want to do anything to upset them or have them disrupt her relationship with the girl.

"I'm beginning to think you have a crush on the man."

"What?" Lucy snapped her attention back to Olivia. "Why would you say that?"

"You're spending an awful lot of time with his daughter, and you're acting kind of funny about him."

She scoffed. "Spending time with Mattie has nothing to do with Graham. She's so serious, I just want to help her loosen up and have fun."

Olivia stayed silent.

"Fine. I can admit the man's attractive." Lucy ignored her sister's growing smile. "But attraction isn't the same thing as a crush. I'm not going to start sending him notes or anything—*Do you like me? Check yes or no.* I mean, he hasn't even pulled my pigtails."

Her comments were met with an exasperated sigh and shaking head.

"So, what happened between you and Bodie when you moved? Are you still talking to him?"

"Sometimes." Lucy shrugged. "There just wasn't anything special there."

"There never is."

"What does that mean?"

"You never go on more than two dates with anyone— three, tops. What's up with that? Why don't you ever date anyone?"

"I date all the—"

"More than a few dates," Olivia interrupted.

"I just don't do the serious thing."

"Why not?"

Lucy didn't want to discuss this. "I just…don't. Look what happened to you."

Olivia glanced at the wedding photo of her and Cash hanging on the wall. They were standing in the back of a pickup truck, kissing. Lucy didn't quite understand the reasoning on that one, but it did make for a great photo. Liv's hand slid across her stomach again. "I'm pretty happy."

"Yeah, now. But before…" Lucy didn't want to bring up all of this.

"It was worth it to get to him. All of that junk was worth it if Cash was the end result."

"Sap."

"Cynic."

"Me? A cynic? Impossible. I'm the most positive person you know. I might be the happiest person in the state of Texas."

"Then why the 'no serious' thing?"

"It's easier that way. I can love everybody, enjoy people, and I don't have to worry about…"

"Getting hurt."

"No! That's not it."

"Then explain it."

She couldn't. Lucy had never been able to. How could she explain what she didn't fully understand herself? It wasn't about getting hurt, like Liv said. It was about having fun and living life as an adventure. Taking each day as a gift and enjoying every minute.

"Have you prayed about it?"

"I pray all of the time." Especially when things got so out of hand she finally remembered God was supposed to be in charge of her life, not her. But Lucy was working on that. Hadn't she just made an attempt to do better this week?

"I meant about dating."

"No, not really." Lucy hadn't prayed about her dating life, but then again, nothing was wrong in that area. Why bother God with it?

"All I'm saying is that sometimes we head down our own path while forgetting to ask God what His plan is. It helps to ask first, then act. Maybe what God has for you is different than what you've decided. What if a relationship were possible with Graham? Would you be open to it?"

Heat burned in Lucy's chest. "That particular subject isn't one I need to ask God about." Unexpected frustration tightened her vocal cords. "Graham's never going to get married again. We just had that conversation a few hours ago. There's nothing between us now and there won't be in the future, so I don't have to waste any of God's time asking about something I already know the answer to."

"Okay." Olivia raised the palms of her hands. "I'll back off. I'm only trying to save you from some of the heartache Cash and I learned the hard way."

Why did Olivia want to push Lucy into the serious relationship *she'd* always wanted? Why couldn't her sister understand that they just didn't want the same things?

Lucy shoved up from the couch. She and Liv could have a conversation like this and still be fine afterward, but right now Lucy needed some space. "If you're pregnant, you must be starving. Do you need some grapes and cheese? To be fed like a queen? I'll get you something."

"I'm fine."

"Then you should rest like Cash said. I'm going to check on Mattie." Lucy tried not to stomp on her way to the front door. She pushed outside and headed for the barn.

That conversation with Olivia reeked like the stuff on Cash's boots at the end of the day. Her sister was being nosy, acting as though the decisions Lucy made were a bad thing. Olivia just didn't understand. She'd always wanted that whole true-love bit, but Lucy had just been less of a dreamer in that area. And she'd never missed it.

Only…hearing of Olivia's pregnancy had sprouted a small seed of doubt in Lucy. Didn't she want that one day? Babies? A husband?

Maybe.

She'd settle for a maybe. But definitely not anytime soon. Lucy knew in order to get to that point, she'd have to let someone in and go on more than three dates, like her sister had said, but she wasn't there yet. Just…not yet.

Lucy spotted Cash and Mattie riding toward the barn and waited for them to approach.

"She did great." Cash lifted Mattie down, and Lucy grabbed her, squeezing the girl in a hug. "I've got a few things to do and then I'll head in. Where's Liv?"

"Inside *resting*." Lucy put Mattie on the ground.

Cash shifted in the saddle, face wreathing in a grin. "She told you?"

She nodded. "Congratulations, McCowboy."

"Thanks. Did she actually listen to me about taking a nap?"

"I don't know. She got all nosy, so I came outside to find Mattie."

"Ah. Sister fun." He tugged on the brim of his hat. "Okay, well, I'll be back in a bit."

She turned her attention to Mattie as he rode away. "So, how was it?"

"Amazing." Mattie twirled in a circle. "It was like flying."

"I'm glad. Were you scared?"

"Nope."

"Brave girl."

"Daddy probably would have been worried about me, but he didn't need to be. I wasn't nervous."

Speaking of Graham, Lucy should probably check in with him and let him know things were going well. And she should invite him to dinner. She got out her phone and texted, then slipped it back into her pocket. She had to get over the weirdness she'd felt after talking to him earlier. So his in-laws didn't love her. So he wasn't getting married again.

So what? Unlike what her sister thought, she and Graham definitely weren't on a path toward a relationship. A friendship? Yes. But all that other stuff, Liv was going to have to let go of.

When his phone rang, Graham set the grocery bags on the kitchen floor and checked the screen. His mom. He answered.

"You went out on a date and didn't tell me?"

"Mom, I didn't go on a date." He tucked the phone between his ear and shoulder and started putting vegetables in the fridge.

"That's not what the Wellings said when I ran into them yesterday."

"They saw me and Mattie with Lucy, and they assumed, Mom. That doesn't make it real. I told them I'm not dating anyone, especially Lucy."

"Who's Lucy?"

Graham moved on to the next bag, sliding whole-grain crackers and snacks for Mattie into the bin he kept for packing school lunches. "She's covering for Hollie, remember?"

"Oh, that's right. Maybe you should ask this Lucy on a date. How old is she? What does she look like?"

She's beautiful. And that has nothing to do with anything.

His mom continued without waiting for an answer. "I don't even know who she is, but I like her already. I have a feeling about this, Graham—"

He groaned, not that his mother noticed. Her *feelings*

were notorious for being overly dramatic and wrong. Graham, his dad and his sisters teased her about them all the time.

"Mom, I'm unpacking groceries. I need to go."

"Fine. You can tell me about her when you come for lunch after church tomorrow."

Without agreeing, Graham said goodbye and hung up. He grabbed the meat to put into the freezer. When his phone rang again, he answered without checking the caller ID. "Mom, I told you I'm not talking about this."

"I am not your mother. I am a snort."

It was Lucy. And she was referencing a Dr. Seuss book. His phone was a three-ring circus today. "What's wrong? Is Mattie okay?"

"Yes, not that you'd know a thing about it. I texted you almost fifteen minutes ago and didn't hear back. I thought maybe someone had abducted you. I figured you'd be on high phone alert in case I called about Mattie."

"I must have missed it while I was driving home. If Mattie's fine, what's up? Want me to swing out and get her?"

"Actually, the Smiths are coming for dinner. Do you want to come? You can just get Mattie then."

Surely his increased pulse rate had to do with seeing friends and nothing to do with the woman on the other end of the phone. Cash and Jack were some of his closest friends in town, though they rarely all got together. Graham could use a night of adult conversation.

"Sure. Sounds good."

She rattled off a time, and they said goodbye. Graham hung up and spoke to the empty kitchen. "There's nothing going on between me and Lucy, so everybody just leave me alone."

He left the rest of the groceries to unpack later and walked into the living room, dropping onto the couch. The photo album of Brooke that Mattie constantly looked through was on the coffee table. Graham grabbed it and opened to Mattie's favorite page. He ran a finger down the photos, sinking into the memories.

He missed her, but with each day Brooke was beginning to feel further and further away. Like a fading photo he couldn't protect. His mom wanted him to move on. The Wellings didn't want him to. Everyone had an opinion, making him feel like a piece of taffy stretched in every direction. But Graham could only deal with his own emotions. And he just wasn't willing to give Brooke up.

If he had his way, he never would.

Chapter 8

"Your dad should be here any minute. In fact, we should probably wash your hands before he arrives." Lucy should at least make an attempt to remove some of the dirt from under Mattie's fingernails.

They went into the bathroom, and Lucy ran the water until it was lukewarm.

"I hope Daddy wasn't lonely without me today." Mattie lathered soap between her hands.

Did normal five-year-olds worry about their parents while they were out having fun? Lucy didn't think so. Just another reason this little girl was one of a kind.

"Did you think he would be? What does your dad do after work and on the weekends?"

Mattie continued to scrub the soap up to her elbows as though she were a surgeon. "Work."

"All of the time?"

"No. He also cleans, and packs my lunches, and goes to Grandpa and Grandma's house—my other grandparents, not the ones you met."

All exciting things. "What does your dad do for fun?"

Her little forehead crinkled and she finally slipped her hands under the water. "What do you mean?"

"Fun. Like does he golf? Run? Hunt?"

Each thing was met with a shake of Mattie's head.

"Watch movies?"

"You mean like *Frozen*?"

"Kind of." Though not really.

"He usually falls asleep during that movie."

"What about watching TV?"

Mattie perked up. "He reads."

Hmm. Lucy flipped the water off, and Mattie used the hand towel.

"And he watches baseball and football sometimes."

Sounded as if Graham rarely relaxed or did anything for himself.

Lucy's conscience raised its hands, screaming for attention. She wanted to ignore it the way she did laundry, but her passionate heart wouldn't let her.

Graham was exactly the type of person who needed someone like her to intervene in his life. Lucy knew without having to peek into Graham's windows that he was the best kind of father. She imagined he read to Mattie every night and packed healthy lunches and was über-calm all of the time. But did he ever have fun? Let loose? According to Mattie, not really. Of course, there was a chance the girl just didn't know, but Lucy doubted it.

Usually, she would be all about bringing a little happy into someone else's life. But diving into Graham's was a bit complicated.

His in-laws didn't like the idea of them spending time together, even if they weren't dating. So how would Lucy ever go about helping him kick back if she couldn't be seen around him?

Unless…the Wellings didn't know.

She could totally help Graham if his in-laws didn't find out.

Mattie flew out of the bathroom, and Lucy followed at a slower pace. She'd have to come up with a plan, though she wasn't sure where to begin.

She shrugged. She'd pray about it. She'd think about it. The idea would come to her.

It always did.

"Thanks for dinner." Graham set a pile of plates by the sink, and Olivia looked up from loading the dishwasher.

"No problem. I'm glad you could come. We'll have to do it again sometime."

"That would be great." Graham had enjoyed dinner. The smaller group setting fit him, and being with Jack and Cash was always easy. They'd reminisced and talked work, sports teams and family. Graham hadn't realized Olivia was pregnant. It had come up in conversation tonight, though Olivia had mentioned they weren't sharing the news publicly yet. Cash and Olivia both looked over the moon, and Graham was happy for them.

The memory of finding out Brooke was pregnant slipped into his mind. After he'd got over his initial shock, Graham had pored over parenting books. He'd thought he was ready for Mattie to be born. Until he'd held Matilda Grace Redmond in his arms for the first time.

Nothing prepared a father for that moment.

His heart hadn't been the same since.

Speaking of his heart, Graham should probably get Mattie and head home. The girl looked as if she'd been dipped in a puddle of mud sometime today and could very much use a bath tonight. But she also looked happy. Sometimes Mattie was so serious, so grown-up, that Graham forgot she was five and *should* be playing in mud puddles.

That was the kind of stuff he'd done as a kid. He'd ridden bikes with the neighbors and his sisters, and had stayed outside playing until dark. He'd come home dirty. And happy. Brooke had been raised differently, though. She'd been an only child, and the Wellings had been strict. When he'd first met her, Graham had thought Brooke would never go for him. She'd been raised with money, and he'd been raised somewhere in the middle class.

But Brooke hadn't been like her parents. She didn't have the same sense of importance they sometimes had. The kind the Wellings had communicated, probably without realizing it, when they'd met Lucy.

Graham wasn't a fan when they acted that way.

Lucy had said she forgave him and them, and Graham hoped it was true. He didn't want her offended. He owed Lucy for today. She definitely brought out a side of his daughter he loved to see. Sometimes he didn't know how to make that same little girl appear himself.

He should thank her, but she was with Olivia and Janie, cooing over the Smiths' newborn daughter. Graham didn't want to interrupt. Instead, he headed upstairs to find Mattie. She and Tucker had been tearing through the house all night.

He found the kids in a bedroom, a basket of toys spread across the floor.

"Mattie, time to clean up." His daughter looked at

him and then went back to playing. Graham knelt beside her. "Did you hear me?"

She nodded. "I don't want to go yet."

"It's late, honey, and you've been here all day." It wasn't like Mattie to argue. She must be exhausted. Graham had heard about all of her activities earlier. She'd been flying high when he'd got here for dinner.

Graham started picking up the toys, and Tucker joined in without being asked. Mattie didn't.

"Mattie, you need to help."

She made a little effort, picking up a couple of things. After they'd tidied everything, Graham scooped her up. He offered Tucker a ride, which he refused, instead running ahead of them out the bedroom door.

Mattie's head rested against his shoulder on the way down the stairs. What would Graham do without his little girl? God had known what He was doing back when Brooke got pregnant. Having a piece of her left behind went a long way toward healing Graham on a daily basis.

He paused between the living room and kitchen. "We're going to take off. Thanks for everything."

Everyone called out goodbyes.

"I'll walk you out." Lucy came over, meeting them by the front door. She slid on a zip-up sweatshirt, then grabbed their coats, draping Mattie's over her shoulders. She opened the door for him and they stepped outside. The dark night sky twinkled with countless stars.

Cool air nipped at them, and Graham snuggled Mattie closer. "Can you thank Ms. Lucy for the fun day?"

Instead, his daughter lunged into Lucy's arms.

Traitor.

He grabbed his jacket from Lucy, slipping it on as they walked. At the car, Graham opened the back door and Lucy put Mattie in her booster seat, helping buckle her in.

She finished saying goodbye and shut the door.

"You're getting pretty good at that." He motioned to the car seat. "Guess stealing them from other people's cars is like a crash course."

Lucy propped her hands on the hips of her faded jeans. Tonight, her hair was in a loose braid over one shoulder. She had on her green Converse shoes and a T-shirt peeking out from under her sweatshirt that said Save Ferris.

Had she dressed casual so she could bum around the ranch with Mattie?

This woman was growing on him.

He pointed to her shirt. "Aren't you too young for that movie?"

Her eyes narrowed, lips curving slightly. Every time they did, Graham felt as though he'd won a prize.

"I like old movies."

"Ah." He rubbed a hand across his chest. "Did you just call *Ferris Bueller's Day Off* an old movie?"

"Well, it is."

"Now I feel ancient."

When Lucy laughed, that victorious feeling skyrocketed.

"So, did you have a good day? Get a lot accomplished?"

"I did." He'd expected to miss Mattie like crazy, but Graham was getting better about her traipsing off with Lucy.

"What did you do?"

"A little work at the office and some at home."

Lucy tilted her head. "Do you ever have fun, Hollywood?"

"What does that name mean?"

She grinned. "That's for me to know and you to endure not knowing."

Seriously. "Yes, I have fun." Not that he could think of any examples at the moment. "It's good to see you back to being yourself."

"How do you know what I'm normally like? We haven't known each other that long."

"It's not hard to tell with you." And it wasn't. Lucy was sunshine and rainbows on the gloomiest day.

"It's good to be back. I'm extremely delightful to be around."

He groaned.

"I can't believe you had most of the day to yourself and you didn't relax and do something enjoyable. What about a movie?"

"By myself?"

"Uh, yeah. Haven't you ever been to the movies by yourself? In the middle of an afternoon? You buy the biggest popcorn and the largest drink, a box of candy, and you settle in—" Lucy waved her hand. "Never mind. I can see I've already lost you. Looks like you definitely need some help in the fun department, Graham Redmond."

"That's not true. I'm perfectly content. I don't need any help having fun."

"I think I'm going to have to step up my position, from best fill-in-on-maternity-leave office person *ever* to Director of Fun."

Panic thrummed in his veins. "Lucy—"

"Did you know there's a business in Colorado where that's an actual position? I would be so good at that job."

Was this what he got for wanting the carefree Lucy back? He'd hoped she would stop being upset about his in-laws, not make him her new pet project. What had he been thinking? Maybe he should go find the Wellings. They'd certainly put a damper on Lucy's good mood.

But even though the woman drove him a bit crazy when she was going full throttle, he did like seeing her happy.

He just didn't want her intruding in his life the way she was threatening to.

"Lucy." He took a step closer. Even with a foot of space between them, the close proximity sent his pulse flying. "I do not—" frustration over his unwanted attraction to Lucy caused his voice to drop "—want or need you messing with my life. Please. Tell me you're listening. Tell me you're not going to do something crazy. I do not need you as the director of fun in my life."

Lucy's lips curved, only this time, it didn't feel like a victory. "We'll have to see about that."

On Monday morning, Lucy laughed as Danielle Abbott, the nurse in Graham's office, squealed and waved her arms with excitement. In the way of nurses, Danielle was calm and put together under the most dire of circumstances. But today something had her in rare form.

"I have never seen you act so giddy. What is going on?"

"I thought we were going to wait a year to get married. A whole year." Danielle propped her hands on her ample hips. "And I was fine with that. At least, I was trying to be fine." She fanned herself with her hand, sending the tips of her short, red-orange hair flying. "Phew, I'm hot. Got myself all worked up."

"So, what changed?" Lucy heard the front door of the office open. She slid from her perch on the reception desk, where she'd been sitting while talking to Danielle.

"Come talk to me when you're done checking him in."

"That's cruel to make me wait."

Danielle chuckled, taking off for her back office area while Lucy greeted Mr. Birl, who was in for a gash instead of a rash this time. The man could come up with all sorts of interesting diseases and issues. Most of the time, he left without so much as a prescription. Lucy had once attempted to convince him on the phone that nothing was wrong with him. It hadn't gone over well. The more she'd tried to talk him out of it, the more he'd come up with. She'd ended up having to schedule him for an extra-long appointment.

After Mr. Birl signed in, Lucy grabbed his chart and walked back into Danielle's space. Large white cabinets and counters lined the sides for processing lab work, with a massive table in the middle that Danielle used for doing paperwork.

Lucy dropped the chart onto the table. "So, what's the rest of the story? What's up?"

Danielle finished applying lip gloss and tossed her purse into one of the lower cupboards. "We moved up the date of the wedding."

"Really? To when?"

"Two weeks from now. Twelve days, more precisely."

"What?" Lucy imagined she must resemble a fish right now, mouth flopping open and shut. "How?"

Instead of looking freaked, Danielle appeared calm and happy. "We've both been through really hard marriages in the past, so we were planning to take extra time with our engagement…after dating for two years already. But we finally decided we don't want to wait. I'm forty-four years old. I'm done waiting. I'm ready.

"We had so much of the wedding already planned that we just needed a place. My uncle has a beautiful home near San Antonio, and we're going to have the wedding there."

"Oh, San Antonio! I've never been." There were all sorts of places in Texas Lucy wanted to visit. She could start there. Not that she was necessarily invited. She'd known Danielle for only a few weeks. "I'm not saying I'm invited," Lucy backpedaled. "I just meant—"

"Are you kidding?" Danielle came around the table. "Of course you're invited. You. Graham. Hollie if she wants to make the drive with a newborn. You're my people."

"Aww." Lucy hugged Danielle, and the woman's arms swallowed her up in a tight grip. Danielle gave the best hugs. "I'm so happy for you. Let me know if you need anything. I'd be happy to help."

"Exactly what kind of help are you offering?"

"Hmm. Well, I can't sew, so nothing like that. And I'm pretty horrible about arranging flowers, so that's out."

Danielle's laugh echoed in the room.

Lucy started checking things off on her fingers. "Can't sing, so no solos. Can't play any instruments. Oh!" She raised her hands. "But I can dance. If you need any lessons, let me know."

"You know, I just might take you up on that. Thanks for the offer, hon. I'd better get Mr. Birl into the exam room. If we get behind with him it will ruin the whole morning."

Danielle grabbed his chart and headed up front.

When she disappeared through the door, Lucy squealed and spun around. While drifting off to sleep last night, she'd been praying over how to implement her new Director of Fun position in Graham's life. This morning, the answer had fallen into her lap.

The two of them being invited to the same out-of-town wedding was a perfect solution to her dilemma. She could get Graham to relax and have fun, and the Wellings would have no idea she and Graham had done anything together.

Lucy couldn't wait to inform Graham they'd be going together.

She assumed he'd be *just* as excited as she was.

Graham winced at the knock on his office door. His head pounded as though someone had recently used it as a bass drum. The afternoon had already been long, and he was only two appointments past lunch. If Walt Birl tried to come back in this afternoon with another made up issue, Graham wasn't sure he could handle it.

"Hey." Lucy poked her head inside. "Can I come in?"

"Sure." Graham unbuttoned his sleeves and rolled them up.

She checked her watch. "Right on time."

"What?"

"Nothing." Wearing black dress pants, a white shirt and red heels that matched her lipstick, her hair down and curling past her shoulders, she looked like all sorts of trouble. Graham definitely should have told her scrubs were mandatory.

To make things worse, she came over and perched on the edge of his desk.

After Saturday night at the ranch, Graham had come to the conclusion that he needed to be careful around Lucy. Keep a bit of distance between the two of them. Partly because he feared she would follow through on her idea to interfere in his life and partly because he just…needed the space.

He was having more and more trouble not being distracted by Lucy. Her involvement in Mattie's life and love for his daughter made it hard for him to keep his thoughts from running beyond friendship. But he didn't want his head going anywhere further than that in regard to Lucy, or anyone else, for that matter.

Graham felt a bit like a child stomping his foot, screaming that he didn't want things to change. But it was true. He didn't. He liked his life. He liked taking care of his daughter and living with the memories of Brooke as his first and only love.

He would fight anything that tried to change those feelings.

Every day, when Lucy turned the phones off and left the office, Graham gave a giant sigh of relief. So the fact that she was inches away from him, looking beautiful and smelling like a sweet mixture of coconut and lime, wasn't helping his already testy mood.

Graham pushed his rolling chair farther from his desk. And Lucy. "What's up?"

"Did you hear Danielle moved the wedding up to two weeks from now?"

He dug his fingers into his temples. "She might have told me something about it this morning. I'm not sure I caught all of it, though. That seems really fast."

"It does, but she's happy."

"Good." He nodded. "That's good, then." If Danielle was happy, Graham didn't have to delve into figuring out why everything had changed.

And Lucy was in his office because...

"We're both invited, so I thought we should ride together since it's going to be down in San Antonio."

"Uh, no."

"Why not?"

"'Why?' is the real question. Don't you have to teach dance that weekend?"

"Dance is in the morning. You know that. We could leave right after class."

"Is this part of your get-me-to-have-fun plan?"

"No." Her arms crossed. "Okay, yes."

She really knew how to hold out. "Why would we need to leave that early on Saturday morning when San Antonio is only an hour away? What time is the wedding?"

"Late afternoon."

"So, my question bears repeating. Why would we leave that early?"

"We? That means you said yes, right?"

"No."

"I'll take that as a yes. We need to leave early so we can have an adventure."

The pounding in his head ramped up to jackhammer speed. "I don't want to have an adventure. I don't have time to have an adventure." Though he sounded like a pouty child, he didn't retract the statements.

"Too bad." Lucy pushed off the desk. "Do you need a prescription, Dr. Redmond? You look like you're in pain."

"I'm fine."

"And crabby." She broke into a smile and turned to leave his office.

His chance to get out of her crazy plan was slipping away. "Wait. I have Mattie. I can't even go to the wedding."

She paused with a hand on the doorknob. "I'm sure Mattie could go. But I also know your parents watch her. This town isn't big enough for secrets."

True.

"And are you really telling me that after Danielle's worked for you since you first opened the clinic, you're not going to attend her wedding?"

He huffed. It was all he had in his arsenal right now. "Fine, I'm going. But not with you."

"Oh, Hollywood. It's sweet when you get all cranky and think you're going to get your way." She beamed. "We'll leave after dance. I'll pick you up."

Chapter 9

"I don't understand why you have to drive." Almost two weeks later, Lucy stood next to her yellow Beetle in Graham's driveway. As threatened, she'd appeared shortly after dance. Wearing a pink, short-sleeved shirt with skinny jeans, colorful heeled sandals and her hair down, she looked as if she could be featured in a magazine ad. She also looked far happier than he felt.

The weather had turned warm after a few days of not getting above sixty, and though the sun heated the back of his green polo shirt, Graham couldn't help a sigh. He'd dropped off Mattie at his mom and dad's right after dance, and the three of them were excited for a day together. He wished he could say the same about spending the day with Lucy. Four times he'd tried to break off the plans for going to the wedding with her. Four times she'd completely ignored him.

Stubborn woman.

He might not stand a chance in an argument with Lucy, but he *was* going to drive. He still had a swipe left on his man card.

"Listen, Duchess, you've already forced me into this day. I'm winning this battle."

"Duchess?"

"Yeah." Graham motioned to her. "You definitely have that regal thing going on where you expect everyone to be at your beck and call. You expect everything to go your way. You—"

"Enough."

His lips twitched. "Don't want me to keep going?"

"Fine." Lucy rolled her eyes and threw her hands into the air. "You can drive. I'll get the stuff."

What stuff?

She yanked open her car door, grabbed something from the backseat, then marched over to his car with her arms full.

Graham followed, wanting to repeat her eye roll about now. "What is all of that?"

She looked at him as though he were crazy. As though the overflowing basket in her arms was self-explanatory. "Road-trip supplies. What else?"

"Road trip? We're only driving an hour away, Lucy."

Her eyes widened. "Exactly."

"Are there games in there?"

When she avoided eye contact with him, he had the answer to that question.

"Maybe," she conceded. "But there's also food."

"I don't like it when people eat in my car."

She reeled back. "You have a child! Are you telling me Mattie never eats a snack in the car?"

"Every so often, but she's very neat. When we get home, I use the garage vacuum to clean the backseat."

"Are you saying that I'm messier than Mattie?"

How to answer that question without inflaming Lucy's already expressive behavior? When he didn't come up with a response, she let out a strangled "Argh." Her head swung back and forth. "Offensive on so many levels. You're just going to have to vacuum after me, too, Hollywood, because I'm bringing snacks. It's not a road trip without them."

"It's not a road trip." The under-his-breath comment set Lucy's lake-blue eyes flashing.

Graham finally opened the back door to his car, and she put the items on the seat. She faced him, confusion evident. "Do you have floor mats on top of floor mats?"

"Yes."

"What for?"

"The top one keeps the bottom one from getting dirty and ruined."

"That's the craziest thing I've ever heard. We can add 'neat freak' to your growing list of descriptions." She went back to her car and returned with a load of clothes and a bag. "My stuff for the wedding," she explained on her way past.

Graham had already laid his black suit, blue shirt, striped tie and dress shoes out in the trunk. One hand was all he'd needed to put his stuff into the car. Lucy, not so much.

"Oh!" She held up a finger. "One more thing."

Only one?

She leaned into her car and grabbed a bright orange purse. "Okay, now I'm ready."

Did she expect him to cheer?

Graham resisted another huff/sigh/whine/stomp of his foot. It was no use fighting Lucy. He just had to get through today. He'd endure Lucy's company and do his best to keep a nice wall between them. One with brick. And ivy. And a moat around it.

They took off, and a short way into the drive, Lucy started digging in her purse. She surfaced with an iPod.

He nodded to it. "What's that for?"

"It plays music. Graham, meet technology." Lucy held the iPod toward him. "Technology, this is Graham."

"I know what an iPod is, Duchess. I'm asking why your iPod is in my car. I have music."

"You know, I think you're meaning to annoy me with that nickname, but I kind of like it. I feel like it fits."

"I'm not surprised."

"And, in answer to your question, I made us a trip playlist. Do you have Bluetooth or do I need to hook up with a cord?"

"Bluetooth."

"Perfect."

"Did you say you made a trip playlist? Is that like making a mix tape?"

"Pretty much. Every good trip has its own song list. Then, when you want to remember the time, you can just listen to the playlist and voilà!"

"Why would we want to remember today?"

"Ouch." Lucy put a hand over her heart. "Are you always this crabby on Saturdays or is this especially for me? Do you need a cup of coffee or something?"

Actually, he could go for a cup. And he had been rather short-tempered this morning. He probably needed to tone it down a bit. "Why? Do you have some in that bag of yours?"

She grinned like a Cheshire cat. "I most certainly do." Lucy twisted between the seats and reached into the back, returning with a thermos and a paper cup. Somehow she managed to pour without spilling.

"Cream?"

"Sure." Graham watched her dig into the bag, this time coming out with a few small half-and-half containers. "Two, please."

She added them to the coffee, then put a cover on the cup and handed it to him.

"You're forgiven for bringing along all of that stuff in the backseat."

Lucy laughed and tossed the coffee thermos into the bag.

"Where's yours?"

"I don't drink coffee."

His jaw dropped. "Is that an actual thing? I always thought people were lying when they said that."

She shook her head, but her lips curved. His pulse did that annoying racing thing, which he ignored. "It's a real thing." She rummaged in her purse, coming up with a soda bottle. "I'm a Diet Coke girl."

"That stuff isn't good for you."

"And coffee is?"

"There have been numerous studies—"

Lucy plugged her ears like a two-year-old. "I don't want to hear it. We all have our vices."

True.

If Lucy didn't drink coffee, that meant she'd gone out to buy those supplies just for him.

"Thanks for this." He held up the cup, then took a sip.

"You're welcome." Lucy tipped her soda bottle to his coffee. "Cheers to our first road trip together." She held up a finger before he could speak. "And if you mumble something about it being our last, it really will be your last, Redmond."

"Yes, ma'am."

"I love this song." Lucy turned up the music and started singing along. "Waited till I had some fun. Don't know why you didn't run. Left you by the house of sun."

"Those aren't the words."

"Who cares?" Lucy continued to sing loudly. "But I wanted to break away. Wished that I could play again. Like I did in the band."

"Me. I care." Graham's comment was drowned out, and despite his total annoyance with the woman next to him, he started to laugh. She was so far off, the phrases didn't even make sense.

"Come on—sing along." Lucy held her soda bottle to his mouth like a microphone.

"No way."

"I'm telling you, you are going to remember this trip whenever you hear this music."

She went back to her off-key singing, and for once, Graham had to admit she was right.

Every time he heard this song, he would think about Lucy and how she looked at this moment, singing her loudest, completely content to ride in a car all day with her snacks and supplies.

She paused from her singing when the next song started. "What's my girl up to today?"

"Hanging with my parents. My nieces and nephews are going over later, too, so Mattie will not miss me one single bit."

"That's good."

"Yep."

"The question is, will you miss her?"

Graham stared straight ahead, hoping Lucy wouldn't notice his face heating at the truth. Because he didn't plan to admit to anyone that for the amount of time he and Lucy had been in the car, Graham hadn't thought about his daughter once. That had to be some kind of father crime or something.

His mind had been occupied with the woman next to him.

And he didn't know what to do about that.

"Admit it. You're having a good time." Lucy took a bite of gelato as she and Graham strolled along San Antonio's beautiful River Walk.

Graham had dressed in jeans, a green polo and brown leather sneakers for their day of adventure. Preppy. Casual. Distracting.

He scooped a spoonful of the hazelnut flavor he'd chosen. "I'm not admitting anything."

"Just look at how many things we've accomplished today, even having dessert before lunch. At least you can check that off your list."

"It wasn't on my list."

Graham definitely had that whole snarly/attractive act down. But the grin tugging on his features was enough of an answer for Lucy. He might not want to admit he was having fun, but she knew he was. They'd already hit the Tower of the Americas. The views had stretched forever, and Graham had been into it, admitting he'd never been before.

At the River Walk, he'd even forgotten to be annoyed for a bit, and the time had been relaxed. Their conversation flowed like the river, from Mattie to work to their childhoods, with easy silence in between.

Lucy was totally winning this day. She'd never seen Graham this chill before. He'd even teased her, smiled and laughed. Twice.

Which turned out to be problematic. Because the man could turn heads even when he was acting snarly, but when he smiled...*good night*.

As if to prove Lucy's point, a woman approaching from the opposite direction had her eyes glued to Graham. *Hello. I'm right here.* Perhaps Lucy should carry a big flag or something to remind people she existed. Not that she and Graham were together, but the woman didn't know that. She should assume they were. She shouldn't be checking out Lucy's not-boyfriend.

The woman tripped on the sidewalk—reason fifty as to why she should have been looking ahead instead of at Lucy's nondate. When she lunged forward, Graham somehow managed to cross the few feet to catch her.

She looked embarrassed, but also secretly pleased.

The tripping move had to have been planned. When the woman gripped Graham's arm for an extra second, Lucy resisted rolling her eyes.

This one's taken, lady.

She bit back the words. Not because they weren't true. Just because they didn't have anything to do with her. Graham was taken, all right, but by his wife. Just because Brooke wasn't alive didn't mean she wasn't in Graham's heart.

Lucy had heard the words come from his lips, and she didn't plan to be so stupid as to ignore the off-limits warning. It was just the reminder she'd needed for keeping things light between them.

After Graham disentangled from the woman, they made their way to the car.

They got in, and Graham put on his aviator sunglasses. "Okay, what's next on your list?"

Lucy pulled the printed paper from her purse. "We don't have a ton of time left. We have to get to the wedding after this one."

"So what is it? I'll put it in the GPS."

"Well, I did a bit of looking…" She had a feeling this next part wouldn't go over well. "Have you ever been to the World's Largest Cowboy Boots?"

Graham looked at her, then out the front window of the parked car. "You're not serious."

"I am."

"You've got the Alamo as an option, and you choose the world's largest boots?"

"We don't have time for the Alamo. That'll have to be a different trip."

He groaned. Closed his eyes for a moment. "They're at a mall, right?"

Must have decided not to fight her. Smart man.

"Yep. North Star Mall." She rattled off the address and Graham punched it into his GPS. They took off, and Lucy hit Play on the iPod list that still had songs left. She wasn't a slacker when it came to the perfect playlist. She'd caught Graham enjoying the music once or twice when he thought she wasn't looking. But no singing—absolutely not.

Lucy could use some real food. She turned and dug into the basket she had in the backseat, pulling out some different snack options—chips (Graham frowned at those), some veggie sticks and two chicken salad sandwiches she'd put into a cooler lunch bag. Graham accepted his sandwich, and they both dug in.

After eating, he glanced at her with one eyebrow

raised. "That was really good. Do you have a hidden talent I don't know about?"

"Nope." She finished her last bite. "I picked them up from The Peach Tree."

"But they weren't in the packaging."

"I was kind of hoping you wouldn't ask and I'd get credit for making them."

His laughter filled the car, creating a warm feeling in Lucy's chest. "Kind of makes you want to go on another road trip with me, doesn't it?"

He glanced in the rearview mirror as he changed lanes, lips quirking. "I wouldn't go that far."

"When are you going to admit you're having fun?"

"When you stop pestering me."

Lucy laughed and slipped her sandals off, putting her bare feet up on the dash.

"*What* are you doing?"

His tone startled her. "What do you mean?"

He motioned to her feet. "Why are you doing that?"

"It's comfortable."

"Well, stop it."

She shifted in her seat to face the crazy man next to her. "Why should I stop?"

"Because I just put on dash protectant, and you're messing it up."

He *had* to be joking. "Dash protectant is not a thing."

"Of course it is."

Wow. A giggle escaped. And she'd thought the floor mats were overdoing it. Still. "It's not like my feet are dirty."

"I wasn't saying your feet were dirty, just that they'll leave a footprint up there."

With a huff, Lucy dropped her feet back to the floor.

"Anyone ever tell you you're a strange man, Graham Redmond?"

"No. Anyone ever tell you that you drive people crazy?"

"Actually, yes." Lucy grinned. "I've heard that one before." Her phone beeped, and she pulled it out of her purse. Olivia knew about the day, and she was likely going nuts without a steady stream of information and updates coming her way.

But it wasn't Liv. It was Bodie. Lucy hadn't heard from him in almost a week. She'd hoped he'd finally accepted that things wouldn't progress between them.

After typing a quick reply, she shoved the phone back in her purse.

"Here it is." Graham drove into the lot, slowing to a stop by the boots.

The size and quirkiness of them standing outside a mall made her chuckle. So worth annoying Graham for this. "They are ginormous."

"Yep."

"You could act a bit more excited about seeing them."

His sigh filled the car. "Fine. Wow. They are amazing. So large. I am impressed. Happy now? Can we go?"

"What?" What was wrong with this man? "We can't leave."

"Why not? You saw them. Isn't that what you wanted?"

"We have to get our picture by them."

Graham's head fell back against his headrest. "Lucy, we don't have time. We need to get to the wedding."

"Oh, come on, gramps. It will be quick."

Surprisingly, Graham gave in and found a parking

spot without an argument. Lucy popped out of the car, waiting to make sure he followed.

They crossed over to the boots, and Lucy stared up in awe. She couldn't believe how huge they were in person.

"Picture." Graham growled the word near her ear. She was losing ground with him. She'd better make this quick.

An older couple stood nearby, and Lucy flagged them down. "Would you mind taking a picture of us?"

"Of course not, sweetie. It's always good to see young love. We were just like you once, weren't we, Arnold?"

Arnold didn't get a chance to do more than nod his head.

"We had the whole world ahead of us back then. Are the two of you on your honeymoon?"

Graham looked as if he'd rather be anywhere else, and this woman thought they were a couple? Laughter bubbled. "Something like that."

"Elaine, don't pester the children." Arnold's reprimand to his wife was adorable, as he was holding her hand and smiling while he said it. They had to be around eighty and so sweet with each other. Lucy didn't have the heart to tell Elaine anything but what she wanted to hear. Though where the woman had come up with the honeymoon assumption, Lucy didn't have a clue. It wasn't as if she or Graham had wedding rings on their left hands.

But if Elaine wanted to see a couple in love, Lucy planned to give her exactly that.

She grabbed Graham's hand and tugged him close, receiving widened, dangerous eyes as a response. This might be the most fun she'd had all day.

"We're not—"

"Oh, come on, honey." Lucy cut Graham off. "Let's

get our picture taken." She handed Elaine her cell phone and went through a five-minute explanation of how to take a photo with it, then pulled Graham toward the boots.

The agitation rolling off him made Lucy's laughter build. He was going to kill her. Which somehow only made the situation more entertaining.

"What are you doing?" Spoken low and near her ear, Graham's words sent shivers down her neck.

"Play along," she whispered back. "I'm just having fun. Let the sweet couple see us happy newlyweds on our honeymoon."

"Lucy."

She tugged Graham next to her and snuggled into his side. When his arm didn't go around her, she lifted it up and put it on her shoulders, then tucked back against his chest.

"You look adorable!" Their cupid was waving one hand as Lucy's phone wobbled precariously in her other hand. "Look here! I'll take a few."

"Smile," Lucy commanded. "Look at the camera."

She could feel Graham glaring at her. "No. You're lying to this woman."

Lucy met his heated gaze. "Graham, she doesn't know us. I'm just trying to make her day. I—"

"I love that with you looking at each other!" Their photographer was still snapping away, acting as if she were on a professional photo shoot. "Now kiss!"

"See?" Graham raised the arm that wasn't around Lucy. "See what you've done now?" He faced the woman, and Lucy just knew he was going to call out the truth and totally ruin the moment. It was just a kiss. Why did he have to make such a big deal out of everything?

Lucy put her hands behind Graham's neck and pulled his head down to meet hers. Just a quick lip-lock was all she needed—enough to satisfy Elaine.

But even with that logic backing her up, Lucy paused with Graham's mouth inches from hers. And then, before she could overanalyze, she went for it, pressing her lips to his.

Graham's mouth and whole body went rigid. Lucy braced for him to pull back and scold her, hoping Elaine wouldn't be able to see the truth of their relationship when he did. But instead of pushing her away, something in Graham's stance softened and his lips stayed on Lucy's.

It wasn't *exactly* a kiss back. But it definitely registered somewhere in the lips-meeting-and-staying department. Lucy didn't know what to call it. She only knew that while she was analyzing the moment, his lips were still on hers. They were soft, and the surprising taste and scent of Graham swirled around her, almost taking her out at the knees.

His hands traveled to her back, and Lucy let out a small sigh. Was he going to pull her closer?

All of a sudden she was cold. Alone. Her body swayed, and she opened her eyes to find Graham standing a foot away from her, looking as though he were standing in the middle of a freeway about to be run down by oncoming traffic.

He didn't speak. His mouth opened. Closed. Oh, man. She might have to take him to the ER. She could see them racing through the automatic doors, envision the conversation now.

He's in shock. Help him, please.
What happened?

We had an almost kiss.

Lucy clung to her amusement. She wanted to laugh. To think about the encounter as a typical Lucy decision and not dwell on the fact that Graham hadn't immediately pulled away.

She didn't want to think about how his lips had felt on hers.

Because then all she'd be able to think about was how she'd like to do it again.

Chapter 10

What had just happened? Had Lucy just *kissed* him? "What was that?"

She winced. "A kiss. For Elaine."

"For Elaine?" His voice was somewhere between snarl and about to lose it.

Lucy took a small step back, palms raised in defense. "It was just—"

"That was quite the kiss, you two." Elaine shoved the phone in his face. When he didn't take it, she offered it to Lucy. "Here's your camera, sweetie."

Lucy was coherent enough to accept it. She exchanged a thank-you and a few more sentences with the couple before Elaine and Arnold left.

Why did Lucy look so calm? Why wasn't she as much of a mess as he was? And again, what had just happened? One moment, Graham had been arguing with Lucy, and the next, their lips had met. And stayed.

Why, why, why had they stayed? Why hadn't he stepped back? Grabbed Lucy's arms and removed her mouth from his?

Because he hadn't wanted to.

That couldn't be right. It had to be that he...hadn't kissed anyone in years. He'd been thinking of Brooke. He'd wished it was her.

Had to be.

When Lucy had yanked him down and kissed him, his first instinct had been logical. Back away and ask her what in the world she was doing. The move had seemed dramatic, even for her. But then, while he'd been contemplating all of that, he'd edged...closer. As if he couldn't stop his hands from sliding around her, as if she'd been made to fit into his arms.

His conscience and logic were having a huge afterparty in his brain right now, raking him over for letting that lip-lock moment continue.

He knew better. Lucy might not, but he did.

"I'm sorry." His words came out strangled, as the situation wasn't really his fault, but he didn't know what else to say. Lucy might be Lucy, but he should have stopped her antics. And he was done wondering why he hadn't. Now he just needed to fix it. He needed it to go away.

"Me, too." She slid her phone into her back pocket. Took another step back. "It was just a joke that got—"

"Out of hand."

"Exactly. No big deal." Then why did she look sort of wounded and shocked at the same time? "We should go." She waved her hand in the direction of the parking lot. "Wedding."

"Right. Wedding."

They walked to the car in silence and got in. Lucy put on her playlist, and Graham punched in the address to Danielle's uncle's house on his GPS.

The whole drive, Graham kept repeating Lucy's words in his mind.

No big deal.
Not once did they feel true.

Lucy wouldn't mind a dance. They'd been at the wedding for hours already—from the outdoor ceremony through the dinner and now into the twilight reception.

So far her nondate had talked to everyone but her.

The whole plan to give Graham a day of fun had backfired. Since their kiss, he'd been unable to look her in the eyes. Not only had she *not* given him a relaxing day off, she'd moved their budding friendship back a few steps.

She stared past the makeshift dance floor under a tree strung with white lights and paper balls, toying with the napkin in front of her.

Danielle's uncle's place looked like something off of Pinterest. The massive lawn stretched from a tall, regal white house down to a man-made lake. A private lake hadn't ranked high on Lucy's need list until tonight. It was gorgeous with hints of sunset reflecting off the water.

"Ms. Lucy, will you dance with us?"

She turned to see two little girls from her dance class standing in front of her. The twins had been the flower girls in the wedding—Danielle's cousin's daughters, if Lucy recalled correctly. They were wearing white taffeta dresses and those little-girl high heels that nights like this were made of.

"Of course." Lucy wasn't going to let the kiss with Graham ruin her whole night.

They walked onto the dance floor and held hands, turning in time to the music. After a few minutes, Lucy's enjoyment grew. The girls were delightful, spin-

ning in order to watch their dresses twirl around them.
She joined in, making the skirt of her yellow lace dress
do the same.

When the music changed and the tempo increased,
the three of them broke out into crazy dance moves, and
Lucy giggled along with the girls. She even threw in a
few robot moves for good measure. By the end of the
song she was feeling far more like herself. One mistake
wouldn't get her down. She'd talk to Graham and apologize again. Somehow she'd convince him to forget all
about her kissing him. Somehow she'd shake the moment from her mind, too.

When the song changed to Beyoncé's "Single Ladies,"
the little girls started singing along. Lucy bent to hear
the words they were using, laughter bubbling when she
deciphered them.

All the singing ladies.

Danielle came flying onto the dance floor to join
them. "I can't believe this song doesn't apply to me anymore!" She glowed with a color makeup couldn't produce. Only a bride could pull off that look.

"I'm so happy for you." Lucy hugged Danielle, thankful she'd become a friend so easily in the past few weeks.

"Thanks, hon. Oh!" Her eyes widened. "We should
have done the bouquet toss to this song. It's perfect.
These are the kind of details that don't get planned when
you do a wedding in two weeks."

"The wedding, the place, everything is perfect. I
thought maybe you were skipping the bouquet toss."
That part of a wedding usually didn't bother Lucy, but
tonight, she wasn't feeling it.

Danielle laughed and shook her finger. "Nice try."

The music switched to something slow, and the current crowd filtered off, a new group taking their place.

Including Graham and the woman he'd been talking to for a while. Lucy watched them as she waved goodbye to the little girls and left the dance floor.

Beautiful, with dark brown hair, the woman was laughing at whatever Graham said. She wore a fitted plum dress that landed just above the knee, simple black heels and a pearl necklace. With Graham rocking a black suit, blue shirt and striped tie, the two of them looked as though they came from the same world and belonged together.

The kind of woman his in-laws would probably approve of.

Lucy glanced down at her fitted yellow lace dress that flared at the waist. She'd paired it with whimsical gold high-heeled sandals and a thin leaf forehead necklace. Earlier, she'd loved the outfit. Now she just felt out of place. Not at the wedding, but in Graham's life. What had she been thinking, trying to help Graham relax and have fun? Why had she thought she could be the one to bring happiness into his life?

Lucy walked over to the outdoor fireplace and snagged one of the blankets stacked on the short brick wall. The day had been gorgeous, temperatures hovering above seventy. Now the heat faded without the sun. With the gas fire pit and outdoor heaters going, none of the guests seemed to notice, though a few had slipped inside. Lucy considered it balmy compared to what she'd be enduring if she were back in Colorado.

She made her way down to the water, stopping to take off her shoes. Slipping her fingers into the heels, she continued walking, the grass tickling her feet.

A wooden dock stretched into the fading light. Lucy walked to the end and sat down, her toes barely nipping into the water. It was cold, and the temperature had her scooting back so that her feet no longer touched. She wrapped the blanket around her shoulders and tugged it close.

Her sigh echoed into the night, the pain that accompanied it surprising her. Unwanted tears surfaced as the events of the afternoon came rushing back. Mainly one event.

What had she done?

Lucy had always been adamant that it wasn't the fear of getting hurt that kept her from serious relationships. She'd fought with her sister over the very subject mere weeks ago.

But Olivia had been right. It was about protecting herself. It was about not letting herself get hurt.

Lucy could finally see it as the truth. But it was a truth that came too late.

Because her attraction to Graham was more than just that. She…was interested in him. She liked him. He drove her crazy. He was insanely neat and detailed — the total opposite of her—and she wanted a repeat of that kiss.

More than one.

She'd gone from *I'm never getting serious* to *I'm in serious trouble* in one instant today.

"No." The word hissed into the night, joining the muted sounds of the party behind her and the silent lake before her. She couldn't turn a one-eighty like that. She couldn't go from nothing to having feelings for Graham, could she?

She went back through the moments in her mind,

from when she'd first met Graham until now, including her sister's wedding last summer. Had it all started way back then? Seeing Graham on the dance floor with Mattie?

She had to be wrong.

Lucy wanted to go back to her innocence again, to believing she didn't date because of her desire for fun. She wanted it to have nothing to do with trying to protect herself.

But the kiss today—albeit an almost kiss—had shattered all of those beliefs.

Graham had a beautiful woman in his arms, but she didn't hold his attention. He'd asked Cherie—an old friend from school—to dance when she'd prompted him. It hadn't been his idea, and truthfully, he wanted to stay away from women in general at the moment. After what had happened with Lucy, who knew what would happen if he got near another one? But since Cherie had openly hinted…it would have been impolite not to ask.

So here he swayed, on a makeshift dance floor underneath a tree dripping with lights. Danielle and Scott danced together a few feet away, both looking so happy. Graham didn't know how they'd made the wedding come together on such short notice, but the place looked fantastic. Intimate and relaxed at the same time. The wedding fit Danielle.

She'd been with him from the beginning of opening the clinic, and Lucy was right. He'd never have missed this. Danielle meant too much to him. He'd danced with her earlier and told her that. She'd laughed away his sincerity, though her eyes had filled with tears. Graham had great people in his life. He'd seen God's presence and provision in so many little and big ways over the past few years. Losing Brooke had been horrible, but he wasn't alone.

While they danced, Cherie chatted and Graham halfway listened. Something about what old classmates were doing now. But the vision of Lucy dancing with the little girls minutes earlier stole into Graham's mind despite his attempts to shake it—much like that kiss.

Lucy was always beautiful. Graham wouldn't be a living, breathing male if he couldn't admit that. But in that moment, she'd been even more breathtaking than usual.

There was something about her Graham couldn't put into words.

She'd been laughing and acting goofy with the girls— not caring what anyone thought. Not realizing that every single man attending the wedding had his eyes on her.

When they'd arrived at Danielle's uncle's house and changed for the wedding, Lucy had got ready with some of Danielle's wedding party. Now she had on a yellow dress and a necklace that went across her forehead. He didn't know what to call it. It was delicate, with tiny gold leaves along the chain. With her hair down and loose curls flowing over her shoulders, she looked like a flower child. As though she should be running through a field barefoot.

But the dress didn't make her. She made the dress.

Graham didn't know what to do with her. He didn't have room in his life for Lucy. He wasn't willing to make space. Not that she was asking him to. He doubted she had any feelings of attraction to him at all. He was too old for her. Lucy would find someone young. She'd marry someday and have kids. But not soon. She had too much life to go out and live. Graham imagined she could easily bounce from city to city without a care. She'd be leaving the office after Hollie came back from maternity leave. And though she drove him crazy at times, he would miss her. He could admit that. But then he'd move on.

"Graham?" Cherie raised one dainty eyebrow. "Are you okay?"

"Fine." He shook his head, wishing the movement would clear thoughts of Lucy from his mind. "Tell me about your new place. Do you like it?"

"I do. I think I'll stay." Her hand slid along the collar of his black suit jacket. "Unless I find a reason not to."

The move made Graham uncomfortable. When his phone buzzed in his pocket, he jumped at the escape. He stopped dancing and checked the call. "It's my mom. I need to take this. She has Mattie."

Cherie nodded, and he escorted her off the dance floor.

Even if the call wasn't about Mattie, he'd take his mom as an interruption right now. As long as she didn't have any "feelings." He'd already had to do some quick explaining about why he absolutely wasn't dating Lucy but they just happened to be going to a wedding together sans Mattie.

Good thing his mother couldn't read minds. This afternoon's incident would send her into a matchmaking tailspin.

He answered just before it went to voice mail. "Mom? Everything okay?"

"It's Dad. Everything is fine. Mattie just wants to say good-night."

Graham heard the shuffling of the phone and then his daughter's voice.

"Night, Daddy. Are you having fun?"

His mouth curved. "You know what? I am. It was a good day." So he and Lucy had locked lips for a second. That didn't mean anything. And he had relaxed today, more than he had in months. Maybe years. "Did you have a good day?"

Her sweet sigh about melted him into a puddle. "The best. I just wanted to check on you before I went to bed."

Wasn't he supposed to be the parent?

They talked for another minute and then said goodbye. Graham ended the call with a grin. He loved that girl. Once again, he was reminded he already had everything he needed. He'd had the love of his life. And he had a daughter who slayed him with her thoughtful, serious little spirit and a God who watched out for him, orchestrating the smallest details.

What had happened with Lucy today didn't change a thing.

I don't like it when you're right.

Lucy pressed Send on the text to her sister and started to put the phone down on the dock before tapping her thumbs over the keys again.

It's really annoying.

If Olivia hadn't poked and prodded, Lucy would likely still have any feelings for Graham deeply buried and locked up. Which meant, even though Olivia had been right, Lucy should absolutely blame her.

Though she had only herself to blame for not listening when her sister had suggested Lucy pray about Graham.

Lucy had been her usual self, thinking she could handle everything on her own, that she had everything under control. But this didn't feel under control.

This felt like riding a roller coaster with a broken seat harness.

Lucy didn't like being wrong. It was a strange occurrence for her.

It also wasn't like her to sit by herself, contemplating a turn of events she definitely hadn't seen coming. She should probably head back to the party. In a minute she would go dance with Danielle and her bridesmaids and have a good time.

After all, that was what she was: the good-time girl. Fun was her motto. She made it happen in her own life and others'. Only, today, the plan had completely backfired and she didn't know what to do about it.

A situation that made her very uncomfortable.

When footsteps sounded on the dock behind her, Lucy didn't turn. Her eyelids fell shut. It would be him. Noble Graham. Of course he would come check on her. Dread of their impending conversation settled like a brick in her stomach. He sat beside her, dangling his feet off the dock but not far enough to let the water touch his black dress shoes.

"You have great taste in shoes."

His quiet laugh answered her. "You okay?"

She felt his eyes on her and forced a smile. "Yep. You?"

He nodded.

She might as well get this over with. "About earlier—"

"Lucy—"

"Let me finish. I'm sorry. I was messing around and I

shouldn't have." She really, really shouldn't have. "Trust me, if I could go back, I would." He had no idea how much she meant that.

"Stop apologizing, Lucy. It's not that big of a deal."

"Right. And that's why you've been avoiding me all night?"

He shrugged. "I just needed a little time to process. That's how my mind works."

She could see that.

"Despite the…ending, I had fun today, Duchess. The most fun I've had in a long time. You were right. I needed this."

She wanted to weep.

"I think today was good for me."

It wasn't today. It was me. I'm good for you. She resisted the desire to whack him across the back of the head and knock the thought into his brain. Instead, she settled for a huge, indulgent sigh.

"Anyway, let's just forget about…earlier."

Forgetting about it sounded like an impossible task. When Graham walked away, she'd have to dive into the water and fish her heart out from under the dock.

His response shouldn't sting, but it did. What had she expected him to say? *Lucy, I was wrong. Maybe there is room for someone else in my life. I just didn't realize it until you.*

Even if he was willing to move on, she wasn't crazy enough to think Graham would go for her in that way. They were too opposite. He was everything put together and she was everything falling apart. And she wouldn't change who she was, even for Graham.

But it would be nice to know that he at least had the potential to feel something for her. That truth stung, too. If Graham moved on with anyone, it would be with someone like Pearls. The woman he'd been dancing with had looked like a perfect fit for him.

"Did you meet someone?" She forced her gaze out to the water and fought the urge to tuck under his arm the way she had earlier today. It was as if she'd been pushed off a cliff. She'd gone from admitting nothing in regard to Graham to admitting everything. She needed to claw her way back up that mountain to her previous innocence. "I saw you dancing with—"

"Cherie? We've known each other since med school. She's a doctor down here now. She knew Brooke."

So he wasn't exactly asking the woman on a date. At least, not that Lucy knew of.

She *really* needed to get these newly discovered feelings under control. Graham had told her straight-out he didn't plan to date or marry. Therefore, this crush she was entertaining was not acceptable. And she *would* be deeming it a crush. It couldn't be more. She hadn't known Graham long enough for it to be more.

She could get over a crush. She could be logical about all of this.

Somehow she had to be. Because Graham was still married to his wife and always would be. Brooke's hold on his heart would go on forever. Lucy even understood it. If she'd lost someone like Graham had, that person would always have a piece of her. It made sense. But if there was any chance of sharing—if there was a possibility Graham could make room for Lucy and Brooke—she'd take that plunge. But Lucy knew there wasn't.

And she didn't stand a chance fighting a memory.

Chapter 11

"It still hurts." On Wednesday night, Mattie sat on the couch gripping a white blanket in her hands, lower lip protruding in an adorable pout.

Graham deposited a mug of warm milk on the coffee table in front of his daughter and held the back of his hand against her forehead. Still a low-grade fever.

"What hurts?"

"Everything, Daddy."

He sank to a sitting position on the coffee table, facing her. She might as well rip out his heart while she was at it. He might be a doctor, he might be able to deal with everyone else's medical problems, but when it came to Mattie, he was a mess.

He hated seeing her sick or in pain—just like he had Brooke. He knew Mattie had a virus that was going around. She had a temperature of 101, aches, pains and a runny nose. But even with that knowledge telling him that in a few days she would be fine, his feelings of helplessness continued to grow.

When Mattie had arrived at the clinic after school today, she'd looked a bit pale. At first, he'd thought it was a midweek thing. Sometimes she was exhausted on Wednesdays, especially going to full-day kindergarten. Plus, the previous weekend had been busy with him being gone all day Saturday and her sleeping over at his parents'.

He'd hoped she was just in need of a lazy movie night and pizza ordered in. But since that time a few hours ago, she'd spiked a fever and seemed to be heading rapidly downhill.

What was he going to do with her tomorrow? She wasn't showing signs of bouncing back overnight and he had to work. It wasn't as if he could cancel his patients for a day.

Graham got out his phone and texted his mom. She would watch Mattie—she always did. But that didn't make it any easier to see his girl sick.

"Do you want orange juice instead of milk? And we can put on *Frozen*." For the millionth time.

Her head swung back and forth.

"Do you want me to make soup?"

"Mommy's soup?"

When Mattie was younger, Graham had called chicken noodle soup "Mommy's soup," and the name had stuck. Not that he made it like Brooke used to. She'd made it from scratch—or at least partially homemade. She used to add dumplings and vegetables. Now Graham bought it premade. He wasn't even sure he had any in the cupboard.

"Let me check if we have some." He went into the kitchen and rummaged through the cupboards, sighing in relief when he found a package. After getting it started on the stove, he returned to the living room. He started the movie and then turned back to Mattie. "I've got the soup going. What else?"

When Mattie's eyes filled with moisture, Graham sank next to her on the couch, scooping her onto his lap. "Honey, I know you don't feel well. I'd do just about anything to make you feel better."

She toyed with her blanket. "I want Lucy."

Graham stiffened. He must have heard her wrong. Or maybe she wanted one of her many stuffed animals, which she was constantly naming after people she knew.

"Is that the white tiger?"

Her small giggle warmed him. "No, Daddy. Ms. Lucy. Do you think she'd come over?"

No. No, he did not. Didn't he see enough of her? Since the weekend, he and Lucy had gone back to work, both adopting a "didn't happen" and "no big deal" approach about the kiss. It was working, but he didn't need to poke a sleeping bear.

"She's probably busy, honey."

"But you could check."

He could check. Hadn't he just said he'd do anything for Mattie? His daughter turned in his lap, looking up at him with those green eyes glimmering like mossy pools. "All right. I'll ask her, but if she can't, no getting upset. I'm sure she has other things going on." That thought gave him a bit of relief. Lucy was a fluttering social butterfly. She'd likely already have plans.

"But she loves me, Daddy."

He couldn't deny that. "You're right. She does." Heat sneaked under his shirt, and he tugged at his collar, fingers meeting the long-sleeved T-shirt he'd changed into after work. The way Lucy loved his daughter might be endearing, but that didn't mean it was a good idea to ask her over.

And he certainly didn't need to be a doctor to diagnose that the idea gave him a rapid pulse and shortness of breath.

Lucy propped her phone on the bathroom counter, putting it on speakerphone so she could continue talking with Bodie while she pulled her hair up. He'd called on Sunday and she hadn't answered, but today, she had.

They'd been on the phone for a while, and she had to admit, it was nice to talk to him again. She did like him. She just wasn't sure anything could come of those feelings. Especially now that she'd figured out how she felt about Graham.

Knowing she couldn't have him felt like looking into a store window and seeing the most beautiful display, and then noticing the small sign hanging from it that said Not for Sale.

Was this what Liv was such a proponent of? This kind of achy feeling? Like being trampled by a horse? Lucy was so going to have a talk with her sister when she saw her tomorrow night.

"Let's go on a date this week."

She twisted her hair on top of her head. "How are we going to do that? You do recall that we live in different states. What are you going to do? Jump on a plane and fly down here?"

"Not a bad idea." His low voice did absolutely nothing to her stomach. So disappointing. She could totally go for a flip or jiggle of excitement. But maybe she needed to push past the lack of instant feelings. At least Bodie showed interest and pursued her. Something that would never happen with Graham.

"I meant over FaceTime. We could have dinner. I'll plan it. What do you say?"

Her cell showed a call from Graham, but Lucy ignored it. The man wasn't good for her. He made her heart all unhappy and hurting. This week at work, she'd made a conscious effort not to yank him into his office, slam the door and kiss him. Really kiss him this time. At least then they'd have something to fight about. Instead, they'd been perfectly nice to each other, leaving Lucy's gut churning with the desire for more. Not necessarily more kisses, though she'd take some of those, too, but more of Graham.

Since her realization about Graham at the wedding, Lucy had finally taken her sister's advice and started praying about him. About herself. About everything, really. What she should do after her job at the clinic ended. How to keep from going any further down sappy-crush lane. Her attempts at remembering to pray might be only slightly better than pathetic, but she was making an effort. That had to count for something, right?

"Lucy, you've pulled away since you moved. Give me another chance. Give us a chance."

What harm could a date with Bodie cause? It might get her mind off Graham for an evening. "Okay."

"Great. Friday night?"

"I haven't been on a Friday-night date in forever."

"Good. Because you should be dating me and nobody else." The mix of humor and determination in his voice made Lucy laugh.

After they hung up, she went into the bedroom of her small above-garage apartment and changed into plaid pajama pants and a long-sleeved T-shirt. She wanted to do nothing tonight. Maybe watch a movie. Eat popcorn for dinner. It seemed like that sort of a night.

When her phone beeped with a text, she hustled back into the bathroom and grabbed it from the counter.

I'm sorry to bother you. M is sick and she wants you. Any chance you're not busy?

Lucy's thumbs hovered over the keys. Seeing Graham probably wasn't in her best interests. Not with her still nursing this crush and daydreaming about kissing him in his office or an exam room too many times a day.

Saying no to Graham was one thing. But how could she say no to her Mattie girl?

When Lucy had entered Mattie's life, it wasn't on a temporary basis. At the time, it'd had nothing to do with Graham. Therefore, her relationship with the little girl should have nothing to do with Graham now.

He didn't affect her *that* much.

Right. Lucy had better not let her sister get hold of that one.

She showed up on his doorstep in typical Lucy style—pink-and-green plaid pajama pants, slippers that looked like knit ballet shoes and her hair piled in a mess on top of her head. It wasn't that cold, yet she looked ready to hunker down for a snowstorm the way she was bundled into her fleece jacket.

"Where is she? Is she okay?"

Graham swung the door farther open for her to come in. "She's fine. She's fighting something and she's emotional. You women seem to do that up-and-down thing when you're sick."

Lucy stepped into the house. "I have no idea what you're talking about. I'm solid as a rock. Haven't cried a day in my life."

"Right. *Even-keeled...* That's a word I would use to describe you."

Her eyes narrowed, lips pursed. His gaze fell to her mouth and stuck like Super Glue.

"I've missed you desperately in the few hours since work, Hollywood. I almost didn't know how I was going to go on without seeing you until morning."

Her sassy response had him fighting a smile, and his stress over Mattie not feeling well kicked down a notch. "I was just thinking the same about you, Duchess."

Graham swung the door shut and took Lucy's coat. She strode across the living room and dropped onto the couch, scooping Mattie's legs over her lap. "What's up, Matilda Grace? Is your dad driving you crazy? Are you faking being sick so that I would come over and rescue you from him?"

Mattie giggled and snuggled into Lucy.

"Dad, I'm hungry."

That was a good sign. Her medicine must be taking the edge off how she was feeling. "You just ate soup. What do you want now? Toast?"

"Chinese food. I want orange chicken."

Lucy held up a hand, which Mattie high-fived. "Best idea ever. Me, too. I'm starving." Both pairs of eyes swung to him, and those symptoms he'd had earlier started in again. They were both beautiful. Mattie's beauty stemmed from her serious nature, from the way she cared about people with a maturity far beyond her years—and the fact that she looked like a miniature Brooke. And Lucy's came from a combination of her effervescent personality, her big heart and the annoying fact that she was gorgeous. Even when she was wearing pajamas with her hair in a messy bun, the sight of her reached in and squeezed the air from his lungs.

What was he going to do with the two of them? They made a formidable team. And he was in trouble.

"Chinese food?" His voice cracked with all the maturity of a twelve-year-old boy. "I'll find the menu." And escape to the kitchen. He'd been right. Inviting Lucy over hadn't been a great idea.

Ever since the weekend, thinking of her in a professional way only was almost impossible.

Thinking of her in other ways—unfortunately—came more easily.

Graham got the take-out menu from the drawer. After asking Lucy what she wanted—which was to share and have a little of everything, big surprise—he called in the order.

He hung up and tossed the menu back in the drawer just as Mattie laughed at something Lucy said. His daughter didn't sound very sick right now. Was Lucy right? Was Mattie pretending not to feel well?

No way. Mattie might love Lucy, but she couldn't fake a fever. It must be the meds—both the Lucy ones and the ibuprofen ones—making a difference.

When he headed back into the living room, Lucy was digging in the cupboard below the TV, half her body disappearing inside the space.

"Help yourself."

She scooted out, hitting her head on the way, then sat back and rubbed the spot, glaring at him.

"You okay?"

Her petulant look increased, lower lip protruding slightly. The desire to kiss away her pout washed over him. Until he remembered his daughter sitting on the couch watching the two of them. And the fact that he wasn't supposed to think of Lucy in that way.

"I'm fine. Mattie wants to play a game. She said they were in here."

"She said correctly."

Lucy reached into the cupboard and pulled a stack of games out, holding them on her lap. "Chutes and Ladders, Candy Land or Monopoly Junior?"

"Monopoly," Mattie answered with authority.

"That's my smart girl." Lucy shoved the other two back into the cupboard. They looked crooked, as though they might fall the next time he opened the door, but Graham resisted fixing them. He'd do it after she left.

Kind of like he'd vacuumed his car after their drive to San Antonio, just as he'd said he would.

Lucy set the game up on the coffee table and Graham turned the movie volume down, leaving it on in the background.

"Do we need to pick up the food?"

"I got it delivered."

"This town has delivery? Does someone show up on a horse?"

"We're not that small, Duchess." Although delivery was a rather new addition.

She laughed at her own joke, and his stomach did that annoying twist it did whenever Lucy was around. No medical terminology could describe it.

He sat on the floor on the other side of the coffee table, and they started the game. Mattie's attention span was a four out of ten at best, and she spent half the time dazed out and watching the movie, the other half being reminded to play. Though Lucy might have improved Mattie's mood, his daughter still wasn't feeling great.

Lucy, on the other hand, was a competitor. If he didn't watch it, she might own his actual house by the end of the night.

"Where'd you learn to play such a mean game of Monopoly?"

"My sister." Lucy took her turn and did not go to jail. "She's supercompetitive and loves to win. I always lost to her. You, on the other hand, are not as formidable an opponent."

He rolled the die. "I'm letting you win."

"I prefer to win my battles without assistance, as you probably already know."

True.

"But I also know that I am fairly and squarely knocking you on your behind, so no worries."

His mouth gave in to a grin. His daughter might be sick, but even with that, Graham knew he didn't want to be anywhere but where he was right now. Playing a game with Lucy and Mattie with a movie on in the background felt…right.

Had he been wrong all of this time? What if his theory on Brooke being the only love of his life was wrong? What if he could have that again? If it felt anywhere near as good as this, he would be a fool not to at least explore the possibility.

Graham would be lying if he didn't admit the kiss with Lucy had crossed his mind more than a few times this week.

But could that momentary lip-lock even be classified as a kiss? He hadn't done much to take part in it. He'd moved in a bit, but he'd cut it off before anything could develop. If he was really going to kiss Lucy, he'd take his time. Thread fingers through her hair, which he imagined would be as soft as it looked, and pull her close. He'd savor the anticipation of his lips a moment from hers, the feel of her—

"Earth. To. Hollywood."

"What?"

"It's your turn."

"Oh." He laughed off his inattention, though the chuckle sounded more like a wounded duck. "Right Sorry."

He took his turn and then Lucy started hers. He might be attracted to Lucy, but there was a difference between kissing her and pursuing a relationship. Even if he did decide to move past the idea that Brooke was his one and only love, he wouldn't let himself move in that direction with Lucy.

She was young. Too young for him. They were total opposites. And she was still his employee—an absolute no in his world.

Totally unprofessional.

Exactly like his thoughts a few seconds ago.

The doorbell rang, and Graham popped up. He grabbed his wallet from the side table and dug money out as he swung the door open.

"How much do I owe you?" He glanced up to see his in-laws standing on his front step.

"Nothing." Phillip attempted a smile, though it looked more like a grimace. "Were you expecting someone?"

"Food." The one syllable sounded strained. If Graham stepped outside and closed the door behind him, maybe the Wellings wouldn't see Lucy.

"Someone besides the owner of a yellow Volkswagen?" Phillip pointed with a thumb over his shoulder.

Then again, maybe not.

Chapter 12

By the scowls lining the Wellings' faces, they'd guessed the owner of the car.

"Come in." Graham forced himself to open the door wider. They glanced over his shoulder, their looks hardening.

He knew what they were seeing without having to look. Lucy and Mattie snuggled up under a white blanket, a game spread across the coffee tuble. An intimate scene Phillip and Belinda wouldn't appreciate.

The Wellings stepped inside, neither taking off their jackets, and the air in the room crackled with tension.

"Hi, Grandma and Grandpa!" Completely oblivious to the friction, Mattie waved from the couch. "Did you know I'm not feeling good so you came to see me like Lucy did?"

Lucy gave a small, tentative wave. The Wellings nodded regally at her, then asked about Mattie. Graham explained her symptoms, uncomfortable silence following.

Poor Lucy shifted on the couch, looking as if she wanted to crawl under the coffee table. Graham didn't blame her. In fact, he might join her.

"Mattie, why don't you show me your room?" She stood, but Mattie stayed under the blanket, confusion lining her features.

"How come? I thought we were going to eat."

"We will in a little bit." She picked Mattie up, and his daughter curled her arms and legs around Lucy. "Don't tell me what color your room is. I'm going to guess." Lucy walked past, eyes averted from him and the Wellings as she and Mattie disappeared up the stairs.

Another apology talk loomed in his future. Heat flared at the thought, spreading across Graham's skin. It shouldn't be this way. Why were Phillip and Belinda so cold to Lucy? Didn't they realize Mattie was in the room? She was a smart girl. Eventually she'd begin to question how her grandparents were acting.

He clamped his teeth together to keep from speaking his mind and motioned for them to move into the living room. They did so quietly, their unease radiating with each step.

The two of them sat on the chairs and Graham took the couch. He waited, not willing to make things easier for them. Not trusting himself to speak. Anger from the last time they'd treated Lucy this way rose up, stifling him.

"Graham." Phillip looked to his wife before continuing. "We heard a rumor yesterday, and we wanted to come straight to the source. We didn't want to believe it. But now that we're here…"

"We heard that you and Lucy went on a date to Danielle's wedding," Belinda continued. "The last time we talked to you about this, you said you weren't interested in dating Lucy."

He inhaled. Exhaled. Struggled for calm. "It wasn't a date."

"But you went to the wedding together, didn't you?"

"Yes, Belinda, we did. But the wedding was out of town. It was more about not driving two cars down than anything else." A half-truth. "And partly about Lucy wanting to do some sightseeing. It was completely innocent and not at all a date." At least the last part of that statement was true.

Why was Graham defending himself? He was thirty-one years old. He had a five-year-old daughter. He could make his own decisions. And what did they have against Lucy anyway?

"I think there's more to this than you're telling us." Belinda was the one carrying the conversation. Was all of this from her?

Graham turned to his father-in-law. "Phillip, are you part of this confrontation?"

He slowly nodded. "She was our only daughter."

An ache flickered in Graham's chest. "I know. And I loved her. I always will. But she's not here anymore. Believe me, if I could bring her back, I would."

"So you are dating Lucy." When Belinda piped up, Graham counted to five before answering.

"No. I'm not." His jaw hurt from clenching his teeth in order to keep from saying more. A full-out confrontation with the Wellings wasn't going to help the situation right now. If he got overly defensive, they'd assume he was dating Lucy no matter what he said.

"Graham, we just want you to be careful. This girl seems young—far too young to be a good influence on our granddaughter."

Graham didn't miss Phillip's emphasis on "our." As

though the Wellings had part ownership or something. As though Graham wasn't the one ultimately in charge of Mattie.

"She probably sees that you're well-off, that you have a good profession. Perhaps she thinks she'll be set for life with you."

"Right." Belinda leaned forward, purse clutched in her hands as though a pickpocket might try to snatch it at any moment. "What do they call those young women who marry older men for money? Trophy wi—"

"Stop." Graham snapped the word out, cutting off Belinda. Yes, he was older than Lucy by seven years, but he didn't think that qualified him as *that* old. At least he hadn't before Belinda mentioned it. And the idea of Lucy going after his money—not that he was a millionaire or anything—was outrageous. He clamped down on the urge to laugh, knowing it definitely wouldn't help the moment. Lucy couldn't care less about all of that. She'd never think twice about his or anyone else's financial status.

If anyone should be accused of something, it was Phillip and Belinda. They were snobby to look down on Lucy or think she'd be after some free ride.

"Lucy's not trying to marry me." Strangely, no relief filled him at the statement. "And she's a great influence on Mattie." But she *was* young. The Wellings were right about that. Hadn't he thought the same thing just minutes ago? But young didn't mean immature. Lucy might always be looking for the next bit of adventure, but there wasn't anything wrong with that. Graham had come to appreciate that about her. He probably shouldn't mention to the Wellings that she'd deemed herself the Director of Fun in his life. He imagined that wouldn't go over well.

Belinda dug a tissue from her purse and dabbed under her eyelashes. Was she faking? Or really that upset? The Wellings had always been strong willed. When he and Brooke had first married, they'd had a few squabbles over holiday schedules, but eventually they'd worked things out. Still, those small disagreements didn't compare to this. He'd never seen them act this way during his marriage to Brooke or even after. The only point of contention since her death was that he refused to be on the board of her foundation.

Phillip leaned forward. "What about Brooke's money?"

Oh. He should have known there was more. Graham's head spun. "Brooke's money—" which had been given to *both* him and Brooke when they'd married "—is going to Mattie. We never touched it. It's in Mattie's trust fund. Her money for college."

Graham hadn't realized he or Lucy could be offended on so many levels in one conversation. Lucy would never take anything from Mattie. That the Wellings could even think it created a bitter taste in his mouth.

Did he know them at all?

"We're not okay with this." Phillip leaned forward, elbows resting on his knees.

Graham stifled a groan. He'd hoped the money discussion would end their doubts.

"You tell us you're not dating her, but not only do we hear you went to a wedding with her, we come over and find her at your house." Phillip's eyebrows thundered together. "In her pajamas, of all things." He spread his hands. "How do you think this looks to us?"

Graham's defense caved a bit. "It probably doesn't

look good. But I don't know how many ways to tell you that you're jumping to conclusions."

"If we're jumping to conclusions now, it's only because we see what's happening and you don't," Phillip stated.

Belinda sniffled. "We want you to stay away from her. We don't believe she's right for you. And if you date her…we're not going to stay around to watch her break both of your hearts."

His world crashed down around him. "What are you saying?"

Belinda glanced to Phillip before continuing. "We're saying it's her or us."

How could they even voice such a thing?

Graham couldn't sit in the same room with them. The temptation to walk out the front door of his own house and escape this nightmare was strong. If the girls weren't upstairs—and hopefully not hearing any of this conversation—he'd consider it. He popped up from the couch and paced behind it.

He wasn't dating Lucy and he didn't plan to, but the Wellings had no business getting involved in his life like this. They were out of line and being completely outrageous. He should tell them to get out of his house right this instant…that they didn't have any right.

But then what? They'd walk out and Mattie would never see them again?

Anger sank into despair. Graham couldn't let that happen. Losing Brooke had been hard enough. Knowing he should have been able to save her but couldn't had broken something inside of him.

He'd never be able to live with himself knowing he

could have stopped Phillip and Belinda from walking out of Mattie's life.

Yes, they were being completely irrational. Judgmental. Inconsiderate. Untrusting.

The list could go on for days.

But a check in his gut told him none of that mattered. Because they were Mattie's grandparents. Despite the way they were acting right now, they loved Mattie dearly. And she loved them back. Which meant he needed to cave to them.

"I'm not going to date Lucy." His voice was low, broken. "I don't know how many ways to say the same thing. You're just going to have to trust me." If he'd already made the decision on his own earlier, why did saying the words now make him feel as though he had a collapsed lung?

At this point, it didn't matter what he felt. Another person wouldn't be ripped from Mattie's life because of him.

Including Lucy.

"I won't date her, but she is going to be in Mattie's life. She's good for Mattie. If you can't see that, then I don't know what to tell you." Standing up for her felt like a small victory, and the sag in his shoulders straightened a little.

The Wellings exchanged a look, as though they were deciding how far to push. Phillip spoke. "How long will this Lucy be working for you?"

Graham ignored the "this" before "Lucy." He had to pick his battles.

"Another two and a half weeks."

The couple communicated with each other again without saying a word. Then Phillip nodded. "Okay.

Deal. We'd prefer no contact at all, but since that's not an option, we'll concede to her being in Mattie's life."

Deal.

Graham felt nauseated, as though he'd just made a shady business agreement in a back alley. He half expected Phillip to offer him a handshake over it. Thankfully he didn't.

The Wellings showed themselves out, and Graham walked around and dropped onto the couch, a flood of feelings coursing through him. Anger. Bitterness. Disappointment.

Before he could analyze that last one, a knock sounded at the door. He grabbed his wallet from the coffee table and went to open it. No surprises greeted him this time. After paying, he called upstairs. The girls came down—Mattie with more excitement than Lucy.

"Where are Grandpa and Grandma?"

"They had to go."

Hurt registered in Mattie's wilting shoulders. Though Graham still felt sickened by the conversation he'd just had with the Wellings, seeing Mattie's response to their quick departure told him he'd done what he needed to do in order to protect her from anything worse in the future.

She peered up at him. "Are we eating in the living room?"

He'd let her eat hanging from the ceiling if that was what she wanted. "Why not?"

"I'll get the plates." Mattie ran into the kitchen, her momentary upset quickly forgotten.

Lucy shoved a jittery hand through her hair, causing a few strands to fall from the bun on top of her head. "I'm completely confused by her. One moment she's running across her room. The next she's crashed in her bed."

"It's the medicine."

"She introduced me to all of her stuffies. There's even one named after me. And her coloring pages are amazing. So detailed for her age. Not that I know what a typical five-year-old draws like, but of course Mattie would do anything better than anyone else. At least, in my opinion."

"Mine, too." Graham rested a hand on her arm to stop her nervous chatter. "It's going to be okay, Lucy."

Worried blue eyes pierced him. "Is it? Do they want me to stay away from Mattie?"

Yes. "I told them that's not an option. You're good for her." *And me.*

"Okay." Lucy's quiet acceptance didn't erase her sad look. Mattie came back into the living room with plates and silverware, and he resisted smoothing the crease pulling at Lucy's mouth.

"You okay?"

"Yep." She crossed her arms, causing his hand to drop from her skin. "You?"

No. He wasn't. Lucy was hurt and he felt as though he'd been to battle. He wanted to tuck her into his arms, kiss the top of her head and make her sad go away.

Exactly what he'd just said he wouldn't do. He had the sinking feeling that all of his excuses for not being interested in Lucy were simply that.

But what could he do about that now? With the Wellings so upset, Graham couldn't develop feelings for Lucy. Mattie would lose two people she loved from her life if he did.

It was best if he kept his thoughts about Lucy centered on friendship and their mutual love for Mattie.

Surely that would be safe.

But even with that plan in mind, he couldn't shake the thought that he'd just made a trade he'd come to regret...his happiness for Mattie's.

Lucy dished a second helping of kung pao chicken and fried rice, then dumped on a packet of soy sauce. She expected a remark from Graham about all of the salt intake, but his commentary had been sadly missing from the evening ever since his in-laws had shown up. Lucy was torn between asking what had happened and not wanting to know.

She waved a hand in front of him. "You still there?" They were sitting on the floor, their plates on the coffee table. A few minutes ago, Mattie had finished a small helping and climbed onto the couch behind Lucy.

Graham had checked her forehead, stated that her fever was back, then returned to eating.

Lucy's back was against the couch, and she could feel Mattie's fingers holding on to her shirt with a slight grip. Endearing little gesture.

"I'm still here."

"You want to talk about it?"

"Nope." Graham tempered his comment with a half smile. "Tell me a story. Something about you I don't know."

Going home would be a better option. The way this man directed her heartstrings was getting pathetic. She wanted to make him smile and laugh. She wanted her Graham back. Whatever Brooke's parents had said to him certainly hadn't gone well.

"I'll say three things. Two true. One made up. You guess which one isn't true."

"Okay." Graham studied her with amusement, and she

fought the desire to lean across the table and give him a smacking kiss. Happy. Angry. Sad. The man looked good wearing any emotion.

Good thing she had this *crush* of hers under control. "I've jumped out of an airplane. I've been to Europe. I've been hunting."

He set his plate to the side and wiped his mouth with a napkin. "That's easy. You've never been hunting."

"Ha! I have been hunting. I haven't jumped out of a plane."

"No way."

"Yes way." Lucy propped a hand under her chin. "Would this face lie?"

Graham chuckled, and no matter who won the game, Lucy already had her victory in the bag.

"What kind of hunting? I'm not sure I believe this scenario. Does this involve an old boyfriend?"

"No." She scoffed. "I wouldn't go hunting for a boy. In junior high, my friend wanted to go with her dad. We were joined at the hip and did everything together, so we both went. I didn't shoot anything." She raised a finger. "But I did go."

"Okay, I believe you."

"You're up, Hollywood."

"Hang on. I'm thinking." He took his time, closing food containers and stacking dishes. Lucy tapped her fingers on the coffee table. She rolled her neck. She could probably teach a dance class and get back before he came up with anything.

Finally Graham stopped cleaning up everything on the coffee table. "I've delivered a baby. I've always lived in Texas. I've never broken a bone."

"I think, despite your cautious nature, that you've definitely broken a bone."

"Actually, I never have."

"What? That doesn't make sense, then, because I'm pretty sure you've always lived in Texas, and you're a doctor, so you must have delivered a baby at some point in your career."

"Technically I haven't always lived in Texas." He looked like a kid who'd just got away with an extra dessert. "One summer I spent a month with my cousin in Idaho."

"That's practically cheating." Not that she cared with that grin claiming his mouth. She loved seeing him happy after whatever had happened with his in-laws. "Next you'll tell me the baby you delivered was Mattie. I'm not sure that counts, either."

His smile fell. "What? No, of course not. Brooke was considered high risk with cystic fibrosis. The two of them had a team of doctors far more qualified than me for Mattie's delivery."

"Oh." Guess that made sense. Although, the way Graham talked…

"Spill, Duchess. I can tell you're thinking something."

Lucy toyed with the edges of the throw she had over her lap. "You're a great doctor, Graham. You do know that, right? I would trust you with my life."

He busied himself collecting their silverware. "How do you know? You're working in the front office, not in on the appointments."

Could he seriously doubt himself?

"I hear plenty." Lucy shrugged. "I know your patients love you, that they trust you and keep coming back."

"I do my best, but I'm still human. Sometimes I wonder…"

"What?"

"Nothing." He shook his head, then motioned to the couch behind Lucy. She glanced over her shoulder to find Mattie asleep, lashes grazing her cheeks, pink skin giving hints of the fever within. She still had one hand near Lucy, as if she'd held on until sleep won.

Lucy turned back to Graham. "I kind of have a thing for her."

"I've noticed." His gaze roamed her face. "It's nice. Thank you. And thanks for coming over. She was a mess before you got here."

Lucy knew the feeling. A bit like she felt now. "You're welcome. Graham, are you sure the Wellings don't want me to stay away from Mattie?" Ever since she'd been upstairs with Mattie, the thought had been clanging around in her head. She'd tried to ignore it. She'd tried to believe what Graham had told her earlier when she came downstairs, but she really needed to know the truth.

If she couldn't see Mattie anymore, Lucy would need someone to sew her shredded heart back together. It was bad enough she harbored these feelings for Graham. Not having either of them in her life might do her in.

"They aren't allowed to think that. I told them you were good for Mattie and that you would be in her life."

Though he'd conveniently avoided answering what the Wellings thought, Lucy accepted his reply. Relief that she wasn't going to lose Mattie rolled down her spine, and she stretched back against the couch before realizing there must be more. "So if it wasn't that, then…"

"I really don't want to talk about it."

"It must have something to do with me. They barely

acknowledged my presence." Lucy felt as though she were poking a hornet's nest, but she couldn't stop herself.

"They just love their daughter, and the thought of me moving on with anyone is hurting them."

Moving on. The thing Graham never planned to do. "So did you tell them—"

"Yes, I did." He looked everywhere but at her, then popped up and grabbed items from the coffee table. "I told them. I mean, of course we know we're not together, that our relationship is built around Mattie and work."

Lucy's heart felt squeezed in a massive fist. What had she expected? She'd hoped she could get through the evening by concentrating on Mattie. She'd thought she could ignore her feelings for Graham, but tonight had made her do anything but. Being with them, all cozy and tucked in—even with Mattie sick—felt right.

Her feelings were going beyond crush into crushing.

Lucy should be thankful that the Wellings had appeared unexpectedly tonight. They'd saved her some heartache. Because despite the fact that Graham must have stood up for her and defended her relationship with Mattie, Lucy knew the truth.

She didn't fit. Not in the Wellings' world, and not with Graham and Mattie.

Chapter 13

During the hour Mattie had been at dance class, Graham had grabbed a coffee and done their grocery shopping for the week. And Lucy thought he never did anything fun.

Thankfully, his little girl had started feeling better late yesterday. Graham had tried to talk Mattie out of dance this morning, telling her she might be a bit weak from having a fever the past few days, but she'd adamantly refused to miss it. He'd let Lucy know when he'd dropped Mattie off this morning that she might not make it through the whole class.

After the week they'd had, Graham wouldn't mind doing nothing besides church for the rest of the weekend. But that wasn't an option.

The last thing he wanted to do was spend his Saturday night with the Wellings after their confrontation on Wednesday. But that was exactly what he had to do. Once a year, they hosted a gala to raise funds for Brooke's charity. All of their rich friends attended, and last year Graham had spent the evening feeling alone in the middle of a crowd. This year would be no different. It was the one thing he agreed to attend for the charity, and the Wellings would never understand his not being there.

His phone rang just as he got out of the car. He shut the door and answered his cell. "Hey, Dad."

"Graham, I hate to be the bearer of bad news…"

"What's wrong?" His mind raced with all kinds of bad scenarios.

"Mom's sick. She has a fever. Her eyes are glassed over and she's going at quarter speed."

"From Mattie." He felt horrible. "I'm sorry, Dad. If she hadn't taken care of Mattie, then she wouldn't—"

"Enough. Your mother will be fine. She loves taking care of Mattie, sick or not. I'm calling because you'd wanted me to go with you tonight, but Mom can't watch Mattie. I can stay home and watch her."

Graham had asked his dad to go with him a few weeks ago, but as the gala drew near, the importance of his father being there was growing. "Don't make me handle all of those people on my own." Especially the Wellings. Since Graham had moved back to Fredericksburg, Dad had become one of his closest friends. Graham wanted a support person there tonight. Someone to keep him from telling the Wellings what he really wanted to say. Someone wise and calm like his father. Mattie's relationship with her grandparents had to come first. No matter what other things Phillip and Belinda accused Graham of.

"I'm fine going, but what are you going to do about Mattie? I already checked with your sisters before I called you and neither of them can watch her."

Graham sighed. He didn't even want to go tonight, and now he had to stick Mattie with a sitter. "I'll find someone." They hung up, and Graham thumbed through the contact list on his phone.

He rarely had to hire anyone with family in town, but there were a few high school girls he could check with. He found the first number and pressed Send. On the fourth ring, a sleepy voice answered.

"Hey, Kieta, this is Graham Redmond. I'm sorry if I woke you up. I'm looking for a babysitter for tonight for Mattie. I know it's late notice—"

"I'm sorry, Dr. Redmond, but there's a big party tonight. You'll probably have a hard time finding someone."

Perfect. "Okay, thanks for letting me know." They hung up, and Graham rubbed the stress from his eyes. He could call the Wellings and tell them he couldn't find a sitter, but knowing them, they'd call a service and send someone to his door.

If he wasn't concerned about sending their currently tumultuous relationship into further turmoil, he'd just cancel for tonight. Nothing would make him happier right now.

"Dad!" Mattie skipped across the sidewalk to him. "Class is over. What are you doing?" He scooped her up, burying his nose in her peach-shampoo hair. After a short hug, Mattie squirmed, forcing him to set her down. She propped her hands on her hips and tapped one toe, a move that reminded him of Lucy. The woman was definitely rubbing off on his daughter.

"What's going on, Daddy? Your face looks all scrunchy."

He wrinkled his nose. "Thanks for the compliment." Her little giggle would never get old. "How did class go? Did you make it all the way through?"

"Of course. Why wouldn't I?"

Kids. They always bounced back faster than adults. "No reason."

"We had to practice for the recital. I can't miss class, Daddy. It's very important. We got to see the dresses today, and they're beautiful." Mattie stretched out the word and spun in a circle, arms wide.

"What recital?"

"The spring recital," Lucy answered, approaching behind Mattie. "It's in two weeks. Mattie's in two dances."

"I didn't know anything about it."

Lucy was wearing her typical leggings and long, fitted T-shirt, though today her hair was in a braid sneaking over her shoulder. She wore pink Converse shoes and she looked…adorable. But not in a little-girl way. Nope. She just looked like beautiful, carefree Lucy.

"At first I didn't tell you about it because I thought you'd say no."

He dropped a hand to his chest in mock offense. "Me? That's crazy." When she smiled, his gaze landed on her lips. He scrambled to distract himself. "Doesn't Mattie need a dress or outfit?"

"Yep."

"Where do we get it?"

"You don't. We order way in advance, and since you were tentative about dance in the beginning—"

"Ha. That's a nice way of putting it."

The skin surrounding her eyes crinkled. "I ordered her stuff without telling you so that she'd have it for recital. I knew we needed to get it right away in order for her to have it in time."

"And so you did it without my knowledge." When Graham had first met Lucy, this conversation would have irked him. Now he just felt relieved. She'd gone behind his back and taken care of everything so that his little girl would have what she needed. "Thank you for doing that."

Lucy visibly relaxed. "You're welcome."

"How much do I owe you?"

"We'll figure it out." She waved a hand. "It's not that big of a deal."

Mattie tugged on his arm. "Daddy, I heard Mrs. Knoll say the dresses were fifty dollars."

He leveled Lucy a look. "I'm paying for the dress."

"That's fine. I wasn't saying you couldn't."

"Okay, good." The conversation stalled. He wanted to say something more about the other night, but words failed him. After Lucy left Wednesday, Graham had fought the feeling that he'd made an even bigger mess out of everything. Not that he knew how to fix any of it.

He was more attracted and more drawn to Lucy with each passing day, but with Phillip and Belinda threatening to walk out of Mattie's life if he dated her, the woman was off-limits.

"I'm going to my grandparents' house tonight, Ms. Lucy." Mattie did a small dance of excitement.

"That's great, Mattie Grace."

"Actually, they can't watch you tonight, Mattie. You're going to have a sitter."

Her lower lip protruded. "I don't want a sitter."

"I don't want you to have one either, but that's the way it has to happen."

Lucy stepped closer. "Why? What's the deal?"

"Nothing." Graham really, really didn't want to talk about any of this with Lucy. "Come on, Mattie. Let's go."

"Why can't Ms. Lucy watch me tonight?" His sweet

little girl crossed her arms and huffed. Actually huffed. Next she'd probably throw herself down on the ground and have one of the fits she'd skipped out on during the first five years of her life.

"Because I'm sure Lucy has plans. Maybe with her sister. Or maybe she even has a…date." The word tasted weird on his tongue, then bowled him right over. Here he was, analyzing whether his feelings for Lucy were changing, and she might be dating someone. She might not think of him as anything more than old. And lame.

Those were two very real possibilities.

"Had a date last night."

That answered that question. The disappointment roaring through him couldn't be a good sign.

"But not tonight." Lucy bent to Mattie's level. "And I think a girls' night is a great idea. We can do our nails, put on makeup—"

"She's not wearing makeup."

She winked at Mattie, then faced Graham. "Come on, Hollywood. You've been doing so much better with just letting me do what I want. A little makeup that washes right off isn't going to hurt."

"I didn't even agree to you watching her. It's out of the question."

Her eyes narrowed. "Why? Don't you trust me?"

"Of course I trust you. It's just, besides the fact that you already do too much for Mattie, this thing tonight… It's for Brooke's charity."

"That's great!"

"With the Wellings."

"Oh." Hurt flashed, but after one look at Mattie, she squared her shoulders. "Well, are they coming to your house before?"

"No."

"Then what time should I be there?"

Only ten minutes behind schedule, Lucy knocked on Graham and Mattie's front door. It had taken her some time this morning to convince Graham that not only would she watch Mattie tonight, but that if he offered to pay her, it would signal the end of their friendship for eternity.

While it was rather stinky to be just the babysitter, at least Lucy got to hang with her favorite little girl. And in lieu of Graham declaring he couldn't live without her, she would take a girls' night with a five-year-old.

"Hey, it's getting cold out here," she yelled at the still-closed front door. And by cold, she meant sixty degrees and drizzling rain. Yikes. She'd grown way too accustomed to the warm Texas weather.

The door flew open. "It is not cold. Aren't you supposed to be used to snow and freezing weather, Colorado girl?"

Graham was wearing a black tux with a crisp white shirt, his bow tie undone and hanging around his neck. *Good night.* Lucy was going to need at least five minutes before she could speak coherently.

His head tilted. "Why are you still standing out there? Quick—get in out of the cold."

"Ha." She managed a strangled response to his sarcasm—her *ha* sounding a little pirate-y and more like a *har-har*. She moved past him, catching a whiff of his cologne as she did. Her eyelids slid shut. She'd got used to how he smelled, being around him so much, but tonight, combined with the tux, *ai yai yai.*

"Where's Mattie?" *Please, go get Mattie. I need her*

to stop me from ruining everything between us by declaring my undying devotion to your cologne.

"She's upstairs." Graham faced the mirror above the small entry table and started tying his bow tie. What man knew how to tie one of those without help? He looked movie-premiere good, and he was headed out to spend the evening in a world Lucy didn't belong in.

Good times on a Saturday night.

At least she'd been able to drop that line earlier about her date with Bodie last night. It wasn't so much that she'd wanted to gauge Graham's response—though that part had been nice—but more that she'd wanted him to know. Because, every so often, she wondered if Graham felt something between them, too. And she just wanted to be honest that she was dating other people. One other person. On one date. Over FaceTime.

Oh, maybe she shouldn't have said anything at all.

But Bodie had been an amazing date, even over a computer screen. He'd had flowers and dinner delivered to her door.

"What's going on with you tonight?" Graham had turned from the mirror and was studying her. "I told you I could have found a sitter. Mattie's not—"

"You ordering us pizza?"

He nodded.

"Then we're good. In fact, the sooner you go, the better. We have girl things to do." She set the bag she'd brought along on the coffee table. It included makeup—despite Graham's protests—movies, nail polish and hair chalk. Lucy didn't think she was brave enough to use that last one on Mattie even though it would wash right out. Graham would lose his mind. On second thought, it might be kind of fun if he saw Mattie in the morning with bright-colored streaks in her hair and thought it was permanent.

"What's in there?"

She tossed a look over her shoulder. "Nothing you need to know about."

Graham followed her into the living room, looking a bit like a lost puppy. "I don't want to go."

Oh, honey. Lucy stepped toward him. "I know things have been tough between you guys, pretty much because of me—"

"That's not true."

She raised an eyebrow and continued. "But you're doing this for Brooke, not them. And for Mattie. You can do it."

He drank her in, and her knees just about went into retirement right then and there. Finally, he sighed and scrubbed a hand across the back of his neck. "You're right."

"Always."

"Right." His tone was low and wry and made her stomach take a roller-coaster ride. "Always." His smile made an appearance. Combined with the tux, the woodsy cologne and the man, she needed to sit down.

She sank to the couch. "So, exciting date for tonight?"

"Yep."

The comment had been meant as a joke, something to get her mind off her close proximity to Graham, but it had backfired big-time. Had he changed his mind about dating? What had happened? Was he really going out with—

"My dad."

Oh. Oh. Oh. Sweet Graham. Lucy loved that he'd go to his father for support. She also loved that she wasn't watching Mattie while Graham went on a date with another woman. "Sounds like a good person to help you survive tonight." In more ways than one. She assumed tonight would be hard for him with thoughts of Brooke bombarding him throughout the evening.

"Hi, Ms. Lucy!" Mattie flew down the stairs and slid across the living room floor in her socks, joining Lucy on the couch.

"Someone's definitely all the way better."

"She's been bouncing off the walls all day. Very un-Mattie-like. I think—" Graham slid his hands into his pants pockets "—she might be a little excited for tonight."

Couch cushions jiggled as Mattie agreed.

"But she also knows she's going to bed at the normal time."

The girl's lower lip slipped into a pout before she switched back to excitement. "Are we going to do nails?"

"As soon as your dad gets out of here."

Mattie popped up from the couch and started shoving Graham toward the door.

"Hey!" His hands rose in the air. "I'm going. Hang on. I have to grab my keys and wallet." He picked them up from the small entry table. "Pizza should be here soon. It's already paid for. And if anything goes wrong, Lucy, just call me—"

"We got it." Mattie gave him one more shove, and Graham opened the front door. "Emergency numbers are on the fridge. We're good, Dad. Later."

"Don't I at least get a kiss?"

Graham leaned down, and Mattie bestowed a smacking smooch on his cheek.

How disappointing. For a second there, Lucy had hoped he'd been talking to her.

Chapter 14

Graham put the key in the lock of his front door, then let his head fall silently to rest on the cool wood. The night had gone much as he'd expected—a lot of schmoozing with people he barely knew. But it had also had some unexpected parts—like the ache that had radiated in his chest all night. Not acid reflux or any other diagnosable illness. Nope. This had been a churning mixture of guilt and loneliness. Because on a night when he should have been thinking about Brooke—and he had, of course—he'd been missing Lucy.

Lucy.

The woman who was in his house right now because she was willing to watch his daughter, willing to walk right into their lives and make an impact in places he didn't remember feeling before.

He was in trouble. For the first time since Brooke, he knew he wanted to move on…and he couldn't. The Wellings made that impossible. Because no matter what Graham selfishly wanted—to walk into his house and sink into kissing Lucy—he wouldn't do that to Mattie.

She'd already lost her mom. She wouldn't lose a relationship with her grandparents because of him.

He gave in to a pathetic sigh before standing upright and turning the key in the lock. Enough wallowing. He'd just discovered—or been willing to admit—these feelings for Lucy. Maybe they weren't that strong. Maybe she didn't reciprocate them and he was frustrated over nothing. After all, she'd had a date last night.

Who had she gone out with? Graham saw her every day of the week between work, dance and church, and he'd never seen her with a guy who looked like a boyfriend.

He stepped into the house.

"Hey." A rumpled Lucy sat up from where she'd been lounging on the couch. "That was a quiet entrance. I was hoping for a blasting boom box being held over your head from the front yard or a lawn-mower ride or something."

Graham dug the stuff from his pockets, depositing it on the front table. "I take it you've been watching '80s movies all night?"

"Since Mattie went to bed."

"You couldn't have fit too many in."

"Just two. But I've seen them all."

"Of course."

He loosened his tie and walked over, dropping into one of the chairs across from the couch.

"Was it that bad?"

He shrugged. "I'd rather have been here."

"Well, that's a given. I am extremely delightful to be around."

Graham rubbed his temples, the slightest curve touching his mouth. "I feel like you've told me that exact thing before."

"Possible, because it's true." Lucy stood and started folding the blanket.

"You don't need to do that."

She ignored him, continuing to tidy up. He should get out of the chair and help her, but he didn't trust himself to be anywhere near her right now.

He still couldn't believe he'd missed her tonight, couldn't believe these feelings had sneaked up on him. Yes, he'd known he was attracted to her. The thought of dating her had crossed his mind before, but he'd really hoped their relationship could revolve around Mattie and stay at friendship level. His reasons for not developing feelings for Lucy—her age, their opposite personalities, the fact that she still worked for him—were all legit.

They just weren't working.

He'd been blind, and because of the Wellings, he needed to figure out how to remain that way.

"Okay, I'm going to go."

Graham stayed where he was. "Thank you for tonight."

"Of course. Like I said before, it's not a problem."

She walked toward him, sitting on the armrest of his chair. Too close. She smelled so good, he just wanted to drink in everything about her. The way her braid fell over one shoulder as she leaned forward, the concerned look pulling on the mouth that could hold his attention for days.

Her hand rested on his forehead. "No fever. Thought maybe you were coming down with what Mattie had."

"I'm fine."

"You're not. You're sad, and I don't like it." She pointed to herself. "Director of Fun, remember?"

"How could I forget?"

"Are you sure you don't have a temp?"

Graham caught her hand on the way to his forehead again and placed a kiss on the inside of her wrist. He shouldn't have, but he hadn't been able to resist. She sucked in a breath and held very still.

After a few seconds, she slid from the chair and stood. "I—"

"You can't fix this, Lucy. It's okay. I'll be okay."

"At least one of us will be." And then she was gone.

"I have a problem."

"What's wrong?" Olivia sounded as if she'd been asleep, and Lucy winced when she checked the time above her rearview mirror.

"I'm sorry. I didn't even realize how late it was. I forget Cash gets up so early—"

"Cash wants to know where you're stranded. He says he'll be right there."

"I'm fine. Not stranded. Boy trouble."

"Oh."

Lucy heard Olivia explain to Cash that nothing was wrong, some shuffling, then a door open and close.

"Okay, I'm out of the room. What's going on?"

"I want him to be happy."

"Sounds like a crime to me. Of course, I was asleep, so there's a chance I'm not following you."

"He kissed my wrist."

"Was he aiming for your mouth?"

"You are seriously snarky when you get woken up."

Olivia's sigh echoed over the phone. "Sorry. I'll try

for silent, but I'm going to need more details. And to know which guy we're talking about."

"There's only one guy."

"Not true. Didn't you just go on a date with Bodie last night?"

Yes. She had. But Lucy would have to tell Bodie that couldn't happen again. Even if Graham didn't reciprocate her feelings, she couldn't continue to date Bodie when she was falling for someone else.

"Graham. When he got back from his dinner-fundraiser thing tonight, he was so sad, Liv."

"I'm sorry."

"Me, too. And I just wanted him to be happy. And then it hit me after I got into the car. Maybe he can be, but just not with me. His in-laws are like a big brick wall between us. I don't know what their deal is, exactly. I only know it can never happen."

"Never say never."

Lucy fought the tears that surfaced without permission. "You know how optimistic I am, but it's not even remotely possible. They don't like me. I'm not good enough for them, their world, their granddaughter…or Graham."

"Has anyone said that to you?"

"Not in words." Lucy sniffled. But sometimes words weren't necessary.

"I am obviously not in agreement with that thinking, but go on."

"I realized if Graham's willing to give up the *I'm never getting married again* thing, maybe he could move on with someone else. He could have a future with someone the Wellings approve of. And then my heart was breaking, because I knew I wanted that happiness for him…even if it's not with me."

"Oh, Lulu. It sounds like you really care about him. Welcome to maturity."

"Maturity stinks."

"Yep. It can. But sometimes it works out in the end."

"I'm not sure this story is going to end that way, Liv. This isn't a fairy tale."

Silence met her, and she swiped at the tear that managed to escape. Lucy wasn't much of a crier. She was going to add this to her list of things to complain about after growing touchy-feely feelings for someone. Why in the world was her sister such a big proponent of this stuff?

"Lulu, you're right. It might not work out. Not everything does. I can only tell you I'll be praying about all of this. And will you do me a favor?"

Strange time to be asking for things. "What is it?"

"This stuff with Graham's in-laws has been wounding for you." Lucy wanted to interrupt and deny it, but Olivia didn't give her a chance. "Just don't forget God created you to be exactly who you are for a reason. How God views you—how much He adores you—that's a truth you should believe."

At the reminder, peace trickled through Lucy. "Good thing I have a wise older sister to take my midnight phone calls."

"If I'm wise, which I doubt, it's only because I've learned from making many, many mistakes. You, my dear sister, are now the lovely recipient of the knowledge gained from my life lessons."

Despite feeling as though she'd lost her heart somewhere back at Graham's house, Lucy's amusement grew.

"First I was almost in tears. Now I'm laughing. Go back to bed, pregnant mama. Thanks for talking me through this."

"Anytime."

"Except maybe not at two in the morning."

"Right. Maybe not then."

"Hurry up, Dad!" Two weeks later, Graham found himself being dragged across the high school parking lot with superhuman strength by a five-year-old girl who refused to be anything less than early for her first dance recital.

"We're on time, I promise." His reassurances were met by silence. "Are you nervous about tonight, Mattie? It's okay if you feel scared and excited at the same time."

She stopped walking and looked at him, bright eyes accentuated behind red glasses. "My stomach hurts."

"That's nerves, honey, and they aren't a bad thing. Sometimes they can be from excitement, too. I know you're going to do great. And no matter what happens, I'll think you're amazing."

She gave him an exasperated look, and he tried his best not to smile. "You have to, Daddy. You don't count."

"Uh, thank you?"

She giggled, grabbed his hand again and took off for the doors. "All of this talking is making us late."

Ten minutes later, they'd found Mattie's group in a classroom staging area where the girls would stay before and after their part of the performance. Coloring books and crayons were spread out on the floor, along with a handful of girls in bright blue tutus. Mattie fit right in, dropping to the ground and chatting with one of the little girls from her class.

"When did she grow up?"

Lucy appeared beside him. "In the last week."

"That's what I was thinking."

They shared a grin.

"Do you need me to stay in here with her?"

"Nope. Go enjoy the show. I have a few mom volunteers who'll be back here helping keep the girls entertained and their hair perfect while we wait for our performances."

"Hair?" Graham panicked. "I didn't do Mattie's hair a certain way. I didn't even know that was a thing."

"Chill." Lucy shook her head, amusement evident. "I've got everything she needs. Curling iron, ginormous bow, more bobby pins than necessary. I'm prepared."

"Okay." He let out a jagged breath.

"Nervous, are we?"

"Me?" He attempted a chuckle but it came out as a wheeze. "No. Maybe." He tugged Lucy away from the girls. "What if she forgets her steps? Or gets stage fright? Are you sure she's ready? The rest of the girls have been in class all year. Mattie's only been going for two months. I don't want her to feel embarrassed if something goes wrong."

"She'll be fine. Relax. I've been praying over this night for her. I think it's a big step for our serious little girl. She's so excited, and I think she's going to do great."

Our little girl.

He wanted to kiss her. Right there, in the middle of a bunch of five- and six-year-olds, he wanted to let his lips find Lucy's and never let her go.

"Graham, there you are!" his mom called from over his shoulder, and then she was next to him. Jabbering to Lucy. Hugging her. Short blond hair dancing around her chin with excitement.

"I'm Nancy Redmond. It's so nice to finally meet you, Lucy. We've heard so much about you from Mattie and Graham. You'll have to come over for lunch on a Sunday so we can get to know you better."

Since his parents attended a different church than he and Mattie did, his mom and dad had never met Lucy. Much to his mother's dismay. Sounded as if she planned to make up for lost time.

Lucy nodded as his mom continued talking, unable to get a word in.

"I'm just so excited to see Mattie dance. Oh, Mattie—hi, love bug!" Like a butterfly flitting from one flower to another, his mom moved to hug Mattie.

"Gary Redmond." Graham's father introduced himself, shaking Lucy's hand. "I might not show it in the same way as my wife, but I'm equally excited to meet you." Graham and his father shared a number of similarities. Both had dark hair, though his dad's had started peppering with gray over the past few years. Their build was also alike. And their minds… By the way his dad currently studied him, Graham feared his feelings for Lucy were an open book. Hopefully the Wellings wouldn't have their magnifying glasses out tonight.

Dad turned back to Lucy. "Thanks for all you've done for Mattie."

"Of course."

They continued talking, and Graham's neck heated, warmth creeping onto his cheeks. He needed to get out of this room. Lucy meeting his parents was giving him false hope that she would fit with his family.

Trouble was, she would. Just not on the Welling side.

"We'd better find our seats."

Everyone said goodbyes, and Graham gave Mattie one last hug. "You're going to do great. I'll be praying for you the whole time."

Mattie nodded, and then Graham walked with his parents into the auditorium. They found Phillip and Belinda at their reserved seats. Everyone greeted each other, then filled in the row. Graham ended up in the aisle seat, his father next to him.

"You never mentioned what Lucy looks like."

He kept his gaze forward, hoping to avoid this conversation.

"Or that you had feelings for her."

A quick glance told him Phillip and Belinda weren't overhearing his father. "I don't, Dad. Or at least I can't."

"Why not?"

"You already know why not. You know what they—" he nodded down the row "—said and did. It will never work. I can't do that to Mattie."

"Do what? Give her a new family? A stepmom?"

The last word echoed in the suddenly silent auditorium as the lights faded. Graham leaned forward enough to check on the Wellings with his peripheral vision. They were conversing with his mom, or rather his mom was talking and they were nodding.

"No. Take someone else away from her. If something happens with Lucy, Mattie will lose having a relationship with her grandparents. We're already barely keeping the turmoil of our current relationship from her."

"I think you're giving them too much power."

"I don't think I have a choice in the matter."

"Of course, you're praying about it and asking for

God's guidance. Not trying to figure out everything on your own."

Graham resisted squirming like a little boy in trouble. "Of course." He had prayed about all of it many times. Graham got up at six every morning and read his Bible and prayed. He lifted up his concerns, trusting God to handle everything. But he couldn't help but wonder if somewhere along the way, maybe he'd stopped believing God could work this out.

At least, in the way Graham wanted Him to.

Besides, he already had so much good in his life. Who was he to ask for more?

Chapter 15

Good thing breathing was an autonomic reflex, because Graham had spent the first half of the performance forgetting to fill his lungs with oxygen.

Mattie had already done one dance earlier in the evening, and she'd absolutely beamed from the stage. She'd even missed a step or two and hadn't flinched once. Most of the girls in Mattie's class had forgotten what they were doing for a portion of the dance, stopping to watch the other girls before remembering they were part of it. After seeing that, Graham had finally relaxed. No one was expecting the little girls to be perfect. In fact, their small missteps were endearing.

Now Mattie was back out on stage for her second dance. She looked so happy, and Graham owed it all to Lucy.

His mind flashed back to that day in the parking lot when Lucy had grabbed Mattie's car seat without asking and completely changed their lives. In the past two weeks, Graham had hoped the feelings he'd developed for Lucy would change.

His wish had come true. They had changed. Just not

in the way he'd wanted. They'd increased. And he didn't have a clue what to do about it. Today had been Lucy's last day of work at his office—and a half day at that, since she'd needed to prepare for tonight's recital. On Monday, Hollie was returning from maternity leave and Lucy wouldn't be working for him anymore. Graham didn't know her plan. And according to the Wellings, he shouldn't care so much.

But he did.

To say he'd miss her would be the understatement of the century.

Mattie stepped forward from the line of girls and did a few steps on her own.

She looked so mature Graham wanted to cry. If only Brooke could see her. She'd be so proud. She would absolutely love this moment.

Would he ever stop missing her? He imagined not. She'd been his best friend in every way possible. What would she think of these feelings he harbored for Lucy? Would she agree with her parents? Or would she see what he saw?

The dance ended, and the girls ran from the stage, their little shoes pattering. Thundering applause sounded as the next group of older girls took the stage for their dance.

She would have wanted me to be happy.

The thought whispered in his mind, then grabbed hold with intensity. Brooke wouldn't have been okay with the tension circling between him and her parents. But she would have wanted him and Mattie to be happy.

The one thought contradicted the other, leaving Graham completely confused. He didn't know how to handle any of this.

What a mess.

God, show me what I'm missing, what I can't see. Show me Your way. Mine isn't working.

The last group exited the stage, and the owner of the dance school came out. Someone presented her with flowers. After that, all of the dancers filed out on stage. Line after line filled the space. Mattie, being one of the smallest, was in the front. The audience gave them a standing ovation as they continued to come out. Mattie's class kept getting pushed forward to give the others more room.

When the last group walked out, everyone inched forward another step. Mattie was right on the edge of the stage, but she didn't seem to realize it. When they started to bow, Graham's nerves went on high alert. But Mattie completed the bow and stood back up, pride and delight mingling on her face.

How he loved that little girl.

The audience continued to clap, and the group on stage started a second bow. Only this time, Mattie tipped forward and lost her balance. She wobbled trying to find her footing, and then she toppled right off the stage.

Lucy watched it happen. One moment, Mattie was on stage taking a bow with her class. The next, she was gone, disappearing as if she'd fallen off the side of a cliff. Lucy shoved forward through the dancers until she reached the front. At the sight of a crumpled Mattie, she heard someone scream. She jumped off the stage and bent over the little girl.

Mattie was crying, and somewhere this registered as a relief. She was alive. Granted, the drop was only a few feet, but Lucy's mind had gone wild with fear.

"Talk to me, Mattie Grace. What hurts?"

"My-my-my arrrrrmmmmm." The last word came out as a wail.

Lucy stroked back curls that had jarred loose. "It's okay. You're going to be okay." The words felt like lies, but she continued to whisper them along with a barrage of prayers.

Please let her be okay. Let there be nothing permanent wrong. Please.

Where was Graham? Lucy didn't know what to do. Should she pick Mattie up? She'd heard too many stories of injuries that shouldn't have been moved, and she didn't want to do anything to make it worse. It was her fault that Mattie was here in the first place.

And then Graham was there, kneeling over the other side of Mattie, asking doctor questions instead of father questions, calm and strong. Graham's hands checked over Mattie, and her subsequent cry when he reached her arm made Lucy's stomach lurch.

Graham's parents were right behind him, along with the Wellings. As usual, the couple didn't acknowledge her, but this time Lucy didn't care. She scooted out of the way so that Mattie's family could surround her.

An ambulance arrived, and Lucy backed farther away as they rolled a stretcher in. Mattie would hate all of this attention. Good thing she wasn't coherent enough to realize a crowd stood around her. Lucy would give anything to be able to protect the girl from all of this and from the pain she must be enduring.

Now Lucy finally understood why Graham acted the way he did about Mattie. After this, she'd apologize for ever doubting him. Maybe they could get Mattie one of those protective bubbles.

The crowd parted as the paramedics, Graham and Mattie's grandparents exited the building. Lucy spotted something red on the floor.

Mattie's glasses.

She picked them up. *God, I know she's not mine, but it feels like she is. Please let her be okay. Let her be okay and I'll leave the two of them alone. I'll back away.*

Lucy didn't know where the thought came from. She only knew she wanted Graham and Mattie to be happy. And while the thought that she wasn't the answer to that equation just about killed her, she knew without a doubt that if walking away was what she needed to do…

She wouldn't hesitate.

Pain medicine was an amazing thing. Mattie had been in the emergency room close to two hours, and she'd gone from wailing in pain to whimpering, and more recently, to being completely distracted by the dilemma of which color cast she wanted for the hairline fracture in her forearm

Pink.

She didn't need surgery, and because the swelling was minimal, they could get it cast in the ER While the fall had been a shock, she was fine other than an additional bump on her head. Graham could breathe. Sort of.

"Daddy, do you want to sign my cast first?"

"Sure."

"And then Grandma."

"I'd be honored, love bug." Graham's mom was the one who had stayed with him. At first, both sets of grandparents had been there, but it had been too many people. After everyone learned Mattie was okay, she'd been covered in kisses and then his dad and the Wellings had left.

"I still get to have my sleepover, right?"

Graham exchanged a wide-eyed look with his mom. He brushed some of the loose curls from Mattie's forehead. "Honey, I don't think that's the best idea."

Tears welled. "But Grandma and I were going to celebrate my first dance recital. And she has miniature tea-cups and marshmallows." Even if Graham did have those things, they wouldn't compare to what his mom had. She was the best at planning special activities with Mattie.

"Maybe we could reschedule?" His mom held Mattie's cup so she could take a sip of water from the straw. "What if we did it next weekend instead?"

Mattie's head swung back and forth, eyes piercing him. "Daddy, you said I could."

"That was before you hurt your arm. Don't you want to sleep in your own bed?" He couldn't imagine being away from her tonight. She might not need him, but he needed her. He wanted to check on her fifty times and see her tousled hair on her pillow.

She contemplated that question. "I do kind of want to see my stuffies. They need to know what happened to me."

He resisted a smile.

"What if I drive you home?" His mom glanced at him, and he nodded. "And we get to have a cup of hot chocolate before bed. I'll tuck you in, but you'll still get to be in your own bed…" She smiled. "Where your father can watch you like a hawk."

"Mom."

She laughed. "What? You are overprotective. In the best way, of course." Her hand patted his cheek. "Between you and your sisters, we endured all kinds of nights of worry. And just look how great you turned out. I always had a feeling—"

"No feelings, Mom. I can't handle hearing about one tonight."

"Just let me say something about Lucy."

He shot his mother a look that said she should know better with Mattie in the room. "Nope. Not happening. None of your feelings are allowed. I should have made that a requirement for you being the one who got to stay."

She huffed, a line splitting her brow. "Fine. But don't say I didn't warn you."

"Warn me about what?" Graham waved a hand. "Never mind. I don't want to know."

"Where is Lucy?" Mattie piped up. "How come I haven't seen her? Why isn't she here?"

"I'm sure she had to finish up recital stuff."

"Oh." Her nose wrinkled. "Okay. But I want to see her soon."

He saluted Mattie. "Yes, ma'am."

She laughed, gluing back together the pieces of his heart that had shattered when she'd fallen off the stage. But the smug look his mother wore wasn't giving him any peace. He should have had his dad stay.

Thankfully, Dr. Kent chose that moment to reappear. "The good news is we have pink. The bad news is I got caught with another patient. Sorry about that."

"No problem. We don't mind waiting." When they'd left the recital, Graham hadn't known the exact nature of Mattie's injury or if it would require surgery. The fact that they'd arrived at the ER to find Dr. Kent—the best orthopedic specialist Graham knew—already on call because of another patient had practically brought Graham to his knees with gratefulness.

An hour later, Mattie's arm was cast and they were ready to head out the door. Pretty impressive by ER standards. No doubt they were getting the royal treatment.

He picked up an exhausted Mattie from the bed and she wrapped around him. He kissed the top of her hair as he walked, feet grinding to a halt when he caught sight of Lucy in the waiting room.

She was curled into a horribly uncomfortable-looking chair, head tipped to her shoulder, sleeping. If his heart could jump from his chest, it would have.

His mom pried Mattie from his arms. "Go." She nodded toward Lucy. "I'm driving Mattie home, remember? Don't mess this up. Not everyone gets a second chance at love."

"It's not like that." His words fell on an empty waiting room as his mom and Mattie disappeared. Graham walked slowly to Lucy, his pulse erratic.

He sat in the chair next to her and allowed himself to slide a hand along her cheek. "Lucy, honey. Wake up."

Her eyelids fluttered open, lips curving in a soft smile. "Hi." Those same eyes widened. "How's Mattie? I was waiting for so long, I just thought I'd rest for a minute and then—"

"She's fine. Just a hairline fracture."

A crease cut through Lucy's forehead. "Just? Just? If I hadn't forced her into dance class, none of this would have happened. You warned me. You said she always got injured in sports, but I told you to let go. I—"

"You were right. I did need to let go."

Her head shook quickly. "No. Not true. We need to

get her a bubble or something. I can't handle her being hurt, Graham. I get it."

His lips slid up. "We're not getting her a bubble." *We.* He liked the sound of that. As if they were a team. "Though it's not a bad idea."

Tears slid down Lucy's cheeks. "Why do my eyes keep doing this?" She swiped away moisture. "I'm not a crier, but my eyes keep leaking. It's annoying."

He reached to the side table and snagged a tissue for her. "After all of my worrying, she did get injured, but you know what? She was still full of excitement about her first recital once her pain medicine kicked in. She wouldn't have traded tonight for anything. She was even telling me about how she could dance with a broken arm and how she was glad it wasn't a foot. If I'd kept her from doing it, she wouldn't have learned all she did these last few weeks. She's really come out of her shell."

Lucy sniffled. "She has. But I'm still so sorry. I wasn't even going to come here, but I just had to know if she was okay. Guess I'd better follow through on my promise."

"What promise?"

"Nothing." Lucy grabbed her purse and stood, her body swaying.

He jumped up and put an arm around her. "I don't think you should be driving, Duchess. You look a bit out of it."

"I'm fine." Her eyelids slid shut and she leaned against him. "It's annoying you always smell so good."

His mouth hitched. "I apologize." He didn't know what had got into her, but Lucy was acting all sorts of strange.

"I didn't sleep well last night. I was thinking about the performance and going over things in my head."

She shuffled her feet, and Graham tightened his hold around her as they walked out the doors.

"I don't function well with a lack of sleep."

"I'm gathering that."

Her arm tucked around his back. "Did I mention you smell good?"

"Once or twice."

She moaned. "It's like I don't have a filter right now."

"Then I should come up with all kinds of questions to ask you." Graham got to his car and opened the passenger door, almost getting Lucy inside before she balked.

"Wait. What are you doing?"

"Driving you home."

"Absolutely not." She backed away from the vehicle. "I have my car here."

"We'll get it tomorrow." He nudged her into the seat. Amazingly she went, though she grumbled the whole way.

He walked around to the driver's side and got in.

She dug through her purse. "Here." She handed him Mattie's glasses.

"Thanks." He put them in the console. "I wondered what happened to those."

"And I can't see you tomorrow."

"Okay." He started the car and drove out of the lot. "Why not?"

"I'm not going to see you or Mattie. I told God if He would help Mattie not to be seriously injured, I'd get out of your lives."

Panic kicked in. "That's not how God works, Lucy, and you know it."

She crossed her arms. Stared out the window. "I know," she whispered, voice burdened with sadness. "But I just needed to feel like I was doing something to make her better. I just need to feel…useful. I don't like waiting for things to get better on their own."

"I know. You're my fix-it girl. But you can't stay away from me and Mattie. We need you… I mean, she needs you." The correction was a lie. He did need Lucy. But what could he do about it? Talk to the Wellings? They didn't show any signs of changing their minds. Tonight, even with how proud they'd been of Mattie and knowing Lucy had been the one to get her into dance, they hadn't mentioned her once. Not one thank-you. Not even an acknowledgment of all she'd done for their granddaughter.

He felt helpless. As though he had two paths before him and he wanted them both. How was he supposed to choose between Lucy and Mattie's grandparents? It was impossible. He needed to drop Lucy off as fast as possible and then run from her. Literally. Even if he had to get out of the car and sprint. Because resisting her was not something he could accomplish right now.

After a few instructions, Graham pulled into the driveway for Lucy's apartment, past the small red house near the street. He parked beside the garage, then shifted toward her.

She wouldn't look at him.

He slid a hand under her chin, gently turning her face to him. "Lucy, you're the best thing that's happened to Mattie in years. Stop beating yourself up about this."

"I'm trying." She mirrored his position, her shoulder against the seat, her face mere inches from his.

He wanted nothing more than to kiss her. But how could he do that when he knew it couldn't go anywhere?

It would be torture to feel her lips on his and never have that experience again. It had been hard enough the last time, and that lip-lock had barely registered on the kissing scale.

Graham grasped for something to veto the thoughts running through his head. The other week, Lucy had mentioned a date. Was she still dating someone? Though the thought shattered him, it would give him the strength he needed to step back from her.

"Lucy, are you dating someone?"

Relief and frustration warred at the thought. *Please say yes. Make it easier for me to walk away from you.* Although, really, would anything make that easier for him to do?

Her head swung from side to side. "Not anymore. You kind of ruined that for me."

"I'm sorry."

Her eyebrow quirked. "Really?"

A wry laugh slipped out. "Not really."

When her lips curved, he couldn't tear his eyes from them. From her. "Lucy." His voice was hoarse, pleading. "I need you to get out of the car."

She didn't move.

"Duchess, for once in your life…" He tried to infuse humor into his tone, but it just came out threaded with desperation. "Will you please listen to me?"

He was asking her to walk away, but how could she?

Graham studied her with serious eyes, and Lucy could see the truth in their evergreen depths. Something—someone—still held him back. Was it Brooke? The Wellings? She only knew whatever it was would break her heart. But even still, she couldn't force herself to run for safety.

Which meant Lucy would be crushed. She should listen to Graham and get out of this car right now. She should yell about the unfairness of it all. Or cry. Definitely cry. But more than she wanted to protect herself, she wanted him.

In this moment, even if she only had this moment, she just wanted to believe they had a chance, that his in-laws or Brooke didn't stand between them.

That she was enough.

She slid one hand across his cheek, fingertips meeting smooth, close-shaved skin. He stayed still, watching her, his breathing as shallow as a Colorado creek bed during a drought. She inched forward. Touched her lips to his. Waited while indecision warred on his face.

And then her name was a groan, and he was kissing her with such tenderness that new tears sprang behind her closed eyelids.

His arms went around her, and she sank into the essence of Graham. The way he smelled, the taste of him. Her fingers roamed behind his neck, sliding into his hair.

She could drown in his kiss and not regret it.

Until tomorrow. Tomorrow, the memory would haunt her.

But tonight…tonight she planned to live in this moment.

Chapter 16

"Wait a minute." Olivia ate a spoonful of her ice cream sundae and propped her feet on Lucy's coffee table. "So if you didn't see Graham this morning after all of that, how'd you get your car back?"

"I jogged to get it."

Liv's head swung from watching the chick flick they'd seen too many times to count to Lucy's spot at the other end of the couch.

She looked up from her bowl of ice cream and met her sister's gaze. "What? It was only a few miles."

"And Graham was okay with that?" Olivia tapped her spoon against her bowl, brow wrinkled. "Maybe I need to change my opinion of the man."

"It had nothing to do with Graham. I needed my car. I got my car. I texted him I didn't need a ride. He probably thought I was getting one from you."

Olivia rolled her eyes. "Good to know that these changes I've been seeing in you aren't all-encompassing."

Lucy laughed.

"So, did you discuss anything after the kiss?"

Lucy set her bowl on the coffee table, digestion suddenly vetoing the idea of more ice cream. "Just that it wouldn't be happening again." Information that hadn't come as a surprise but still hurt. Graham had told her nothing could come of their kiss.

The man had kissed her until she couldn't breathe or think straight, then tried to apologize.

She'd wanted to cry and slap him and kiss him all over again. An unusual combination. But she'd settled on accepting. Why? Because she'd known going into that kiss it wouldn't lead anywhere.

"What?" Olivia shrieked. "You can't just leave it like that."

"Actually, we can."

Flashing blue eyes that were an exact match for Lucy's bored into her with impressive heat.

"It's…complicated."

"Did you at least tell him you love him?"

Good thing she'd stopped eating or Lucy would have choked. "I don't—" Lucy sat back against the couch cushions. "I can't love him."

Liv's eyebrows scrunched together. "Why not?"

"I'm not…enough. There's something holding him back. And I'm certain part of it, if not all, is his in-laws. We don't stand a chance at a relationship with them between us. And…" Lucy trailed off.

"And what?"

"I'm not sure I am right for Graham and Mattie. I want them, but…what if the Wellings' obvious misgivings about me are right? I'm young and not exactly mature. Could a relationship with Graham and me even work? I mean, it's not like I'm mom material."

Olivia let out a disgusted snort. "Says who?" She

looked ready to pop up from the couch and hunt down the person who dared to offend her little sister. Bless her.

"Probably everyone. Again, including his in-laws."

"What did I tell you about that?" With a growl, Olivia set her bowl on the coffee table. It landed with a clatter. "It doesn't matter what his in-laws think. It matters what God thinks. The Wellings are wrong, Lulu."

Lucy had her doubts. "Even if that's true, what can I do about it?"

Silence reigned. The fact that Liv looked at a loss for answers didn't encourage Lucy in the least.

"I thought you knew everything, big sister."

"I don't. But I have learned to pray before doing." She grinned. "Most of the time."

Lucy thought she had, too. But it turned out she really, really stank at asking God for help. She still struggled against the tendency to do everything on her own. And whenever she did get into the habit of praying and asking first, she always ended up snatching things back and attempting to do them herself again. Just like after the recital, thinking she could fix everything by not seeing Graham or Mattie. Why couldn't she just hand things over and trust God? Why did she think she could handle everything on her own? If the past few weeks were any indication, she definitely could not.

"I still think you love him."

"Like you so willingly admitted you loved Cash? I remember visiting, sister. I think everyone knew you loved him before you did."

Instead of taking offense, Liv just laughed. "Probably true. Nice try changing the subject."

"I don't—" Lucy huffed, ready to deny that she loved

Graham, but the words caught in her throat. She hadn't...
She couldn't...

No.

The realization washed over her with a certainty she
couldn't ignore. Oh, stink. How had she let that happen?
She'd known not to let her feelings for Graham progress, but they'd just gone on and done their own thing,
tumbling all the way to heartbreak land.

Her eyes closed. "Fine. I love him." Guess all of that
wanting him to be happy even if it wasn't with her did
stem from her growing love for Graham and Mattie.
Fluttering started in her stomach. "I love him."

A smile formed, then dropped like a stone. "But I still
can't have him." She turned to Liv. "Will you *please* stop
making me feel things? You're the worst sister ever."

"And by that you mean the best?" Olivia beamed, and
they both laughed, though Lucy's ended on a pathetic
note. She might love Graham, but she didn't have a clue
what to do about it.

As the movie progressed, Lucy's mind wouldn't settle. One tempting but nerve-racking idea kept taking
hold. There was something she could do with her recently discovered feelings. She could tell Graham. Give
him the words as a gift. He might not be able or willing
to say them back to her...but wasn't the point of love to
give it away?

Never had a text sent him into cardiac arrest before,
but Graham was pretty sure the one he'd received from
Lucy ten minutes ago on his way out of church had done
exactly that.

I need you.

Lucy Grayson—the girl who had turned his life upside down, the one he'd kissed two nights ago and hadn't stopped thinking about since—never needed anyone.

The text had included an address, so he'd replied that he and Mattie would head in her direction. Graham had asked what was wrong, but he'd yet to receive an answer from Lucy. Surely his elevated blood pressure would come down once he found out she was okay.

Graham spotted Lucy's car and parked two spots over. "Mattie, I'll be right outside the car. Just stay buckled in."

"But I want to see Lucy."

"You will. Just give me a sec."

He popped out, striding in her direction.

Was she having car trouble? Another flat tire? What in the world had happened?

She was standing by the passenger door of her car. Smiling. Heart attack number two of his day.

"What's wrong?" He stopped in front of her, grabbing her hands. They were freezing, and it wasn't cold out. "Lucy, what's going on? I'm going nuts here."

Her smile was like sunshine. He shouldn't look at it, but he couldn't tear away.

"How's Mattie?" She waved at the backseat of his car, and Mattie grinned, waving back with her non-cast arm.

"Really?" Exasperation laced his tone. "That's how we're going to play a desperate text and me finding you on the side of the road?"

"You didn't find me. I asked you to come. And I'm in a parking spot, not on the side of the road." Again, her lips curved as though she harbored a tantalizing secret. "And, yes, that's what I want to know."

He knew better than to fight this woman. "Mattie's

great. She did way better than I expected the last two nights. We even made it to church this morning."

"I know." Her head tilted. "I saw you across the way, but the two of you were surrounded by a crowd."

A rush of pride gripped him. "It's a bit surprising, but I think she might be learning to enjoy the attention." Mattie was changing, opening up, and most if not all of the credit for that went to the woman currently standing in front of him. The one confusing him with her cryptic texts and giddy behavior.

"Smart girl."

"So, any chance you're going to tell me what's going on now?"

Whatever it was, Lucy certainly found it amusing. "I guess." She released a mock sigh. "You know how you walk over those grate things in the ground and think, man, it sure would be awful to drop your keys in there?"

"No." This woman was crazy. "I've never thought that."

"Yes, you have! Everyone has thought that."

"Lucy." At her name grinding between his teeth, she pointed to the ground.

"I actually did that. I stopped after church to grab a sandwich and a Diet Coke, and then *bam*, down they went."

He glanced to where she was pointing, then bent to peer closer. Sure enough, a pink ballet-slipper keychain was wedged a few feet down in a pile of muck. A bit of trash. Some food.

When he straightened, she was beaming again. Was she going to start bouncing on her toes next? "Did you drop them on purpose?"

"No." Her eyes widened with innocence. "It was an accident."

"Then why are you so happy about it?"

"At first, I was just upset. I was trying to decide whether to walk home—if I had an extra set of keys there—"

"Why would you do that? Of course you should call—"

"Wait!" She held up a hand. "And then I realized something." The look on her face softened from humor to something entirely different. She edged slightly closer, bringing with her the smell of lime and coconut. "I realized I *wanted* to ask you to help me. I wanted to be rescued. By you."

His hand lifted involuntarily, tucking a loose curl behind her ear. "You asked for help? And you wanted to?"

She nodded.

Who knew what a heady feeling that thought could invoke? His mouth hovered way too close to hers. "I should get Mattie out of the car. She wants to see you. Plus, I have no doubt if I don't, in the next few seconds, I'm going to be kissing you." The past two nights, he'd barely slept between checking on Mattie and thinking about that kiss from Friday night. *Kisses.*

Goose bumps erupted on Lucy's arms, and Graham rubbed his hands across her bare skin. She was wearing a sundress, gray on top, colorful zigzag stripes on the bottom. As always, she looked gorgeous.

Graham had spent the past day and a half thinking about her, processing whether a relationship between them might be possible.

Was there a chance for them? The weight of that question rested on his shoulders. He couldn't tell Lucy how he felt about her until he'd dealt with the Wellings. And he wasn't exactly sure how to do that. Another thought that had kept him awake.

"Kissing." Her head swung back and forth and those lips smoothed together. "Can't have that."

"Unfortunately not." Or maybe just *not yet*.

Somehow, he managed to drag himself away from her, go to his car and open the back door for Mattie. She scrambled out, shooting him a look that said the minute he'd left her in there had been far too long.

She vaulted into Lucy's arms. "Are you coming to lunch with us? Daddy said I get to have a celebration lunch and I want you to come."

Lucy had crouched for a hug, and now she met his gaze over the top of Mattie's head. "I'm not so sure—"

"We should celebrate two things. Mattie's dance recital and your recent…groundbreaking decision."

Her eyes crinkled. After another Mattie squeeze, she stood, her hand still wrapped around his daughter's. A seriousness rare for Lucy tugged at her features. "Are you sure that's a good idea? I know there's things—"

"It's just lunch." That wasn't true, and they both knew it. They had things to discuss, to figure out, but he just wanted to spend a little time with her. Hollie would be back from maternity leave tomorrow, and Graham likely wouldn't see much of Lucy this week. The thought was enough to make him consider begging.

She nodded. "Okay. It's just lunch."

They loaded into his car. "We'll have to get a hanger or something to get the keys out. So, food or keys first?"

Mattie and Lucy exchanged a grin, both answering "Food" at the same time.

"Let's go to our place, Daddy."

"Which one's our place?"

"The one we went to with Lucy before. The one with ice cream."

Our place. Lucy smiled, and Graham wanted to lean over and kiss the spot where it creased her cheek. The idea of it being *their* place swept in and took hold. Graham was done trying to stay away from Lucy. If rescuing her from lost keys made him this happy, he couldn't fight how he felt any longer.

He needed to talk to Phillip and Belinda.

After the short drive there, the three of them piled out of the car. Mattie held Lucy's hand, and Graham barely resisted doing the same.

He wanted this—the three of them together. He just wasn't sure how to get it. Would the Wellings even listen to him?

His gut churned at the thought. Graham needed to orchestrate things right, because he didn't want to lose anyone from Mattie's life. Somehow he had to figure out how to get through to the couple.

They were almost to the register when Mattie started hopping on one foot. "Dad, I have to go potty."

"I'll take her," Lucy said. "Order me that sandwich again." And before he could protest, they were gone.

He shouldn't have been surprised when Phillip and Belinda opened the door of the restaurant and stepped inside. Graham knew they ate out every Sunday after church, and—how could he forget?—he'd even run into them here before. Still, when Mattie had suggested it, the Wellings showing up had never crossed his mind.

Of course, he'd been preoccupied with thoughts of Lucy. She had that effect on him.

At first, the sight of them sent him into a small panic.

They would be irate about him being here with Lucy after their previous conversation. But then…that fear turned into something else.

Excitement.

He wanted to talk to them. Why not now? Waiting wasn't going to get him any closer to having Lucy in his life. Graham was done tiptoeing around them. They had to be able to talk calmly and work this out.

He left his place in line and strode over to them. "Phillip, Belinda." He greeted them with stiff hugs. "Could I speak to you outside for a minute?"

They nodded, looks instantly changing to concern. Once outside, Graham fumbled for words. Perhaps he should have given himself some time to figure out what he wanted to say and how to say it.

"Where's Mattie?"

He hadn't thought about that question being asked so quickly, though it made perfect sense. "She's…using the restroom."

"Oh." Belinda nodded. "And is her arm okay? How's she feeling?"

"She's doing well. We went to late church. She wanted to go, I think to show off her cast." His mouth quirked at that, but he quickly came back to what he wanted to talk to them about. "But Mattie's not in the restroom by herself."

Now their faces twisted with confusion. And really— he resisted an eye roll—he could have come up with a better intro than that.

"She's with Lucy."

Phillip glanced to his wife, then Graham. "Isn't Lucy done working for you?"

What did that have to do with anything? "Friday was her last day. Hollie comes back on Monday."

"Then why is Lucy here with you? You're not holding up your end of the deal. You said after Lucy stopped working for you, she'd be out of your life."

Graham choked on his breath. Scrubbed a hand over the back of his neck. "I never said that. You assumed. That was never part of our deal."

"Grandpa, Grandma!" Mattie's squeal echoed down Main Street. She flew by Graham in a blur, lurching into her grandfather's arms. He chuckled and began asking Mattie questions about her arm as Lucy stopped next to Graham, confusion marring her brow.

"What did you just say about a deal? What's going on?"

Panic filled his mouth with a metallic taste. This wasn't going according to plan. Not that he'd had a great one of those when he'd stepped outside in the first place.

Graham needed to talk to Lucy. Alone.

He tried to steady his voice, though it didn't obey. "Phillip, Belinda. Can you take Mattie inside and order?"

The couple stared, their wounded looks flashing between him and Lucy.

"I'll be right there. Please."

After what felt like an hour, they acquiesced. Graham waited for the restaurant door to shut before facing Lucy.

He reached for her hand. Held on. "Remember when the Wellings were upset the night they came over and you were there?"

She nodded.

"They were concerned about me dating."

"You said that."

A sigh rumbled through his chest. "But I didn't tell

you the rest of it. They said if I dated you, they'd walk out of Mattie's life. And I couldn't do that to her. I couldn't let her lose another person. And so I promised not to date you."

She pulled her hand away from his as though his touch scalded. "You...you made a deal over me?"

"It wasn't like that."

A wounded sound tore from her throat. "Did you or did you not make an agreement with them about me and then not tell me about it?" Though quiet and controlled, her words pierced like a knife.

He wanted to lie so badly. He needed time to explain. Needed her to stop looking at him with so much hurt bursting from her blue eyes. "Yes, but you have to understand—"

"I understand." Her wooden response slayed him. Tears glistened, but she blinked them away, replacing them with a vacant look that scared him even more. "I knew I wasn't good enough for them. But I had no idea you felt the same way."

"That's not true." Graham's world was spinning out of control. "You know I don't think that way about you."

"If you were willing to use me as a bargaining chip, then yes, you do." Fingertips pressed against her lips. "And I had to go and fall in love with you."

What? His throat constricted, but she didn't give him any time to deal with that comment.

"I'd wanted to tell you, wanted you to know how much I felt for you even though I knew you couldn't say it back to me." Her eyelids momentarily shuttered. "Now I know why."

His fingers itched to reach for her, to hold her there.

Knowing she wouldn't tolerate his touch, Graham fisted his hands by his sides.

"I was going to tell you that you should move on without me. I wanted you to be happy. To find someone they approved of." She motioned toward the restaurant. "I'd hoped you wouldn't go back to the place you were in before, that you'd get married and have more kids." Her head shook as though she could wish away the pain written on her face. "I knew better. I knew better than to fall in love."

She took a step back.

He panicked. "Lucy, please listen to me. I didn't know what else to do. They didn't give me any choice. I couldn't—"

"Goodbye, Graham." She turned and walked away. With each step, a piece of him crumbled.

"Wait!" he called out. "Your keys. We need to get them out. At least let me drive you—"

She whirled in his direction, what felt like miles of sidewalk separating them. "Don't worry, noble Graham. I'll take care of it myself." Her shoulders straightened, mouth weighed down with sadness that resonated in his bones. "I always do." She sounded hollow. No tears. No yelling at him.

He wanted to go after her, to make her listen. He wanted to be the person she called when she needed help. But he'd ruined any chance of rescuing Lucy. *For the rest of my life?*

Had he lost her forever? That goodbye had been full of finality. Graham shook off the thought because it was drowning him, snaking around his chest and squeezing until he couldn't breathe.

He got out his cell and texted Cash.

Your SIL is walking down Main near Adams. Needs help
getting keys out of a drain.

The next bit was harder to type.

Won't let me help her.

She would have, five minutes ago. Before Graham
had thrown away any hope of a future between them.
He couldn't believe he'd failed her.

And the fact that she loved him…had loved him, at
least. What was the point of doing life without Lucy?

Mattie.

He dug his fingers into his temples, but nothing qui-
eted the humming pain that had taken over his body.

Mattie would be distraught. She loved Lucy fiercely.
He'd done all of this to prevent Mattie from losing another person, yet now that was exactly what had happened.

He wasn't the only one suffering in this scenario.

His phone buzzed with a reply text.

Got it. Liv's on the way Trouble between you 2?

A wry breath puffed out of him.

Something like that.

Cash's reply came quickly.

Been there, done that. Hang in there. Grayson girls usually come around.

Graham wanted to believe his friend so badly, but hope felt too far out of reach.

That was that. Olivia would help Lucy. Graham was no longer a necessary part of her life. He had been for about two minutes. And maybe it would have lasted if he'd handled things better or stood up to his in-laws earlier.

He should never have let things escalate the way they had. Though he still didn't have answers, he only knew he'd failed to figure it out before it was too late.

A failure. He knew the feeling well. He let it wrap around him, accepting the blame he deserved.

All of those things Lucy had said about him moving on and not going back…getting married. Having more kids.

What she didn't know—what she would never know now—was that this time he didn't need a few hours to process. He already agreed with her. He *was* meant to do all of those things. He was just meant to do them with her.

Chapter 17

Olivia paused in the doorway to Lucy's bedroom. "Any chance you've stopped wallowing between the time I walked out of your room five minutes ago and my return?"

Considering that it was Saturday evening and Lucy was still lounging in bed dressed in orange striped pajama pants and a white long-sleeved T-shirt, the answer to Olivia's question should most likely be no.

"I'm not wallowing. A girl should be able to stay in her pajamas all day if she wants to. It's not a crime. And who even uses that word anyway? Wallow. It sounds funny. Like something a fish would do."

Her sister dropped onto the other side of the bed, facing her. "Fish don't wallow. They swim."

"Enough with that word! I hereby ban all words that start with *W* for the rest of the night."

"Oh, Lulu." An amused sigh slipped from Olivia. "You're definitely snarky enough to drive any man away."

"Hey! I didn't drive him away. He made a deal over me." A new ache started in Lucy's chest, right next to the wound that had been ripped open last Sunday. "Like I was a chess piece," she whispered. "Or a business merger."

"Yeah. I'm not a big fan of that, either. But don't you know him better than that? Don't you think he had reasons? I agree he shouldn't have done that, but he was just trying to protect Mattie—"

"I get that part of it." Lucy would do anything for Mattie, too, so she understood Graham had been put in a hard place. "But how could he not tell me? How could he have an agreement with them about me and not say a thing? How could he trade me like that? I just feel…"

Used. Worthless. Lucy swallowed the words. "I knew I wasn't good enough for the Wellings, and that was hard enough. But Graham?" Those annoying tears she'd been fighting all week tried to return, but she blinked them away.

Enough of this. So she'd been hurt. She needed to pull herself back together. And she certainly wasn't going to admit she was doing the *W* word her sister had mentioned.

How could Lucy miss something so much that she'd never had? It had been six days since that awful moment with Graham and his in-laws, and she hadn't seen or heard from him since. And since she no longer worked at his office…not a glimpse of him all week.

Six days somehow equaled a year in her math world.

She was mad at him and she missed him all at the same time. She wanted to yell at him. She wanted him to show up on her doorstep and kiss her, to hear him say he'd fixed everything with his in-laws and he was a jerk of the biggest sort.

But even if he did all of those things…she still

couldn't let go of how she'd felt in that moment. He'd made her feel like the yucky stuff that had been sticking to her keys when she'd finally retrieved them from under the grate.

How could she just forget that?

It would be like forgetting about Mattie, and Lucy knew after this week that was something she could never do.

The spring dance session had ended after last week's recital, so she hadn't seen Mattie since the confrontation with Graham. Lucy missed the girl and was desperate to know if she was okay.

Was Mattie and Graham's relationship with the Wellings intact? And why did Lucy care so much? The couple had been nothing but horrible to her, but still, she didn't want anything to stand between them and their granddaughter.

Maybe tonight, after Olivia left, Lucy would go over to Graham's to check on Mattie. Make sure things were okay between her and the Wellings. And if they weren't? Lucy would march over there and set the couple straight. Forget hiding out. Nobody put Lucy in a corner. It was time to hit the dance floor again. Just minus the partner she'd hoped to have.

Except…before Lucy stormed over there attempting to fix everything herself, she would pray about it. It still might not be her first instinct to stop and ask God for help, but she planned to train herself the way a person would train a puppy.

Olivia would probably start studying numerous devotionals, verses and books, but Lucy had trouble with all that. One word seemed possible for her. So one word was what she'd chosen. It was the one that had been knocking her over the head for the past few weeks, and she'd finally recognized God's direction.

Ask.

And so she was working on it. It had been a long time coming, this change in her. But she'd finally hit bottom. Finally realized she couldn't do everything on her own. A simple paper sat on her nightstand, the word *Ask* scrawled in her handwriting. Her reminder to do exactly that. And each morning for the past week, Lucy had paused before doing anything else in her day and asked God for help.

Her prayers weren't eloquent. They were more the accumulation of many years of thinking she could handle it all herself. And the new realization that she couldn't.

Some days, she didn't even know what she was asking for.

Maybe God preferred it that way, without all of her suggestions and solutions added in.

"You've had a week to process," Olivia said, breaking into her thoughts. "What are you going to do now? You can't keep living like this. Don't you think you need to forgive Graham even if you two aren't together?"

Lucy scooted farther under her covers. "I didn't bug you when you were a mess over Cash."

"True. But Janie did. She was all over me about it."

"Even if I do forgive him, that doesn't change anything between me and the Wellings." She sighed, though it came out as more of a wheeze. "I feel strange." She rubbed a hand over her throat. "Kind of itchy or something." Of course, with the amount of weird things they'd eaten tonight—total junk-food nation—she could very easily feel sick.

Or it could be the fact that she'd lost the man and the

little girl she loved. For a second, at the restaurant, she'd let herself believe.

Believe she and Graham had a chance of making things work.

Believe she could be mom material.

Why had she got so involved? When she'd moved here, she'd had a plan, and it hadn't looked like this. There was a reason she didn't do serious. Because it stinking hurt.

The first time she'd met the Wellings, Lucy should have started distancing herself from Mattie and Graham.

"Lucy." Olivia leaned forward. "I think you're breaking out in hives. Are you allergic to something we ate tonight?"

"How should I know? We ate a bunch of junk and then topped it off with dessert. Who knows what was in all of it?"

Her sister's brow creased. "I think you need to go to the hospital."

"What? I'm fine."

"You're not fine. Does your throat feel tight, like you can't get air through?"

"Maybe." Panic began to beat in her veins. "Yes."

Olivia was already running from the room. "I'm grabbing you some Benadryl in case it helps. Let's go!"

Lucy should call Graham. He'd know what to do. But, then again, did he even care? It wasn't as if she'd heard from him this week. She didn't need him or his help. She pushed off the covers and popped out of bed, causing the paper from her nightstand to flutter to the floor.

Ask.

The blatant reminder was just what she needed. Lucy

might not have Graham, but she did have God. And He could handle every request she sent His way.

Including her strange combination of symptoms: hives, a swollen throat and a broken heart.

"So, you've been bright and full of sunshine this week." Graham's father handed him a dish he'd just washed, and Graham dried. "Reminds me of that stage you went through in high school when you turned caveman and stopped talking to us for a year. Then one morning your door opened and you were back. It was the strangest thing."

The serving dish clanked as Graham stacked it in the cupboard. Maybe he could just pretend not to hear his dad talking.

"Have you decided what you're going to do?"

Then again, maybe not. "No." Frustration seeped out in a deep sigh. "What can I do? Lucy's mad at me and I deserve it. I was a jerk to have an agreement with the Wellings and not tell her what was going on. Phillip and Belinda are upset and barely speaking to me, though thankfully they are still talking to Mattie. How can I choose? Not that Lucy would even have me at this point. My hands are tied. If I fight for Lucy, Mattie misses out on a relationship with the Wellings. If I choose the Wellings, Mattie and I both miss out on a relationship with Lucy."

There were a lot of bad things about this situation, but the worst part was that both of his girls were hurting and Graham couldn't fix it. That he'd caused it.

Ever since losing Brooke he'd felt a sense of failure. Could he have done more? What had he missed? Now it all came rushing back. He wanted to fix this. He wanted

Lucy *and* Mattie *and* the Wellings to be happy, but after a week of thinking, praying and begging God for guidance, he still didn't know what to do.

"I can't fathom losing a child like the Wellings did, and an only child at that. They must be hurting so much."

"I know. That's why I can't hurt them more."

The water sloshed in the sink, joining the sound of Graham's mom reading to Mattie in the living room. Being at his parents' house always felt comfortable, but tonight it only reminded Graham of what he'd begun to hope he'd have with Lucy.

A home. A family. A person. He just wanted another person meant for him. Was that so much to ask? According to the Wellings, and now Lucy, yes.

"Have you tried talking to them calmly? Outside of them finding you with Lucy?" His dad handed him a bowl.

Graham contemplated that question, a bit surprised by the answer. "No. I guess not."

"Maybe you should try it."

"Dad, they've been so…not themselves. So harsh about Lucy. I don't think that conversation would end well."

Another minute went by in silence.

"Of course, you'll never know unless you try. Plus, I think part of their issue is that you never told them how you feel about Lucy. They just kept finding you with her after you said you weren't dating her."

Exactly what Graham had hoped to talk to them about at the bakery before his life had crashed and burned for the second time. And now all he could think about was how Lucy would love that he'd just inadvertently thought a phrase from *Top Gun*.

"This conversation proves I share way too much with you."

His dad chuckled.

But the man was right. Graham hadn't been honest with the Wellings. Not once had he sat down with Belinda and Phillip and been truthful about his feelings for Lucy—partly because he'd been too busy denying how he really felt.

All of this time, he'd blamed the Wellings for keeping them apart. And while they obviously had reservations about him moving on, Graham believed they were more wounded about missing their daughter than anything else. Each time they'd found him with Lucy—just like last week—it had come as a shock to them.

Things might be different if he'd changed his response to them. He could have said *I think I do have feelings for Lucy, but no matter what happens, you'll always be in Mattie's life.*

He could have reassured them instead of getting defensive.

Graham's phone buzzed in his pocket and he checked the screen. It was the after-hours answering service for the clinic.

He answered.

"Dr. Redmond, Bill Fitzer's son called and said his dad just went back into the hospital. They were hoping you could check on him. He knows he's not technically your patient, but—"

"I'll go. Thanks for letting me know." After a few more details, they disconnected.

Dad dried his hands on the towel. "I heard. Go on. We'll keep Mattie." He paused. "You're a good doctor, you know that?"

Where had that come from? "You're my dad. You have to say that."

"You care, Graham. That's most of the battle right there. Not every doctor would go to the hospital during their free time to see a patient who's no longer their patient."

"I guess."

"You do know there was nothing more you could have done for Brooke, right?"

Graham's pulse stuttered.

"Everyone worked so hard to save her. Including you. You did everything you could." His gaze held Graham's. "I've just felt lately like I needed to tell you that."

Tears formed at the backs of Graham's eyes, but he fought them and won.

"You loved her well, Graham. It's okay to move on."

"I want to, but—" He shrugged. First he had to figure out how to accomplish that.

"And when—" his dad paused, a small smile creasing his mouth "—or *if* you talk to the Wellings, you do have a secret weapon. A God who moves mountains and changes hearts. Even hardened ones. Mom and I have been praying over your relationship with Lucy ever since you met her."

Graham rubbed a hand over his chest, heart thudding under his fingertips.

"Your mom had a feeling Lucy was the next one for you." Dad grinned. "And this time I agreed with her. So just…don't give up yet."

Suddenly Graham was incredibly grateful for his mother's intuition. Emotion gripped him again, and he cleared his throat before speaking. "Thanks, Dad. I'd better go."

"If you need to stay out and take care of some other things…" His dad went back to doing dishes. "Go right ahead. Mattie will be just fine."

An hour later, Graham stepped into the hospital hallway after finishing his visit with Bill and his family. Bill had started seeing a nephrologist to treat his kidney disease months ago, yet for whatever reason, he always wanted to discuss his treatment options with Graham.

And Graham was learning to accept that.

His thoughts ricocheted as he walked. He was alone. He could go talk to…anyone he wanted to talk to. Like a certain person he'd missed so much this week that a constant ache had weighed down his body, making him wonder if he was sick. He'd finally realized his symptoms were simply from missing Lucy.

Having Hollie back from maternity leave was great. No one did the job quite like her. But Graham wasn't sure he could go another day, another hour without seeing Lucy. Even if she just yelled at him or slapped him, it would be worth it to catch a glimpse of her.

As he walked by the coffee machine, Graham heard his name. He turned to see Olivia.

"Hey." She approached, blowing into a paper coffee cup. "Cash is just in the restroom and then we're headed back in to see her."

His head tilted, brow pinched. "Headed in to see… who?"

The way Olivia's expression went from surprise to concern would have been comical if it didn't tighten something in Graham's gut.

"You're not here to see Lucy?"

Pinpricks raced across his skin as he took a step toward her. "What?"

"Lucy's in the ER." Olivia reached out, putting a hand on his arm for a second as if to calm him. The move didn't work. "I thought maybe she'd let you know."

"No." He struggled for oxygen. "She didn't. Your sister's not exactly the kind to tell anyone when she's hurt or in trouble." Especially him.

She laughed. "So true."

Strange time to be acting so happy. The panic thrumming through him must have been visible on his face, because Olivia squeezed his arm again. "She's okay, Graham."

She couldn't be that okay if she was in the ER. "What's wrong? What happened?"

"She had an allergic reaction."

Before the words were fully spoken, he was headed for the ER.

"Don't you dare break her heart again, Graham Redmond! I'll send Cash after you if you do!"

Graham turned back, the overwhelming need to see Lucy only slightly outweighed by the desire to clarify Olivia's allegiance. If he didn't have her support, he didn't stand a chance with Lucy.

"You aren't going to tell her to run as far from me as she can get? She listens to you and cares what you think. You must want to throttle me for hurting her."

"I did." Olivia's shoulders lifted. "But you'll be relieved to know I'm all about second chances. I have a God and a husband who did the same for me." She made a shooing motion with her hand. "Now get out of here already. It's going to take everything you've got to win her back."

Graham didn't doubt her for a second.

Moments later, he burst into the ER, scanning for

someone to help him. When he didn't find anyone, he started peeking into treatment rooms. He could always play his doctor card if someone caught him.

A mess of blond curls spread on a pillow made him stop.

He slowly edged inside. Lucy was lying still, eyes closed, her breathing steady. He attempted to follow suit.

She smelled like summer and lime and everything he never knew he needed.

He studied her skin. Her color looked good. At this point, they were probably watching for a recurrence of her symptoms.

The doctor part of Graham knew she should be fine. But the other part of him—the part that couldn't imagine his life without the woman tucked under a blanket who'd just started snoring like a three-hundred-pound man with sleep apnea—wanted reassurances.

He wanted promises.

But Graham knew better than anyone that life didn't work that way. He stood by her bed for a number of minutes and watched her sleep, wishing he could wake her with a kiss. Wondering how she'd react if he did.

I love you. The thought seeped into him slowly, warming him. He loved her. He wasn't giving her up.

Which meant right now there was something he had to do…and unfortunately it wasn't watching Lucy sleep. But in the future, if this next conversation went well, that was a job Graham definitely wanted to apply for.

Chapter 18

"I haven't been honest with the two of you." Graham was sitting in the Wellings' living room, and the couple had their rapt attention on him. He'd never been so nervous in all of his life. It felt as though everything depended on this moment, on his ability to convince them to accept Lucy.

He took a calming breath, experiencing a rush of peace when he remembered what his dad had said. His parents were praying. Graham wasn't fighting this battle on his own.

"I wasn't even honest with myself about my feelings. I never thought I'd want to remarry. I had a great marriage with Brooke, and I didn't think that could happen twice. I was content with what I'd had and with being a dad to Mattie. But then Lucy came along." Graham begged for guidance from God, knowing his next words would wound. "I really didn't mean to fall in love with her. That wasn't the plan. But I did. And so did Mattie."

Silence reigned. Belinda wiped a tear with her fingertip.

"I'm willing to give you back Mattie's money if it

helps. That's not what Lucy wants. She doesn't even know that money exists, nor would she care. She might come off young and a bit impetuous, and yes, she's not like Brooke, but then… Brooke was one of a kind. And so is Lucy. I'm not trying to steal your memories of Brooke from you. I don't want to hurt you. And I don't want Mattie to lose you from her life because I want to have a relationship with Lucy."

Emotion clogged his throat. "Please don't make me choose between you and Lucy. Mattie needs all of you in her life."

Belinda snagged a tissue, wiping a now steady stream of tears. "It hurts that you would choose her over us. It feels like losing Brooke all over again."

Graham got up and moved next to his mother-in-law on the couch. "I don't want to choose. I want all of you in Mattie's life and my life. I ache for you as parents. I can't imagine losing Mattie. Part of the reason I didn't say anything about Lucy to you earlier is because I didn't want to hurt you. I'm so sorry. I just can't keep burying these feelings."

When Belinda's hand snaked out slowly to squeeze his, the smallest bit of hope sparked.

"So." Phillip shifted in his wingback chair, the same pain on Belinda's face etched on his. "If you and this Lucy have a relationship, you'd still want us in Mattie's life?"

"Of course. I never considered otherwise. I just thought you disliked Lucy so much that you wouldn't be in our lives if I remarried."

"We don't really know Lucy." Belinda looked at her husband. "And we just… We were worried that another woman might come in and steal you and Mattie away from us." Her sob broke him. "And the two of you are all we have left."

"You'll always have us. Nothing is going to change that. And once you get to know Lucy, you'll realize she would never think that way. You're Mattie's grandparents. I don't ever want you to feel shut out of her life. In fact, maybe we can start a better schedule for you with Mattie. A sleepover once a month or something so you're seeing her consistently."

She sniffed. "A date night for you and Lucy."

Graham sighed. He'd thought they were getting somewhere.

"I didn't mean that how it sounded." Belinda squeezed his hand again as if the action could communicate what she couldn't. "I meant, it would be nice for you to have the time with Lucy, especially if she's walking right into a family instead of starting one on her own."

That was the closest thing to acceptance Graham had ever heard. Definitely not the response he'd feared or expected. His dad was right. Prayer worked. Without it, this conversation wouldn't be happening.

"We don't want the money back." Phillip leaned forward. "We gave it to you to do as you both saw fit, and we don't need to know what happens to it. If it's going to Mattie's college, that's great. But—" he shook his head "—I, for one, never need to talk about the money again."

Graham nodded. "Okay. One more thing." Phillip and Belinda both tensed. "I'm sorry I never joined the board for Brooke's charity. I'm willing, if you still want me."

"Really?" Both of them looked at him wide-eyed.

"I want another connection, another way to prove to you that inviting Lucy into our lives doesn't mean you're going to lose Mattie."

"Or you." Belinda's mouth gave in to a slight curve. The first smile Graham had seen from either of them since he'd walked through the door.

"Or me."

"Of course we want you on the board." Concern wrinkled Belinda's brow. "But, Graham, what about this Lucy? Will she ever be able to forgive us? We were horrible to her. We were just hurting so much seeing you move on."

"I think she'll understand and forgive you. She's pretty great that way." The assurance was partly for them, partly for him. If she didn't, he was going to be a huge mess. "But, Belinda?"

"Yes?"

"I think the first step toward mending your relationship with Lucy is to stop putting *this* in front of her name."

"They think it was the mango in the sherbet." Lucy sat in her hospital bed, holding court with Cash and Olivia in the visitor chairs.

Lucy might be a proponent of doing things on her own, but she was going to have to adjust that opinion once again. Everyone should have a sidekick that could fly through traffic fast enough to save their life.

"No mango ever again. It was freaky." Liv wiped a tear. "On the way to the hospital you got so quiet." When Olivia sniffled again and more moisture rolled down her cheeks, Cash pulled a handkerchief from his pocket and offered it to her. For some reason this made her laugh through her tears. "I thought I was going to lose you. I didn't know what to do. Pull over and call an ambulance? Keep driving?"

Cash wrapped an arm around Olivia, pressing a kiss to the top of her head. "I'm thankful you're both okay since I'm sure you weren't exactly obeying traffic laws."

"For reals, McCowboy. What would you do without a wonderful sister-in-law like me? Your life would be incomplete."

The comment earned a grin from him and a groan from her sister.

"You're definitely feeling better."

"I am, especially since I slept a bit."

"Speaking of sleeping, did you have any visitors while we were getting coffee?"

Lucy ignored the pang of disappointment. It wasn't as if she'd sent the text she'd written on her phone earlier.

I need you shouldn't have to be said twice.

"Nope. No visitors."

Olivia and Cash shared a look Lucy couldn't decipher. "Give it time, Liv." Lucy didn't understand Cash's comment, but she let it slide.

"What are you two still doing here anyway?" She made a shooing motion. "It's late. You don't need to wait for me."

"We can stay," Olivia protested.

"Absolutely not."

"What happens when they discharge you?"

"Leave me a set of keys. I feel fine and I can drive myself home."

Cash shrugged. "We do have two vehicles here." He stood and tugged Olivia up with him. "Come on. Lucy's right. She's fine. You heard it straight from the doctor. And I'm guessing you're about as emotionally exhausted right now as can be."

Olivia covered a yawn. "Not true. I'm a rock."

"Yep. You are." He grinned, and the way he looked at her sister made Lucy fight a rush of emotion.

"Okay, enough sap, you two. Have you forgotten I recently had my heart broken? Get out of here before you mess me up again."

They came over and gave her hugs, and once they'd gone, Lucy snuggled under the light blanket on her bed. For a moment earlier, when she'd woken up, she'd been positive that she could smell Graham. That he'd been here.

Maybe the medicine had messed with her mind.

Now Lucy felt completely fine and wanted to get out of the hospital. But since the ER moved at a snail's pace, she assumed she had a wait on her hands.

"Did someone order a doctor?" Graham peeked into her room.

"Hey." Lucy sat up against her pillows. Those mad-at-him/please-kiss-me feelings came rushing back. "What are you doing here?"

"Technically, I am your doctor."

"No, you're not."

"You worked in my office, Lucy. I think that counts as close enough to a patient."

Oh. How disappointing. He'd come to see her because he was Graham and he was noble. He was right to come, though, because they had to learn to be friends again and function around each other. Especially if Lucy planned to stay in this town.

And due to the news she'd found out this week—that the owner of the dance school she worked at wanted to sell the business within the next few years—that possibility was getting more and more definite.

Lucy could do this. She could get through a conversation with Graham. Then the next one *had* to be easier.

"I know I'm not exactly your favorite person right now, but I figured these were extenuating circumstances." Instead of sitting in a chair, he perched on the edge of her bed. Her pulse started drumming like crazy at his close proximity and the fact that she hadn't inhaled him in almost a week.

When his hand found hers and held on, the machine monitoring Lucy's heart betrayed her, broadcasting her body's reaction to his touch.

"How are you feeling?"

"Much better."

"I'm glad to hear that." His hand switched from cradling hers to entwining fingers. "Lucy, I love you."

Her mouth slacked open and her throat closed off again. A rush of goose bumps spread across her skin, but she tamped down any excitement at hearing those words from him.

Love wasn't enough.

Not with how the Wellings felt about her, and Graham bargaining over her.

"Phillip and Belinda are going to apologize to you. They were upset about me moving on because it made them feel like they were losing Brooke all over again. They thought us being in a relationship would take me and Mattie away from them."

Indignation straightened her spine. "I would never do that."

"I know. That's what I told them."

"And they…accepted that?"

He nodded slowly, and something close to hope started flapping wings in her chest. Lucy shoved it down again. He'd hurt her. How could she just forget about that?

"Lucy, I'm sorry I made a deal with the Wellings and didn't tell you what was really going on. I was so busy denying my feelings for you I didn't even realize what I'd done." He tucked a piece of her hair behind her ear, fingers lingering against her cheek and wreaking havoc on her emotions. "Until it was too late."

It's not too late.

Yes, it is.

The thoughts warred as Liv's advice came rushing back.

Forgive him.

Lucy could have everything she wanted. Or none of it.

Graham's hold on her hand loosened, his shoulders wearing the same hurt she felt coursing through her. Was he going to leave?

Panic rose up, screaming for attention. How could she even consider letting him go? She might not want to need anyone, but she needed this man.

"You hurt me, Hollywood."

Regret clung to his features. "I know. And I'm so sorry. I never want you to feel like that again. The things that make you *you* are exactly what I love about you. I'll do anything I can to make it up to you. To prove how I really feel about you."

Anything.

Ideas started forming.

"Like another road trip? That purse I wanted?"

His low chuckle warmed her from the toes up, and the heart monitor started giving away her every emotion again.

"Can you turn that thing off?"

Graham did something to the machine and the screen went blank.

"That was so not like you, breaking rules, turning things off that are supposed to be on."

He just grinned and sat back on the edge of the bed. "I won't do anything to mess with you being okay. I kind of have a thing for you."

"You do?"

"Yep. And I wonder if you noticed I said I love you." His head tilted. "I didn't hear a response to that, though I know for certain you said you loved me once before."

"That conversation was a week ago." She tried desperately to keep her lips from curving. "So much has changed since then."

His eyes narrowed. "Still counts as good for me. I'm holding you to it."

"You're awfully demanding." His lips were dropping to hers, and she was having a hard time concentrating on anything else.

"And somehow, even in a hospital bed, you're beautiful."

He kissed her.

It was a good thing her heart monitor had been turned off. His kiss was gentle—almost reverent. He memorized her face with his lips, and Lucy fell into the knowledge that something had changed between them. Now, along with the tingling current that always ebbed, there was also a strength. A sense that she was safe. She'd never known before what it felt like to have everything she wanted within reach.

Good night. She couldn't give in that easily. Lucy placed her hands on his chest and pushed, but he gave her only a few inches of space.

"Do you think this is some kind of done deal or something?"

His mouth curved, causing her stomach to tap-dance. "Yep."

"Well, it's not."

"Okay." He stood and started disconnecting wires and cords.

"What are you doing?"

"Getting you out of here."

She clutched the blanket. He couldn't do that, could he?

"By the way, are you in pajamas?"

"Yeah. I was wearing them when the reaction happened."

"Why?"

"I was wallowing."

His brow furrowed. "I'm sorry if you were wallowing because of me. I'm sorry I didn't talk to the Wellings earlier, that I didn't fight for you. For us. Although, I'm not sure that conversation would have gone so well without an extreme amount of prayer. I'm still in shock that it did. Isn't it funny how we ask God for something and then we're surprised when He answers us?"

Recognition of that truth settled in her soul. "I do that all the time." This. This was why she needed to ask God to handle things instead of trying to do everything on her own. She'd wanted this, but God had made this happen. Not her. She'd always thought she had to do everything on her own. But when that got stripped away from her, she'd found the God she'd been missing. The one who didn't need her to be in charge. The one who, turned out, already had everything under control.

Graham continued to mess with all of the stuff connected to her. Removed her IV.

"Don't I need that?"

"Nope. You're not even getting medicine through it anymore."

"Then why am I here?"

"You won't be for long."

Suddenly she was being lifted from the bed. Graham was cradling her, carrying her out of the ER.

"Tight security around here. I'm being abducted and no one even blinks."

"I don't think anyone would be upset to find out your future husband—who's a doctor—is taking you. Plus…" His grin turned sheepish. "I checked with the doctor before I came in to see you and got all of your paperwork. You're fine. And I already got you an EpiPen."

Of course he had.

Did he just say *future husband*?

Giddiness threaded through her. "Who says I'm marrying you?"

"I do."

Her arms were wrapped around his neck, and Lucy had to admit, she was enjoying the ride. "You'd better check your sources. Last I heard, a man usually asks a woman to marry him. He doesn't demand it caveman style. What makes you think I'm going to marry you, anyway?"

"This." He slid her down until her feet touched the ground, one hand holding her against him, one wrapped into her hair. He kissed her until she could hardly stand before pulling back. "And the fact that I love you and you love me, and when you're done being snarky, you're going to admit it."

"Oh." Her voice was as wobbly as her legs. She slipped her hands behind his neck, pulling him down for another kiss. "I do love you. You're easy to love."

Too soon, he inched back again, sliding his hands to her shoulders. His evergreen eyes were filled with so much love she considered heading back to her hospital bed for a hit of oxygen.

"Lucy, will you marry me and Mattie? We have this big hole that only you can fill. We need you."

Her stupid eyes were leaking. "I knew you were for me. I just didn't know if I was going to get to keep you."

"Keep me. Please. I'm a mess without you."

"Yes." She touched his face, wondering over the fact that she was being proposed to in a hospital hallway and she couldn't envision a more romantic scenario. "I'd wanted to fix this. To make sure the Wellings' relationship was back on track with Mattie. But you and God fixed it instead of me."

"God gets all the credit. There's no other explanation for how that conversation went so well." His hands slid down her arms, warmth seeping through her long-sleeved T-shirt. "And I thought I had to save everyone, that everything rested on my shoulders. But then you came along and saved me and Mattie when we didn't even know we needed it."

"My heart is beating all wild again."

He scooped her back into his arms. "It's because you love me. But just to be safe, I'd better carry you out of here."

Lucy looked up at the man she wanted for forever and let go of a contented sigh.

Being rescued wasn't such a bad thing after all.

Epilogue

Three weeks later, Lucy met Graham and Mattie at the bottom of her apartment steps. Since little eyes were watching, Lucy's first instinct—jumping into Graham's arms—was a no go. Instead, she settled for a nice long hug from each of them.

"So, Mattie Grace, where are we going?"

Mattie shook her head, eyes sparkling behind her red glasses. "Dad says we can't tell."

Graham held out his hand. "I need your car keys."

"What? Why?"

"Because my car is washed, and yours isn't."

"I think I'm offended, but I'll forgive you if you tell me where we're going."

His mouth curved. "Duchess, I already told you—you're on a need-to-know basis."

"But I need to know!"

He put his hands on her shoulders and directed her to the passenger seat of her car. "Get in. We have to do something." He started backing out of her door, then popped back in to place a kiss on her cheek. "Close your eyes." His whisper made her skin tingle.

"Fine." She complied, unable to keep the smile from her face. Graham had told her casual—that was all she knew—so she'd paired black skinny jeans with a flowy white shirt and pink Chucks. She heard the trunk open and a bunch of scrambling, some finagling of what she assumed was a car seat going into the back. After a minute, the car door shut.

"Okay, you can open them now." Graham grinned at Mattie in the rearview mirror and started the car. The two of them were dressed casually, like her—Mattie in a yellow sundress and boots, and Graham in jeans and a button-up shirt. Lucy's curiosity hovered near boiling. Where could they be headed?

He drove out of town, and she somehow resisted asking questions. Finally, they reached a turnoff. Gorgeous bluebonnets stretched before them, and white and yellow flowers also speckled the roadside and fields. Lucy agreed with Mattie's excitement coming from the backseat. It was unlike anything she'd ever seen before.

"This is a good surprise." She shared a smile with Graham.

"It's going to get—"

"Hey!" Graham cut off Mattie's next words, and she giggled from the backseat.

After a few minutes driving slowly along with other cars looking at the wildflowers, Graham signaled and turned onto a small dirt road, driving the car around a patch of trees and then parking.

"This doesn't look like a well-worn path. Are we trespassing or something?" So not something Graham would do, but none of the other cars had turned.

Graham laughed. "We're good. I have my sources. And patients."

"And your patients let you tromp around on their land?"

"Yep. Come on." He hopped out, and Lucy followed him and a bouncing Mattie to the trunk. They opened it, revealing a picnic spread. A brown basket brimming with fruit, cheese, meat and crackers. A cooler filled with drinks. Graham grabbed a plaid blanket and spread it out, the amazing flowers a backdrop all around them.

In the past three weeks, Graham and Lucy had gone on a few dates by themselves, and although those dates had been nice—okay, they'd been wonderful and Olivia had been teasing Lucy about walking around wearing a silly grin—this one was equally great in a whole different way. This felt like a glimpse of what was to come. In between bites of food, Mattie ran around in the field, looking like a wild flower child. She'd blossomed so much in a short amount of time. It was as if she finally knew she was safe—that all of her people were getting along.

Lucy had also made progress with the Wellings over the past few weeks. Their interactions weren't perfect, but they were all making an effort. And Lucy knew the chance to be with Graham and Mattie was worth the extra work she would continue to put forth with the couple.

After they ate, Graham stood and held out his hand to her. "Should we take a walk?"

"Sure." They took the dirt path—only two tire tracks cutting through the field popping with color.

"I have something to show you." Graham twined his fingers with hers, touching the gorgeous engagement ring he'd given her a few days after proposing at the hospital. She'd always known the man had good taste.

They rounded the bend and a beautiful dark wood barn came into view. What was going on?

Mattie ran up ahead, then came flying back to them, excitement evident.

Graham squeezed Lucy's hand. "So, what do you think?"

She scanned the landscape. A gorgeous barn in the middle of a field of wildflowers. She didn't quite know how to answer his question.

"It's beautiful."

"It's being remodeled into a place to hold weddings."

Oh. Now she liked it even better.

"I've seen the plans for the inside, and it's going to be amazing. I'll show them to you and then you can decide."

"I'd like to see them, but I already know I love it."

"Are you sure? I know wedding stuff is a big deal."

"I pretty much just want to have a huge party and invite everyone I know."

"Why am I not surprised?" A grin claimed his mouth. "We could be the first wedding here."

"Patient-doctor privilege?"

He nodded.

"Where do we sign up?"

Mattie clapped and spun in circles. "We're going to get married here, and I'm going to have a white dress. Then you'll be ours, Lucy. Daddy told me that's how a wedding works."

She scooped Mattie into a hug, meeting Graham's gaze over the top of her head. "I'm already yours." The smile that met hers warmed her from the inside out. "Cover your eyes, Mattie Grace."

"Why?"

"Because I want to kiss your dad."

"Eww!" Mattie shoved her hands over her eyes, and Lucy leaned into Graham.

"It's a good thing you asked me to marry you."

Humor tugged on his lips. "Oh, yeah? Why's that?"

"Because I kind of have a thing for you two." She kissed him, though not for as long as she would have liked. There would be plenty of time for those kisses in the days, weeks and years to come. She peppered Mattie's cheeks with smooches, and Graham joined in. The girl screamed and tried to squirm away from them, giggling with a belly laugh that made Lucy's heart go gooey.

The Mattie effect was still in full force.

When Lucy let go, Mattie dropped to the ground and ran ahead, still yelling and laughing as if she was being chased.

Graham tugged Lucy against his chest, and she slid her arms around his waist. When Mattie disappeared around the bend in front of them, his lips found the sensitive spot just under her ear. Turned out that whole patience thing wasn't really her gig. "I think finding the perfect place to have our wedding deserves a real kiss. Am I right?"

Strong arms tightened around her, his curved mouth hovering over hers. "Always."

* * * * *

**IF YOU ENJOYED THIS BOOK
WE THINK YOU WILL ALSO LOVE**

LOVE INSPIRED
INSPIRATIONAL ROMANCE

Uplifting stories of faith, forgiveness and hope.

Fall in love with stories where faith helps
guide you through life's challenges, and discover
the promise of a new beginning.

6 NEW BOOKS AVAILABLE EVERY MONTH!

Love Harlequin romance?

DISCOVER.

Be the first to find out about promotions,
news and exclusive content!

Facebook.com/HarlequinBooks

Twitter.com/HarlequinBooks

Instagram.com/HarlequinBooks

Pinterest.com/HarlequinBooks

YouTube.com/HarlequinBooks

ReaderService.com

EXPLORE.

Sign up for the Harlequin e-newsletter and
download a free book from any series at
TryHarlequin.com

CONNECT.

Join our Harlequin community to
share your thoughts and connect
with other romance readers!
Facebook.com/groups/HarlequinConnection

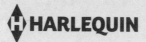

HARLEQUIN

Heartfelt or thrilling, passionate or uplifting—Harlequin is more than just happily-ever-after.

With twelve different series to choose from and new books available every month, you are sure to find stories that will move you, uplift you, inspire and delight you.